Everyone has a story... but not all of them are true.

"WATCH OUT, GRISHAM."
—*The Sydney Morning Herald*

continued . . .

UNDERTOW

"Bauer (the nom de plume of Australian TV executive Kimberly Scott) credibly navigates multiple segments of Boston society as she fashions a complex plot from simple elements."
—Publishers Weekly

"An impressive debut. Written with urgency . . . The climaxes and about-turns and surprises just keep coming until the final showdown . . . Watch out, Grisham."
—The Sydney Morning Herald

"A creditable, enthralling legal suspense drama following firmly in the footsteps of Grisham and Patterson."
—Good Reading

"*Undertow* is all handled with dexterity and no little style . . . [Bauer's] locations have the right sense of place, her plotting is economical and concise . . . Bauer is credibly packaged."
—The Australian

"Bauer has done a Grisham, producing a fast-paced and suspenseful legal thriller."
—The Melbourne Age

"Sydney Bauer has hit the crime scene in fine style with a legal thriller that is confronting, touching on relevant and controversial issues with absolute confidence. This is the kind of story that legal thriller fans everywhere would eat up with a spoon and then go looking for more."
—Australian Crime Writers' Association

"One of the most accomplished Australian crime novels to date. Look out, John Grisham." *—Sisters in Crime Australia*

"A deeply compelling political/legal thriller . . . with a series of ingenious twists."
—Crime Down Under

"Bauer's eye for detail never lets her down. Her obviously thorough research is carefully integrated and never just for effect." *—Bookseller and Publisher Magazine*

ALIBI

SYDNEY BAUER

JOVE BOOKS, NEW YORK

THE BERKLEY PUBLISHING GROUP
Published by the Penguin Group
Penguin Group (USA) Inc.
375 Hudson Street, New York, New York 10014, USA
Penguin Group (Canada), 90 Eglinton Avenue East, Suite 700, Toronto, Ontario M4P 2Y3, Canada
(a division of Pearson Penguin Canada Inc.)
Penguin Books Ltd., 80 Strand, London WC2R 0RL, England
Penguin Group Ireland, 25 St. Stephen's Green, Dublin 2, Ireland (a division of Penguin Books Ltd.)
Penguin Group (Australia), 250 Camberwell Road, Camberwell, Victoria 3124, Australia
(a division of Pearson Australia Group Pty. Ltd.)
Penguin Books India Pvt. Ltd., 11 Community Centre, Panchsheel Park, New Delhi—110 017, India
Penguin Group (NZ), 67 Apollo Drive, Rosedale, North Shore 0632, New Zealand
(a division of Pearson New Zealand Ltd.)
Penguin Books (South Africa) (Pty.) Ltd., 24 Sturdee Avenue, Rosebank, Johannesburg 2196, South Africa

Penguin Books Ltd., Registered Offices: 80 Strand, London WC2R 0RL, England

This is a work of fiction. Names, characters, places, and incidents either are the product of the author's imagination or are used fictitiously, and any resemblance to actual persons, living or dead, business establishments, events, or locales is entirely coincidental. The publisher does not have any control over and does not assume any responsibility for author or third-party websites or their content.

ALIBI

A Jove Book / published by arrangement with the author

PRINTING HISTORY
Pan Macmillan Australia trade paperback edition / 2008
Jove mass-market edition / August 2009

Copyright © 2008 by Sydney Bauer.
Cover art and design by Springer Design Group.
Text design by Tiffany Estreicher.

ISBN: 978-0-515-14659-2

JOVE®
Jove Books are published by The Berkley Publishing Group,
a division of Penguin Group (USA) Inc.,
375 Hudson Street, New York, New York 10014.
JOVE® is a registered trademark of Penguin Group (USA) Inc.
The "J" design is a trademark of Penguin Group (USA) Inc.

PRINTED IN THE UNITED STATES OF AMERICA

10 9 8 7 6 5 4 3 2 1

ALIBI

PROLOGUE

"Once there was a young Japanese princess," said Jessica Nagoshi, the thick cotton sheets now stretching across her middle as she twisted to meet his eye, "who was picked up by a powerful wave and carried to a deserted island far away from her father's home." They were in New York, at the Plaza no less—two of the Ivy League elite, hiding out from the rest of the world in the middle of the busiest city on earth.

"The princess was lonely and sad," she went on, as James turned his head, his arm now reaching across her shoulders so that he might pull her close. "And wished with all her heart that she would be rescued, but many years passed until someone came to her aid."

Jessica was prone to stories such as these—simple yet telling tales of Japanese folklore that gave him a rare insight into not so much *what* but *how* this clever, complex girl was thinking.

"Let me guess," said James then, his green eyes lost in her own deep brown ones, the lamps in their executive suite dimmed but the curtains stretched wide apart so that the room was now flooded with the lights of the city beyond. "It was her knight in shining armor."

"No, James." She shook her head, and he realized how much he had grown to love the way she would feign frustration at his simplistic "Western" generalizations. "In fact, there were four warriors who came to her aid—one carrying a sword, one riding a crane, a third astride a tortoise and a fourth holding a cherry blossom and wearing the smile of the gods."

"*'Rescue me and I shall be your bride,'* said the princess, after which all four warriors stepped forward to state their case.

"And so the warrior carrying the sword said: *'Allow me to rescue you, for I have the strength of minions,'* while the warrior riding the crane argued, *'But I sit upon a crane which will assure us a life of good fortune,'* and the third man, astride the tortoise, promised the princess good health and longevity, while the fourth remained silent, offering her only a branch of cherry blossom as a symbol of life's transience."

"So who did she choose?" asked a now intrigued James, shifting on the mattress so that he might rise onto his elbow.

"The fourth warrior of course," she said. "The only one who would bring her happiness, no matter how short-lived."

James frowned then, looking down upon her—at her smooth skin and perfect lips, at her dark almond eyes and long black hair, which fell across the pillow in waves. It had only been two months since they first met, and strangely enough, he felt like he knew everything and nothing about her all at the very same time. She was not like the other girls at Deane—the beautiful, well-connected intellectuals, the daughters of old money and the progressive nouveau riche.

"What are you saying, Jess?" he asked after a time. "That you want me to rescue you? That you want me to offer you that cherry blossom and promise you happiness for as long as it will last? Because if you do, I . . ."

"I do not need to be rescued, James," she said then, as if he had failed to grasp her point. "But the garden I live in is small."

"I don't understand," he replied. "You of all people have the world at your feet."

"Then maybe I am asking too much."

They lay in silence for a while, the street noise beyond cosseting them in anonymity.

"I want to meet your father," said James at last. "Tomorrow."

"Shhh," she whispered, lifting her long narrow finger before stretching her neck to meet his lips with hers. *"Asu no koto o ieba, tenjo de nezumi ga warau.* Nobody knows what tomorrow might bring." And he kissed her in return.

"Jessica," he said. "I want you to know . . . that whatever happens, you are . . . I am . . ."

"It is all right," she interrupted. "In case you have not noticed, I made my decision weeks ago, by the riverbank on that morning filled with color. For as my mother once told me, it is the choices that we *don't* make in life that we live to regret—not the ones that we do."

1

"Okay," said Boston attorney-at-law David Cavanaugh as he took his girlfriend by the arm and led her inside the warm cocoon that was O'Sullivan's Bar in riverside Cambridge. "It's official. I am old, Sara Davis—over the hill, past it, seriously on the wrong side of thirty."

David took Sara's coat and looked around the student bar. It was cozy and dark and filled with good-looking twenty-somethings, all knocking back beers and wines and other alcoholic concoctions of various colors in long slender glass bottles.

"David," said his fellow attorney girlfriend. "I wouldn't call thirty-seven over the hill. And besides, you're fit, healthy and still pretty hot—for an old geezer that is."

David grabbed both ends of the wool knit scarf that hung around Sara's neck and pulled her close, kissing her squarely on her lips, which were tinged with a hint of blue despite the now tepid surroundings.

"You're cold," he said. "I'll get us a drink."

"Let me find Jake first," she said. "He is the reason we are here after all."

David had met thirty-one-year-old Sara Davis almost two years ago when she asked him to represent her boss, Rayna Martin, in what turned out to be one of the biggest hate trials of the decade. David had made many good friends—and enemies—during the course of that high-profile trial, and even better, had fallen in love with his long-haired, brown-skinned, turquoise-eyed co-counsel.

Last year Sara agreed to join David's law firm—Wright, Wallace and Gertz—run by David's boss, friend and mentor

Arthur Wright, and since then they had taken on a range of cases together, including the high-profile defense of Professor Stuart Montgomery, the man accused of killing the vice president of the United States.

"There he is," shouted Sara, in an attempt to be heard over the din as she pointed to the far back corner of the hotel. "You grab the drinks and meet me over there."

■ ■ ■

While David headed to the bar Sara jockeyed her way down to the back, ignoring the various stares and proclamations of love by at least two drunken college boys who, she knew, would definitely be feeling it in the morning.

She wrestled her way into the tightly knit group as politely as possible before coming face-to-face with one of the three men she loved most in the world—her little brother, Jake Davis.

"Hey bro," she said wrapping her arms around her blond-haired, blue-eyed sibling. Sara had been adopted by her parents six years before they surprised everyone by giving birth to a second child the natural way. "Congratulations, kiddo. This new job is huge, right? Who would have thought, my scruffy little brother the big corporate executive."

"Thanks, Sara," said Jake, pulling her into his circle of friends. "But it's only an internship, and I still have to finish my . . ."

"I know, I know. But it is seriously great, Jake. I'm allowed to be proud of you. That's what big sisters do."

Earlier in the year, twenty-five-year-old Jake had completed the much respected Massachusetts Institute of Technology's Sloan's Undergraduate Program in Management Science at the top of his class. This meant he could pretty much choose his career path from a long list of alternatives including consulting, commercial and investment banking, financial analysis, commercial marketing, software engineering or new product management.

He had decided on continuing his post-graduate studies by taking on a further degree in international business law, a course he would now have to complete part-time considering he had just been offered a high five-figure internship by Credit Suisse First Boston.

"So here he is," said David, putting down the three beers on a now-sticky walnut bar table before joining the huddle to shake Jake's hand. "The budding Donald Trump. So how long before I can hit you up for a loan?"

"Actually," said Jake, "I was gonna ask you guys to lend me a coupla bucks tonight. With only a few days of freedom left, the boys are in the mood for partying and I figure we better make the most if it."

"The most of what?" Sara smiled. "Us having more money than you, or you being able to cry destitute little brother just one last time?"

"Both." Jake laughed.

"Fair enough," said David, pulling out his wallet.

Jake was right, the crowd was obviously in for a long night. The new college year started the following week and, judging by the festive mood around them, this lot were going to milk this unusually cold final week of summer vacation dry—literally.

"Let me introduce you to my friends," said Jake with one arm around his sister and the other draped over David's shoulder.

"Look out, guys," he said, turning to his circle of drinking buddies. "There are two lawyers in the house so no talk about tax evasion strategy until after my sister and her boyfriend here leave." Jake smiled before downing most of his freshly poured beer and proceeding to give the introductions. "Seriously, Sis," he said, turning back to Sara again, "I am so glad you guys made it."

"Wouldn't miss it for the world," Sara said, smiling at her brother.

· · ·

A little over an hour later the crowd started to disperse, with talk of clubbing here and hooking up there. David and Sara were just about to leave when an expensively dressed, good-looking young man with short dark hair and pale green eyes made his way through the group to their cozy little corner at the far end of the room.

"Hey, Jake," said the boy, shaking Jake's hand with enthusiasm. David noticed the young man was a little rocky on his feet. "I heard your news. That's just great, man. Seriously. I just hope it rubs off."

"Thanks, James. You'll be next. Don't worry."

"Not without your tutoring I won't. You'll still have time to fit me in, won't you?" said the boy, now steadying himself on the back of Sara's stool.

"Sure," said Jake as he turned to gesture at Sara and David. "And even better I might be able to hook you up with an even more experienced . . ."

"I don't believe this," said James then, a fresh expression of recognition lighting up his bright green eyes.

Jake smiled. "This is my sister, Sara, and you obviously know of her boyfriend David . . ."

"Cavanaugh," said James then, his eyes now set on David as he shook Sara's hand before pumping David's palm with enthusiasm.

"Nice to meet you," said Sara with a smile that suggested she was highly amused by this young man's obvious fascination with David.

"Mr. Cavanaugh," said James. "I . . . well, in a strange way you are responsible for my making Law Review. I wrote my competition essay, the one that saw me selected to Deane Law Review, on *Commonwealth v. Martin*. And then, in my second year I wrote a manuscript on *US v. Montgomery*, which was published on the front page."

"I read it," said David. And he had. He remembered thinking the kid that had written it saw possibilities in precedent that even he had overlooked. "And I thought it was terrific. Apart from the fact that you probably credited me with a fair bit more insight than I was entitled to."

"No, sir," said James. "Attorneys like you, Mr. Cavanaugh, without trying to sound like a total kiss-ass, are why I chose law in the first place."

"Thanks, James," said a now embarrassed David. "And if you ever need any help, any advice, Jake has my numbers so . . ."

"That would be amazing. Thanks so much," James said before turning back to Jake. "Geez man, you didn't tell me you knew David Cavanaugh."

"I try to keep it a secret," said Jake. "You know, in case the paparazzi start going through my rubbish."

They all laughed.

"Well, anyways," said James. "Like I said, Jake, any time you have would be most appreciated."

"Don't worry, we'll work something out," Jake told him.

"Besides, you guys at Deane have so many connections you were practically born in Harborside offices. Right?"

James punched Jake's shoulder in mock admonishment.

"Miss Davis, Mr. Cavanaugh," he said then. "It's been a pleasure."

"It's Sara and David." Sara smiled. "And it's been great to meet you too, James."

"Thanks. And . . . just so you know, a group of us are headed over to the Lincoln. I can leave your names at the door if you like."

"Thanks but no thanks," said Jake. "I'm not sure the Lincoln Club is ready for us yet," he said, referring to the exclusive watering hole. "Promise to call me though."

"Thanks, man," said James. "And congrats again."

"Wow," said Sara as the young man made his way back to his friends. "Who the hell was *that*—besides David's number one groupie?"

"James Matheson as in Matheson Bailey," replied her brother. Matheson Bailey were a well-known institution of merchant bankers and James' father, Jed, was the CEO. "I posted a tutoring ad on the Deane notice board about a year ago and he was one of the first to call. He is just about to start his final year of law." Jake finished his beer and went on. "Majoring in economics. I tutor him once a week."

"The Lincoln Club? Deane?" said David, noting both institutions' exclusive reputations. "When I was at BC we used to say Harvard was for the intellectually rich and Deane for the rich intellectuals."

And he was right. Deane University was officially the most expensive college in the country with average tuition fees at around $70,000 per year.

"Not that his paper wasn't amazing—it was certainly a hell of a lot better than anything I could have written in law school."

"And what were you writing in law school, Mr. Cavanaugh?" joked Sara.

"Oh, I don't know, mortgage checks, bar tabs." David had worked at a smoky bar in South Boston to pay for his tuition at Boston College.

"Yeah, well," said Jake. "James Matheson may be loaded,

and connected, and a serious chick magnet to boot, but like David says he's also incredibly smart. You think I got a career ahead of me—just wait till you see what that guy can do. The kid is so savvy it scares me sometimes, the way he thinks, analyzes, identifies ways to manipulate the system."

"Sounds like a corporate lawyer to me," joked David.

"Tell me about it," said Jake. "That kid is going places, believe you me."

2

Saturday, September 12

Sammy Ito was a fortunate man.

He acknowledged this blessing, as he did every morning, as he slid the long silver key into the freshly polished lock of the carefully painted dry oak garden shed door at the top of Mr. Nagoshi's extensive Wellesley estate, Japanese Garden.

Sammy was a *uekiya*. A third generation *uekiya*, from a family of similarly fortunate gardeners who took honor in tending some of the most beautiful Japanese gardens a man ever had the privilege to till. He understood and respected the principles of *wa*, or balance, that less is more, that *ma*, or space, defined the elements around it and that carefully placed *ishi*, or rocks, played a superior role to plantings, or *shukusai*, in a garden where *mizu* (water) and *okimono* (ornaments) worked together to create the true spirit of *in* and *yo*, or as the Chinese put it, yin and yang.

It was 6 a.m. The low-lying condensation that so often followed a cool and cloudless night sat peacefully above his beautiful responsibilities like a guardian—waiting for Sammy to come with the sun, and tend to them until darkness claimed them again.

He began as he always did—retrieving his pad and pencil from the shed, walking the garden, assessing its needs and making notes on his priorities for the day. He would start at the water basin, or *chozu*, which sat at the base of a running stream, filling and emptying simultaneously as the clack of its bamboo water chute marked the passage of time.

For the next half hour he would continue south, past a series of stones placed vertically, arched, reclining and horizontally in sets of threes, fives and sevens before moving east to assess the Japanese native plants (cherries, bamboo and maples). Finally, feeling the lift in his heart as he neared the greenhouse, or *onshitsu*, he thanked Buddha once again for the honorable gift before him.

People said they were a myth—a subject of fable that lurked undiscovered in some yet to be charted tropical jungle. But Sammy Ito knew differently as he entered the enclosure and surveyed the *Telipogon portillae*, or totally black orchid, which grew in full splendor before him.

He had seen many imposters—the *encyclia cochleatea*, the *dracula vampira*, the *polystachya transvaalensis* and various other hybrids that made a mockery of the original's beauty. For none of these were the true color of the night, none had the pure darkness of bloom as the priceless specimen he now beheld.

And then he saw it. The stone of death.

It was one of the Three Bad Stones, along with the withered or misshapen Diseased Stone and misfit Pauper's Stone, which brought hardship and misfortune to its master's house. The Death Stone was a stone that was obviously a vertical used as a horizontal, or vice versa, like an epitaph propping up the dead.

And in this case, it was.

For as Sammy Ito, master *uekiya*, walked around his precious black orchid, he saw evidence of the greatest act of evil. There she lay, all pale-skinned and blue-lipped, her neck placed at a devilish angle on the upturned vertical that acted like a pillow to her colorless corpse.

Sammy said a prayer, trying not to focus on the haunting dark marks that circled her neck like a snake or the X-shaped indentation that crossed her forehead like a warning. Then he dropped his notepad and turned and ran, not realizing that his calls of "*Akuryo, akuryo*" ("Evil, evil") were loud enough to shock the living from their sleep and cloud his so far fortunate life with a vision so dark it would be marked on his soul forever.

3

"Jesus, Frank," said Lieutenant Joe Mannix as he nodded at the uniform who lifted the tape so that he could meet with fellow homicide detective Frank McKay at the top of John Nagoshi's white pebble drive. "What in the hell are you wearing?"

"What?" said the fifty-something McKay.

"The sweater."

"It's not a sweater it's a skivvy."

"It's also . . . yellow," said Joe.

"It's also warm."

"You look like one of those guys from that kids' group," said Joe, following McKay's lead as he pointed around the side of the house toward the back garden gate.

"The Wiggles," said Frank.

"That's them."

"I still don't see the problem, Chief," McKay countered.

"No problem, Frank, except the Wiggles' expertise is dancing for kids in diapers and yours is . . ."

"Dead people," said Frank, looking down and shaking his head. "Don't remind me."

It was a ritual, maybe not a conscious one, but a routine nevertheless. Mannix and McKay often played this game of tit for tat just before they faced the horrifying realities of their chosen profession, and judging by the look on McKay's face, this one was in the "splinter" category—meaning one that got under your skin and left a scar as a permanent reminder of the iniquity of mankind.

Normally McKay would have been teamed with his regular partner, Detective Susan Leigh, but the determined young Leigh, whose drive and enthusiasm were motivated just as much by a desire to "do good" as they were by ambition, had recently been accepted as a new recruit by the FBI.

"Geez," said Mannix, who, truth be told, was actually enjoying playing grassroots detective while the department organized a replacement for Leigh. "This is some backyard."

McKay shut the garden gate behind them, leaving Mannix to take in the huge horticultural expanse before them. The sun had risen to a crisp, clear day, cutting across the frost and removing at least some of the bite from the early fall chill.

"Like something off of a postcard, ain't it?" McKay nodded. "According to the gardener," he said, flipping open his notebook, "a Mr. Samuel Ito, who discovered the vic, Mr. Nagoshi is a stickler for detail."

"So I hear," said Joe, noting Nagoshi's reputation as a successful and hard-nosed corporate chief. "And the girl?"

"Over there," said Frank, pointing at the greenhouse and shaking his head again. "We're looking at a real son-of-a-bitch for this one, boss."

"Aren't they all, Frank?" said Mannix.

"True," replied his friend, taking out his handkerchief to cover his nose and indicating it might be best if his superior did the same. "But some more so than others."

The two men entered the greenhouse and immediately noted the rise in temperature. The air was thick and moist and saturated with the smell of death. The crime scene was frenetic, but the conversation muted—perhaps out of concentration, or respect, or plain old-fashioned disgust. Joe nodded at the men from Boston PD's Crime Scene Response Unit before approaching the tall, familiar, blond-haired man standing directly over the victim.

"Hey Gus," said Joe to Swedish-born Gustav Svenson, Boston's chief medical examiner.

"Lieutenant . . . Detective," said Svenson, turning toward them, and in doing so providing Mannix with a full view of the twisted figure before him.

"Jesus," said Joe.

"Jah," said Svenson in his clipped Nordic English. "A tragedy, no?" All three looked down upon the body of Jessica Nagoshi, her long slender frame contorted in an unnatural curve that started at her pale slender feet, turned as it reached her thighs and arched at her elongated torso before taking a sudden impossible twist at her porcelain neck, which crooked inward and upward toward her head, which lay side up on the upturned stone.

She was fully clothed in a white shirt, blue sweater and pleated red-checked skirt that rested just above her knees. All that was missing were her shoes and stockings or socks, which were nowhere to be seen in the hothouse. Her long black hair flowed outward behind her face as if it had been pulled back and styled in a mermaidlike arrangement. Her bloodshot, dark brown eyes were wide, her once-red lips now drained of color.

"So what you got, Gus?" asked Joe, forcing himself to stay focused on the job. Disassociation was part of his trade, but every now and again you got one that forced you to "feel" it. And somehow this kid seemed to be . . .

"Jessica Nagoshi, nineteen," said Svenson, interrupting his thoughts. "Early assessment suggests death by asphyxiation or more specifically in this case, death by manual strangulation."

"He used his hands?" asked Frank, taking notes.

"I think yes," said Gus. "There are no ligature marks." He pointed to the girl's bruised neck. "If ligature, you would most likely see horizontal mark across the neck in the region of the lower end of the thyroid cartilage—and even the smoothest of ligatures leave furrows. Now note the thickness of the bruising," Gus went on. "And the irregular hollows most likely caused by uneven pressure from a palm or a thumb. My guess is autopsy will find fractures of the hyoid bone and thyroid cartilage, due to compression of these structures against the cervical vertebrae . . . which is unusual."

"What do you mean 'unusual'?" asked Mannix.

"Because of her age," said Gus. "The hyoid is a little U-shaped bone just on top of the thyroid cartilage and it forms the big part of the larynx. As we get older, our cartilage and the hyoid bone get calcified and manual strangulation is more likely to cause a hyoid fracture. In our teens, both of these structures are very pliable . . . like . . . how you say—putty. If a young person is strangled, they most likely not suffer a fracture of any of the bones of the neck—unless the force was . . ."

"Extreme," finished McKay.

"Yes."

They stood in silence for a moment, taking it all in.

"What about sexual assault?" asked Joe.

"No—at least no obvious indication. Rape kit will be done however, and I will do further examination in autopsy."

"Any signs of struggle?" asked Frank. "Don't they usually go hand in hand with manual strangulation?"

"Yes," confirmed Gus. "You are right, Detective. Victims of manual strangulation almost always have associated injuries such as scratches to the face or neck, or bruising to the extremities. But not in this case."

"The blow to the head," said Mannix.

"Yes," replied the ME. "Two blows actually, one on top of the other. Most likely she was unconscious before strangulation began—and even if she wasn't, the bruising indicates she was strangled from behind so . . ."

Gus moved to the side to point to the abandoned garden hoe being photographed by the CSR team several feet from the body. Joe noted it appeared to have blood on both of its ends.

"Body matter and hair on both the top and bottom end of the garden tool suggest this was the instrument that leave two specific impressions on the forehead . . . here," said Svenson, turning back to the body, "and here. One is long and narrow like the handle end, the other wide and thick like the . . ."

"Bottom of the hoe," finished Frank.

"Yes. And bruising suggests the blows successive—from different angles."

"Hold on a minute," said Joe. "Why the hell would the perp swap ends—and change angle?"

"And hands," said Svenson.

"Come again?" said Frank.

"Of course the autopsy will tell me more, but I believe that one blow was made with force from the right hand and the other from the left."

"Two killers?" asked Joe.

"Or one who is ambidextrous. Whatever the case, the blows followed each other. *Bang, bang*," said Gus, making them jump. "*Bang, bang*," he said again. "Not *Bang* . . . pause . . . *bang*. You see?"

"Ah, yeah. We got it, Gus," said McKay, scratching his head. "It just doesn't seem to make any sense."

"No," said Gus. "Difficult to explain."

"What about this rock?" asked Joe.

"Stone," said Frank, correcting his boss. "According to the gardener this stone comes from outside, it is number two of a set of three. He says it is meant to be upright but someone laid it on its side making it a . . ." Frank hesitated.

"A what?" asked Joe.

"A Death Stone," he managed.

"Geez," said Mannix.

"The stone was an afterthought," said Gus. "The blood flow pattern from the victim's head suggest it was placed under her head after death."

"Like a pillow," said Joe.

"Exactly," said Svenson.

"Sweet dreams," said McKay.

4

Twenty minutes later, just as Joe Mannix was heading back toward the Nagoshi residence to speak to the dead girl's father, David Cavanaugh was eight miles east, jogging across the Boston College rugby field, getting ready to pack down in a scrum just inside the opposition's half.

It was the first game of the season, and judging by the fitness levels of the Boston College old boys and their Northeastern counterparts, most of these ex-law school peers had done very little training over the summer—if any.

"Jesus," said David's friend Jay Negley, a big, blond chunk of a man who now worked for the Public Defender's Office. "What the hell are they thinking scheduling the first game for 8 a.m.?" This was the umpteenth time Negley had complained about their early morning call, and David and his teammate Tony Bishop were getting tired of it.

"They told us, Jay," said David, looking back at his lumbering friend. "It's a one-off. The freshmen have the field for the rest of the afternoon for some sort of orientation thing."

"Since when do a pack of wet-eared freshies take precedent over alumni?" asked Negley.

"Seems to me you asked the same question in reverse about seventeen years ago," said David.

"Yeah, well, at least I'm consistent." Jay grinned.

"Anyway, Negley," piped in Tony Bishop, who was definitely looking fitter than most of his maroon-and-yellow-jerseyed teammates, "no one asked you to pub crawl with your public defender buddies until three a.m."

"It was the boss's birthday. What are ya gonna do?"

"Work isn't everything," said Bishop as they reached the halfway line—a comment that sent David and Jay into fits of laughter considering Bishop, the blue-chip corporate attorney with a big harbor-view office and a paycheck to match, had built an entire lifestyle out of working as many $500-plus billable hours as possible.

"What?" said Bishop blank-faced before releasing one of his killer smiles. "All right, you got me there, boys."

The scrum packed down hard with the usual grunt of testosterone, David and Tony taking their positions in the back row, with Jay—a front row prop—locking shoulders with the equally brawny boys from Northeastern.

The Northeastern halfback fed the ball into the scrum and watched and waited for his teammates to boot it back for the inside center to receive out the other end and put the ball into play. But Jay managed to hook the ball with his right foot and send it in the other direction, back toward Tony and the rest of the Boston College pack. It was a good move. In a game like rugby, possession was everything. Now if only they could . . .

Just then a beeping noise cut through the grunts with a sharp high-pitched squeal—and Tony, who obviously felt the vibration of his pager in his right pocket, lost concentration, collapsing the scrum in one almighty heap.

"Shit!" he said as the ref gave a penalty to the other team. *"Shit!"* he said again as he read the look of frustration in his fellow teammates' eyes. "Sorry, boys," he said as he got to his feet just as the hooter sounded for halftime.

"So work isn't everything, hey Bishop?" teased Negley, catching up to his two friends as they left the field for the much needed ten-minute break. "At least I do my sucking up on my own time. Not in the middle of the first game of the season, against one of the better teams in this goddamned . . ."

"What is it?" asked David, interrupting his speak-before-he-thinks friend. They stopped on the sideline, David grabbing three water bottles from an assortment of iced drinks in a cooler at the edge of the field.

"What the . . . ," said Tony, finally getting a chance to read the message on his pager screen. "I don't believe this."

"What's going on?" asked David again.

"A client—a big client. His kid has just been murdered."

"Murdered? Who?" asked David.

"John Nagoshi's kid."

"Of Nagoshi Incorporated?" asked Jay.

"Yeah. His daughter's a student at Deane, a real looker too . . . I mean, she was a good-looking kid before . . . *Shit!* I gotta go."

"Now hold on, dude," said Negley. "I'm sorry for the girl and all, but since when do the victims need lawyers? Isn't that the DA's job?"

"Not when the dead girl's father is CEO and majority shareholder of a multibillion-dollar corporation. When this gets out, the share price could plummet, and believe me this is not one client you want to . . ." Tony was obviously thinking out loud.

"So where are you going?" asked David, watching Bishop collect his things.

"Home to shower and change, and then to the office—the partners want to brainstorm."

"On the girl's murder, or its financial repercussions?" asked David, unable to help himself. The debate of dollars versus morality in their chosen profession was an ongoing one between him and his fellow law school alumni.

Tony said nothing, just rolled his eyes. "Either way, you guys are gonna have to manage without me."

"Jesus, Bishop," said Negley. "You're gonna pay for this."

"Nah," said Bishop. "Sad but true fact, my man, as of now I am billing Mr. Nagoshi his usual rate. Sorry, guys," he said again. "But them's the breaks in the big bad world of corporate reality."

And then he slapped David on the back and punched Negley in the arm before racing across the field, jumping into his 911 convertible and taking off like his life depended on it.

5

"Lieutenant Mannix, Detective McKay," said the middle-aged butler with the Japanese-British accent. "My name is Harold Sumi. Please come in. Mr. Nagoshi is expecting you. I shall tell him you are here."

The first thing Joe noted was that the man knew exactly who they were. The second was that he greeted them more like attendees at an executive conference than homicide detectives about to partake in the details of a young girl's murder. And the third was that Mr. Sumi was focusing on their shoes, his head making a slight sideways gesture toward the front sandstone steps beside them. It was true, their shoes were a little muddied from their walk in the garden and this discreet gesture was obviously an "invitation" to remove their footwear before proceeding into the house.

Joe stepped back outside and looked down to see a number of other pairs placed neatly by the doorway—two pairs of worn, black Boston PD uniform issue (the shoeless officers would be doing a routine check of the house to look for any signs of breaking and entering, theft and so forth), and a shiny dark brown pair made from expensive Italian leather. Mannix and McKay discarded their footwear, Frank carefully placing his in symmetry with the other shoes that were lined up like sentries just to the side of the enormous double front doors, and they moved into the entryway, which was a large, limestone floored area with a double-vaulted ceiling.

The furnishings were a mixture of Asian and Western— cool-colored antique vases sitting on expensive classical European side tables, intricate Japanese artwork hanging over authentic handwoven Middle Eastern rugs, subtle modern downlights complemented by more traditional lantern-style wall illuminations. The effect was rich but not cluttered, ordered but not austere, cultured but not alienating. In other words, it screamed of good taste, international sophistication and an interior designer's budget from heaven.

Mr. Sumi bowed again before leading them across the entrance hall to the two hand-carved double doors, which he gently pushed aside to reveal an extensive living area, larger than the entire bottom floor of Joe Mannix's heavily mortgaged four bedroom colonial in West Roxbury.

The decor in this larger room was just as impressive—and, despite the massive oriental-style chandelier that hung above them, humble in some way. It was as if all the trappings of Mr. Nagoshi's obvious wealth were symbolic of a gratitude for his good fortune, as if this man took nothing for granted, and appreciated quality over abundance and humility over the grandiose.

"Detectives," said John Nagoshi, who excused himself from what was obviously a private conversation with a silver-haired, shoeless man in an expensive European suit, to walk swiftly across the room to meet them.

Nagoshi was of medium height, slim build with short dark hair showing not a trace of gray. His steps were light, his manner gracious, but the entire package said "confidence" to Joe, which was a strange first impression given the man's only daughter had been strangled to death just hours before.

"Mr. Nagoshi," said Joe, extending his hand and for some reason feeling an unusual level of vulnerability in the man's presence—particularly without his shoes. "I am Lieutenant Mannix and this is my fellow homicide detective, Frank McKay."

"Yes, I know," said Nagoshi, bowing slightly as he shook Frank's hand. "Do come in, detectives. Take a seat, please. This is my attorney, Mr. Gareth Coolidge of Williams, Coolidge and Harrison." Joe and Frank shook the attorney's hand.

"And my son, Peter," he said, gesturing toward a serious-faced young man sitting in an armchair at the far corner of the room. Peter Nagoshi nodded without bothering to get up, so Joe and Frank simply raised a hand in acknowledgment.

"Can I offer you some refreshments?" asked Nagoshi as the detectives took their seats.

"A coffee. Black, if that's okay," said Joe.

"Same, but with milk and three sugars." McKay bowed, and Joe wondered if it was contagious. Mr. Sumi immediately left the room.

All of these social graces were making Mannix nervous. He had seen plenty of unconventional reactions to murder, but this was not a morning tea, nor a civilized business meeting. It was a post-mortem interview following the host's daughter's death.

"Mr. Nagoshi," he began, now anxious to get started. "We are sorry for your loss but often the period immediately following a serious criminal offense such as this one is critical. Fresh crime scenes provide the most reliable evidence, and I am afraid the same goes for post-crime interviews."

"I believe you are right about the importance of haste, Lieutenant Mannix, and you can obviously appreciate my level of dedication to solving this matter."

Mannix said nothing. He had never heard a parent refer to a child's murder in such a way before.

"Right," said Joe, clearing his throat. "So as you can appreciate, I need to ask some questions—of you and your son and your wife, and anyone else who lives in, or was here, at your house last night."

Nagoshi nodded. "Peter and I are at your service, Lieutenant, but my wife passed away seven years ago."

"Oh. I'm sorry, sir. I didn't . . ."

"No need to apologize, Lieutenant. It was after her death that we moved to the United States—to New York. We have an apartment there where my company has its American headquarters, and six years ago I purchased this home here in Wellesley so that I might be close to my children while they attend university."

"And Peter," Joe said, raising his voice a little so that the young man, who had made no attempt to join the group around the coffee table at the center of the room, might hear him. "You were home last night?"

"Yes," said Peter Nagoshi, still not moving an inch. "I have my own private study adjoining my bedroom. I was working for much of the evening."

Joe noted the boy's accent was even stronger than his father's.

"And you did not hear or see anything untoward?"

"No," he said, before looking at his watch and returning his arm to his lap once again.

Joe stole a glance at Frank, who raised his eyebrows ever so slightly in return.

"I am sorry," said Nagoshi then, and Joe was not sure if he was apologizing to him for his son's standoffish behavior or to his son for holding him up. "I am afraid Peter has some rather urgent business calls to make on my behalf, so if you will excuse him briefly I am sure he will make himself available to answer any further questions as soon as the calls are completed."

Joe nodded as a determined Peter Nagoshi stood and left the room.

"I hope you do not object to my attorney being present during these interviews," John Nagoshi went on, gesturing at Coolidge who had made himself at home on an antique embroidered armchair.

"No, sir," said Joe, because at this point there was nothing else he could say.

"All right then."

"Okay," said Joe, shifting in his seat. "I need you to tell me as much as possible about your daughter, Mr. Nagoshi—and more specifically what you know to have been her movements in the past twenty-four hours. Do not discount anything as insignificant or too trivial to divulge," Joe went on. "And please make sure your answers are completely frank and devoid of any family censorship, which of course is a natural response when trying to protect the memory of a child."

Mannix met Nagoshi's eye but saw nothing but intense concentration.

"Please be assured," Joe continued, "that any sensitive information you share will be treated with the utmost discretion, but also know that if our investigation requires us to dig up some family dirt, then that is just the way it's got to be. In return I can assure you we will do anything and everything within our power to find Jessica's killer." They had been in the room for almost fifteen minutes and this was the first time anyone had said her name. "And that, Mr. Nagoshi, is a promise."

"I understand, Lieutenant," said Nagoshi without hesitation.

"You did not know my daughter so I appreciate you might assume there may be some . . . ah . . . dirt to be excavated. That will not be the case, but regardless of this, I can assure *you*, we are at your service." Nagoshi nodded again. "Please proceed."

And so it began.

6

Three hours later, just as the "freshies" were "taking over" the Boston College fields, another first-year orientation ceremony was taking place on the hallowed grounds of Deane. And impressive they were.

Deane University—named after the Massachusetts-born and -educated Nobel Prize winner Richard Cleaver Deane and spread over some four hundred acres of stately pines and rolling hills—was located in Wellesley, only twelve miles from downtown Boston. Cited as one of the "Most Beautiful Campuses in the Country" by the respected *Princeton Review*, the university was built around a surprisingly clear lake where canvasback ducks and black swans cruised under wooden bridges beside the whitewashed gazebos that dotted the extensive grounds like ornaments. The labs and lecture halls were housed in historic redbrick buildings with freshly painted shutters and granite entryways. Every classroom was fitted out with the latest technological facilities, and every dorm took in a view of what could only be described as "College Utopia."

Today's little "do" was being held in the School of Law's main reception hall, where the large glass bifold doors had been slid aside to their perimeters, allowing the sunshine and fresh air to flood into the sanctified meeting place. Here first-year law students could show the appropriate degree of awe at the wood paneled, honor roll–decorated walls, and older students, academia and trustee members could congratulate them for being among the privileged "chosen few."

"I am sure you have all read the blurb," said the Law School's dean, Brian Johns, who was standing at the ornate black oak lectern, front and center and elevated on a stage at the top of the room, "that Deane University is a premier private liberal University featuring highly selective undergraduate and graduate programs in numerous areas of the arts and sciences, business and law. But Deane—and its highly respected law school in particular—is more than that, as you are about to discover.

"True, you are 500 of the 5000 who applied, many of you having already completed an undergraduate degree at Deane, and others gracing our very special campus for the very first time. True, you come from colleges where you were ranked as some of the most academically gifted in the country, and true your Law School Admission Test scores were some of the best in the nation.

"You have achieved with the best of them and therefore deserve the best from us—and you shall receive it, in the form of state-of-the-art amenities, technologically advanced research facilities and, most importantly, a faculty made up of some of the most brilliant academics ever to come together with one all-important common goal."

Johns paused for effect, his jolly round face flush with the wonderment of it all.

"We are determined to give you—and our statistics tell us we *will* give you—every chance of graduating to become leaders in your chosen fields and trailblazers for those who follow. *But . . .* " Johns took a breath, obviously savoring the silence in the overcrowded room, continued, "more importantly, you are now members of the *Deane School of Law family*—a family dedicated to nurturing good citizenship, compassion and all-around decent Americans dedicated to using their already considerable talents and soon-to-be accumulated skills for the betterment of themselves, their family, their fellow students, their country and the international community as a whole. These are the qualities we seek in you . . ."

"Along with about seventy grand in fees and another big fat bundle in 'compulsory donations,' " whispered Heath Westinghouse into James Matheson's ear.

"And I know you will not disappoint us," finished Johns as the crowd clapped and cheered enthusiastically before moving outside to enjoy a sumptuous afternoon tea on the expansive lakeside lawns.

"What a load of crap," said Matheson, who had been dragged by Heath to this beginning of semester routine. "Why the hell did I agree to skip kayak practice in favor of this nauseating sales pitch?" he asked, grabbing a fresh apricot pastry from a white tableclothed trestle.

"Because you are my friend, and my father is on the Board of Trustees and he is partner in one of the most respected law firms in Boston, and you are third-year law, and . . ."

"Yeah well, after this afternoon I am not sure I want to spend my life in an office next to you, Westinghouse," said Matheson, who had just completed a summer internship at his friend's father's prestigious firm, practically guaranteeing him a permanent position with the blue-chip establishment when he graduated next spring. "And besides, like I told you last night, David Cavanaugh offered to help me out with my studies. Maybe he'll convince me to go with criminal law instead of . . ."

"Cavanaugh may be your goddamned hero, Matheson, but something tells me the close to six-figure first-year income my dad will be offering might convince you that there is more money in live bodies than dead ones," said his tall, blond-haired friend looking out at the picturesque scene before them.

"Well, Mr. Westinghouse," said James in his best Boston Brahmin accent, "if I wasn't such an honest man, I would take offense at such a comment."

"Who's taking offense?" said a well-dressed, pale-skinned, red-haired young man from behind them.

"No one," said Matheson, shaking his friend H. Edgar Simpson's hand. "Heath just called me superficial. That's all."

"Good for him," said Simpson with a smile. "And good for you too."

The three young men laughed before heading down toward the lake where one of the gazebos had been turned into a make-shift café serving fresh teas and espressos in Deane-logoed white china cups.

"All right, enough messing around," said Westinghouse at last. "Did you bone Barbie or not?"

James Matheson knew this was coming. The last time he saw his two college buddies he was on the receiving end of some pretty serious attention from Barbara Rousseau—one of the most beautiful, and up until the end of last semester, untouchable girls at Deane.

Barbara was a third-year sociology major, a French exchange student whose perfect long legs were right now on their way back to Paris—or more specifically, the Sorbonne, where they would no doubt tread the historic halls of the famous French university sending shivers down the spine of every red-blooded French boy within eyeshot. She had been at Deane for two years—her dad being some big French American diplomat, and her mom an ex-supermodel who still looked hot enough to be Barbara's older sister.

At the end of last semester, word got around that blond-haired Barbara, better known as "Marseille Barbie" thanks to her likeness to the plastic princess, had broken up with longtime boyfriend and college jock, Jason Speed. Needless to say, the male population of Deane celebrated, but then commiserated given it was the beginning of summer, which gave them little time and zero campus accessibility to capitalize on Barbie's newly realized emancipation.

All seemed lost, until last night at the Lincoln Club, when on the very eve of her flight back to Paris, she started coming on to one James Matheson, giving every other male in the room that contradictory sensation of elation and regret—elation that Barbie had given another one of their local boys a chance before saying "*au revoir*," and regret that the boy she picked had not been them.

"*You* banged Barbie?" asked H. Edgar, who, James thought, had probably been too drunk to even notice last night's potential hookup.

James looked at his friend, and for a brief moment felt a strange sensation of irritation as it registered how out of place this lowbrow colloquialism sounded coming from the mouth of his normally cerebral, calculating, highly opinionated friend. There was also something about the way he had asked the question—with the emphasis on *you*—as if there was no way Barbara Rousseau would go for a guy like . . .

"None of your business," said James, maintaining the smile he knew he should in response to such testosterone-driven inquiries.

"Come on, Matheson," said Heath, his own good looks and recent tan from a summer in the Cape making him, from the female students' perspectives, the male version of Marseilles Barbie. "Did you sleep with her or not?"

James rolled his eyes. "What does it matter? By now Barbara is half a world away."

"You *did,* didn't you?" said Heath, slapping his friend on the back. "I can tell by the look on your face."

"Let's just say I gave her a going-away present," said James, telling them exactly what they wanted to hear. "A sort of thanks for coming from all her American admirers."

"And did she?" asked Heath.

"Did she what?"

"Say thanks for coming?"

"Jesus, man, you are sick."

"Are your parents around?" asked James of H. Edgar then, in an attempt to change the subject.

"No, they left for Europe on Wednesday." Simpson's father was an ex-multinational CEO who now made a substantial post-retirement income by lecturing other prominent businessmen around the world in corporate management and international business relations. "Mother had some philosophy conference in London and Dad had some dinner with Lloyds so . . ."

"How are you feeling by the way?" asked Westinghouse. "The last time I saw you you were staggering up your ridiculously long circular drive. I waited outside until you made it to the door, figuring you might have kept going around and around, not knowing where to get off."

"Very funny," said H. Edgar, who resided in his parents' expansive Chestnut Hill estate. "And since you are asking, I feel like crap. Mitchell Ward wants some sort of favor from my father, so he kept serving me doubles," he said of the Lincoln Club bartender, who was also a scholarship student at Deane.

"Didn't your dad get him the job at the Lincoln in the first place?" asked Matheson.

"He did," replied Simpson.

"Ungrateful SOB." Heath grinned. "He should have been serving you triples."

The three of them laughed again as they grabbed another coffee and headed back outside toward the lake.

It had been like this ever since the day they had met at Deane's School of Law Main Admissions Hall just over two years ago. They had found themselves lining up to enroll in exactly the same classes and hit it off instantly as only three ambitious, commercially driven, privileged young men seem to do.

They had become instant friends, sharing similar upbringings with the same intellectual talents and corresponding lofty goals. They were trust fund babies of the highest order, never having any doubt where they belonged—at top private schools, in prestigious colleges and law schools, and eventually walking the hallowed halls of blue-chip law firms, influential merchant banks or multimillion dollar corporations. Their Ivy League banter had taken on a life of its own—a sort of cerebral dialect that was shaped by their surroundings but contained words, phrases and self-assured opinions that set them apart from the less fortunate of the fortunate. When first overheard, it might have come across as some overt attempt to consolidate their superiority, but, in fact, it was the opposite—more an appropriate way for three similar young men to communicate in a world where privilege had set them apart through no fault of their own.

James contemplated this thought as he followed his two caffeine drinking pals across the freshly mown lawns and wondered, in that second, just how "real" their bond actually was. Did they click because they were similar people who were destined to be friends for life, or because their "mirrored existence" had created a false common ground that, if removed, would shatter their camaraderie in seconds.

They are my best friends, he thought, *but I lied to them about Barbie.* More to the point, he knew, he had not told them about *her*—but that was understandable, given her requests to the contrary and the fact she was . . .

But James' thoughts were interrupted by the scream of a young girl, prompting him and his two friends to look farther down the gentle sloping levee toward a nearby footbridge where a second year by the name of Meredith Wentworth was now hugging two other girls who seemed to be just as distressed.

"What the hell is that all about?" asked Westinghouse.

"Who knows?" said James. They walked over to find out.

"Hey, Meredith," called James, who had last seen the under-age strawberry blond knocking back wine coolers at the Lincoln. "What's up? Are you okay?"

"Oh, James," said Meredith, turning toward the three boys. "It's Jess, she . . ."

"Jess Nagoshi? What about her?" said James, immediately feeling the involuntary gush of air abandoning his lungs in one almighty gasp.

"She's dead—*murdered*!" cried Meredith. A mascara-stained tear landed squarely on her crisp white collar. "Jennifer Baker lives down the block from the Nagoshis and she said the place was crawling with police. Apparently they found her this morning—at home, in her garden or something. I can't believe this." The girl sobbed some more. "This is a living nightmare, James. Like . . . last night she was so happy. You guys saw her. She was so sweet, so smart, so . . ."

"No," said James.

"Shit," said Westinghouse.

"Her father is going to have a fucking fit," said Simpson, and in that instant, James felt the bile rise in his throat, like a flare setting a torch to his dreams and obliterating them into one huge cloud of nothing.

7

"I am sorry, Mr. Crookshank," said twenty-six-year-old Peter Nagoshi. "But it really is not good enough."

Nagoshi America Incorporated President Bob Crookshank sat back in his ergonomically designed swivel chair—his large profile framed by a window taking in the expanse of the Manhattan skyline and Central Park below—and shook his head in the hope that what he had just heard was not, well . . . what he had just heard.

Just moments ago he had embraced these two men, held them tight, close, in a gesture of empathy. He had seen Mr. Nagoshi and his son—who had followed him to corporate functions like an obedient puppy ever since he graduated law/master in business administration earlier in the year—several times over the past few weeks, but always in the less intimate settings of boardroom meetings or corporate presentations. So this was the first time he had had a real opportunity to express his personal condolences to the two men, and given that he was born and bred in Texas, he did it the only way he knew how.

So much for compassion. Now they were booting his ass.

"What exactly are you saying, Peter?" asked Crookshank.

"That your productivity is down four percent Bob, your sales down seven and your overall profit margin shrinking by the minute. Need I remind you, Bob, that Nagoshi America Inc. is a publicly listed company and as of this morning the NYSE listed its shares at forty-one dollars. That is an all-time low for the past twelve months, Bob, and a long journey from the company's high of fifty-seven dollars just two years ago."

Shit, thought Crookshank. That goddamned fifty-seven high had been plaguing him ever since he took over the American division of Nagoshi Inc. just eighteen months ago. It was an impossible figure to maintain and was only reached due to the collapse of a major competitor.

Still, he had to admit, his division of the international conglomerate was not exactly reaping harvests of gold. Peter Nagoshi's figures were correct, but every president had his down times and this just happened to be one of . . .

"John," he began, making the decision to bypass the smartass son and appeal to the reason of experience. "It's a blip in the graph, that's all. Our new head of sales is a real go-getter. I poached him from Sony so he knows his shit. We're just about to initiate a new marketing campaign for the Notebook 3000 and, with all due respect, the share price was up to forty-eight a little over a month ago, just prior to the death of . . ."

Fuck! He stopped himself right there. *What a fucking stupid thing to say.*

"You're right, Bob," said John Nagoshi, sitting firm in one of the two large leather sofa chairs in Bob Crookshank's forty-fifth floor Madison Avenue office. "My daughter's passing did result in, ah—what did you call it, Bob? A *blip* in the graph. And that blip was felt internationally. But I find it hard to understand why all other divisions recovered instantaneously, while the US continued to, shall we say, blip on?

"No, Bob." Nagoshi fixed a smile on his face. "I am sorry, but my son is right. In fact, I am here to inform you that I will be taking over the presidency of Nagoshi America immediately, and working closely with my son until he is ready to . . ."

"What?" asked Crookshank, incredulous, his normally hearty skin blanching an even deeper shade of crimson. "Forgive me, Mr. Nagoshi, sir, but the suggestion that your son is in the position to assume such an important role is nothing short of ridiculous."

Crookshank was a physical being who, to be honest, right now felt like beating the shit out of his average-heighted boss and similarly lightweight offspring. But he took a moment, calmed himself and did his best to limit his bodily response by rising from the matching two-seater across from his two visitors and pacing the room.

"Mr. Nagoshi," he said after a breath, "Peter is barely out of diapers. I mean . . . law school. He is young and inexperienced.

"I made a commitment to you people," he said, immediately realizing this last comment may seem offensive. But he'd spent the past eighteen months dealing with the daily frustrations of US–Japanese cultural differences so, if it came out that way, then . . .

"I have worked damned hard under the circumstances," he went on. "And, I must say, have found your disinterest in discussing my range of progressive recommendations to be nothing short of insulting. I have expanded our household products division, consolidated our growth into telecommunications and . . ."

But when he picked up his pace to turn back across what the company interior decorator had referred to as his "inspirational but functional minimalist workplace," he saw that Nagoshi and his equally stealthy spawn were already on their feet and halfway across the coffee-colored carpet to the frosted-glass door. He still had no idea how they did that—moved like fucking cats without making a goddamned sound. It just wasn't normal.

"Thank you for your kind wishes of sympathy, Bob," said Nagoshi as he turned to bow before opening the door.

And with that, they left, leaving Bob to his million-dollar view and his ridiculously uncomfortable furniture, shutting the door behind them slowly, softly and without a trace of any audible click.

■ ■ ■

"You did well, *segare*," John Nagoshi said to his son as soon as they were safely inside the private confines of their car moving south along Madison Avenue. John Nagoshi motioned for his driver to pull out into the thick Manhattan traffic and make their way back to their two-story apartment on Central Park West.

"Thank you, Father," said Peter. "We are well placed."

"Yes. Regardless of Crookshank's incompetence, the forecast for the future is bright."

And it was.

Despite the death of his daughter, as Mr. Crookshank so inappropriately pointed out, Nagoshi Inc. was just last week named in the Forbes 500 comprehensive ranking of the world's biggest companies, at number 138—up twenty-seven places from the year before.

The list, which spanned fifty-one countries and twenty-seven industries and was measured by a composite of sales, profits, assets and market value, named Nagoshi Inc. the seventh most successful company in Japan—behind Toyota, Nippon, Honda, Nissan, Tokyo Electric and Sony. Its nearest market competitor was way back at number 205, just where it belonged.

Annual sales of their myriad of products, including everything from refrigerators and washing machines to DVD cameras and multimedia systems, computers and printers, cell phones and fax machines, were now at about eighty-five billion, with assets of over seventy-seven billion. They currently employed some 350,000 people worldwide with the company having 985 subsidiaries, including 486 overseas companies.

If there was one thing John Nagoshi had learned from his grandfather Nagoshi Isako who, together with his younger brother, Yoji, had founded Nagoshi Inc. over eighty years ago when they opened a small electrical repairs shop in a Tokyo marketplace, was that expansion was key to success. But his wise elder also taught him that sensing his surroundings, feeling when it was time for growth and time for stillness, was the only way to prevent the disappointment of failure.

"The animals observe their environment," his grandfather used to say. "They sense the ups and downs of the seasons. They feel the changes in the weather—the hot, the cold, the wet, the dry. They store food in times of plenty so that they can feed their young in times of famine. They know their enemies and assess their power and so learn when it is time to attack and time to walk away. Know this, *magomusuko*, respect all beings around you, and you shall be rewarded."

And his grandfather had been right. Observing, respecting and most importantly timing the push for growth was paramount to achieving your goals.

And that was why the next few months were so important.

While Nagoshi Inc. had established itself as a world leader in the area of household appliances, home entertainment products, technology software and hardware, and more recently telecommunications, it did not go unnoticed that Japan's most successful manufacturers were in the business of making cars. John Nagoshi had done what his grandfather had advised—stopped, listened, felt, observed, and now he knew in his heart that this was the time to push forward into the multibillion-dollar world of automobile production. The company was strong, the overheads down, the market ripe for a new alternative—and John Nagoshi, who had spent the past four years waiting for this moment, was on the verge of announcing to the world Nagoshi Inc.'s far-reaching expansion plans.

He wanted his grandfather's name emblazoned on the finest automobiles Japan, or indeed the world, had ever produced. He wanted to hand his children—his *child*—an empire born out of devotion but run with intelligence and sensitivity to both the strengths of capitalism and the basics of solidarity. He also felt it was time he gave the Toyotas, Hondas and Nissans a run for their yen. And so . . .

If they were to launch their new initiative at the beginning of the year, less than three months from now, they needed to rid themselves of burdens and consolidate their strengths—in matters of business, in matters of life and, in their case, in matters of death. This last thought crossed John Nagoshi's mind and with it came a wave of disappointment. Jessica's life had not gone as he planned. The Japanese had always seen mourning as an integral part of life, but he had not had time to grieve his daughter's passing, and now this acknowledgment of incompletion sat inside him like a boulder in the middle of a stream. He knew he must allow his spirit to recognize her death, but this was difficult given the demands of his work and the inability of the authorities to identify her killer. His grandfather had taught him patience, but his soul was demanding answers with an ever-increasing fervor.

"Crookshank was a mistake," said Peter, refocusing his father's thoughts on the situation at hand. And in that moment Nagoshi wondered if Peter had not just postponed his own process of grief, but forgotten the obligation to do so.

"Yes," said his father, perhaps sensing that applying himself to work was the only way Peter knew of mourning his sister. When his mother passed away, Peter responded by achieving the highest marks possible in his university entrance exams—marks high enough to gain him entry to the highly respected *Todai* or

Tokyo University—an institution he attended briefly before transferring to Deane.

"Appointing Mr. Crookshank was an error of judgment," Nagoshi went on, raising his voice over the customary din of honking horns and emergency vehicle sirens as he gazed out upon the sea of yellow taxis, private cars and pedestrians that negotiated the minefield that was midtown Manhattan. "But we agreed at the time that cultural sensitivities warranted us considering a local leader."

"We were wrong," said Peter, gazing out the opposite window at the standstill traffic, a look of pure intolerance on his smooth-skinned face.

"Yes, *segare*. But it bought us time. You have graduated magna cum laude. You have my support and my knowledge is yours as always. We keep no secrets, my son. That is how it should be."

Peter said nothing, just nodded. "Consolidation has begun then," he said a few moments later, and John Nagoshi took pride in knowing that he and his offspring breathed as one.

"Not just consolidation, *segare*, accountability. Crookshank was simple. One puff of wind and the dying leaf is gone to be replaced by fresh foliage. The other matter will take a greater effort. It is time for some answers, *segare*. Six weeks and still nothing. It is not acceptable."

Peter nodded as their car negotiated a right-hand turn on West Fifty-ninth toward Columbus Circle.

"She was a Nagoshi—my daughter, your sister," said the elder Nagoshi. "We cannot move forward until justice is recognized."

"Justice," scoffed Peter. "It is a joke, Father. Their efforts are incorrectly motivated. Mr. Katz is more concerned with individual progression than prosecuting the devils. How strange that Americans swear by the ethics of democracy, and champion the concept of teamwork, but live their lives dedicated to the benefit of the individual. They see personal ascent as a right, but it is a curse of selfishness and brings municipal downfall."

Nagoshi nodded. His children had been raised in Tokyo under their mother's care until her untimely death, when Nagoshi, determined to foster the international growth of his business but refusing to neglect his familial responsibilities, moved them all to New York.

Here Jessica, aged twelve at the time, attended the most exclusive international schools, all within blocks of their parkside apartment while Peter, then nineteen, began his graduate education at Deane—living under the supervision of Nagoshi's butler, Harold Sumi, in the Nagoshi's newly purchased estate at Wellesley during the week, and flying back to the Big Apple in the Nagoshi company jet on weekends. In other words, they were educated in a Western system but schooled in the traditions of their mother country—just as Nagoshi had always planned.

Together the two heirs to Nagoshi Inc. had made a potentially powerful team—Peter with his ambition and business sense, Jessica with her open intelligence and ability to embrace all that was American. As the children grew and Jessica graduated from high school, Nagoshi spent more and more time at their larger Wellesley estate, so that his children were not polluted by the trappings of American university dormitory life, so that he might watch over them during this important stage of their development, and they might join him on regular commutes to the company base in New York where they would sit in on conferences and meetings—quiet, observant, respectful.

Despite Peter having spent most of his adult life in America, his father knew that, unlike his sister, he was Japanese at heart—at *soul*. Even now his son preferred to read in Japanese rather than English, his only physical discipline came in the form of the Japanese martial art of *Bujinkan* and he often chose his native tongue over his adopted brogue in the confines of their private homes.

His American "friends" were acquaintances, his Tokyo connections expansive, and he showed no desire whatsoever to find a position for himself within the American societal structure. And as a result of his nationalistic attitudes, his grasp of English was almost completely "formal"—a dialogue learned from books, lectures and academic texts, rather than everyday conversation. In short, his command of the English language—or more accurately the *American* language—was somewhat strained.

Nagoshi was proud of his son's respect for their heritage, but he also knew such unwavering patriotism did not come without consequence. He realized Peter's inability—or perhaps sub-liminal unwillingness—to "acclimatize" to a nation that domi-nated the world economy had its drawbacks. And that is why he watched him so closely, guiding him every step of the way.

Jessica on the other hand had understood every nuance, ev-ery gesture, every shade of this technicolor society they call the USA. But that was not to be—*she* was not to be—and now was not the time to dwell on such irreversible matters.

Whatever the case, Nagoshi knew that this period in his son's development was critical. Peter had his imperfections, but his saving grace was his hunger to foster and grow his family's company to the best of his ability.

In the very least Nagoshi hoped his son was smart enough to understand the benefits of feigned assimilation. For it was such manufactured sincerity that had seen Nagoshi rise beyond the competition and become one of the few Japanese *kinmusha* to take their place on the world business stage.

"You are right about the selfish motivations of the Assistant District Attorney my son," Nagoshi said at last. "My sources tell me Lieutenant Mannix comes with high regard, but Mr. Katz made a note of his superiority and I believe his desire to control has masked his ability to listen."

"Mr. Katz is an egotist, Father," said Peter. "He is a rooster who likes to plume his feathers, an *unuboreya* who looks to himself before others."

John Nagoshi nodded. Perhaps his son was not so bad at reading Americans after all.

"You are right, *segare*. And enough is enough. I am going to set up a meeting for Wednesday," the older Nagoshi said, "to discuss any new developments in the case. If I am correct, Mr. Katz will involve the police—if only so he can blame his lack of progress on others. We shall observe them then, and decide on a course of action."

Peter nodded.

"Don't worry, Peter, one way or another we will finalize this matter."

"I know, Father," said Peter. "I know."

8

I am so close, thought Suffolk County Acting District Attorney Roger "The Kat" Katz after shutting his office door and telling his amoeba of a secretary that he did not want to be disturbed for the next half hour.

So goddamned close.

He felt the power within his grasp, and it wasn't just because his boss had taken an extended leave of absence to care for her mother who, as far as he could tell, was so far down the Alzheimer's highway to nowhere that she probably didn't even know it was her own daughter who had taken a dive on her career to sit with the old woman day in and day out. More fool her.

No, it was more than that. This Nagoshi trial was a gift—the perfect case at the perfect time. Sometimes you just got lucky.

Fucking Mannix, came the next logical consideration in his self-motivated train of thought. If Mannix and his useless freak of a deputy would pull out their goddamned fingers and give him someone, something—hell, anything—to work with, then maybe he would be just where he was destined to be. But they had nothing—bar a couple of unidentified latent fingerprints, a partial shoe print and an extensive interview log with the girl's family, friends, admirers, fellow students and so forth, which told them absolutely zip.

The call from Nagoshi was not unexpected. Katz had begun by phoning the CEO every day, but then had to reduce his call frequency to every second day and then every third, as there was nothing new to report. And he was furious at Mannix for putting him in such a position. In any other circumstance he would be relishing the opportunity to ingratiate himself with one of the world's most successful businessmen, but in recent weeks he had had to avoid him.

He took a deep breath, leaned back in his dark brown leather chair, and looked around his modest but meticulously arranged office—the wood-paneled walls, high Victorian ceiling, deep green carpet and serious lack of window space. Despite its insufficient size, he had to admit it carried an aura of success—and not just because of the black-and-white photos that hung on the wall behind him as a reminder of the many celebrated personalities who had admired his work—attorney generals, senators, governors and even the odd movie star. No, the air of accomplishment in this twelve by twelve was largely due to the fact that Katz was the man behind the antique cedar desk, and there were very few attorneys on either side of the legal fence—State or defense—who had the balls to mess with him.

He ran his hands over his shiny dark hair and his tongue over his straight white teeth—involuntary habits that assured his good grooming in the absence of a mirror. And then he felt a slight furrow form in his smooth olive-skinned brow as he realized how patient he had been. He had been playing bridesmaid to his less than competent superior, Suffolk County DA Loretta Scaturro for seven long years, which was definitely long enough. He had won her two elections by providing the balls to her banality, giving her platform the edge it lacked, promising and achieving a new high in criminal convictions and devoting his talents to kicking some serious lowlife butt. He treated every case like it was a battle—refusing the pussy plea bargains and going for broke in sensational and highly publicized trials. He fostered his reputation for intolerance and called for long sentences, most of the time nailing the maximum. And he continued to take the ultimate pleasure in watching defense attorney after defense attorney scurry from his courtroom wondering how in the hell their "surefire acquittal client" ended up with a pat on the back and life without parole.

Katz felt himself smile. The self-recognition was deserved, and definitely felt good. Of course there had been glitches—such as the horrendous Rayna Martin trial two years ago. But that was only because his moralistic boss had been afraid to commit to some unconventional but necessary interpretations of the law. Not to mention the fact that Martin's lawyer, David Cavanaugh, was good friends with Joe Mannix—the lead investigator on the case.

Which brought him back to Mannix. There was no love lost between the two lawmen. In fact, Katz knew that Mannix hated his guts. But Katz was no stranger to animosity and most of the time he thrived on it, and so . . . It was time Mannix and McKay got their acts together. They had to deliver and they had to do it now. For the Nagoshi case was Katz's ticket to the big time, and there was no way a couple of middle-class cops were going to ruin this for him.

No way.

9

"I swear to God, H. Edgar," said a red-faced Heath Westinghouse as he pushed hard against the double glass doors from Tort Room B and bounded out into the parquetry floored corridor beyond. "That man is out to get us. Did you see the way he targeted us?

"'Perhaps you are unfamiliar with the concept of the need for inventive approaches to capital growth, Mr. Westinghouse,'" mimicked Westinghouse. "I mean, what the hell was *that* supposed to mean?"

"He's just jealous," said H. Edgar.

"You bet your ass he's jealous. He has one of those 'short' man, 'poor' man, 'I'm a little asshole with a minuscule dick' man complexes whereby his sole purpose in life is to persecute those more fortunate. What a freaking pig."

They were talking about Professor Karl D. Heffer—a new member of the faculty who was teaching a recently introduced series of subjects related to corporate law and the concepts of entrepreneurial application. The aim was to teach the budding attorneys ways of "thinking out of the box"—looking for new ways for both client and attorney to make fresh capital on top of the existing billing practices.

"You have to come at it from his perspective, my friend," said H. Edgar. "The man probably comes from some middle-class burb in Iowa. He's small, overweight and seriously lacking in any compensatory form of charisma. He sees us sitting there and thinks we've had it easy—that we have sat on our proverbials for the past twenty-odd years getting Mommy and Daddy to fund our entire parasitic existence."

"The fuck they did. If I recall correctly, it wasn't my dad

scoring top one percent in the SATs or touchdowns on the football field."

"Exactly, but the chip on his less-than-substantial shoulders tells him otherwise."

Heath stopped then, right in the middle of the main building front doors, to turn to his all-too-sensible friend. Right now he was simply wishing he had chosen the "Regulation of Financial Institutions" elective like his other law school friend James Matheson, rather than stupidly corralling himself in Heffer's stable and being forced to listen to the likes of some big assed, miniature brained professorial impostor.

"How the hell can you be so calm about this?" he said at last. "Heffer is not just slandering us, but our parents."

H. Edgar said nothing, just paused for a moment as if trying to decide the best way to explain things to his obviously frustrated friend. Then he took Heath's arm, guiding him beyond the door and out of earshot of the river of students flowing in and out of the building on their way to their next class.

"Don't you see, Westinghouse?" he said at last. "Heffer is ripe for the picking. These sorts of Epsilons can't be told the truth of things, they need to be *shown*." H. Edgar loved calling those he considered inferior "Epsilons," after the lowest of the intellectual low in Aldous Huxley's *Brave New World*.

"What do you mean *shown*?" asked Heath.

"He insinuates we have no entrepreneurial skills because we are from families of privilege. He thinks we lack the ability to do anything inspirational simply because our parents are successful. It is a case of blatant 'wealthism.'" H. Edgar had once assured him this was a valid term coined by some dude with a PhD in social justice.

"So what do you suggest we do?" asked Westinghouse.

"We use his ludicrous assignment," said H. Edgar, his pale blue eyes now shining with the glow of what had to be a brilliant idea taking form in the recesses of his highly inventive brain. "And show him just how entrepreneurial we are."

Heffer had just given them a project whereby they had to work in pairs to come up with new and unusual ways to make money independent of a typical law firm's usual means of income. While just hypothetical, the students had to outline their ideas in detail—showing concept, aims, execution and results, listing all outlays and incomings as if their schemes actually existed.

The pair realizing the highest profit at the end of their imaginary strategy would gain a distinction and course credits as well as a sign-off from the professor to "make" law review. Becoming a law review member was the be-all and end-all at Deane, and most other prestigious law schools around the country. More important, it was a huge asset on your applications to blue-chip law firms, and a must-have for the hallowed Top Ten. James Matheson had already scored himself a front-page article on the Montgomery case and the entire student body had been talking about it for weeks.

"You want to come up with something spectacular for his banal assignment?" asked Westinghouse. "Somehow I don't think that's gonna change his mind about us being spoiled little . . ."

"It will if we come up with the money for real."

"What?" said Westinghouse with a half-smile, wondering what the hell was the scheme his conniving friend had come up with now. "You want us to work in imaginary law firms and realize an actual profit."

"If you remember, Westinghouse," said H. Edgar, now pulling his friend farther down the walkway toward Building C and their next lecture on corporate finance and taxation, "the professor's hypothesis did not specify that we had to work in an existing firm, just that we operated within the legal fraternity to make legitimately acquired funds."

"And how do you suppose we . . . ?"

"Jesus, Westinghouse," said H. Edgar, looking at his watch, quickening his step and urging his friend to speed up alongside him. "I'm not a fucking computer. I need a little time to think about it."

"Well," said Heath, his sour mood now eased by his friend's uncanny ability to whip intellectual ass, "think away, my friend, because whatever you are proposing, you can count me in."

10

"Been a while since you dragged me here," said David Cavanaugh, as he approached his friend Joe Mannix at the end of the bar of one of Joe's preferred drinking spots, a small, smoky Irish pub in South Boston known as The Idle Hour.

"Not that I'm complaining, but what's wrong with Bristow's?" he asked, running his hand through his sleet-soaked, sandy-colored hair. "At least it's close, and the clientele are . . . um," he paused to look around, ". . . still breathing."

"Very funny," said Joe, already on his second beer and shifting slightly in his seat to allow his attorney friend to slide onto the other well-worn green velvet stool beside him.

David knew Joe liked it here—the cozy, dark wood-grain ceilings, the stained glass windows, the 1950s jukebox, the regular clientele, and the thirty-odd clocks fixed on 6 p.m., which allowed happy hour to run forever. He also knew this was the kind of place Joe suggested when he needed to talk—in private.

David took off his scarf, gloves and coat before ordering two Heinekens, which prompted a strange look from the pepper-haired barman who spent the next three minutes trying to find the icy green bottles way at the back of the cooler. They sat in silence, enjoying the first few sips of the freshly opened brew— David knowing that if Joe had called him here to tell him something, he would need to do it in his own time.

"Late October and already as cold as hell," said David.

"Yeah. Apparently they're predicting another blizzard, like the one in '78. All I remember from that seven-day snowstorm was not being able to leave the house for a week."

"Jesus, that's all we need."

"How's Sara?" asked Joe after a pause.

"Great," answered David with enthusiasm. "She's working on setting up a pro bono arm of the firm. Her background at AACSAM means she has a lot of experience with clients who might not necessarily be able to afford private representation. In fact, she already has her first client—a young waitress being sexually harassed by her restaurant owner boss."

Before Sara joined their firm last year, she had been employed by AACSAM, the African-American Community Service Agency of Massachusetts. While working at the respected community service agency, Sara spent her days helping African-Americans and other minority groups negotiate everything from legal aid and insurance payouts to health benefits and educational assistance.

"She'll kick ass," said Joe. "She has the heart for it."

"That she does," said David.

They sat in silence for a moment, settling for two more beers from the tap—the new stronger, harsher lager somewhat jarring after the light imported brew—before David sensed Joe was still unsure as to whether or not he would share what he had intended to when he called David and asked him to this little get-together earlier that afternoon.

More often than not, Joe's inclination to clam up was due to his desire to protect David, his professional obligations and the possible repercussions of brainstorming with a cop. David was a defense attorney after all, and Mannix, despite his abhorrence for ADA Katz, was meant to be an extension of the prosecutor's team.

But whatever was bugging Joe tonight, David was sure there could be no conflict of interest. David's only current case was a health insurance dispute, and Sara was working on the pro bono thing so . . .

He knew his detective friend had been working on the high-profile Nagoshi case, but he also knew there had been no arrest, and according to his other friend and sometime drinking buddy, *Boston Tribune* deputy editor Marc Rigotti, no new public release of information. But maybe that was the problem, David thought. Maybe Joe was jammed up because there was nothing to report. Which also meant he was probably . . .

"I'm feeling some heat," said Joe, interrupting David's reverie and finishing his thought all at the same time.

"The Nagoshi case?" asked David, just as Elvis Presley's "A Fool Such as I" hit the jukebox turntable.

Joe said nothing, just nodded.

"So what's the problem?" prompted David.

When Joe put down his drink and turned to face his friend, David noticed how tired he was looking. His normally olive Italian-American skin was a sallow shade of gray, and his dark brown eyes ringed with the telltale signs of exhaustion.

"I can't get a read on this one, David. The case is so . . . clean." Joe shook his head before going on. "The girl was about to start her third year at Deane, she was aiming to go to law school, so all her subjects are pre-law—except for art history, which she studied independently at some fancy art school in Fenway.

"She was smart, friendly and popular in an upbeat sort of way. Her family are strangely calm but extremely cooperative, her friends are forthcoming about the girl's genuineness and her teachers do nothing but rave about her."

"Boyfriends?"

"None as far as anyone knows—and Frank and I must have interviewed over a hundred people on this one. Besides, her father is the controlling type so I doubt any kind of illicit tryst would get past him—nor the older brother for that matter, who, as far as I can tell, is twenty-six going on fifty—a chip off the old block."

"Last twenty-four hours?" David asked, his brain now snapping into investigatory mode.

"Nothing extraordinary. It was the last Friday before classes resumed so she went shopping on her own for school stuff in the morning, then to some French art film with two girlfriends in the afternoon—and out that night with same said female friends."

"Underaged drinker?"

"Most are, but not in this case," said Mannix. "She went to the Lincoln Club and met up with some college friends, but from what the bartender says, she was drinking sodas. The Lincoln is considered a family club so underage entry is allowed as long as they are not consuming alcohol."

"You mean it turns a blind eye to the robust drinking habits of the Ivy League offspring of wealthy member parents."

Joe shrugged again.

"Come on, Joe. These kids are probably covering half of the Lincoln's exorbitant Beacon Hill rent. I've heard about that place on a Friday night. My guess is half the clientele is underage and most of them are chugging back imported beers and expensive wine coolers at seven dollars a pop."

Another shrug. "What can I tell you?" asked Joe. "It's not like *we* never . . ."

"Fair enough," said David, realizing this was the second time in the past couple of months that he suddenly felt old.

"So what did the autopsy tell you?" David went on, getting them back on track.

"That she hadn't been drinking, for starters," said Joe, instinctively draining his own glass until all that was left was froth. "As far as the cause of death goes, Gus was spot on. Jessica Nagoshi died from manual strangulation, but not before someone clobbered her on the head with both ends of a garden hoe."

"Both ends?"

"Yeah." Mannix shrugged. "Go figure. The girl got it *wham, wham*—top and bottom ends—one blow from the right and a second from the left."

"Two perps?"

"Unlikely, but Gus says the blows applied equal pressure so maybe someone ambidextrous."

David paused. He could tell this ambiguity annoyed Joe, and it puzzled him as well.

"What about physical evidence?"

"The Nagoshis run a tight ship. Their staff are all from Tokyo and have been with them for years, including the gardener who is straight up. There were only four sets of clean regular prints in the greenhouse: the three family members—the mother died seven years ago—and the gardener. There were however two separate unidentifiable prints, the first one on the rock the perp used as her death pillow, and the second on the glass near the greenhouse door. Both are smudged and the one on the rock is pretty much unreadable."

"I know your CSR guys are the best, Joe, but have you thought of getting the FBI to . . ."

"The two prints are down at Quantico as we speak. I called

Susan Leigh and she is gonna make sure they get the full treatment. Our guys lifted them with the latest technology—glue
fuming, photometric stereo imaging and so on—so in the very
least, the FBI lab guys have the best raw materials available."

David knew of these two techniques. Glue, or cyanoacry-
late, fuming was a process whereby the fumes from heated
glue are directed onto a surface using a fuming chamber and a
small fan. Fingerprint powder is then applied to make the prints
visible. The technique worked on most smooth surfaces, including human skin and glass.

The photometric stereo imaging would have been used on
the rock because it was a superior method for lifting prints off
rough surfaces. From what David could remember, it used different angles of light to enhance the recovery of the print by
reducing the variations in the background surface.

"Anything else?" David went on.

"A partial shoe print, which appears to be a size eleven and
have the Nike logo in its tread. It doesn't match any of the family member's or gardener's shoes but it's a basic trainer print,
most likely from an average sized man, which narrows my
search down to roughly one quarter of the male population in
Boston."

"You holding anything back?" asked David, referring to an
old homicide cop's trick of keeping some small detail from the
press in an effort to flush out perps who accidentally "flip" on
said detail, not realizing it had been kept under wraps.

"Two things, actually," said Joe. "The first is, well, we
haven't even told the family, so . . ."

"I understand," said David, knowing when not to push.

"As for the second," Joe continued, "the perp took her
shoes."

"Hmmm," said David. He had heard of "trophy" killings
where murderers took some of the victim's possessions as me-
mentos, but in cases such as these, the stealth of clothing usually went hand in hand with some kind of sexual assault. But
according to what David had read, the Nagoshi girl had not been
raped. He turned to Joe.

"There was no evidence of sexual assault, right?"

"None."

"Then the shoe thing is kind of . . ."

"Weird, I know," said Joe, signaling for two more lagers. "I rang Simba and asked if we could put a profiler on it. See if it means anything."

"Simba" was the nickname of the FBI's Boston Field Office Special Agent in Charge, Leo King—a brown-haired, wide-eyed investigative genius and, better still, a good and trusted friend.

David nodded as he accepted the fresh drink from the now satisfied bartender and took a long sip. He noticed the brew was softening with practice, or maybe they were just getting a little drunk.

"That it?" he asked after a while.

"Pretty much," said Joe. "We've been through the girl's room and college locker and found nothing untoward. She was a straight-A student, on the university lacrosse team and pretty good at the art stuff. She liked to draw—sketch things. In fact . . ."

Joe bent down to his worn leather briefcase and pulled out what appeared to be a large sketch pad in a plastic evidence bag from one of the many inside flaps. He reached into his pocket and retrieved a pair of plastic evidence gloves, slipping them on in seconds—a practice he no doubt could do in his sleep, considering his daily dealings with death.

"What did she draw?" asked David, pulling his stool a little closer to get a look at Jessica Nagoshi's work.

"Portraits, nature scenes, stuff like that. She was studying French Impressionism and from what her art teacher told us, had a thing for . . . um . . ." Joe dove back into his briefcase to fish out his equally weathered notebook. "Pierre Auguste Renoir—the famous French guy who lived in the late eighteen hundreds. She copied a lot of his artwork in sketches, and I may be no art expert, but they look pretty good to me."

David watched as Joe leafed through the book and was seriously impressed. Jessica Nagoshi was one talented kid. He saw page after page of Jessica's delicate handiwork with the original portrait's name, and date of the artwork's completion, at the base of the page: *Little Miss Romaine Lacaux—1864, In the Summer—1868, The Dancer—1874, Girl with a Watering-Can—1876.*

There were large works and smaller ones, each capturing

the subject matter, mood and lighting of nineteenth-century France. Jessica's attention to detail was striking. She had the knack of complementing an expert's work as opposed to making it look like a practiced imitation or tracing, almost as if she had seen these scenes through Renoir's eyes, just as he did, almost a century and a half ago.

Joe then flipped the page again, revealing a sketch with a different subject matter. This one was not a portrait and had no title or date at the base. It was also a less structured, gentler interpretation, as if her pencil had taken a route of its own, freed from the boundaries set by a previous Impressionist master.

"What's that?" asked David, gesturing toward the sketch of a striking, dark-petaled flower.

"Black orchid. This is one of her own. The flower grows in the family greenhouse, not far from where we found her."

"I thought black orchids were a myth," said David, remembering reading some article about a couple of not-so-savvy plant smugglers who dyed orchid leaves with black ink, trying to pass off the pale-colored versions as their darker counterparts.

"Not a myth," countered Joe. "But rare as hen's teeth. The Nagoshis' gardener told me this particular bloom is worth thousands of bucks. In fact, at first we thought Jessica might have walked in on a thief trying to bag the plant, but the orchid was left untouched."

"Might be worth checking it for prints," said David, who could tell by Joe's expression that the thought may not have occurred to him.

"I told the CSR guys to lift everything but I didn't specify the plant life. Maybe they forgot the flower. It's not exactly an obvious place to . . ." said Joe.

"No," said David. "But it's doable. In fact, a lab tech from Philly once told me petals are the perfect surface for latent print lifting because they are smooth and soft and slightly moist. He also says they have little hairlike things on their surface that compress with contact and can sometimes provide a perfect print re-creation."

David watched as Joe made a note. It was worth a try.

Joe took another drink before flicking quickly through the rest of the book, and David glimpsed page after page of what looked to be some amazing reproductions. He stole a quick glance at Mannix, and saw how close the normally detached investigator was getting to this one. The sketchbook's corners were crinkled with signs of repeated turning and David guessed Joe had spent many an hour doing exactly what he was doing now—looking for some sort of clue, or hidden message, from the hand of the girl whose life it was his job to avenge. *This one has got to him*, thought David, feeling more than a tinge of concern for his dedicated friend.

And then something caught his eye. A quick flick of a sketch that showed traces of the same fluidity expressed in the drawing of the rare black orchid.

"Wait," said David, grabbing Joe's arm. "Go back," he said. "Further, before the one of the girl combing her hair."

Joe flipped backward and stopped at the portrait of a young man. It was drawn from a diagonal, showing most of the right side of his face and part of his left. The boy's expression was calm but focused, as if he was listening to something important and absorbed by the wonder of what he heard. His hair was short and dark, his skin shaded to appear tanned, his jaw strong, his eyes pale.

"God," said David then.

"What is it?" said Joe.

David hesitated. For some reason he felt an odd reluctance to share what he was thinking, which was ridiculous given Joe was a friend and this was a murder investigation, and even if he was right it did not mean that the boy in the sketch had anything to do with Jessica Nagoshi's death.

"I know this kid, Joe," he said at last, grabbing a bar napkin and taking the sketchbook from his friend's gloved hands. "At least I think it's him. I met him out one night. He is a friend of Sara's brother. A law student. He called me up after. We met a couple of times for coffee. I have been helping him with his studies."

"What?" asked Joe, clearly walking that fine line detectives often walked—between frustration and breakthrough, between disappointment and hope. "But I showed John Nagoshi the sketchbook and he didn't recognize anyone . . . Who the hell is this kid, David?"

While logic reminded David that the simple sketch meant

nothing, he also wondered what the consequences of his next utterance could be—for him and for Joe and for the good-looking kid in the skillfully drafted image before him. He was a young man David had come to like, admire even, perhaps even seen traces of himself in—the young man he had been back in his senior year at law school, loaded with idealism and with a world of possibilities at his feet.

"His name is James," he said at last. "James Matheson. He is in his last year of law at Deane. The night I first met him he was drinking at a Cambridge bar with his law school buddies—and it was the same night that Jessica Nagoshi was killed."

David looked at Joe then, and he could see the newfound interest in his eyes.

"And later, just before he left, he asked us if we wanted to join them. They were planning to make a night of it, their last big fling before the new semester began."

"Jesus," said Joe then. "He told you where he was going."

And David nodded. "He was headed to the Lincoln Club," he said then, looking down at the drawing once more, now feeling the highly illogical and yet undeniable twang of guilt. "It's him, Joe. I am sure of it."

11

It was early. Peter Nagoshi had only slept for four hours—a routine to which his body had now become accustomed given his increasingly senior role in a multinational company. He had been woken at five by a telephone call, and the information that was delivered had not pleased him. In fact, he was quietly seething with fury—at Mr. Kwon and his inability to control those determined to jeopardize the progress of their manufacturing operations in China.

The Nagoshi heir rose from his bed and retrieved his green silk robe from the antique Japanese oak closet. He put on his matching silk slippers and walked across the plush handwoven rug to the bedroom door. From here he proceeded down the hallway to the stairwell, ignoring the framed Japanese scrolls that hung in chronological order on the corridor walls—scrolls he would often stop to read, admire and draw inspiration from. But not today.

This morning he slipped down the hall of the exceptionally large two story apartment, taking the marble stairs two at a time before going into the kitchen for his ritual morning coffee. It was his only Western vice—coffee—strong and rich and, dare he admit it, effectively filling him with the energy he needed to face mornings such as these.

He gazed out the kitchen window. The city was still a sea of lights—the rectangular expanse that was Central Park cutting a dark divide across midtown Manhattan. His father was still asleep and he did not want to disturb him.

The Chinese. Yes, they were a problem. He had been unwise to underestimate the scope of unrest in Guangdong. Perhaps he should have stopped to read the scrolls this morning after all, for they documented the magnificent victories of the Sino-

Japanese War of 1894—of Japan's mastery in embracing the
need for advancement and China's archaic and self-destructive
determination to cling to the world of the ancients. Even then,
all those years ago, Japan had been wise enough to drain
knowledge from the West and perfect and adapt it to major
Japanese advantage, sending hordes of its diplomatic and military officials abroad to evaluate and mimic the strengths of
European armies, learning from British, French and German
advisors so as to construct their own powerful terrestrial and
naval forces.

So, what had started out as a squabble between Japan and
China as to the sovereignty of Korea, ended in the massive an-
nihilation of the Chinese forces when the Qing Dynasty's foolish
belief that the Chinese "strength in superior numbers" would
be enough to stop the driving force of a modern Japanese military. China's inability to embrace change, her disdain for the
pro-Japanese reformists in Korea, her refusal to acknowledge
the need for modernization had seen her stuck in the Third
World ditch she still found herself languishing in to this very
day. Peter Nagoshi was no fan of the West, but like his astute
ancestors before him, he had learned how to absorb their knowledge and discern the relevant from the refuse. He was a Nagoshi
after all.

Peter poured himself another cup of coffee before contem-
plating the irony of it all. The head of his Chinese operations,
Mr. Kwon Si, told him it was the West who had forced this
problem upon them in the first place, and in many ways he was
correct. It was the modern world that demanded "productivity"
and "profit" but also cried out for the principles of "solidarity"
and "human rights"—two philosophies that do not always sing
so harmoniously together. It was true the 300 workers at Nagoshi
Inc.'s Guangdong plant were overworked and underpaid. These
people were largely unskilled peasants who, in the scheme of
things, were fortunate to have any form of employment at all.
Peter's reformist instructions six months ago to cut salaries and
increase hours, to base pay on level of productivity and to remove any workers over the age of fifty-five were proving to be
extremely profitable. Output was up fifteen percent and costs
reduced by twenty, with all earnings going toward the launch
of their new automobile initiative—an initiative he had argued

should be based in China where land was cheap and labor was industrious.

Now Mr. Kwon, who had seemed only too happy to incorporate Peter's plans last May (with the promise of a small commission for every percentage point of growth—and a promotion to Senior VP of Operations once his father confirmed China as their major automobile manufacturing base)—had the impudence to suggest that his changes were a mistake, a shift in perspective that only materialized when a small group of American Solidarity Global militants had decided to use Nagoshi as their latest whipping boy.

Peter had acted quickly. He had neutralized the threat by claiming their accusations that the Chinese workers were forced to toil for over twelve hours a day for substandard pay were false—even going to such lengths as allowing three SG activists to enter their plant and interview a controlled number of workers on a specified day and time, so that they might compile their much sought after "employees' assessment report." He had done so well, in fact, that his father knew nothing of it. All the senior Nagoshi was shown were the productivity figures to which he had responded with a forceful, "Well done, *segare*." It was the Chinese growth that had secured him the promise of the company's US presidency after all, and there was no way he would allow Mr. Kwon's news of Solidarity Global's latest requests to hijack his progress.

According to Kwon, they had requested further information regarding the hours of night shift workers and confirmation of additional pay for overtime. They had also told the Chinese manager that their report would not be discussed with Nagoshi Inc. as previously suggested, but released on their website, in the form of an international press release, without warning. In other words, they were leaving Peter no room to negotiate, and the consequences could be devastating.

For once his hands were tied. He had thought the problem died with her—but perhaps, that had been an unwise and potentially costly presumption.

12

I should have never said it, thought James Matheson as his paddle sliced through the smooth silver water of the Charles River, enabling his metallic blue kayak to slide over the glassy surface at record speed. *I should never have lied about Barbara. It was a mistake and it will come back to haunt me,* he told himself for the hundredth time. He had suspected it from the outset, and now he *felt* it for sure.

He upped his rotation, pushing his aching arms even farther, forcing his screaming shoulders to rise to a new plane of pain where his picturesque surroundings slipped past him in a blur and the burn of lactic acid sent the self-admonishment away, at least for a while. He shot under the Anderson Memorial Bridge at record speed, leaving his fellow kayak team members far behind, before at last starting to slow. He could not do this forever and eventually he would have to face what he had done—or rather failed to do in the wake of her death.

He had spent the past six weeks convincing himself that it did not matter—that Jess was gone and would never know what had come to pass. But deep down he knew that hiding from the truth was not the answer, and at the very least he should honor her memory by telling the police what he knew.

James lifted his paddle from the water and allowed the kayak to glide. He closed his eyes and tilted his neck backward, feeling the icy wind bite at the perspiration on his brow and sting the reality of the situation into his brain. He went over that night again, wondering if anyone could have picked up their connection. If anyone could sense, feel, see what they had meant to each other purely by their proximity in a large but crowded room. The secrecy had been difficult from the outset, especially in those early days when he could think of nothing else. But it was as she wanted, and so he had obliged, for she was strong and beautiful and persuasive and in the end he knew she had been right.

He took a breath, his brain now trying to focus on the one immediate priority he knew he had to face—that if the police came to question him, his alibi would not stick. He knew this and yet was still afraid to come forward and tell them the truth about what she had meant to him. For when it came down to it, he was honest enough to admit, he was terrified beyond all imagination that his "perfect" life would end.

James Matheson's privileged existence had started the minute he was born. He grew up the only child in a reasonably happy home, spent summers at the Cape and winters in Aspen and attended the best private schools his affluent parents could afford. His parents had an unusual relationship in that they were still together but had lived apart at various intervals to further their respective careers. In fact, when he was twelve he had moved to Australia with his mother who was offered the chance to study for a doctorate in psychiatry at the respected University of New South Wales.

In Sydney he attended an exclusive boys' school, lived in a harborside home and trained with some of the best swim coaches in the country. He spent his mornings at squad, his weekdays studying to get the grades required to gain international admission to Deane and his weekends catching waves, playing rugby, downing schooners and chasing some of the prettiest girls on the face of the planet. As soon as he finished his Higher School Certificate, scoring a near perfect 99.9, he made the trip back to his father's home in Brookline where he took up residence in the renovated pool house. His mother stayed on in Sydney, making regular trips to the US, her career having soared to the point where she was currently considered one of the most experienced psychiatrists in the South Pacific region.

Since graduating with an economics degree at Deane, he had breezed through the first two years of law, slid through three "appropriate" relationships with attractive, intelligent and "connected" girls, achieved regular personal best times in the pool and kicked ass on the river in his blessed blue kayak. His life was, in a word, perfect. It was as if his own personal screenplay had been written even before he was conceived. And he had made sure that it never wavered from the script; in fact he had embellished it with overachievements—personally, academically, athletically.

And then he had met her, Jess Nagoshi, the girl who entered his world like an unexpected summer storm and changed his life forever. She was like no one he had met before—and most likely would ever meet again.

James shut his eyes once again as he felt the anger well up inside him—the now familiar heat of rage rising from the dead weight in his stomach to constrict the breathing in his chest. *It is the ultimate paradox,* he thought, the fact that on one hand he knew what he had to do—what a man such as he was meant to do—and on the other was hesitating for fear of upsetting the balance of his predictably flawless existence. A catch-22 with the best of them. A lose/lose when all he had ever known was win/win and win again.

But in the end he realized there was only one answer, only one way to save himself from a life of never-ending regret. And so he turned his kayak around and headed back to the Deane University boat shed, wincing as his now stiff limbs cried out in protest. And then he picked up the pace . . . one, two, one, two . . . until his brain was doused in the comfort of the mind-numbing repetition and his body comforted by the growing sensation of pain.

. . .

Six months earlier

"Are you trying to set some kind of record?" she had asked. They were the first words she had ever spoken to him, in that calm, inquisitive voice.

He had not even noticed her. It was early, before seven, and he had just returned to the boat shed following a solo paddle down the river.

He loved this time of morning, the solitude of dawn, those moments between darkness and light when, somehow satisfied with their allocated allotment, the shadows gave way to a rising sun and the ever-promising possibilities of what lay ahead.

"I'm sorry?" he said, squinting up the levee to where she

sat, knees to her chest, a sketchbook and pencil discarded beside her. "You took it out pretty hard this morning," she said, "like you were in a hurry, running to, or away, from something."

"It's called training," he said, placing his kayak and paddle on the rack before grabbing a towel from his gym bag. "The Compton Cup is in a couple of weeks so . . ."

"So you like to win," she interrupted.

"I, ah . . . I suppose I do. Anything wrong with that . . . um . . . ?"

"Jessica." She smiled. "And no, there is nothing wrong with that, James Matheson, just so long as you gain more than the kudos. You know, so that it makes a difference," she said bringing her palm to her chest. "In here."

He looked at her then, not knowing what in the hell to say. She was so still, so perfect that she might have formed the centerpiece of some classic Asian masterpiece.

"Do I know you?" he asked, realizing she had referred to him by name.

"No. I come here mornings, you know, to sketch the dawn. I'm studying Renoir and he was a master at light and how it soaks the world in color and clarity."

"You an art major?" he asked, putting his towel around his waist from some instinctive need to cover himself in front of her.

"No, pre-law actually, the art is a welcome diversion. My father is John Nagoshi," she said matter-of-factly, like it was part of her makeup—just as she had black hair, brown eyes, straight teeth and long, porcelain-skinned legs.

"Why do you like being alone so much?" she asked, surprising him again with her frankness.

"Who says I like to be . . . ?"

"Of course you do. That's why you kayak and swim and spend so much time sitting in the back row at tutorials."

"Maybe all the front-row seats are taken," he said, now walking up the bank toward her.

"No. They're not," she said.

And then she said nothing, as if waiting for him to go on.

"I like the water," he said after a time, perhaps trying to justify himself. "It makes me feel . . ."

"At one with the world, I know," she interrupted him again. "Did you know water is one of the five Japanese *Godai*, the great elements of life? It represents all things flowing, formless and constant—like our emotions, our adaptability, our suppleness and even our magnetism."

"Ah . . . no, I didn't."

"Well, you do now."

He stood there for a moment, now right in front of her, the only sounds coming from the water that dripped from his body onto the fallen maple leaves that covered the levee in a choppy sea of red.

"I have to go," she said, grabbing her things and rising to her feet so quickly that his natural impulse was to take a step back. Which he did not do.

She smiled at him then and he found himself studying her— her flawless skin, perfect narrow face and clear almond eyes. And then he opened his mouth to ask her something—a question he knew he needed to ask before his brain even registered exactly what it might be—only to have her cut him off again.

"Don't worry," she said as she raised her slender right arm and flicked a random fallen leaf from his left shoulder. "I'll be back. This was nice." And then she turned and started walking up the hill.

"I am glad to finally meet you, James Matheson," she said without turning around. "You are just as I expected."

13

"Jesus Christ, Frank," said Joe Mannix, turning to face his detective partner who was bent over and seated next to him on the plush purple sofa just outside of Dean Brian Johns' expensively decorated office. "What the hell are you doing?"

Detective Frank McKay tilted his neck and looked up at his boss with his usual "*no capisce*" expression as he retrieved the red tartan lunch box from his faux leather briefcase and proceeded to open it up.

"What?" said McKay, proceeding to undo the neatly applied cling wrap on his tuna salad sandwich. "Didn't you hear the bell, Chief? It's lunchtime. The Dean's secretary said he'd be at least fifteen minutes. You know what I'm like if I miss a meal, boss. And tracking down this kid could take all afternoon."

"For Christ's sake, McKay. The bell wasn't meant for you. You're a detective, not a freshman whose mom still packs his lunch in some quaint little carry case. And it smells like shit by the way. So just can it, okay?"

"All right already," said McKay. And Joe knew he had gone too hard on the annoyingly endearing detective who usually amused Joe with his unconventional take on "appropriate." But he guessed Frank knew his short temper had more to do with this case than with the tuna because he packed up the fish and put it away without another word.

They waited a full twenty minutes, listening to Brahms, Handel or one of those other European geniuses whose music seemed to go on forever. And then, when Johns was finally available, waited a further fifteen while he consulted once again with Deane's legal advisors before giving his official permission for them to reenter the grounds and further question the students.

Once that was done—and Mannix and McKay reinforced their promise not to "request that any student accompany them off campus without full permission from the school and the said students' parents or guardians"—they were allowed to check with administration as to the whereabouts of one James Matheson who, it was soon revealed, was currently at kayak training and could most likely be contactable once he returned to the campus boathouse.

"Do you want me to leave a message for him to come to the Dean's office as soon as practice is over?" asked Johns' administration coordinator, a tall, thin, pinched-faced woman whose hair was the color of a rusty drainpipe.

"No thanks," said Mannix, preferring to catch the boy off guard. "If you could give us directions we'll save Mr. Matheson the trip and meet him at the boat shed."

"It's a boathouse, not a shed, Detective, and you may proceed as you wish," said the woman with a fresh squeeze of lemon on her lips. "Here's a campus map. The boathouse is on the southern side of the campus past the Medical School and the College of Humanities. But if you intend on walking I'd hurry. Practice finishes at one, and Mr. Matheson will most likely want to shower before his afternoon classes."

"He lives on campus?" asked McKay.

"No, in Brookline. But the sports complex on the western side of the campus has an extensive shower area where many of our athletes like to freshen up after training."

"Right," said Frank. "Well, that's a lot of helpful information Mrs. . . ."

"It's Ms. Humfries—with an 'f,'" said "Lemons."

"Well, thank you, Ms. Humfries with an 'f,'" returned Frank with a smile. "It's been a pleasure."

Humfries, perhaps taken a little aback by Frank's impressive manners, also managed a smile—at least Joe thought it was a smile—barely one notch up from a wince.

"Not a problem, Detective," she said. "And please don't hesitate to call if there is anything else you require."

"Will do," said McKay who gave Ms. Humfries another appreciative nod before following his boss out of the office.

"I think you might have made yourself a friend, Frank," said Joe, now realizing he was smiling as well.

"Nah," said McKay. "I just figure a woman like that goes about her job professionally and efficiently, day in day out, without so much as a thank-you. She's just looking for a little respect."

"Aren't we all, Frank?" said Joe, himself now grateful for Frank McKay's unique view on life. "Aren't we all?"

• • •

The kid was on a soapbox—literally, on a soapbox. It even had the branded logo of "Imperial Leather" on its side, and Joe guessed his elevated position was not so much so that he could be heard—because his bullhorn speaker was taking care of that—but more so that he could be seen.

"What the hell is going on there?" asked Frank, who had talked his boss into grabbing two coffees and a matching pair of doughnuts at the campus canteen before striding south across the dewy emerald lawns of Deane.

"Some sort of rally," said Mannix, his breath blowing clouds of condensation into the chilly fall air. "Check out the master of ceremonies." Joe stopped to look at the freckle-faced kid on the soapbox. "He can't be more than . . ."

"Twelve by the looks of things," finished McKay.

Joe knew they would have to make quick time to catch James Matheson at the boat shed, but there was something about this kid that was compelling. He had placed himself, and said box, smack in the middle of the campus courtyard, a thoroughfare for students leaving what must have been a total of six or more buildings congregated around the campus in a semicircular formation. He was loud without sounding aggressive, his tone sympathetic but forceful, so much so that Mannix found himself readjusting his hearing to tune in to the boy's soliloquy—something about workers' rights and Third World degradation.

"In Taiwan, children as young as six are toiling in retail factories owned by multimillion-dollar companies whose executives spend more on a tie than they do on the annual wage of their Asian workers," said the boy. "In China, toy manufacturers who make annual profits of over forty million dollars per year are paying their staff twelve cents an hour per fourteen-hour day. In Thailand, Burmese migrant garment factory workers are being paid fifty baht—that's less than two American dollars—per day to work in filthy, dangerous, overcrowded conditions where factory fires have killed over 1200 people in the past twelve months. And in Indonesia, a multibillion-dollar sporting goods company operates a factory where young female workers have been asked to trade sexual favors to gain employment . . . and the list goes on."

The boy stopped to shake his mop of unruly light brown hair, his words obviously hanging heavy on the shoulders of the fine young elite who stood, cell phones pocketed and textbooks hiked, stock-still in front of him.

"The thing is," said the boy, now scratching his head before moving on. "The only person, the only *single*, *solitary* human being who can help these workers and their families, is *you*."

The boy looked up then before extending the thin arm not supporting the bulbous bullhorn toward the growing crowd of students who were now obviously mesmerized by the content and delivery of his emotive oration.

"You, and you, and you, and *you*," he said pointing at individuals as he went. "Each and every one of you can impact upon these people's downtrodden existence. A small contribution of your time, and maybe your spare change, is all it takes to raise awareness and make a difference."

The kid lowered his speaker and raised both hands in a "that says it all" gesture before nodding the shaggy mop once again and continuing.

"As Bono says: 'Where you live should no longer determine whether you live' and 'distance should not decide who is your brother and who is not.'"

"We all come here to feed our brains. We all come here to pad out our resumes. We all come here to fill our social calendars, but that doesn't mean we can't satisfy our souls at the very same time. So grab a brochure, fill in a membership form, make a donation, give whatever you can and help get the word out that it is not okay to treat workers like slaves just because they happen to be born on a continent that has fallen prey to the rampant greed of the multinationals." The boy paused again, the silence around him deafening. "Make a difference," he said, before smiling at the crowd in front of him. "Make a difference for them—and more importantly for yourselves. Thank you."

. . .

"Who the hell is Bono?" asked Frank, diverting Mannix's attention away from the boy who had jumped from his wooden podium to hand out the brochures.

"Jesus, Frank," Joe rolled his eyes. "Where have you been for the past fifteen years? He's Irish, the singer—U2."

"No, Chief, not me. Can't hold a tune to save myself, and my father was Scottish."

"For fuck's sake," said Joe, realizing it wasn't worth the effort and pulling his partner back on route toward the southern end of the campus. "Sometimes I wonder if you'll ever come down from Planet McKay and grace us with your company in the real world."

"Detectives . . . !"

Joe was interrupted by a voice from behind and turned to see the soapbox kid running down toward them. The kid extended that skinny arm again, and gave them both a double pump, an almost ludicrously "grown-up" greeting that surprised Joe with its intensity.

"Sawyer Jones, Solidarity Global," he said.

"Frank McKay, Boston Municipal," returned Frank.

Joe gave Frank a sideways glance. He could see the kid was rubbing his fellow detective the wrong way—and he had to admit, despite the kid's obviously noble motives, he was coming off a little cocky.

"I'm sorry, detectives. I recognized you from your previous visits," said Jones unfazed. "I saw you watching me. The subject of workers' rights interest you, Detective?" he said, turning to Joe.

"A lot of things interest me, Sawyer," said Joe, turning to move on and indicating if the kid wanted to press this, he would have to stay with them. "But ninety-nine percent of them I don't have the time for."

"My guess is Jess Nagoshi is in the other one percent then," said Jones, forcing Joe to stop in his tracks.

"What do you know about Jessica Nagoshi?" asked Joe, wondering what the hell game this kid was playing. Jones obviously read the edge in his voice and attempted a smile before moving on.

"Look, I'm sorry, detective . . ."

"Lieutenant . . . Mannix," said Joe.

"Lieutenant," resumed Sawyer. "Jessica was a friend. We had some of the same classes last semester. I'm pre-law as well. I'm going to major in the human rights and international varieties."

"Good for you," said Frank who pointed at his watch, indicating to Mannix that they needed to get going. The two detectives started walking again, forcing Jones' shorter legs to work in double time in order to keep up.

"You got something to tell us, kid?" asked Joe at last.

"I guess that depends on what you want to know," replied Sawyer.

"Like . . ." prompted Frank.

"Like that Jess was a member of Solidarity Global, that she had a particular interest in China, that she was angered by the abuse of Third World workers and that she was willing to take a personal stand against the multinationals who perpetrated such abuse."

"Her father owns a multinational, kid," said Frank. "Just how angry is she supposed to get?"

Jones said nothing which, for some reason, piqued Mannix's interest. He knew talkers like this kid and nine times out of ten, when they fell silent, that was when they usually had something to say.

"Look, Sawyer," said Joe, stopping to turn to the boy once more. "If you've got something to tell us, then you owe it to your good friend Jessica to spit it out. If not, we've got someone to see so . . ."

Joe saw the kid hesitate, almost if he was having his own internal war with the definition of "principle." *He knows something, or in the very least suspects something*, thought Joe, but even a confident kid like Sawyer was having trouble organizing his opinions on this one.

"Kid," said Joe, his eyes locking with Sawyer's huge brown pools before looking up briefly to see the boat shed at the near western end of the levee. "Here's my card. I think maybe you should get your thoughts together and give me a call. Okay?"

"Ah . . . sure," said Sawyer, taking the card before following Mannix's eyes toward the boathouse where a group of young men were now stowing their kayaks on racks on the side wall of the freshly painted wood shingle structure.

And then Joe saw it—a fresh spark of recognition in the boy's eyes—as if a new piece of the jigsaw puzzle had fallen into place in that bright, young, overcrowded head of his, creating a picture that did not sit well in the world of Sawyer Jones, intellectual crusader.

"You're here to talk to James Matheson, aren't you?" he asked at last.

"What makes you say that?" returned Frank, stealing a glance at Joe before turning to face Jones.

"He didn't do it," said Jones now, taking his own small, slow steps in retreat, an expression of what appeared to be disappointment now descending upon his innocent boyish features.

Sawyer looked at them then, before turning to move slowly back up the riverbank, with one more thing to say. "James loved her, detectives," he said, his back to them now, his voice low and resolved and filled with traces of what Joe believed to be regret.

"And Jess . . . well, Jess loved him just as much in return."

14

Myrtle McGee's was packed. The popular harborside cafe was abuzz with the usual lunchtime crowd of health-conscious workers all clamoring to place their order and nab a seat, or grab their fresh salad baguettes and homemade rhubarb pie as takeout, before trekking back to their offices in Government Center or Downtown Crossing or the Financial District.

There was no Myrtle. In fact, Mick McGee, the café's Irish-born, carrot-topped proprietor and chief cook, looked more like a retired army recruit than a health-conscious homemaker. But according to Mick, his clientele liked the idea of some sweet old Irish lass working with deliciously fresh produce beyond his lime green counter and multicolored chalkboard menus—and if the myth brought in the customers, then who was he to destroy the fantasy?

"Ah . . . Davy, my boy," said Mick as he threw an extra carrot into a swilling juice concoction that looked more like a multicolored vitamin tablet than a palatable beverage. "Want to try my latest combination? It's carrot, celery and beetroot with a handful of wheatgrass and a smidgen of mint."

"Geez, sounds tempting, Mick," said David, finally reaching the crowded counter front. "But I might play it safe and go for a fresh orange and pineapple instead."

"Same here, Mick," said Tony Bishop who wormed his way up next to his attorney friend. "And how about two of your famous Mexican chicken rolls to go? There is no way we are bagging a seat in here today," he said, looking around.

"Maybe we are in the wrong business after all, DC," said Bishop, turning to David. "Seems like there could be more cash in melons than mergers. What do you say, Mick?"

Mick looked up from his juicer to survey the "thriving" enterprise before him.

"To be sure, Mr. Bishop." He grinned. "And a lot less stress. No monkey suit and a breathtaking harbor view to boot. I am looking for a breakfast hand by the way—if you're interested."

"That's a definite *no*, Mick." David smiled, answering for his friend. "Unless the job comes with a six-figure bonus and a company Porsche."

"Not this week, lad." Mick laughed, handing them their juices and generous chicken wraps. "But I'll keep Mr. Bishop here in mind if anything else comes up."

David and Tony took their lunches, said good-bye to Mick and began negotiating their way back out of Myrtle's and down toward Christopher Columbus Park at the northern end of Boston Harbor. They took a seat on the grass, enjoying the midday sunshine and the welcome lull in the recent spate of biting offshore winds.

"I don't know how he does it," said Tony as he unwrapped his oversized roll.

"Who?" asked David.

"Mick. The guy is up at five a.m., works through until at least six. Doesn't have time to scratch himself and all for what? Eighty grand a year tops? I make more than that by the time I've brushed my teeth in the morning."

"He's happy," said David who was used to his corporate lawyer friend's somewhat materialistic outlook on life. "He built Myrtle's from scratch. He's got a lot to be proud of."

"Pride didn't pay for my three-bedroom apartment in Copley," said Tony. "And I still feel pretty good every time I take the elevator to the penthouse floor."

David smiled and glanced at his friend. "Whatever works, bud," he said.

They sat in silence for a while, finishing their lunches before David turned to his friend again. He noticed Tony was looking out toward the water, an almost daydream-like expression on his strong dark features. He was also looking a little tired—gray circles framing his deep brown eyes. Tony was definitely not in his normal ten-miles-a-minute mode today. In fact, on closer examination he looked exactly like Joe Mannix had the night before—downright exhausted.

"So what's up?" asked David, guessing he already knew. "You've missed two rugby games in a row and Deakin sucks in the backs. You still propping up the Nagoshi share price, or have you moved on to some other poor suffering multimillion-dollar enterprise?"

"Hmmm." Bishop sighed. "See there's the irony, DC. Nagoshi Inc. did suffer a moderate slump after the daughter's death, but it has recovered with a bonus. Better still, yesterday they sacked their American president, a Texan named Bob Crookshank, and the share price went *up* two points."

"Yeah, I think I read something about that," said David, draining the rest of his juice. "But I thought high-level layoffs usually sent stock plummeting."

"They do," said Tony. "But I swear to God, DC, this company is invincible—or rather John Nagoshi is invincible."

"How so?" David was curious now, if not in the least because of his recent conversation with Mannix regarding the seemingly unsolvable Jessica Nagoshi case.

"Well, Nagoshi dumps Crookshank," Tony went on. "But at the same time announces he is stepping in as temporary US president until they find an appropriate replacement. Rumor has it he is priming his son Peter to eventually take over the company, and the American presidency would be a great place to start."

"But isn't the kid just out of law school?"

"Yeah, but so what? Look at the Murdoch kids. They are young, but super-smart. Age isn't such an issue anymore, DC. In fact, youth can be an asset, especially when Dad is a fit fifty and bound to be around doling out sound advice for the next thirty years."

"So this Peter is being primed to . . ."

"Peter and Jessica were both being primed to be future company leaders. In fact, together they made a pretty hot team. Both smart, hardworking, and from what I hear, Jessica's approachability took the edge off Peter's arrogance."

Tony looked up, as if sensing he had said too much. No matter how mercenary Tony might be, he never betrayed a client's confidence—and David respected him for that.

But then Tony smiled, and David knew his friend was aware that anything he said remained between the two of them. They had acted as sounding boards for each other since college and neither had ever come close to taking advantage of their friendship. In fact just last year David had helped Tony's nephew beat a drug rap that saw Tony's congressman brother's political career at risk. David had gone out on a limb for his high-powered friend and knew that when it came down to it, Tony would do the same for him.

"So," David went on, guessing his friend needed to talk about this, "is the son up to the job—minus the less intimidating daughter?"

"Yes and no," said Tony, shaking his head. "It's hard to say. Peter is very, ah . . . *Japanese* for want of a better description, and that's not a racially based criticism by the way, more a corporate observation."

"How so?" said David, genuinely intrigued.

"Well," Tony began, now removing his jacket as the sun slid west and hit their backs with a new intensity. "It's like this."

Tony went on to explain that when his firm took on the Nagoshi account a couple of years ago, the firm's senior partner and Nagoshi's personal lawyer Gareth Coolidge arranged for the legal team working on the account to take a course in American–Japanese business relations. They worked with a Japanese localization analyst who taught them the intricacies of Japanese–American cultural differences in an effort to reduce any confusion and prevent any embarrassing and potentially financially damaging miscommunications.

"So give me an example," said David. "What kind of stuff did you learn?"

"Well, first up," Tony explained, "you have to remember that our two cultures are diametrically opposed. America, thanks to its colonial beginnings, grew as a loosely knit society on a vast land where people moved to new frontiers to avoid being stepped on. They came from all different ethnic backgrounds and did not know what to expect of one another. So, they stayed out of one another's business and in this relative isolation, individualism became paramount. Independence and self-determination were the keys to survival and became the backbone of our ethos.

"Japanese society, on the other hand," Tony went on, "is traditionally close-knit, with crowded living conditions requiring inhabitants who are attentive, responsive and reserved, just to avoid stepping on one another's toes. In other words, in Japan, *your* problem is *my* problem. You follow?"

"I think so."

"So then, just after World War II, we missed an opportunity. A post–Pearl Harbor/Hiroshima Japan was in the mood for reform—for reconciliation and rebirth—and we were more than happy to tell them just how great democracy can be. The Japanese saw the US in a phase of prosperity and embraced democracy in the hope they could rebuild themselves to find similar fortune. But they embraced *their* version of democracy—the textbook version—which once again . . ."

"Is a culturally different one from our own."

"Right again."

Tony went on to explain how the Japanese defined "democracy" at its base meaning—as a system that gives everyone equal rights to participate in the decision-making process—but soon discovered that American democracy is more about the right to individual advancement. He told David how Americans often point out that the Japanese do not know what democracy really is, while the Japanese find it strange to see the authoritarian nature of American society.

"I get you," said David. "A communication gaffe from the get-go—but how does all this affect your approach to someone like Nagoshi?"

"Good question," said Tony, now adjusting his position on the grass to face his friend front-on. "In fact, that was exactly what I was wondering as I was sitting in some conference room with a 'localization analyst' instead of billing three-figure hours at my desk. But what I soon discovered was that disregarding these cultural anomalies was tantamount to career suicide. The value of our legal advice depends on us understanding their motives, and they understanding ours—which can so easily be misread by both sides.

"Take language, for example," said Tony, now squinting into the descending afternoon sun. "Pronunciation, sentence structure, syntax, semantics, and the difference in the way Japanese and English handle expressions of respect and humility . . . everything about English is different from Japanese and when we add accents and colloquialisms the problem multiplies tenfold.

"And then you have the nonverbal stuff," he continued, obviously eager to get his point across, his voice raising a little, his pace upping a beat. "Like knowing a nod is not necessarily a 'yes,' that a '*hai*'—the Japanese word for 'yes'—is often used to indicate they are listening but not that they agree."

"Wow," said David. "I see what you mean."

Tony nodded. "We're a hands-on bunch, DC. So we shake and hug and pat on the back, whereas the Japanese may find this an invasion of their personal space. They don't like to maintain eye contact and we find that uncomfortable," he added without taking a breath. "We talk the leg off a chair while the Japanese prefer concise verbal communications. We are encouraged to be clear and assertive while they are brought up to read the more subtle unspoken signals.

"So my point is . . . it can be . . ."

David could see his friend was running out of steam and wondered why all of this "information" on Japanese relations had spewed from his friend's normally neatly organized conscience this afternoon. Tony was agitated—there was no doubt about it. But David wasn't sure if he should press for the real meaning behind his impromptu sociology lecture, or leave it to Tony to decide when, and how much to . . .

"I don't trust him," said Tony at last, his eyes now set on a Massachusetts Bay Transport Authority shuttle boat heading across the harbor to Logan Airport.

"Who Tony?" asked David quietly. "Who don't you trust?"

"The kid, Peter," he said, still following the shuttle's path. "His father is sensitive to the needs of communication and he treats people with respect. John Nagoshi is a good man and runs his company as such, but his son is an arrogant prick with a total disregard for others."

Tony stopped there and David said nothing, giving his friend time to consider exactly how much he wanted to share.

"He's ambitious, David," Tony said at last, before turning to his friend again, "almost to the point of fanaticism. He's cold and condescending and opinionated and self-assured—and worse still, I fear he is making decisions without consulting his father. And if that's the case, I don't know if I should tell Coolidge that . . ."

"You know for sure he is sidestepping the dad?"

"Last week we had a board meeting to go over division profit margins and Peter asks to be excused so he can check some release dates with the American sales director in New York, a local guy named Jeff McGrath. But I go out to get some additional paperwork and I hear him on Coolidge's office line talking to some dude in Chinese, the aggression in his voice unmistakable."

"Well, maybe he made two calls, one to McGrath and one to . . ."

"No, only the one, and it was to China. After everyone left I went into Coolidge's office and pressed 'last call made,' and it was to Nagoshi Inc.'s manufacturing plant in Guangdong."

"Tony, there could be a million reasons why Peter Nagoshi . . ."

"Last week I went over the figures from China and found some significant anomalies—and lots of them. Like reduced outgoings, higher production levels, ballooning profit margins, unaccounted for payments to his Chinese head of operations."

"So maybe the boss got a bonus for a job well done."

"Guangdong is Peter's jurisdiction, David, but his father is still in charge. I checked with the latest output results and noted John Nagoshi had been sent a brief on China's improvements, but in a watered-down form. You have to know this kid, David. He will stop at nothing to rule his father's empire single-handedly. He has this determination, this look in his eye, this decided lack of anything resembling a conscience."

David looked at his friend again and suddenly—just like that—realized what was actually troubling his longtime friend.

"Oh my God," said David at last. "You think Peter's ambition is uncontainable—so much so that he is willing to lie to his father, hoodwink his lawyers and go to any lengths to achieve his individual goals."

"Let's just say whenever I saw the brother and sister together, it certainly appeared like there was no love lost between them. Peter seemed wary of his sister. People seemed to gravitate to her and maybe he was concerned her popularity might undermine his determination to lead his father's company."

"You think he murdered her, don't you?" David asked at last. "You think he killed her or had her killed so that he could . . ."

"I don't know, DC," interrupted Tony, his face now drained of color. "But I have to admit, for want of a better explanation, which it seems the police are at a loss to come up with, the thought has crossed my mind."

15

He saw them coming. No, he felt them coming before he even looked up. And when he did, when he stacked his paddle and lifted his head to see Jessica's humanitarian friend point him out to the two cops, he felt a shudder of fear radiate throughout his entire body.

They had come for him, James thought. He had run out of time.

He looked down again, even started a conversation with a fellow kayaker as he put on his shoes so that their appearance would look like a total surprise. He did up his laces, collected himself, ignored the excretion of sweat stinging his underarms and threw on his kayak team jersey with all the casualness that a self-assured college kid such as himself should display. He was going to stick to the stereotype, he knew, as they headed down the bank toward him. He was going to play out the charade exactly as expected, just as he supposed he always knew he would.

"James Matheson?" said the dark-haired one, flashing his gold shield in the early afternoon sun.

"Yes," said James with an appropriate look of interest on his olive-skinned face.

"Lieutenant Joseph Mannix, Boston PD—and this here is Detective Frank McKay. You got a minute?"

"Sure," said James. "I'll catch you later, man," he called to his teammate over his shoulder as casually as possible. "Tomorrow, same time, right?"

"Ah . . . you got it," said the friend, unable to conceal his curiosity.

James instinctively walked farther up the riverbank, away from the boathouse crowd and the now growing group of curious onlookers. His gait was relaxed, as if a pair of homicide detectives made regular visits to Mr. Easygoing Young Man on Campus after every kayak practice—*"Just popped in for a chat—to shoot the breeze, kick the shit and tackle the troubles of the world."*

No biggie right? No biggie at all.

. . .

"How can I help you, detectives?" said Matheson, a fixed smile on his even-featured face.

Joe looked at Frank. "Detective McKay and I are investigating the murder of Jessica Nagoshi." And then he stopped short.

Years of experience had taught Mannix that silence was an interrogator's most efficient tool—and assessing how those silences were filled was the key to evaluating a subject's motives.

"Right," said James, shaking his head. "That was, you know . . . so incredibly sad. Jessica was a nice kid from what I hear."

"You didn't know her?"

"Well, yeah, sort of. But she was a couple of years below me and we didn't have that many classes together. We did share a few lectures though, at least I think I saw her in one or two—and I'd see her out every now and again, but that was about it."

"You see her the night that she died?" asked Frank.

"Actually yeah, I think I did. She was at the Lincoln with some girlfriends."

Joe said nothing.

"Geez," said the kid, barely missing a beat. "Just goes to show you. You never know, right? Carpe diem and all that."

"You talk to her at the Lincoln Club?" asked Joe.

"Ah, to be honest I can't remember," said Matheson, scratching his head. "We may have said 'hey' to each other."

"Did you see her leave?" This from Frank.

"Not really. But there must have been a point when she went home because I don't think she was there when we left."

"We?" asked Frank.

"Yeah, me and my friends Heath Westinghouse and H. Edgar Simpson—both third-year law students here at Deane."

"So you three went home together?"

"Not exactly. We all left the Club at about one—and Westinghouse dropped H. Edgar home. But I . . . well . . ."

"You what, James?" asked Joe.

Matheson looked down, scuffing his feet in the moist levee dirt, a contrived half smile on his face.

"You scored, is that it?" Frank smiled in return. "Come on, kid. We were all twenty-two once. At least I think I was."

James responded with a nervous laugh. "Well, it's not like me and my friends set out to . . . you know, find a girl to beat it up with?"

"Is that what they call it these days?" said Joe, shaking his head in mock disbelief and maintaining the big boy banter.

"Among other things." Matheson laughed. "Anyways, I guess you could say I got lucky."

"This lucky got a name?" asked Frank.

"Sure," said Matheson, now running his hands through his thick short hair. The kid kept changing feet and shifting his weight this way and that. He was nervous as all hell, thought Joe. A bona fide sack of stress.

"But if you don't mind, detectives, I'd rather not give it up. The girl just broke up with her ex and well . . . if he found out she . . . so soon after . . . I don't think it would be fair to either of them."

"Sure, James," said Joe. "We get it. So there's nothing else you can tell us about Jessica—about that night at the Lincoln Club, about anyone else she may have been interested in, or someone who wanted to, ah . . . 'beat it up' with her?"

"Geez," the kid said again, now looking up, as if searching for an answer in the clouds. "Not really. I mean she was a pretty girl. I am sure there were guys who . . ."

Just then Joe bent down to pick up his briefcase. He did this slowly, wanting the kid to follow his movements and suffer every second in the process.

"What's that?" asked James, the curiosity obviously proving too much as Mannix pulled the drawing pad from his bag.

"Jessica's sketchbook," answered Joe. "She was pretty good. Here, take a look."

James Matheson edged closer to Joe, and Mannix could swear he felt the kid shaking. Joe flipped through the sketches—slowly, deliberately, until stopping at the portrait.

"That look like someone you know?" asked Frank.

"Wow . . . sure," said James, scratching his head again and

taking a small step back. "It looks a lot like me." He smiled, as if flattered and confused all at the same time.

"It *is* you, James," said Joe. "She even captured the light in your pale green eyes. See?" Joe advanced again.

"Sure," he said again, taking another step back while nodding in double-time.

"You have any idea why she would . . . ?"

"No," interrupted the kid, his voice raising a notch. "I mean," he took a breath, "I guess she was bored in some economics lecture or something, and took to drawing the closest, equally disinterested subject in the room. No idea why she chose my mug though. I mean, there are plenty more interesting faces at Deane."

"Now, kid," said Frank, surprising the boy with a jovial punch in the arm, the mere suggestion at physical contact making the boy flinch. "If I looked like you in college, I would have been 'wrestling it up' as often as . . ."

"It's 'beating it up,'" said James, a little too quickly before slipping on that smile again. "Beating it up—you know, the freshmen even call it banging the bootie."

"Hmmm." Frank smiled. "I think if I suggested either of those options to Mrs. McKay, she'd bang my bootie right out the front door."

The boy smiled again, his perfect teeth fixed in a jaw-breaking clinch.

"Anyway," James said again. "If there's nothing else, detectives, I really gotta get cleaned up before afternoon classes. The professors here are pretty tough. Half of them lock the doors if you're one minute late."

"Sure, kid," said Joe. "Just wanted to check on the sketch and all. I am afraid we don't have that many leads so . . ."

"I understand, detectives. It's not a problem," said James, his bag already over his shoulder, his feet already retracing his steps back down the riverfront. "And good luck, you know. With solving the case, I mean."

"Sure, kid," repeated Joe. "And thanks for your time."

• • •

The pair of them watched him go, Matheson's head down, his steps short and anxious.

"Geez," said Frank.

"I know," said Joe.

They realized they were being watched by the scattering of students just leaving the boat shed, so they walked in silence, back up the levee and toward the northern end of campus where the main entrance was located. They were halfway up the bank when Joe stopped, grabbing Frank's arm from behind before turning him on the spot and gesturing for him to follow him back down the levee.

"I think I dropped my pen," he said. But he hadn't, despite the fact that he was now crouching down, sifting aside a leaf or two to examine the mud beneath them. "Nikes," he said then, pointing to the partial, average-sized shoe print showing the just visible logo in the shape of that famous *swoosh*.

And then Joe saw Frank nod, before he met Joe's eye and lifted his finger as if to indicate there was one last thing. Frank got to his feet and then walked, jogged, back to the boathouse, which was now, thankfully, deserted. Joe followed him, his feet sliding on the slick autumn leaves, stopping finally on the northern side of the shed, the kayaks and paddles now neatly stacked layer upon layer on the whitewashed exterior wall.

Frank hesitated, saying nothing, taking in the neatly racked sporting equipment before reaching out for the closest paddle and facing his boss once again. Then he proceeded to mimic a kayaker's action—one, two, one, two—the circular downward motion that forced the streamlined vessels to slice through the water at surprisingly high speeds. And then he did it again, but this time with force, a look of anger and determination on his face. "Wham, wham," he said. *"Wham, wham!"* he said again, this time louder and faster, the force coming directly from his gut.

"Well I'll be," said Joe, looking at his friend as the tiny pieces suddenly fell perfectly into place. "Well, I'll fucking be."

16

"This is the best," said Jake Davis, fishing another crispy onion ring from the gingham-lined side basket. "Seriously, I haven't eaten so well in weeks."

David and Sara had arranged to meet Jake at Antico Forno, a popular gourmet pizza restaurant in the city's historical North End. The colorful Italian Salem Street eatery was famous for its thin-crust pizzas with a list of topping combinations that read like the *Encyclopedia Britannica*. After fifteen minutes of debate, they had settled for an extra large wood-fired sausage, tomato, mozzarella and ricotta with some garlic bread and onion rings on the side. Topped off with a bottle of merlot, David couldn't think of a finer meal on the planet—and all for under twenty bucks apiece.

"What is it with guys and pizza?" joked Sara. "It's like you all have some built-in genetic need for Italian cholesterol at least once a week."

"They'll never understand," said David, smiling at Sara's younger brother.

"That's okay," said Jake. "All the more for us, right?"

And with that Jake lifted his glass to 'clink' with David's, prompting Sara to roll her eyes before grabbing her own glass of red and taking a slow sip.

David enjoyed Jake's company. So much so in fact that the three of them, sitting there together, relaxed, felt suspiciously like family, which in a way he supposed Jake was—or in the very least, he hoped would be one day. He looked at the brother and sister across the table—nothing and everything alike. Jake with his mop of light blond hair, now combed down and across in an attempt to tame it for his long hours on the conservative corporate beat. Sara and her long, wavy, chestnut brown tresses, her mocha skin glowing, her pale blue eyes shining indigo in the lavender candlelight. They were physical extremes and yet so perfectly attuned to one another, their mannerisms identical, their laughs in sync. He realized then that what he was actually feeling was a slight tinge of envy, for while David was close to his younger, Massachusetts General nursing sister, Lisa, he rarely found the time to catch up with her. And his older brother Sean was . . . well, he was a shipyard worker hundreds of miles away in David's hometown of Newark. *Hundreds of miles away, and a million miles apart,* thought David, Sean having inherited their late father's tough, silent edge and David and Lisa more like their idealistic mom.

Was it really almost twenty years ago that he had left New Jersey to study law in Boston? A wide-eyed, sandy-haired, enthusiastic high school grad determined to uphold justice, defend the innocent and kick some serious courtroom butt? He could see his older brother's face now—the disappointment, the resentment at his having decided against joining the family shipping business. It was as if he was letting them down—and, in a way, he supposed he was.

All of which made him think of another law student with, no doubt, similar visions of grandeur. He had not spoken to Mannix in the past twenty-four hours, but he knew his detective friend would have tracked down James Matheson today in an effort to discover what, if any, role he played in the Nagoshi girl's demise. Strangely enough, he felt an all-consuming hope that the boy was innocent. That the enthusiastic, intelligent, passionate student he had, truth be told, *enjoyed* sharing his thoughts and theories with had nothing to do with the violent actions that took place in that greenhouse several weeks ago— which made his mind take another tack to Tony Bishop, and his suspicions about . . .

"A penny for . . ." said Sara, reaching across the table to lay her hand on his.

"Oh, sorry," said David, squeezing her hand before turning to Jake. "I was just thinking about that kid—you know, James Matheson. I gather Sara told you we hooked up for a coffee. He had some questions about criminal law and evidence that I attempted to help him out with."

"Sure," said Jake, taking another huge bite of the stringy

wedge in his right hand. "In fact, James told me you'd been great—and that he was going to call you up for another chat sometime soon. But what made you think of him?"

David hesitated, knowing it was not his place to give too much away. "Nothing really. I was just thinking of the night that we met and how I felt really old because these days, more often than not, I limit myself to a few wines over dinner." He lifted his glass. "While guys such as yourself and Matheson can drink 'til dawn and still function perfectly well the following . . ."

"Uh-uh," said Jake, shaking his head. "I had a wicked hangover after that particular drinking fest. And the guys from Deane, well, don't you remember? That was the night the Nagoshi girl was killed so they were all pretty upset the following day."

"You spoke to James the next day?" asked David.

"Yeah, he called to try and lock me down for a tutoring time. He said everyone was crushed."

David nodded.

"It's weird how things work out, isn't it?" said Sara, stealing a sideways glance at David. "You know—Jake tutoring Matheson, Matheson meeting you, Matheson knowing the Nagoshi daughter, our friend Joe investigating her murder, you catching up with Joe . . ."

David sensed what she was getting at. Sara knew that he had had a drink with Joe the previous evening and the fact that he had not been particularly forthcoming about the nature of their "chat" had probably piqued her curiosity. She respected the fact that he and Joe shared a mutual trust, but, considering where Joe and David's hidden confidences had led them during the Montgomery trial, she also tended to get a little nervous when David chose not to divulge the nature of their conversations.

"Hang on a minute." Jake smiled. "Is this some game of 'Six Degrees of Separation'? Because if it is you only have two degrees left before you have to get to Kevin Bacon. And seriously, man, I really can't see where this one is going."

"Very funny," said David.

Sara looked directly at him, that familiar *you know something you're not telling me* expression on her flawless face.

"Spill it, David," said Sara. "What gives?"

"It's nothing. I had a beer with Joe and he told me they were scrambling for leads on the girl's murder. I just thought Jake's friend might have known her. I mean, he was going to the Lincoln Club that night and Jessica Nagoshi was seen there before she was . . ."

"You're helping Joe with the investigation," said Sara. A statement, not a question.

"No, Sara. Seriously, I'm not."

"Hmmm." She narrowed her eyes and took another sip of her wine before, to his relief, looking at him with a smile. "Why is it I find that hard to believe?"

"I have no idea." He returned the smile.

"Well," interrupted Jake, "James Matheson is one smart bastard but there is no way he had anything to do with Jessica Nagoshi's murder—*if* that is what you are suggesting. He's actually a very likable guy. I get the feeling there is a heart under all that Ralph Lauren. Which is more than I can say for his friends who are . . ."

"Are what?" asked David.

"Two rich wankers named Westinghouse and E. Ledger or H. Edgar or something like that. The Westinghouse kid is okay, just believes his own publicity. But the other one is a conceited piece of work. So far up himself he practically eats his own breakfast for dinner."

"Jake!" said Sara, ever the older sister.

"Sorry, sis." Jake grinned.

"He's probably right, Sara," said David, taking it all in. "I knew kids like that in college." And then he said nothing, just picked up another pizza wedge and bit into the thick topping.

"What?" he said, realizing Sara's eyes had not left him since he brought up the Matheson boy.

"Nothing," she said.

"Come on, Sara," said David with a grin. "I was just shooting the breeze. I'm curious by nature. You know me."

"You're right," she said, leaning across the table to wipe a stray string of cheese from his chin and kiss him squarely on the lips. "I *do* know you, and that is exactly why I know we haven't heard the last of this." He kissed her back.

"Did you know Kevin Bacon went to Deane?" he said at last.

"That's bullshit," said Jake.

"Yeah," said David. "But it was worth a shot."

17

Heath Westinghouse was totally pumped. It was only 9:52 on a Wednesday morning and here he was, flat on his back, his hips elevated, moving back and forward to a rhythm set by one of the most beautiful girls on campus by the name of Charity Summers. And there she was, rocking away, her perfectly shaped double D–cup breasts bouncing up and down like two taut miniature basketballs above him. Her long blond hair lashed his chest intermittently as she arched her back and stretched her long pale neck, releasing bursts of "oohs" and "ahs," reminding him that he was the definition of a young American alpha male, in a sea of similarly blessed, but not quite as exceptional, beings at the hallowed university around him.

No doubt about it, he thought as Charity bent to run her long pink tongue down his hairless buffed chest, those glorious breasts now rubbing back and forward against his flexed torso and making it hard for him to maintain the thought his brain had just begun to contemplate which, he believed, went something like this . . .

The last time he saw Charity she was seeing some rich senator's arts major son named "Wes." In fact, every time he had seen her, she had been either on Wes' puny arm or "towing an anchor"—which was freshman talk for being shadowed by some fat, unattractive girlfriend who never left her side when Wes was not around. Heath even suspected Wes was paying the "anchor" to play bodyguard while he was mixing it with his equally as inferior arts degree friends, which would be typical of the ball-less billionaire asshole who thought his dad's DC address and Capitol Hill connections won him a woman like Charity and all the kudos that went with it.

Of course he had heard Charity was a "knob snob"—the type of girl who only went for rich or powerful guys because of the money and connections they could provide. But seriously, even if she was, who gives a fuck?

I sure as hell don't, he managed to finish his rambling, pleasure-driven train of thought just as Charity sat up and drove those strong narrow hips down upon him resulting in his experiencing the best goddamned orgasm he had had since . . . well, since the last time he banged Charity about a week ago.

And then, there was a knock on the door.

"Who is it?" called Charity, which was her prerogative given they were going at it in her dorm. It was probably that pesky "anchor" he had thought about earlier. She was probably hoping to keep the towing gig until the next rich asshole came along and put her right back on the payroll.

"Westinghouse," said the voice behind the door, prompting Heath to feel both pleased (that it was not the anchor) and pissed (at being interrupted) all at the very same time. "Westinghouse, if you are in there I need you to get the hell out here."

"H. Edgar," said Heath, recognizing his friend's voice and rising to his elbows to shake the post-beating bliss from his brain. "Fuck off. I'm busy."

"No way. Tell little Miss Charity you can renew your donation later." Westinghouse had to muffle a laugh at that one. "I need to talk to you now."

"Your friend's a prick," said Charity, climbing off him, her substantial breasts now covered by the sheet she dragged along with her.

"I know." Heath smiled, jumping up to put on his pants.

"I don't know why you stay friends with him," she said. "I mean, he's nowhere near as hot as you, or your other friend for that matter."

"Honey," said Heath. "No one is as hot as me." He said this tongue-in-cheek so as not to sound smug, but was pretty sure she agreed with him just the same. "I have some free time tomorrow morning. What do you say, same time, same place?"

She looked at him then, as if unsure how to answer, before cutting to the chase. "You got invited to the President's Halloween Ball, right?"

"Sure, my dad's on the Board of Trustees."

The President's Annual Halloween Ball was a massive event for Deane—a black-tie celebration frequented by alumni that included some of the most influential businessmen and politicians in the country.

"You got a date?" she asked.

"I do now." He smiled, realizing she *was* a knob snob after all and still not giving a fuck.

"Okay then, tomorrow." She smiled, allowing the sheet to drop ever so slightly below her right nipple. "But tell your creepy little friend he's not invited."

"Done," he said, lacing her hand behind her neck and pulling her close to stick his tongue down her soft pink throat one last time before heading toward the door. "Something to remember me by," he said, prompting her to drop the sheet, arch her back and place her hands on her hips.

"Just so you won't forget," she said in reply. And with that, feeling the front of his pants starting to stand to attention once again, he took one last look before opening the door and bounding out into the hallway.

■ ■ ■

"Move it, Westinghouse," said H. Edgar, unable to contain the annoyance in his voice.

"Jesus, H. Edgar," said Westinghouse as Simpson dragged him out of the side entrance of the lakeside girls' dorms. "What's the rush, man? I was just about to ask Charity to . . ."

"We're late for Heffer's lecture," said H. Edgar.

"What?" Westinghouse threw up his hands, only to have them forced down again as Simpson slammed his friend's copy of *Law and the Entrepreneur* against his chest.

"You mean to tell me," Westinghouse went on, "that you dragged me out of the bed of one of the most incredible women on campus just so that I wouldn't be late for another round of unjustified abuse from that communist asshole."

"That communist asshole is giving out the details of his assignment today, remember? You know, the one where we are gonna burn his Marxist butt and shit all over his 'wealthiest' theories regarding our personal intellectual worth as independent from our parents' substantial means and influence." Simpson took a breath. "We miss this lecture, he won't allow us to submit the assignment. No assignment, no law review, no socialist ass-kicking. You got that so far, or is your bourgeois brain still deferring to your dick?"

"H. Edgar," said Westinghouse, now keeping time with his friend, "one mention of Heffer shut my poor dick up for good."

"Good, because you'll want a clear head when I tell you what else I found out this morning."

"What?" said Westinghouse, now obviously intrigued.

"The cops were on campus again yesterday."

"Really?" said Westinghouse, now double-stepping to keep up with his friend as they strode across the main quad. "So did they arrest someone? I always thought the Nagoshi girl was done by one of those quiet intellectual psychopaths. She was smart from what I hear, and those girls always attract the weird ones with the high IQs who are more turned on by a girl's aptitude than her ass."

"They were here to see James." H. Edgar glanced sideways as he said this, trying to gauge his friend's reaction and, concluded from his expression, that Matheson hadn't told him either.

"*What?*" said Westinghouse, stopping short. "I saw James last night and he said nothing about . . ."

"I know," interrupted H. Edgar. "I saw him before 'Agency and Partnership' this morning and he didn't mention a thing to me either."

"What did they want?" asked Westinghouse, starting to move again as Simpson picked up the pace.

"How the fuck should I know?"

"Who told you?"

"Davenport."

"The senior with no neck."

"Yeah, that's him. He was at the boathouse when they sought James out."

"We gotta find him, H. Edgar," said Westinghouse, now grabbing his friend's arm just as they were about to enter a red-brick building monikered "Law 1B." "We have to find out what they wanted."

"One thing at a time, Westinghouse," said H. Edgar, knowing his friend would follow his direction. "First Heffer, then Matheson."

H. Edgar studied Westinghouse's face, waiting for it to move through its usual predictable cycle of uncertainty, disappointment and then acceptance.

"All right," said Westinghouse, at last pushing at one of the front glass double doors before starting to move inside. "But your scheme to fry Heffer better be good. James is our friend, H. Edgar. He may need our help."

"I know," said H. Edgar. "But don't worry, Westinghouse, Matheson knows we've got his back."

"Which we do, right?"

"No question."

"Because his problems are our problems."

"Absolutely."

"And that's just what friends are for."

"Right," said Simpson, checking his watch and walking into Heffer's lecture room exactly on time. "Whatever it is, we'll be there for him. In fact, if we three put our heads together, who knows what we can come up with."

18

Roger Katz put down the phone and took a long, slow breath. And sure enough, there it was—that sweet, seductive smell attributed to success. All of a sudden the air seemed thick with it, which was no surprise considering the nature of his recent call, and the identity of the person who had engaged him.

Massachusetts Attorney General Patrick Sweeney was nothing short of effusive in his praise for the Acting DA. He had called to congratulate Katz on his *"capable leadership"* in Scaturro's absence, on his *"impeccable record"* as a dedicated prosecutor, and then had suggested in no uncertain terms that his future was one of great promise.

"The thing is, Roger," he had begun, *"if DA Scaturro decides to step down, I want you to know that you have my support. You would be a more than worthy successor to her post, Roger, and the County is lucky to have you. Having said that,"* he had continued, *"I believe I should add that my motives are purely selfish. For ultimately, I know, with a few years of experience as the County's top law enforcer under your belt, a man like you would be a major asset at the State Attorney General's office."*

And there it was—plain and simple—a bona fide "feeler" to gauge Katz's interest in representing the Commonwealth on a higher, more significant level. The Massachusetts AG was not just the top legal advisor to the state government, but also the chief law enforcement officer in the whole goddamned state. Of course, then Sweeney had gone on to ask about his progress in the Nagoshi case—a juxtaposition not lost on the savvy ADA. And maybe that was why the recall of Katz's unsubstantiated assurance that *"an arrest was imminent"* was quickly turning that sweet smell sour.

The truth was, he was stuck in a hole—a hole dug by that

incompetent Mannix, a pit he must climb from quickly given that the Nagoshis were due in his conference room in a little under an hour. Men like Mannix weren't forgers of justice; they were weak, sympathetic procrastinators who stalled the criminal process by adhering to some touchy-feely bullshit that apprehending a perp was not justified until they had *proof* said perp committed the crime. But Katz didn't need proof, at least not at this early stage of the game. He just needed a target, someone for him to work on, someone for the press to name in association with the crime and play their subtle role in convicting a man in the eyes of the great American public long before the suspect ever set foot in a courtroom.

Justice wasn't about the truth, it was about the most likely scenario. And nine times out of ten that was as close as you were ever going to get. Reasonable doubt was all a matter of opinion, after all, and when Katz tried a case, any "reasonable" notion of innocence was slaughtered about half an hour into the trial—just as the Acting DA sat down, after making his flawless opening statement.

Strictly speaking (and despite Sweeney's generous reference to him as such) he was not the Acting DA. He was still, at least on paper, the Assistant District Attorney kindly minding his boss's temporarily vacated position while she was off spoonfeeding some absentminded old bird who had no idea whether she was Arthur or Martha. Scaturro had not physically offered her resignation, but her extended leave was becoming longer than the Great Wall of China and to all intents and purposes he was executing the top job with a lot more skill and finesse than his minority-hugging superior ever had the charisma to achieve. And that's why Mannix's disregard for his current level of authority pissed him off so much—that and the fact that John Nagoshi and his cardboard-faced son would be demanding answers by nightfall.

Enough was enough, he told himself as he picked up his sterling silver letter opener to check his reflection in its narrow polished surface. *Timing is everything,* he reinforced as he lifted the blade upward to check his hair which, as usual, sat slick and flat and stylish, with not a single dark strand out of place.

If he played his cards right, he would be elected DA before the following year was out—a stepping-stone that, with

Sweeney's support, could well lead to a coveted post at the Attorney General's Office at One Ashburton Place. It was time for Mannix to deliver—not tomorrow or the next day, but now! In fact he made the decision, right then and there, that he would not permit Mannix to leave his conference room without offering up a name. For that is all he would need. One poor sod and he would be on his way to victory—the rest falling neatly and deservedly into place.

∎ ∎ ∎

"Mannix," snapped Joe as he picked up his direct line, and David could tell he had caught his friend at a bad time.

"It's David. You sound busy. I'll call you later."

"No. I mean, yes . . . I am busy, but I thought you were Katz so I . . ."

"No need to explain."

If anyone understood why Joe would be avoiding Roger Katz it was David. He and Katz had a history, a *long* one, that went way beyond their courtroom battles and into the far reaches of their drastically opposing use, and in Katz's case, abuse, of the law.

"Listen, David. I gotta run," said Joe. "I'm late for a meeting with the Kat and the Nagoshis."

David heard the anxiety in his voice, and felt a similar urgency as he sensed how important it was that he tell Joe what he had learned about James Matheson and Peter Nagoshi, before Joe headed downtown for his audience with the overzealous ADA.

"You check out the Matheson kid?" he asked.

"Yeah."

"And . . . ?"

"He owns a pair of Nikes and has one of the best 'one, two' kayak motions at Deane."

David paused. "That's not enough, Joe."

"Maybe not, but it's all the little things put together that end up building a case like this, David."

David knew Joe was right. "What is he saying?" he asked then.

"All the right things while coming across as guilty as a kid in a candy store. He says he barely knew the girl while another witness claims he was in love with her."

David paused as he took this in, knowing he had to decide quickly which way he was going to go. "I spoke to Sara's brother," he said then, realizing there was no time for procrastination.

"David," said Joe with a sigh. "I asked you not to . . ."

"Don't worry," said David, "I didn't give anything away, Joe. Jake says Matheson is a good guy. And from what I know of the kid I tend to agree. Jake says he has a heart, and in his opinion there is no way he would . . ."

"We all have hearts, David," said Joe. "It's just that some of them beat to a murderer's drum."

David paused.

"You got something else to say?" asked Mannix, perhaps sensing David's hesitancy to elaborate further.

"Has anyone considered Jessica Nagoshi may have been murdered, not because of who she was but because of what she might have become?" David was trying his best to give Mannix "something" without betraying Tony Bishop's trust. There had to be a way to plant the seed in Joe's mind, he thought.

"What?" said Mannix.

"She was a pretty girl, Joe, and there are plenty of pretty girls at Deane, but not all of them have John Nagoshi as their father."

"Jesus, David," said Mannix, obviously getting tired of playing "*read the hidden meaning.*" "What the hell are you saying?"

"I'm saying that maybe it goes beyond James Matheson and some innocent teenage sketch—that maybe her future role in her father's company was enough to set . . ."

"She was only nineteen, David, and a long way from becoming a corporate threat."

"Her brother is only twenty-six and he has just been named as Nagoshi's next US president."

Joe said nothing.

"Look," said David at last, "I know you know what you are doing, Joe, so if you say Matheson is the guy, then I am wrong and Matheson is the guy. All I am saying is maybe you should look at little closer at Nagoshi Inc.—and specifically its Chinese operations."

He stopped after saying this, wondering if he had gone too far. But something told him this is exactly what Tony Bishop had wanted him to do—consciously or subconsciously—when he began his conversation with him twenty-four hours ago.

"China?" said Joe, and David could have sworn he heard a trace of recognition in Joe's voice, as if a "loose" connection was now not looking so loose after all.

"Yeah," said David. "Check the employment records, the salaries and so forth."

"Who told you this?"

"Call it an informed hunch."

Mannix paused.

"I gotta go," he said at last.

"Okay," said David, before deciding to ask one more question. "By the way, have you told Katz of your suspicions—you know, about Matheson?"

"Not yet."

"You about to?"

"Well . . . now I'm not so sure."

"Okay," said David, finding himself strangely relieved at Mannix's reconsideration.

"Why the hell do you do this to me, David?"

"Because you do it to me."

19

Five months earlier

The next time James saw Jessica Nagoshi, he came face to "foot" with her feet—her long, slender, narrow feet, which hung gracefully before him, arched and pointed in a ballet dancer's pose. It was late and he had just finished his final lap. The pool was officially closed for the night but he had stayed behind having promised his coach he would exit via the back entrance.

And there she was, shoeless—her feet dangling in the water before him. He looked up to see her perched high above him on block number four, her perfect face tinted aqua through the azure lenses of his blue racing goggles.

"Hello," she said.

"Hi," he said, now holding on to the stainless steel backstroker's rung underneath the white tiled block before him. "I haven't seen you," he said, removing his goggles at last. "At the river I mean. You said you would . . ."

"I had to go to New York," she said. "Family business and all that. My father likes to involve us in company developments."

James nodded. "What are you doing here?" he asked.

"Posting some leaflets on the Sports Center bulletin board—Solidarity Global," she said, holding up a sample. "I saw you swimming alone in the pool so I told my friend Sawyer I would finish up—post the pool boards on my own so that he could move on to the senior girls' dorms."

"Lucky Sawyer," he said.

"He won't even notice," she replied, before dismissing the subject and moving on. "I used to do this as a kid."

"What, post brochures?" he said.

"No," she said, returning his smile. "Take off my shoes and dangle my feet in the backyard pond."

"You had a pond in your backyard?" he asked.

"Still do," she said before looking him squarely in the eye. "Are you getting out?"

"Why, are you coming in?" he countered, speaking on impulse.

"Is it warm?" she asked.

"Warm enough."

"All right then," she said before standing to peel off her Deane issue T-shirt, revealing a pale blue sports bra underneath. She stripped to her underpants—a matching blue set—and released her long dark ponytail. She stood on top of the block and lifted her arms in front of her, and then without hesitation, she dived, her body curving high above his head and landing sleekly farther down the lane, piercing the water without a splash and disappearing from view.

He immediately dived down to meet her, as if needing to check that this wasn't a dream, that this girl—this totally surprising, unpredictable, incredibly beautiful girl—was still there somewhere ahead in the blue expanse before him. And then he reached her, unsure of what to do next, just as she turned to face him, her eyes wide and unblinking, her smile innocent and inviting all at the same time. And in that moment he realized he was looking at the most striking thing he had ever seen—here, below the water, where everything else seemed to . . .

She kicked then, quickly, arching her back and heading to the surface. And so he took her lead, forcing himself upward, finally meeting her face-to-face, the water sliding off her smooth pale skin under the harsh white light of the domed fluorescent overheads.

"Jessica . . . I . . . you . . . I don't know what to . . . ?"

"Have you ever heard of the Japanese proverb '*Ko-in ya no gotoshi*'?" she asked, her voice slightly echoing, her breath light on his face as they trod water, inches apart in the middle of the deserted Deane Memorial Pool.

"I . . ." he began. "To be honest, I probably wouldn't know if I had."

"It means 'time flies like an arrow,' " she said. "And it's true, James. My mother died when I was a child and now I want some control over . . ." She stopped then, as if unsure as to how to go on.

"Are you afraid to stop swimming?" she asked him, changing the subject again.

"I'm not sure," he said, surprised at his own admission.

"Me neither," she said.

He wanted to touch her then, to pull her close and hold her tight but the sound of the overheads plunging them into darkness made them both look up before facing each other once again, their breathing now deep and pronounced in a new level of silence enhanced by the dark.

"Why me?" he asked at last.

"I don't know. Perhaps it is your eyes. *Me wa kokoro no kagami*," she said.

He shook his head.

" 'The eyes are the mirror of the soul.' "

He said nothing, just looked at her, willing her not to break the moment for fear there might not be another.

"I want to see you again," he said.

She smiled. "I have to go away for the summer—back to New York. But we are both intelligent beings, James, so I am sure we can think of some way to organize a get-together."

And he felt a shiver of hope rise through his body.

"I'll be back as soon as I can," she continued before shifting in the water again and diving under the nearest set of lane ropes. "And you'll be . . . ?" she asked as she emerged again.

"Right here," he said.

"What?" she said before diving and emerging again. "Swimming in the dark in the middle of the night?" She smiled as she reached the edge of the pool.

"Probably." He nodded, returning the smile.

"That's okay," she said, using her long arms to pull herself from the water and turning around to face him one last time. "It just means I'll know exactly where to find you."

• • •

And so here he was. Just as she had predicted. It may not be night but he was here nevertheless, enveloped by the endless comfort of the long, warm stretches of blue. He had always been drawn to the water, and over the past month it had become an obsession—whether on his slick azure kayak carving up the deep green waters of the Charles River, or hiding behind his reflective goggles in the Deane Memorial Pool. He knew what he was doing as he closed his eyes and kicked off from the wall, using his legs to torpedo through the water and dolphin-kick a further five meters before bringing his right arm back to start on his third kilometer of freestyle. He was somehow ac-knowledging the memory and trying to banish it all at the very same time. He needed time to think, and normally the solitude of the long black line that stretched endlessly before him as-sisted in clearing his head but today, for some reason, all it did was remind him of Jessica—and her long silken hair, flowing and slick like an endless river of . . .

His lungs started to burn, he had not taken a breath for al-most an entire lap, in fact he had dived *down*, toward that line, feeling an all-encompassing need to touch it. He was almost there, right at the bottom of the diver's end when weakness be-trayed him and his lungs screamed for air and his natural in-stinct for survival turned him around and dragged him upward toward the surface. And that was when he saw them—two blurred but recognizable forms that hung suspended like in-truders beyond a rain-splattered window above.

"Hey," he said, as he broke the surface, took a deep breath, pulled off his goggles and reached for Westinghouse's out-stretched arm. "What are you guys doing here?"

"What do you think?" said Westinghouse, handing him his towel as he climbed out of the pool. James stole a glance at H. Edgar, who stepped instinctively back, obviously not wanting his new suede Hogans to be stained by the splash.

"Why didn't you tell us?" Westinghouse went on, as James peeled the swim cap from his head and ran his hands over his short dark hair.

"Tell you what?"

"About the cops, you Epsilon." James cringed. For some reason he hated it when Heath used H. Edgar's cerebral ver-nacular.

"Oh, that," he said smiling. "It was nothing. The cops have no leads on the Jessica Nagoshi thing, so they are going back to question a lot of the gang that were at the Lincoln that night."

"They haven't talked to me," said Heath.

"Nor me," said Simpson, the first words to come out of his mouth.

"Well, shit," said James, managing a smile. "Maybe they went to the best-looking guy in the house first."

"But they didn't come to me," said Heath again, with just the slightest trace of a grin.

"What did you tell them?" Westinghouse went on.

"The truth. That we saw her there, that she was a nice kid, that she probably had lots of admirers. That she left before us."

"You spoke to her that night," said Simpson. "I saw you."

"Yeah. I told the cops I said 'Hey,'" said James, signaling for them to move to the side of the pool where he had left his training gear.

"Maybe the cops thought she had the hots for you," said Westinghouse.

"Nah," said James, shaking his head.

"Maybe she saw you talking to Barbara and got the hint," said H. Edgar, prompting James' head to turn instinctively and face his friend front on.

"No," he said almost too quickly. "Jessica had left before then. I'm sure of it." And then he saw the look in H. Edgar's eye—one of realization or victory even—like he had caught him out in a lie, or confirmed something he had suspected.

"Anyway," said James, forcing that smile again as he pulled on his track pants and drew his windbreaker over his head. "It was no big deal. In fact, I wish I could have helped them more."

"So that's it then," said Westinghouse, handing James his towel so that he could stack it in his swim bag. "Fuck, H. Edgar," he said turning to his red-haired friend. "No wonder he didn't tell us. That story is about as exciting as the geology majors' end of semester Hawaiian party."

"And you would know this because . . . ?" H. Edgar smiled.

"Good point," said Westinghouse.

As Westinghouse punched Simpson in the arm James studied his opinionated friend's features, wondering what slant he had put on "Matheson's little visit from the cops" to his best friend Heath. He linked eyes with Simpson for a second before Simpson's pale face broke into a "reassuring" smile.

"We're just glad you're okay, man," he said, slapping James

on the shoulder. "You know what cops are like these days. Just as easy to fake a scenario than prove one."

"I thought that was what us lawyers did." Westinghouse smiled as James shouldered his bag and the three of them turned to leave the complex together.

"No," said H. Edgar. "We don't fake, Westinghouse, we *create*, and make a shitload of money in the process."

20

The stage was set the minute Joe Mannix and Frank McKay entered the conference room. The first thing Joe noticed was the seating arrangements—Katz at the head of the long antique cherrywood table, John Nagoshi to his right, Peter Nagoshi next to his father (and Joe could not help but study the younger Nagoshi as he entered the room, his smooth expressionless face barely turning to acknowledge their entrance), and across the table FBI Boston Field Office Special Agent in Charge Leo King and Special Agent Ned Jacobs—the Feeb's resident profiler. Then at the opposite end of the table, the end closest to the door, directly facing Katz, two seats had been placed side by side, squashed in between the table's thick hand-carved legs.

It reminded Joe of the big Italian dinner parties he had endured when he was a kid—how the adults took up the head and the sides of the table and the kids were jammed into the far end where two oversized chairs wrestled for space and the two subordinates in them banged elbows with smaller plates, smaller cutlery and the general acknowledgment that they were to be seen and not heard. Unless called upon by one of the grownups in the room to respond to a specific demand.

It was cold. This room was always cold, thought Joe. Katz had the air-conditioning jacked up to the max despite the cooler than average temperatures outside. A junior in the DA's office once told him the Kat had heard about David Letterman's theory on maintaining a "meat locker" mentality—how the successful TV show host demanded his green room and studio be kept at icebox temperatures to keep his guests and audience alert. Except Katz wasn't Letterman. And Joe and Frank sure as hell weren't Brad Pitt and Angelina Jolie.

"Sorry we're late," said Mannix, noting the glare of disapproval on Katz's clean-shaven face. "I had to take a call." His eyes tracked instinctively toward the still stony-faced Peter Nagoshi.

"We were about to start without you," said Katz, cutting Joe off and establishing his authority from the outset. "In fact, we had just decided Agent Jacobs here should begin by giving us his profiler report. Given the police have not been forthcoming with any solid suspects to date, we thought perhaps, in the very least, a hypothetical one might be a good place to start."

And there it was, thought Joe. Blame Transferral 101. Joe had in fact heard Agent Jacobs' report a few weeks earlier, and he had used what he could to narrow his search. In fact, Joe knew the only reason the genuinely impressive Jacobs was at this meeting was so that Katz could play Joe as the incompetent fool in comparison, and in all honesty, Joe expected no less from the self-serving, ass-preserving, gutless ADA.

Joe glanced at Leo King—a dedicated and trusted friend who gave him a subtle roll of his eyes before introducing FBI Profiler Special Agent Ned Jacobs. Jacobs then proceeded to open the folder in front of him, look directly at the Nagoshis and, out of an intuitive sense of courtesy, begin by explaining the profiling process in detail.

"First up," said Jacobs with a smile. "I should explain that us profilers are not clairvoyants. We have no special powers or supernatural insights, and do not keep crystal balls or tarot cards in our two by four lockers at Quantico."

Jacobs was a kind-faced African-American, and Joe realized the top-notch communicator was cleverly taking the edge off the room by providing the Nagoshis with sound and helpful information.

"There are only about forty of us in total," Jacobs went on. "Forty of about thirteen thousand agents. But that doesn't necessarily make us special. It just means we fit the bill for this type of job—we have trained extensively in areas such as forensic sciences, forensic pathology, sex crime investigations and interview and interrogation techniques, and then undertaken further studies in behavioral analysis.

"As profilers we assess a crime scene and embark on a process we call 'criminal investigative analysis,' which in layman's terms means study all the evidence and come up with a possible

profile of the offender based on his or her psychopathology—
the behavioral and psychological indicators that are left at a violent crime scene as a result of the offender's physical, sexual,
and in some cases verbal interaction with his or her victims."

Jacobs stopped then, taking a sip from the ice-filled glass
before him.

"The good news is, we have assisted the Bureau and other
law enforcement agencies in making hundreds of arrests by
giving our fellow agents and police detectives guidelines for
their search and investigations. The not-so-good news is that
we have our limitations. We cannot hand the investigators the
offender—merely provide another tool to assist them in narrowing their search."

"And in the case of my sister?" asked Peter Nagoshi with
just the slightest hint of irritation—and Joe could have sworn
his father shifted ever so slightly in his seat.

"Right," said Jacobs, obviously reading the Nagoshi son's
impatience and realizing it was time to cut to the chase. "In
Jessica's case the first obstacle we face as profilers is that the
crime appears to be a one-off. Profilers get much clearer results
when analyzing the work of serial killers who leave a trail of
behavioral clues at each crime. Stand-alone offenses are not so
easy, but I am fairly confident I have some basic information
that can assist the police in their investigations."

Peter Nagoshi nodded for Jacobs to continue as the amiable
agent looked down at his notes.

"Given the approach to the murder and the statistical information available to us regarding attacks of this kind in this
area, I believe the offender to be a white male, aged between
twenty and thirty. I believe him to be controlling and organized, to the point of being meticulous."

"How so?" asked John Nagoshi, speaking for the first time.

"The crime scene was sanitary, the offender left almost no
forensic evidence, the body although distorted was organized
in a resting position, her hair was placed neatly away from her
face and the method of murder in itself was reasonably 'clean.'

"The placement of the stone as a pillow appears to be something of an afterthought suggesting either a knowledge of the
cultural significance of the rock itself—or more likely, in my
opinion, a sense of familiarity with . . ."

"One moment, Special Agent Jacobs," interrupted John Nagoshi, obviously wanting to take in every detail. "You said the murder was clean? I would call murder many things, but I do not believe there is anything hygienic about taking a young girl's life."

"Yes, sir, I agree," said Jacobs. "But in this case I am speaking literally rather than psychologically. Strangulation does not pollute a crime scene, Mr. Nagoshi, with blood and other messy body fluids. It leaves the victim looking as if in a state of sleep. It can be a killer's way of 'preserving his victim,' leaving his memory of her largely intact."

"What about the blows to the head?" asked Katz.

"Acts of rage. The two blows Jessica endured were, in my opinion, the result of some emotional or psychological trigger, some revelation or physical action or new piece of information she shared with her killer, which led the normally controlled individual to lash out in anger. The blows disabled her and the strangulation silenced her cleanly, neatly, quietly."

"Are you saying my daughter was familiar with her killer, Agent Jacobs?" asked John Nagoshi who, Joe was surprised to see, seemed a little taken aback by this suggestion.

"Almost certainly. First there was the placement of the stone I mentioned earlier. Its use as a pillow, motivated by either the killer's knowledge of it being, as your gardener explained, a 'death stone,' or more likely, in my opinion, a symbolic gesture suggesting that the offender knew her well enough to wish to see her at peace in death.

"Then there was the taking of the stockings and shoes and the fact that the removal of such intimate items indicates familiarity." Jacobs paused. "Jessica knew her killer, Mr. Nagoshi. I am sure of it."

There was silence then as John Nagoshi nodded, and despite his stoic expression, Joe sensed this new piece of information did not sit well with the respected corporate chief.

"What else does the taking of shoes tell us?" asked Katz, determined to keep control of Jacobs' report.

"All sorts of things but none of them definitive. Subconsciously the killer may have wanted to restrict Jessica from taking a certain road, from going somewhere, doing something, making a decision that might either alter his preferred course or have taken her away from him. Physically he may have had some connection to that part of her body, which indicates a sexual attraction the offender did not, at least at the time, pursue."

"But she was not raped," said John Nagoshi.

"No," said Jacobs. "But that does not mean the killer did not have intimate feelings for your daughter. In fact my guess is there was a strong physical attraction on his part—but one that, at least at that point in time, was not returned."

"So he is what?" asked Katz. "Cowardly, impotent, weak?"

"On the contrary," said Jacobs, shaking his head. "I believe him to be confident, adaptable, intelligent. My guess is the lack of sexual contact on the night of the crime was more a case of his trying to protect himself. Sexual crimes can be some of the easiest to solve because of the exchange of bodily fluids. I believe the killer considered this. He did what he did out of anger but within moments of the crime was calm enough to move into damage control."

Jacobs stopped then and closed his file, his many "possibilities" still hanging in the air like teasers to an unsolvable whodunit.

John Nagoshi placed his hands on the table before him, his back straight, his demeanor even, before looking directly at Roger Katz to say: "Forgive me, Mr. Katz. I appreciate Special Agent Jacobs' expertise and the trouble he has gone to in studying my daughter's killer. But I do not see how this transforms into action.

"My daughter was young, intelligent and pleasing to the eye. I am her father, Mr. Katz, but not naive enough not to understand she was a profitable catch in more ways than one. There must be some other way to identify this man. What about the fingerprints, the shoe print, the . . ."

"The shoe print was only a partial, Mr. Nagoshi," said Leo King. "It looked to be a Nike but half of the students at Deane wear the same type of shoe. As for the fingerprints, they are of no use to us until we have something or someone to compare them to. Our people in Quantico have worked overtime on them and I can assure you they are extremely pleased with their ability to enhance their clarity given their deteriorated state at the scene. But the offender, whoever he is, does not have a record. We have run the prints through our Integrated Automated Fingerprint Identification System, checked every local, state, federal and government database available. We even ran them through Interpol. But our killer is a first timer—or in the very least, has never been caught before."

"Then there must be something more," said John Nagoshi. "Lieutenant Mannix," he said, turning to Joe. "You told me many weeks ago that the police obtained some evidence they were keeping silent in the interest of the investigation. At the time I agreed. I know we live our lives in the eyes of the public and, as such, respected your judgment when you suggested it was best Peter and I not know of such a detail." Nagoshi took a short breath before shifting in his seat once more and going on.

"She was my daughter, Lieutenant, and while I am no investigator, I am schooled in the arts of discovery for profit. Perhaps if I knew this detail, my son and I could shed some light on the matter."

"I don't know if that is such a good idea," began Roger Katz who, Joe guessed, was afraid of the powerful man's reaction to what he knew would be a shocking revelation—and perhaps even more fearful of any repercussions on his part, given he had "caved in" to Joe's insistence that this evidentiary detail be withheld.

But Nagoshi was not listening. He was focused on Mannix, his eyes unwavering, his determination clear.

Joe met the man's gaze, seeing now for the first time, deep below his controlled façade, the basic primal need for a father to avenge his daughter's death. He had seen it before, too many times, and in the end, he realized, John Nagoshi was no different than any other parent who had suffered the ultimate loss. He needed the truth, and more to the point, he deserved it.

"Mr. Nagoshi," said Joe, stealing a quick glance at Frank and Leo, who both gave slight nods in agreement before moving on, "there is a detail, a significant one, but I am afraid it has not helped us identify your daughter's killer. We have found no evidence of her being in a physical relationship. No proof that suggested she was . . ."

"What is it?" snapped Peter, with no effort to hide his frustration. Joe looked to the son before turning to the father again, knowing it was he who would feel the full impact of what he had to say.

"I am afraid, Mr. Nagoshi, that on the night of Jessica's death, the killer stole more than one life."

"A serial killer?" said Nagoshi. "But Agent Jacobs said . . . I do not understand."

"No, sir," said Joe, realizing there was only one way to say what needed to be said. "Jessica was pregnant, Mr. Nagoshi. When the murderer struck, he killed your daughter *and* your grandchild—two lives for the price of one. I am sorry, sir. I am very sorry."

What happened next was a surprise to them all. Peter Nagoshi leapt from his seat and yelled *"Baita!"* sending his heavy antique chair teetering on its hind legs before knocking it backward toward the floor.

Roger Katz responded immediately, standing to move around the table and calm the obviously distressed Nagoshi son, but in the process he managed to knock the corner of his hard leather binder, which slid at an angle toward the water pitcher at his end of the table. The pitcher smashed sideways, sending water and ice cascading down the long conference table in one almighty gush before breaking into several tributaries that tracked across the table, slid off the edges into people's laps and poured silently down onto the American-made "Persian" rug, which soaked up the liquid like a thick, hungry sponge.

"This cannot be true! Baita," said Peter again, his father now ignoring the wet patch on his suit pants to stand and settle his offspring who, as far as Mannix could tell, was either extremely distressed by this latest piece of news or, more to the point, accusing Joe of telling an outright lie.

"Peter," said John Nagoshi, subtly stepping around the obstacle that was a floundering Roger Katz to hold his son by both shoulders before leaning in and whispering quietly in his ear in Japanese.

A respectful Special Agent Jacobs and Detective McKay diverted their gaze and retrieved some paper towels from a side table before proceeding to mop up the remaining water that now sat like bubbles on the glossy varnished table.

And then Peter Nagoshi nodded, now leaving his father's huddle to face the room and say: "Forgive me, gentlemen, I am afraid this revelation is unexpected. This is a difficult time for my family and I apologize for any impropriety."

The older Nagoshi indicated for his son to retake his seat—
and the rest of the room followed in unison.

"I mean you no disrespect, Lieutenant Mannix," Peter Nagoshi went on, his red cheeks flush, his breathing now deep.
"And I understand your reasoning that police investigators must
sometimes operate in secrecy. But if what you say is true, I do
not agree that this was a detail to be kept from us. Jessica was
my sister, her child was my niece or nephew—my father's
grandchild—a Nagoshi heir.

"We have not honored this child by mourning its loss," said
the younger Nagoshi, his voice now rising a notch. "Rather it has
been used as a pawn in your so far fruitless investigations and
we . . ."

"Peter," said John Nagoshi before turning to Mannix himself. "I apologize for my son's reactions, Lieutenant. But I have
to say I agree with him. This is a significant truth and I am
afraid I do not see how . . ."

"Mr. Nagoshi is right," said Katz, prompting Joe, Frank and
Leo to do a double take toward the sycophantic ADA at the
head of the table. "This detail should not have been kept from
his family.

"I can assure you, Mr. Nagoshi," the Kat went on, now turning to the corporate giant with an expression that suggested
both sympathy and determination, "I did not agree with this
obviously unsuccessful tactic, but I am afraid the DA's office is
often at the mercy of investigators whose job it is to provide the
raw material for a case that . . ."

"Who was the father of this child, Lieutenant?" interrupted
Nagoshi, still focusing on Joe.

"We have no idea, sir," said Joe. "We have a DNA sample
from the fetus but once again we need something to compare
it to."

"How far along was she?"

"Thirteen weeks, sir," said Joe. "But just because your
daughter was pregnant, does not mean the father of the child
was her killer. Our medical examiner stressed there was no
evidence of rape either on the night of your daughter's death or
previously, which suggests any sexual relations she had had in
the past were consensual."

Peter Nagoshi bristled in his seat and Joe took a breath before going on. "Look Mr. Nagoshi, I am sorry this detail was withheld from you and your son, but in all honesty I still believe it should be kept within the four walls of this room. We do not want a situation where every asshole in town is claiming to be the father of your unborn grandchild and believe me, there are scum out there low enough to waste our time with such rubbish in some ridiculous attempt to get their hands on your fortune.

"Furthermore," Joe went on before Katz could interrupt, "I still believe this detail can help us find the offender. If Special Agent Jacobs is right, then maybe it was the news of her pregnancy that rocked the killer's world. Maybe it was this unborn child that sent the murderer over the edge and if that is the case then . . ."

"Two million dollars," said Nagoshi.

"I'm sorry, sir?" said Mannix.

"Two million American dollars for information that leads to the arrest of the man who murdered my family. One million for each life, Lieutenant, a tawdry amount is it not?"

The room fell silent again, until . . .

"Mr. Nagoshi," said Katz, his eyes wide at just the mention of such a substantial reward, "I think that is a *very* good idea. It could just be the key to . . ."

"No," said Joe, now completely exasperated by the unexpected turn of events at this evening's meeting. "Forgive me, sir, but that is a *huge* mistake. For every idiot who will come out of the woodwork claiming to be Jessica's lover, there will be another thousand concocting fanciful crap just so they can get their hands on the reward."

"I shall trust your judgment that the pregnancy should be kept quiet, Lieutenant," said Nagoshi. "But monetary incentives are my area of expertise and I am afraid you have no jurisdiction as to how I allocate my finances. The reward stands, Lieutenant. I shall contact the press today and if you do not wish the Boston Police to be the relevant point of contact, then I shall set up my own team of investigators to . . . as you say, sift through the *koe-dame*."

Joe looked at him then, the others in the room virtually forgotten, the two of them negotiating like broker to broker, expert to expert, man to man.

"All right, Mr. Nagoshi," said Joe at last. "You win. But I

want to ask one favor—one small favor before we send out an invitation to every greedy piece of scum this side of Maine to bombard this investigation with bullshit."

Joe took a breath, not sure what he was about to do was right. He had not intended to mention James Matheson at this meeting, especially after his recent conversation with David. But this evening's events had been anything but predictable, and right now he would do everything he could to prevent this case—a case he and Frank were slowly and carefully unraveling—from turning into the three-ring circus from hell. "There is a new lead, sir," Joe went on, carefully choosing his words. "A young man who we believe may have had some form of personal relationship with your daughter."

"What?" said a now red-faced Roger Katz.

"Detective McKay and I have spent the past twenty-four hours making some discreet inquiries about this boy," said Mannix, ignoring the now furious ADA. "And I want to make it clear that, at least at this point, we have no evidence to suggest he is guilty.

"He is popular, intelligent, independently wealthy and one of the highest performers at Deane's School of Law— scholastically and athletically. We also believe he has an alibi and with all due respect, sir, we need at least until the weekend to check it out."

Joe stopped there, taking a sip of water to cool his now dry throat before taking another breath and moving on. "So that's the deal, Mr. Nagoshi. It's now Wednesday evening. Forty-eight hours and you get to post your reward. We come up blank, you put up your money. Two more days and you have it your way. Just give us a chance to . . ."

"All right, Lieutenant," said Nagoshi, "I accept your deal. But you must also promise me a full report on this boy before the week is out."

"I can assure you, Mr. Nagoshi," interrupted Katz, "I will make sure Lieutenant Mannix provides you with . . ."

"It's a deal," said Mannix, ignoring the ADA yet again, his eyes never leaving the Japanese businessman who now stood to walk across the room and shake Joe's outstretched hand.

21

Sawyer Jones was in his Deane University dorm room, sitting on the edge of his single metal-framed bed and facing toward the large, open bay window that gave uninterrupted passage to the cool, biting southeasterly breeze. It was late. The lights were off but the moon cast a single beam through the window and Sawyer had squeezed his lithe frame into the path of said beam in an almost primitive urge for natural illumination. He looked at his bedside digital for the tenth time in the past hour. A quarter after midnight and he was already counting the hours until the sun crept over the horizon like a welcome visitor promising warmth and activity and banishing the shadows of the endless night that brought nothing but loneliness and regret.

It was his birthday. As of fifteen minutes ago, Sawyer was seventeen years of age.

Seventeen, he said to himself. At the very least it sounded older than sixteen, but then Sawyer's age had been playing tricks on him since he was a child, since he was tested and assessed and labeled as "exceptionally gifted" by a never-ending succession of fascinated educational experts who viewed him as the intellectual specimen from heaven.

"He read Dickens at five," his New Hampshire blue-chip tax attorney father would tell the experts—paying more attention to their attention than he did to his actual son. *"He conquered calculus by seven, Pythagoras by eight, the theory of relativity by nine and the molecular breakdown of DNA by the age of eleven."*

His fellow Deane students had no idea and he had no intention of telling them. The university administrators knew, of course, but he had asked that his age and gifted status remain confidential and they saw no need to protest as long as his grades were satisfactory, which of course they were.

He *looked* sixteen, but given his high grades and ingrained ability to "mix it with the big kids," his boyish features were taken as just that. In fact, his angelic appearance fit perfectly on the face of one who spent all of his spare time trying to right the wrongs of this burgeoning bourgeois world. It was almost as if he were born to it. He was passionate about helping those less fortunate, that was fair to say, but Sawyer was passionate about everything he took on, and that was part of the problem. His role as Solidarity Global Youth Director had given him a worthy outlet for his overactive social conscience, and selfishly, a means of making friends.

Friends, he said to himself. *From the Greek "philos," meaning fondness*. Even now he found his brain was in overdrive, a coping mechanism no doubt, given the depth of his despair, the burden of his loss, the intensity of his *guilt*. Jessica was his friend. Dear, sweet, beautiful Jess who saw him for what he was and accepted him with all his quirks and hidden eccentricities. He even had his own secret name for her—J No—which was extremely teen of him, and therefore, perhaps, not so inappropriate after all. His motives for "conscripting" her were selfish—and she knew it. But she assumed such selfishness sprung from his desire to parade her, the daughter of one of the biggest multinational chief executives on the planet, as an advocate for international workers' rights. The stories of injustice troubled her, but her knowledge that her father's policy of optimal working conditions for all Nagoshi Inc. employees made her proud and determined to see other global corporations follow suit.

True, her status as a corporate princess was a drawcard, but if he was truly honest with himself, Sawyer would have to admit that, in the end, it was not about her father. It was, at least eventually, and probably from the outset, all about her. For Sawyer loved her the minute he set eyes on her a little over a year ago. That long, smooth hair, perfect porcelain skin, bright almond eyes and sparkling smile. And he loved her even more as he got to know her spiritually and intellectually—their analytical sparring elevated him to a new level of cerebral and emotional bliss. And that was why he felt so sick, rotten to his very core. He was nauseous, dizzy, hot, cold, dry, thirsty, hyped, exhausted and, as was *so* typical of the "bona fide intellectual genius" that was Sawyer Hudson Jones, fully operational all at the very same time. But despite appearances, sitting here in the murky gloom of obscurity, the guilt was all consuming. It sat like a parasite eating away at his insides. Feeding on his shame, his remorse, his *inconsolable sorrow*. It lay low in his belly throughout the day and consumed his entire body in the long, black, solitary hours of darkness.

Sawyer glanced at his bedside clock. 12:35 a.m. He had to prepare an agenda for the SG fundraising meeting scheduled before classes at 7:30 and had not yet put pen to paper. He was an intelligent person. And while he knew there was no way to rewrite history, he reasoned there must be a way to, in the very least, atone for what he had done.

That's it! he said to himself now, feeling warm reassurance from the familiar format of "problem and solution." There was no puzzle beyond Sawyer's grasp, he had never, *ever* experienced the frustration of being unable to answer a question, unravel a riddle, demystify an enigma.

Peto reperio verum-i—seek a solution and you will find the truth.

And so Sawyer decided he would start with a shower. He summoned all of his strength and rose from his bed—his legs finding their balance, his lungs consuming the fresh night air, his eyes refocusing on the twinkling fairy lights that graced the Deane University gazebos like fireflies sitting in circles. But it was his stomach that would not follow suit. For just as Sawyer was about to announce himself ready for another day, his gut wrenched like a garbage compactor, forcing its meager contents upward so that he barely had time to race to his tiny bathroom before purging himself of the sickness that bled like a river inside.

22

"*Nagoshi Incorporated Chief Executive Officer John Nagoshi is on the verge of offering a record seven-figure reward for information leading to the arrest of his teenage daughter's killer, according to a reliable source involved with the case,*" David read aloud from Marc Rigotti's piece on the front page of this morning's *Tribune*. David had just arrived at Myrtle's, Joe having called late last night to ask if he would meet him for an early morning coffee, and had barely taken off his coat before an obviously furious Joe pushed the paper in front of him, and said, "Get a load of this."

"*The reward, according to the source,*" David went on, "*will be offered as early as Friday in an attempt to draw new information on the brutal murder of nineteen-year-old Deane University student, Jessica Nagoshi, who was strangled to death in the greenhouse of her father's expansive Wellesley estate almost two months ago.*"

"*It is believed this unusual move was suggested by Mr. Nagoshi—and supported by Suffolk County Assistant District Attorney Roger Katz, who according to the source, has had grave concerns with the lack of progress made by Boston homicide detectives since Miss Nagoshi's death.*"

David looked up at Joe, a new flush of rage now coloring his detective friend's unshaven face.

"*'John Nagoshi is a successful executive with unparalleled business acumen,'*" David continued quoting after a nod from Joe. "*'And he knows that money talks,' said the source who did not wish to be named. ADA Katz, who has promised to prosecute the case personally if and when it gets to trial, has been patient with the police but knows that time is of the essence.*

"*When asked if ADA Katz would be seeking the highest*

penalty available in the State of Massachusetts for first degree
murder in the Nagoshi case, which is life without parole, the
source answered a definitive, 'Absolutely.'

"Blah, blah, blah," said David in disgust as he looked up
from the paper, which had allotted a further three pages to this
new revelation in the up until now stagnant Nagoshi case.
"Jesus, Joe. You and I both know there is no source. This is
Katz talking. He would have given Rigotti the quotes on the
condition he wasn't to be attributed."

Joe said nothing, just gave David a shrug that said *Tell me*
something I don't know.

"Is it true though?" David went on. "A reward of millions?"

"Afraid so," said Joe, his now white-knuckled hand wrapped
tightly around what remained of his bottomless cup of Mick's
strong Brazilian coffee. "Nagoshi proposed the reward in the
meeting last night, but I managed to stall him, at least until the
weekend, giving Frank and me the time to make a few more
inquiries about the Matheson kid.

"There were only seven of us in the room, David, including
Leo and a Feeb friend, me and Frank and the Nagoshi father
and son. The Nagoshis gave me their word they would hold off
announcing the reward until Saturday, and I trust them, but Katz
was still reeling from my winning a few points with the famous
businessman so his bruised ego, and disregard for the law, has
blown this case wide open for every fucking lunatic in the city
to put up their hand for a playing role."

"Shit," said David. "What an asshole."

Joe said nothing, just gave him the same indignant shrug. At
that point Mick came over to their table, placing a second mug
of hot black coffee in front of David before slapping Joe on the
back and heading back toward the counter. Mick had known
the two men for years, and was intuitive enough to sense when
they needed to be left alone.

"So what are you going to do?" asked David at last.

"Kick Katz's ass to hell and back," said Joe. "I have been
trying his cell for the past hour, even got his secretary to try to
raise him at home. But the prick is not picking up."

"No, I meant about the reward."

"The only thing I can do. Pull everyone I can off normal
duty to man the Crime Stoppers line."

David nodded before going on. "I know you want to burn the Kat, Joe, but your going off the rails is exactly what he wants you to do. Don't give him the satisfaction. He's not worth it."

Joe looked up at his friend then, perhaps realizing he was right. "Since when did you become the voice of reason?" Mannix asked at last.

"Since I dedicated my career to making the Kat sweat," said David with a half smile.

David picked up his coffee and took a long slow drink, allowing the dark, bitter fluid to warm the chill left by the early morning's single figure temperatures. He wanted to ask Joe about the investigation—or more specifically his progress regarding his inquiries into James Matheson—but he didn't want to overstep his . . .

"What's this shit about China?" asked Joe, interrupting his thoughts.

David put down his mug.

"I don't want to put you—or any source you may have—on the spot, David," Joe went on. "But I'm behind the eight ball here."

David considered him then, wondering how much of Tony Bishop's conversation he should relay. "I heard there may be some trouble regarding Nagoshi Inc.'s bottom line," he said. "But not in a negative sense—more like the opposite. According to a friend, the Nagoshi's Chinese operation is booming, but the numbers don't add up."

"And this relates to Jessica's death . . . how?" asked a frustrated Joe.

"I have no idea. But my friend also says Jessica was being primed as a dual company leader along with her older brother. And the brother is apparently kind of driven."

Joe looked at him then, obviously wondering if David was insinuating what he thought he was insinuating, before shaking his head to say: "It doesn't fit."

"How so?" asked David.

"Jessica was nineteen. Her brother is a little highly strung but I checked him out weeks ago and by all accounts he is a loyal family member—personally and professionally. And according to the father, who was up late making business calls on the night of Jessica's death, Peter did not leave the main house for the entire evening. I saw him last night, David. The guy may look like an emotional zombie, but he reacted with passion when we told him about the evidence we had been withholding. Besides, this wasn't about ambition. It was a crime of passion."

"But there was no evidence of sexual abuse and the girl had no boyfriend and . . ."

"She was pregnant," said Mannix.

"Oh," said David, looking Mannix in the eye, nodding his head in understanding.

"So is James Matheson the . . ."

"No idea," pre-empted Joe. "And even if he is, it doesn't mean he killed the girl."

"No," said David. "It doesn't. In fact, it could mean the opposite. You said the kid came across as nervous during your interview. Maybe he's just shook up, from the loss of it all."

"Or maybe the girl pressured him and he decided to get rid of Jessica and her little bundle of baggage before they could interrupt his all too perfect life."

They sat quietly for a while, choosing not to speak while a group of young workers hovered over the table next to them before deciding on a bigger booth at the far end of the increasingly busy café.

"Matheson says he has an alibi. Says he was banging some girl."

And David shook his head. "And does the alibi check out?"

"I'm about to find out."

Joe finished his coffee and the two men sat silently for a moment before Joe looked up again. "You asked Sara's brother about Matheson, right?"

"Yeah. He said he was straight up."

"And from what you know of him . . . ?"

"He seems like a good kid—enthusiastic, interested, grateful."

"He ever talk about his friends?"

"No, but Jake mentioned them. Apparently they are a band of three—all rich, smart and connected."

"I need the friends to help me corroborate Matheson's alibi. I want to get to them before I speak to Matheson again—catch them off guard, do it low-key."

"Don't know how low-key you are gonna get after this

morning, Joe," said David, pointing toward the newspaper. "My guess is the *Tribune* is already doing the rounds of Deane's hallowed dorms and cafeterias."

"Then I'd better make tracks," said Joe, grabbing his jacket from the back of his chair and throwing a ten dollar bill on the table.

"Joe?" said David as his friend put on his coat. "Let me ask you something. And you don't even have to answer if you don't want to. But my gut tells me you're worried the Matheson kid is in danger of being played—because the Nagoshis need someone to blame and Katz needs his much celebrated day in court."

Joe said nothing.

"You think he's innocent?"

"I have no idea," said Joe. "But everyone deserves a fair trial, David, and I am afraid whoever we arrest is gonna be branded guilty before we even have a chance to clip on the cuffs.

"Let's face it," Joe continued, shaking his head, "Matheson is the sexy option. We arrest him and Katz has his perfect nemesis. He'll go to town trying to prove the District Attorney's Office—under his leadership—does not discriminate between rich and poor. Matheson will become the poster boy upon which he will launch his coup to take over Scaturro's job permanently. I don't trust him on this one, David. He's got something up his sleeve, and that scares the hell out of me."

David nodded. There was no doubt in his mind that Joe was right, and it scared the hell out of him too. He knew his friend was worried about the nature of this case—and the fact that it could well turn into one of those terrifying public phenomena that take on a life of their own, leaving the accused high and dry and making a mockery of "innocent until proven guilty" and the so-called impartial system of justice.

"It's too early to worry yet, Joe," said David, trying to alleviate his friend's fears as much as anything else. "Matheson's alibi will probably stick."

"Yeah, well, the kid's got something to hide."

23

Heath Westinghouse was repulsed. There was really no other way to put it. Here he was, one of the nation's elite, sitting in this overcrowded lecture hall, inspired by the water-struck redbrick walls, walnut-grain desks, classic amphitheater structure and impressive stained glass windows that turned the white morning light into a rainbow of colors as if by magic—and he was forced to look at him!

Professor Karl D. Heffer was undoubtedly the most unattractive human being Heath had ever laid eyes on. His physical repulsiveness was made all the worse by his poor sense of dress in a university where even the scholarship students were self-aware enough to spend a decent proportion of their meager earnings on clothing. It really was deplorable—so much so that he was considering sending an e-mail to the dean suggesting the man's current personal appearance was at such a level that it detracted from his ability to . . .

"Mr. Westinghouse," boomed Heffer, Heath refocusing just in time to see the shower of spit fly from his yellow-toothed mouth like the gush from a sperm whale's blowhole. "Perhaps you could offer a comment on my previous hypothesis? I have no doubt your designer ears have teamed up with that brilliant brain of yours to trigger the necessary synapses required to reason, evaluate and respond to my layman's supposition."

"Ah," began Heath, obviously having no idea what Heffer had been talking about. "I agree, sir," he said, not being able to think of any other valid response. But then he sensed the mood around him—the disappointment! The loss of opportunity! He had let the masses down with his pathetic response and so promptly made up for it with a quick: "I agree I have damn fine ears, Professor, and my synapses are firing just fine this morning. Thank you so much for asking."

Heath knew it was childish but he did take delight in the familiar shade of purple now blossoming on Heffer's spotty cheeks. He could tell H. Edgar, who was shaking his head ever so slightly in the seat beside him, was wavering between stifling one of his conceited little laughs and kicking Heath for aggravating the professor to the point where repercussions would be unavoidable. But Heath was beyond caring. The man was disgusting, faculty fuck of the month or not.

Heffer opened his mouth only to be silenced by the sound of the end of lesson bell, at which Heath collected his books and dragged H. Edgar toward the far right-hand stairs so that he might make good his escape.

"Mr. Westinghouse, Mr. Simpson," Heffer bellowed.

"Jesus," said Heath.

"It's your fucking fault," whispered H. Edgar before turning to Heffer to say, "Yes, Professor, how can we help you?"

Heffer lifted his hand and used his plump pointer finger to beckon them both toward him, the smirk on his face obviously telegraphing the payback Heffer was no doubt brewing in his vindictive little brain.

"Feeling particularly clever this morning are we, Mr. Westinghouse?" he asked as they approached his desk.

"No more than usual, sir," said Westinghouse, not necessarily meaning to be smug but sounding that way nonetheless.

"I see you two have paired up for my assignment," said the professor. "You have already devised a business plan, I hope."

"Yes, sir," said H. Edgar before Heath could interrupt.

"Dare I say I shall be particularly interested in assessing your project," said Heffer, his cheeks now transformed from a deep mortified mauve to a self-righteous rosy hue. "I did mention the assignment will account for fifty percent of your marks this semester, did I not?"

"Yes, Professor," H. Edgar answered again, "which is a shame really, considering the confidence we have in our proposal."

"Hmmm," said Heffer with a haughty little titter. "You'll need to be focused then, free of distractions. No extracurricular activities and all that."

"We'll be living like monks, sir," said Simpson, "until our assignment is complete."

"Good," said Heffer with a smirk, and Heath could not help but think the sarcastic swine had something up his sleeve.

"Off you go then," he said, prompting H. Edgar to grab his friend's shirtsleeve and steer him toward the side exit.

"Oh!" said Heffer just as Westinghouse tugged on the thick colonial doors. "I almost forgot. There are some men here to see you. Two rather impatient Boston Police Detectives, to be exact."

"What?" said Heath, letting the door slam before him. Simpson dropped Westinghouse's arm and swiveled back to face the professor.

"I told them I would go to find you just before the class began," Heffer went on. "But forgive me, dear boys, it completely slipped my mind, what with all that cerebral energy emanating from Mr. Westinghouse's synapses and all. I imagine they are still there though. They certainly sounded very keen to speak with you both."

"They asked for us personally?" asked Simpson.

"Indeed." Heffer smiled.

"Shit," said Heath, unable to hold it in.

"Nothing to worry about, I hope?" said Heffer, his face now contorted in an expression of mock concern. "No." He smiled, exposing the ingrained nicotine stains on his uneven overbite. "Of course not!

"Well, hurry along then. Not very gentleman-like to keep the men waiting—especially when they are two homicide detectives with rather dour demeanors.

"Good luck then," he added, at last waving them away like two insignificant insects. "On the assignment, I mean. I am sure your minds will be free to focus 100 percent on the task at hand, and you shall be patenting your brilliant proposal before the year is out."

• • •

"All right, listen to me," said H. Edgar to his friend, as they bounded down the corridor toward the law faculty offices. "Don't tell them anything, okay? Just listen, be polite and let me take the lead."

"What the fuck are you talking about?" asked Westinghouse. "We have nothing to hide. James said they were interviewing a lot of people who were at the Lincoln that night, we are probably just the next two on their list."

"Matheson was lying," said H. Edgar.

"What?" said Heath, stopping short, turning to face his friend.

"He was lying, Westinghouse," said H. Edgar, pushing Heath into a quieter alcove beside a bank of lockers. "And that guy can't lie to save himself."

"He's our friend," said Heath. "Why are you . . . ?"

"I'm trying to help him, you idiot," snapped Simpson. "For some reason these detectives have it in their brains that James had some connection with Jessica Nagoshi. And they're right. I saw them together last semester, one night at the pool. He didn't know I was there."

"What? Were they . . ."

"Not at that point but my guess is they did, and had been for the best part of the summer."

"Fuck. Why didn't he tell us?"

"I have no idea. At the time I suppose it did not seem relevant."

"So do you think the cops think James is involved somehow?"

And then Simpson saw his friend's eyes light up—like he had a solution to all of their problems.

"Hold on a second. James was with Barbara that night, remember? He has an alibi."

"I know," said Simpson. "But Barbara is somewhere in Europe and it will take them time to find her. If James is arrested his reputation will be ruined forever. Do you think your father's firm would employ someone who was even remotely connected to a murder—and a high-profile one at that? Think about it, Heath. We have to play this thing carefully."

Heath nodded. "Maybe we *should* call my dad," he offered, referring to his powerful attorney father. "Maybe we shouldn't talk to these guys without an attorney in the room—an attorney with our best interests at heart."

"No!" bit out H. Edgar. "At least, not yet."

Simpson looked at his friend then and realized he would have to calm him before they spoke to the police. Westinghouse was one clever son-of-a-bitch but he had no diplomatic censor whatsoever. With Westinghouse it was a case of what you see is what you get, which he was sure the women found endearing, but Simpson saw it as a major flaw that would no doubt impede his friend's progress in the legal world where discretion, tact and subtlety were everything.

"Listen, Westinghouse," he said again, grabbing his friend's forearm in an effort to stress the point. "You saw this morning's paper."

Simpson had collected his own copy of the *Tribune* off his front lawn at dawn, and his brain had been ticking ever since. As soon as he arrived on campus, he had dragged Westinghouse to the Law School coffeehouse so that he might read it for himself. Westinghouse had grabbed the last copy on the stand (with word of mouth already spreading that today's issue was a "must read" for all at Deane) but, considering they were already running late for their class with Heffer, they had not yet had a chance to discuss it—meaning Simpson knew he would have to get Westinghouse up to speed, and quickly.

"The cops are embarrassed, red faced, humiliated by their failure to find Jessica Nagoshi's killer. And these half-assed excuses for law enforcement personnel have one agenda, to make an arrest and clear their names before any more shit hits the fan. They don't give a fuck who it is, Westinghouse, just so long as it is a warm body they can parade in front of the media to justify their pathetic existence." H. Edgar looked into Westinghouse's blue eyes then and knew he was coming around.

"No, if this thing needs to be handled, it will be handled on our terms. So just shut the fuck up and let me do the talking, okay?"

"All right," said Heath, shaking his right arm free from Simpson's grip.

"But H. Edgar, you do know what you're doing, right? You have a plan?"

"A plan?" said H. Edgar, now signaling for the somewhat calmer Westinghouse to follow him up the hallway. "I always have a plan, Westinghouse. And this one," he said with a slight sideways smile, "this one is big enough to blow them all away."

24

"Did you know that we are standing on an international landmark?" asked Sara, removing her red overcoat, allowing the midday sun to soak through her white fitted shirt and obviously enjoying this impromptu lunchtime escape to Boston's historic Public Gardens.

"My feet are international landmarks?" asked David.

"No, this bridge," said Sara with a smile as she pointed downward at the picturesque sandstone and blue-painted bridge that crossed the garden's pond at its narrowest point. "It's the smallest suspension bridge in the world."

"Wow," said David, throwing his arm around her. "Let's hope it holds then. I am not wearing my swim trunks and I hear that swans are very territorial." He pulled her into a hug and she squeezed him right back.

It had been Sara's idea to get out of the office, grab an early lunch and go for a walk through Boston Common down to America's oldest public park. She had been working flat out on the sexual harassment civil suit and David knew she felt bad about spending every spare second at her office. They made their way toward Commonwealth Avenue and the Arlington Street entrance where the George Washington statue rose high above the manicured flower beds. From there they circled north toward Beacon, toward the famous *Make Way for Ducklings* miniature bronze statues that waddled in suspended animation as a tribute to the Robert McCloskey children's story of the same name.

"So what is it?" asked Sara at last, swinging David's hand as she held it tightly in her own.

"Sorry?" asked David.

"What's on your mind?" she said, squinting into the early

afternoon sun to look up at him. "Something is bothering you, David, has been all morning and experience tells me your breakfast with Joe may have everything to do with it."

David said nothing.

"Come on, David," she said. "Last year we made a promise never to keep things from each other, remember?"

And he did. It was during the Montgomery case when his first wife, Karin, had asked him to represent her husband, noted Washington heart surgeon, Professor Stuart Montgomery, who had been accused of killing the vice president of the USA.

"I'm sorry," he said. "You're right. Joe is in trouble—caught between a rock and a hard place on this Nagoshi thing."

"Is it the reward—the one they speculated on in the paper this morning?"

"Partly," said David.

"Wanna talk about it?" she asked, and he could tell she was trying her hardest not to push. But in her voice he heard that familiar tinge of fear—fear that he was walking down that lonely road where he shut her out, jeopardized her trust, and all with the misguided belief that she needed protecting from the big bad evils of the world.

"It's about James Matheson," he said at last, knowing Sara, who Joe also trusted 110 percent, deserved to hear what was bothering him. "I am afraid the kid is in a whole heap of trouble."

"I knew I hadn't heard the end of that," she said, shaking her head as she looked up at him again. "So tell me everything—from the beginning."

And so he did, starting with Joe's frustration with his inability to identify a bona fide suspect, before moving on to the lifelike portrait in Jessica Nagoshi's sketch pad. He told her of Tony Bishop's insinuations, Katz's determination and Joe's fury at the Kat's "leak" of the supposed seven-figure reward in this morning's *Tribune*. He spoke about Joe's description of Matheson's nervousness, his choice of sneakers, kayaking abilities and alibi claims and Joe's current whereabouts—being Deane University where he was most likely in the process of questioning Matheson's friends. He ended with Joe's concerns that Matheson, guilty or not, was on the fast track to becoming public enemy no. 1, given what he knew would be Katz's personal passion to use the kid as a stepping-stone to the permanent position of district attorney.

"At the moment, at least from Joe's point of view, it's all just a big fat bundle of frustrating 'what-ifs,'" finished David. "*What if* Matheson's alibi does not stick, *what if* he is the baby's father, *what if* Katz managed to get a quick grand jury indictment and nail Matheson to the wall for what will be portrayed in the press as a heartless murder of a young, pregnant girl?"

Sara stopped then, before turning to him, her expression pure affection with perhaps a touch of pride. "He ask for your help?"

"No. Not that there is anything I can do except listen."

"That's a help in itself."

"In this case, I'm not so sure."

"You're a good man, David," she said at last, pulling him toward her. "And don't worry. Joe is a smart guy. He'll do everything he can to make sure this thing plays out fair and square."

"You're right," said David, kissing her on the forehead, finally managing a smile in return. "Joe's one of the best detectives in the country—and I'll bet, before the week is out, he'll have this whole thing totally under control."

25

"I feel like one of those fish," said Frank McKay, shifting in the musty green leather chair in the corner of Professor Karl Heffer's office.

The small room was a mess—a dusty, cluttered conclave that belied the spacious lecture halls and expansive grounds around it, as if proudly establishing itself as the most congested corner in the entire university complex.

"What?" said Joe Mannix, pushing several copies of heavy texts titled *International Business Practice* and *Theory of the Modern Corporation* aside so that he might gain a better view of his fellow homicide detective, who sat looking out the window on the far side of the room.

"One of those fish—you know, the ugly fish."

"I am not sure I want to hear this," said Joe, glancing at his watch again. It was 12:15 p.m. They had been waiting for over an hour and a half.

"When Kay and I were on our honeymoon in Hawaii," Frank went on, "we went to this bar where they had one of those huge fish tanks behind the bar—you know, one of those big tropical numbers where the water is warm, the fish all pretty colors and the coral glowing like neon at the bottom of the tank."

Joe did not comment. There really wasn't any point.

"Anyways," said Frank, "Kay glances up over her pina colada and says, 'Frank, get a load of that ugly fish!' and by George she was right. In fact, she was being kind to the little brown bastard. This thing was one of the most unattractive specimens of marine life I had ever seen and it stuck out among all the beautiful fish like a turd in a rose garden."

Jesus, thought Joe.

"So Kay says to the guy behind the bar, 'I feel sorry for that little one, the one that looks like a scrunched up cigar. He looks all alone. None of those pretty fish want to play with him.'

"And the barman says, 'Don't feel sorry for him, ma'am. He's a puffer fish. He may be butt ugly but when he gets riled he expands to ten times his normal size and kicks some serious butt. The tropicals are scared to death of him. They may not want to admit it, but the puffer is in control, 100 percent.' "

Joe looked at his friend then, realizing that in his own way McKay was trying to ease his fears. Joe knew he was drawing an analogy from their affluent surroundings—the tank being Deane, the picturesque fish being the beautiful young things that paraded around campus like princes and princesses. And they were the puffer fish, all disheveled and jaded and out of place—but holding an unspoken power over the privileged of Deane, as representatives of the law and all that it represented.

"It just hit me," said Joe, wanting to express his gratitude but realizing the only way to do so was to slip into the banter they knew so well. Joe had known Frank for years and had always admired his ability to diffuse a situation with his own special "Frankness."

"What is it, Chief?" asked Frank.

"Your wife. Her name is Kay."

"Yeah."

"Kay McKay."

"Yeah."

"Nothing wrong with that," said Joe after a pause.

"No, Chief. Nothing at all."

Seconds later they were interrupted by the click of the door and the subsequent entrance of two of the "beautiful people" themselves—their expressions all earnestness and sincerity, their gait purposeful and self-assured. The shorter red-haired boy entered first, his arm extended in a gesture of cooperation before pumping each detective's hand with determination. "Detectives, we are so sorry to have kept you waiting. My name is H. Edgar Simpson and this is my friend Heath Westinghouse. Please, retain your seats and tell us exactly how we can help you. We are at your service, gentlemen. What is it you need to know?"

• • •

"This Heffer," Joe began as the boys pulled over two wooden chairs and placed them side by side in front of the now closed door. "He ride your ass?" It was a simple question, but one that would establish many things.

Firstly, it suggested Joe was open to setting himself on their level, sympathetic to their situation as students, but also as adults—he was not here to lecture but to discuss. Secondly, it showed them Joe meant business—no euphemisms, no pleasantries, man to man, straight up. Thirdly, it begged some sort of explanation as to their tardiness—like did the professor demand they stay until his class was over or was the delay a tactic on their part? And finally it enabled Joe to gauge a sense of the boys' attitudes, or more specifically their level of respect for a man like Heffer who, despite his obvious eccentricities, was older, more experienced and "superior" to them, at least on the ladder of Deane academia.

"Professor Heffer is new to this university, Lieutenant," said H. Edgar after a pause. It was as if the kid was also gauging Joe's motives, and reading every one to a "T." "And I am afraid he sometimes gets a little flustered. It was he who failed to notify us of your presence, if that is what you are asking, at least until after class, when we made haste to prevent you any further inconvenience."

"That's very nice of you," said Joe with a half smile, as if in appreciation for Simpson's thoughtfulness. "But you didn't answer my question. Does the Professor ride your ass?"

"No, Lieutenant," said Simpson returning the smile. "Our 'asses,' as you so aptly put it, are generally unrideable."

"A pair of bucking broncos, eh?" said Frank.

"Not exactly, Detective." H. Edgar smiled. "If you want to consider an equine analogy I suppose you would say we are two Arabians, steered only by those we believe will enhance our personal development."

"I see." Frank nodded as if enlightened. "Come to think of it, I do remember reading that Arabians pick their owners rather than the other way around."

"Exactly," said Simpson.

This kid had balls, thought Joe, no doubt about it. He was telling them in no uncertain terms that Messrs Simpson and Westinghouse were not to be trifled with. They were masters of their universe, directors of their destinies, bastions of their own incredible strength of mind.

"Forgive me, Lieutenant . . . Detective," H. Edgar went on, "but I am sure you did not invite us here to ponder Professor Heffer's ability or lack thereof to intimidate his students. Correct me if I am wrong, but I believe you are here to discuss Jessica Nagoshi—and more specifically her relationship with our good friend James Matheson. Am I right?"

Joe glanced at Frank. This one was a doozie.

"I thought so," said Simpson, not waiting for a reply. "Well, let's be clear from the outset, shall we? Obviously you can appreciate we came here on our own recognizance, and as you can see, there is no lawyer present to advise us in regard to any statement we might provide. That is our decision, Detectives, a show of good faith, because as you may or may not be aware, Mr. Westinghouse here comes from a line of respected attorneys, including his father, Mr. Gordon Westinghouse of Westinghouse, Lloyd and Greene. And if we felt we needed such representation, this meeting would not be taking place, at least not now, in this . . . ah," he said looking around him, ". . . most uncomfortable of settings."

Joe said nothing. This kid was too good. He wanted him to go on.

"So, you may ask us about James and we shall tell you what we know. But if we feel our rights, or those of our friend, are being compromised, we shall get up and leave the room without hesitation. Agreed?" he asked with one of the most conceited, self-righteous expressions Joe had ever seen—and that was saying something.

"Anyone ever tell you you'd make a good lawyer, Edgar?" asked Joe, knowing full well the kid was obviously arrogant enough to take this comment as a form of admiration.

"Yes, sir." Simpson smiled. "And it is H. Edgar, by the way."

And so they began.

Within minutes Simpson and Westinghouse's one word/ same phrase answers had established that these two boys were exactly what they purported to be—smart. Their use of one word definitives and repeated references to lack of recall were the responses of seasoned legal experts.

What time did you arrive at the Lincoln? 11:15 p.m. *What time did Jessica Nagoshi arrive?* They did not recall. *Was she drinking?* They did not recall. *Were they drinking?* Yes. *Was she with a male companion?* They did not recall. *Did they see anyone make advances toward her?* No. *What time did she leave?* They did not recall. *Did she leave alone?* They did not recall. *Was James Matheson talking to her?* They did not recall. *Did James Matheson have a previous relationship with her?* They believed the two to have been acquaintances. *Had they seen Jessica and James together on previous occasions?* They did not recall. *Did James leave with them?* They left the Club premises together, yes. *At what time?* 1 a.m. *But did he then go home with somebody else?*

This last one stopped them in their tracks. Joe saw a slight tic at the corner of Simpson's left eye and knew that whatever was about to come out of his mouth was most likely going to be a lie.

"Lieutenant Mannix," said H. Edgar after a pause, "I know you most likely did not attend a university."

A put-down if there ever was one, thought Joe.

"Your prerogative, of course. Indeed if it weren't for the fine work of our esteemed police force us budding lawyers would be out of a job before we even sat for the bar." Cue smile. "But I am sure that your experiences at the police academy were not that different to our experiences here at Deane—in a social, interactive sense I mean. You studied, you trained, you tolerated your superiors and you made friends. You shared confidences, developed trusts and no doubt swapped stories of your conquests in regards to the female gender.

"It happens everywhere, Detectives, young men in the prime of their lives boasting or commiserating, depending on their success or failure." H. Edgar looked at his tall blond friend then, and Westinghouse responded with a nod as if their testosterone bond was proof of Simpson's "universal theory."

"James did go home with someone else that night," said H. Edgar. "Her name is Barbara Rousseau—a French exchange student who has since returned to Paris. I am sure if you contacted her she would be able to confirm this. I am not sure of her exact whereabouts but I am confident you fine investigators will be able to track her down."

Frank took down the girl's name while Joe's eyes remained fixed on the two boys in front of him.

"Now if there are no other questions, Detectives, I believe we are late for our next tutorial."

"Nothing else," said Joe. "Unless your silent partner here has anything else to add."

"No, sir," said Westinghouse. "Mr. Simpson and I are on the same page. I agree with everything he has said and once again, we apologize for keeping you waiting."

"No problem," said Joe.

And then the pair turned to leave—just as Frank thought of one more thing to ask.

"Hey, kid," he said, calling to Simpson who turned just as he was about to walk out the door.

"Yes, Detective?"

"What's with the H?"

"I beg your pardon?"

"The H, you know, in H. Edgar."

"My mother has a PhD in philosophy, Detective. She graduated from Harvard magna cum laude. I was named for one of her academic forefathers—a Greek philosopher, one of the greatest intellectual minds in history."

And then Frank smiled—a smile that grew until it exploded onto a beam on his wide, rosy-cheeked face.

"Your name is Homer—Homer Simpson!" he said at last. And now, despite himself, Joe found he was smiling too.

"Yes, Detective, and I am proud of it, sir."

"Well, obviously."

26

"I tell you what, H. Edgar," whispered Heath Westinghouse as they moved quickly down the law faculty corridor. "You may be a little odd sometimes, but you kick ass like nobody I have ever met."

"Shut up," said H. Edgar.

They slowed their step as they saw one of the faculty approaching from the other end of the hall, and did their best to look for all the world like two respectful young intellectuals returning from a visit to one of their learned superiors.

"Good afternoon, Professor Todd," said Simpson, nodding at his Advanced Torts teacher.

"Mr. Simpson, Mr. Westinghouse," said Todd in acknowledgment.

H. Edgar's heart was racing. He had done it! He had opened the fucking door and taken one huge step through, allowing it to close behind them. There was no going back now. The plan was in motion, and it was inspired. No! It was more than inspired, it was unparalleled, exceptional—downright fucking *brilliant*! Of course, it was extremely complex and must be carried out with the greatest of focus and commitment. But he had been over it a million times since he first read the article a little after 6 a.m.—that was barely seven hours ago and already all of his ducks were in a row. Now it was just a matter of telling them where to march.

"This way," he said to Westinghouse, steering him toward a closed office door with the name *Toni Mansfield—Professor of Law, B.A., M.A.T.* painted on the front glass. Simpson grabbed the handle, pulled Heath inside and shut the door behind him.

"Jesus, H. Edgar," said Heath. "What's with all this cloak and dagger shit?"

"We are meant to be in Mansfield's class right now," said H. Edgar. "So we know we won't be interrupted."

"What's to interrupt?" asked Westinghouse, obviously now completely confused and perhaps a little tired of being pushed around.

"How much do you want to get back at Heffer?" asked Simpson, gesturing for Westinghouse to move away from the door so they would not be spotted through the frosted glass.

"More than anything. You know that."

"And how committed are you to burning that bastard's ass?"

"Like I said."

"Then what do you say about us taking his assignment to a new level and making some real money—to the tune of around $700,000 apiece?"

"What?" Now Westinghouse was smiling. "How the hell are we going to do that?"

"You trust me, right?" said Simpson.

"Sure."

"And our friendship is . . ." H. Edgar stopped to rephrase. "I mean, you and me and James are . . ."

"Tight. Brothers. You know that."

"All right then. Now listen to me. We don't have much time. Maybe forty-eight hours at the outset."

"What?" said Westinghouse again, his face now a contortion of pure bewilderment. "Why forty-eight hours?"

"Because I figure that's how long it will take for the cops to find Barbara and confirm James' alibi. It would have been less of course. It'll take those detectives two minutes to get her forwarding address and phone number from admin. But she's not in Paris right now. She's in Switzerland on some cross-country skiing thing with her friends from the Sorbonne. I rang this morning, checked it out. Her little trip buys us some time."

"Wait. Slow down. What are you saying H. Edgar?" said Westinghouse, shaking his head. "I thought this was about Heffer?"

"It is—at least in the sense that the satisfaction we get from . . ."

"Then why did you check on Barbara?" interrupted Westinghouse. "And what has any of this got to do with James?"

"James is the key to all this," said H. Edgar, now thinking

aloud. "Listen to me, Westinghouse. Tonight I have arranged for us to meet James at The Fringe. We need to be seen there together, but after that you must not talk to him. You cannot see him. No contact, nothing, at least until the cops confirm his alibi."

Westinghouse was looking more uneasy by the minute. Simpson knew he may have missed that much underestimated "manipulation" gene, but he was sharp, and the reality of what Simpson was saying was no doubt slowly coming together in the recesses of his brain.

"Saturday morning," said Simpson. "We'll need your father."

"Saturday night is the President's Halloween Ball, dude. Everyone who is anyone is flying into town. My dad will be schmoozing all day. He . . ."

"We leave it any longer, Barbara steps up, and our window of opportunity closes."

And then it hit him. Simpson could see it in his eyes. The pure genius of it all.

"The reward money!" he said at last. "The two million split . . ."

"Three ways," said Simpson.

"No way, H. Edgar. James will never forgive us. He will be . . ."

"Cleared of suspicion as soon as those two detectives track down Barbara," finished H. Edgar. "Cleared of suspicion and $700,000 richer."

"We're going to claim the reward?" said Westinghouse. "You and me and . . ."

"Matheson."

"He'll never go for it."

"Yes, Heath. Yes, he will."

"He doesn't need the money."

"Neither do we."

They stood there for a moment, saying nothing, Westinghouse taking it all in, Simpson watching him come around, little by little, bit by bit.

"No. It doesn't add up. The police will know we are riding them as soon as they talk to Barbara."

"Yes, but we trade our information with conditions—that

what we give them is enough for an arrest, not contingent on a conviction."

"Arrest?" said Heath at last, shaking his head. "This is way beyond anything we discussed. I don't know if we should do this. We could be branded as snitches of the highest order, money hungry Judases who are willing to sell out their friend for . . ." Westinghouse took a breath before going on. "An hour ago you told me James could not afford to be arrested, at least publicly, and you were right. It will ruin his potential career. Shit like that sticks, H. Edgar, even if you are as innocent as a virgin in a nunnery."

"But that's the beauty of it, Westinghouse. Your father will broker the deal. He'll demand confidentiality. He will insist James be given the chance to turn himself in quietly—which he will. The supply of our statements will be contingent on an agreement of no public release of information for at least forty-eight hours. James will be protected. No one will ever be the wiser. The terms will be unnegotiable. The money wired to untraceable accounts. The cops will never know about the three-way split and James will walk free, his reputation intact and $700,000 in his pocket."

Heath stopped then, weighing it all up, ready to be tipped, one way or the other.

"Think about it, Heath," said H. Edgar at last. "The pure brilliance of it all—a real opportunity to test our superior intellect. I really don't think this has ever been done before, an accused man claiming his own reward. It is really quite beautiful, don't you think?"

"But we just told the cops . . ."

"Nothing," snapped Simpson. "We . . . *I* . . . told them nothing, or weren't you listening?"

Westinghouse was starting to frustrate him, but he knew he had to tone it down, massage his friend's anxieties, relieve his fears, appeal to his hatred for . . .

"Heffer's cause will be lost, his fight defunct. This is nothing if not entrepreneurial."

"But won't he just turn us into the police for providing false information . . . which is *what* by the way? How do we hang our best friend when we know he didn't do it?"

"Details, Westinghouse. It's all in here," he said, pointing to his head.

"Look," he said now, leaning in close. "This is a once in a lifetime opportunity and there is no time to waver, Westinghouse. You are either with us or you are not."

"*Us?*" said Heath, his own voice now raising a notch. "James already knows about this?"

"Of course. We spoke early this morning."

"Then why didn't you tell me as much in the first place?"

"Because I needed you to be calm, focused, in front of those two cops. And the less you knew at that point the better."

Westinghouse frowned.

"Look, Heath," said H. Edgar, determined to bring his friend back on board. "There is no way I would suggest this if I didn't have James' approval. For without his cooperation, this whole thing turns to shit. So . . ." asked a determined Simpson. "Are you with us or are you . . ."

"You're *sure* James is down with this?"

"Positive."

"And Barbara will make this all go away?"

"Straight after we pull off the negotiation of the century."

And then Simpson saw it, the smile in Westinghouse's pale blue eyes.

"Fuck it," he said. "I'm in."

27

"I apologize, Detectives," said Mrs. Humfries with an "f." "It really is not like Sawyer to be late."

"You sure he got the message?" asked Mannix, tired of waiting for upstart college kids who apparently thought their precious daily schedule was beyond interruption—even when summoned by the goddamned Boston PD.

"Yes, Lieutenant," said Humfries, talking to Joe but looking at Frank with that disconcerting smile/wince on her narrow pallid face. "I paged him over two hours ago, when you first arrived."

"Students have pagers?" asked Frank.

"Some, yes," said Humfries, who, no doubt thanks to Frank, was a fair bit more "honey" than "lemons" this afternoon. "Sawyer's role as youth director of Solidarity Global makes him eligible for a university pager, like the ones the faculty carry. He came to the office moments after the page. I told him you wanted to see him and he said he would be back forthwith. Which obviously he . . ."

"Is not," finished Joe, unable to hide his frustration.

It was now after two—*2 p.m!*—and Joe felt the pressure building up around him. He knew the reward deadline was now invalid thanks to Katz's selfish "leak" to this morning's *Tribune*, but he could not help but feel there was another timer at work here—a silent, invisible meter ticking down to zero when they would find themselves squeezed into a corner from which there was no escape.

The interview with Simpson and Westinghouse had been nothing short of extraordinary. The Simpson kid was possibly the most egotistical subject Joe had ever had the displeasure of questioning. He was arrogant, conceited, condescending and cool. The Westinghouse kid was another matter, however, and Joe saw the jitters behind his superior façade despite his friend's complete hijack of this morning's conversation. Of course all this would mean jack shit if Matheson's alibi checked out. And thanks to Mrs. Humfries forwarding address and contact information on Barbara Rousseau, this should be resolved, one way or another, before the day was out.

Now all they had to do was wait for the soapbox kid to show his mop of a head and come clean on his cryptic dialogue of a few days ago. After all, he was the one who told them James was in love with Jessica.

"Detectives," said a voice from the door, and in that second Joe could have sworn it was the voice of the soapbox kid. But he was wrong, this kid had the same confident tone but he was a she—and over six feet tall.

"Hello," she said, moving forward. "My name is Valerie Winston-Smith and I am Deputy Youth Director of Solidarity Global—Sawyer's 2IC."

Jesus, thought Joe, *did everyone who entered Deane have to pass a course in "Confident as All Hell 101" before they let you in the front gates?*

"It's nice to meet you, Valerie," said Frank, no doubt sensing Joe's frustrations. "I'm Detective McKay and this is Lieutenant Mannix. Is Sawyer with you?"

"I am afraid not," she said, now standing close enough to tower over the two men. "But he asked me to give you this," she said, handing them a recycled envelope with the well known SG logo—a sphere representing the earth with two horizontal lines representing the symbol for equality cutting through it—on the far left-hand corner.

Joe opened the note.

"*Tomorrow. Noon. New England Aquarium. Shark Tank,*" Joe read to himself, allowing Frank to do the same as he looked over his shoulder.

"Is that it?" asked Joe, looking up at Valerie.

"Yes, Lieutenant," said Valerie, sliding her tortoiseshell glasses back up her long slim nose. "And he wanted me to wait so that I might text him your response before I returned to class."

Joe glanced at Frank. "Listen here, Long Tall Sally," he said then, sick and tired of a pack of smart-ass, conceited rich kids trying to run his show. "You have five seconds to tell me exactly where Tom Hanks Junior is skulking before I call in the entire Boston PD to scour this entire campus and have his ass in for questioning."

Joe could see the vertically blessed Valerie physically shake in her two flat boots.

"I . . . he is not on campus," she managed. "As soon as he gave me this note he packed up and left and said he wouldn't be back until tomorrow."

"Does Jones live on campus?" asked Frank of Lemons.

"Yes, Detective," said a now wide-eyed Humfries.

"But he's not in his dorm," said Valerie. "I just called his direct extension before I came in here and there was no answer so . . ."

"Shit," said Joe, just as Frank shrugged and pointed to the handwritten note in his hand. "This is crazy," he added, talking directly to Frank, way past caring if Valerie or Humfries overheard, "the fact that we have to humor this cocky kid by keeping his ludicrous appointment next to a bunch of man-eating fish—at twelve noon *tomorrow* no less."

Frank nodded before turning to Valerie. "Tell him we'll see him there," he said at last.

"All right then, Detectives, I'll let him know," said Valerie, nodding at them both before swiveling on the balls of her extremely long feet and running out the door.

"Fuck," said Joe, ignoring Lemon's scowl.

"Jesus," said Frank, doing pretty much the same. "But it's already late afternoon and we got other priorities besides chasing the kid all over Boston for the rest of the day."

Joe nodded. "This ride is getting crazier by the minute, Frank," he said, as they headed toward the door.

"Couldn't agree more, Chief. I mean . . . puffers are one thing, but sharks—well, they are a whole different kettle of fish altogether."

28

"Fishermen," said John Nagoshi as he leaned back in his black leather chair at the head of the long mahogany conference room table. Nagoshi and his son had returned to their New York base early that morning, and had been in an exhilaratingly positive board meeting for most of the day, thanks to Peter's incredible progress in China.

"I beg your pardon, Father?" said Peter, sitting straight in his seat at the other end of the now quiet conference room.

"Fishermen, my son. They used to say the Chinese were born and bred only to fish but they were wrong. It seems they are also more than adept at building cars—and driving them as well. You were right, *segare*. Basing our first automobile plant in China was an excellent idea."

"Thank you, Father," said Peter, with a bow.

John Nagoshi was, in fact, more than pleased with the day's developments. Recently, he had to admit, he had been concerned about his son's somewhat erratic behavior—especially following the uncharacteristic outburst in Mr. Katz's office barely twenty-four hours ago (after which Nagoshi found himself extremely grateful that no one else present could speak Japanese). But his performance in front of the board today was nothing short of brilliant. His presentation was confident, well prepared and extremely encouraging. There was no doubt he had allayed any fears regarding his right to the position as company heir.

Jessica was gone, but her killer would soon be arrested. Nagoshi was sure that Roger Katz had leaked the reward to the press for personal gain, and he had left a message at Lieutenant Mannix's office assuring him he had kept his word. But in all honesty he was not disappointed with the early release of the story. If anything, it might help Mannix confirm this young boy's guilt and finally enable them to put Jessica—and her unborn child—to rest.

"It is late," said Nagoshi at last. "I am going to call for the car. Will you accompany me home, my son?"

"No thank you, Father. I still have some matters to address."

Nagoshi nodded. "Do not stay too late, *segare*. The week has been long." And then he got up to leave.

"Peter," he said, turning away from the magnificent backdrop of the Manhattan skyline in front of him to face his son front on. Nagoshi and his offspring had a strong relationship, but he feared the lack of motherly love and Peter's seeming inability to show emotion had left their bond somewhat devoid of any physical displays of affection. He loved his son, as he had his daughter, and now, while he still ached at the loss of one, he was mindful to acknowledge his feelings for the other.

"I am sorry, son, about Jessica. But please, do not be angry with her. We are all allowed mistakes in our lives and this child, well . . . no matter how it was conceived, it was still my grandchild."

"It is not your fault, Father," said Peter, now standing from his seat, his face stoic, focused, clear.

"I asked the lieutenant," Nagoshi went on. "Before we left last night, I asked him if my grandchild was a boy or girl."

"Yes, Father."

"It was a boy, Peter. I was going to have a grandson—and you a nephew."

"I see. I am sorry, Father."

"Do not be, my son," said Nagoshi before walking across the room to place his hands on his only living child's shoulders. "For there will be others. You will lead this company to greatness—you and your children and their children after that."

And then John Nagoshi did something he had not done in years. He extended his arms to reach behind his son's shoulders and pulled him close in a firm, if not somewhat awkward, embrace. "I love you, *segare*. Never forget that is true. For you are a Nagoshi and I am proud to call you my son."

As soon as his father had left the room Peter Nagoshi took a

long, slow, deep breath. He then straightened his suit of the
creases left by his father's unexpected show of emotion, and
began walking across the mocha-colored carpet toward the
expansive eastern windows at the far side of the room. The
lights were dimmed, but all about him was clear—the room
now saturated by the illuminations of the never sleeping city
beyond. And in that moment, just as he reached his father's end
of the boardroom table, he found himself turning the larger
chief executive chair around so that he might sit in the president's berth and replay the day's victory while looking out on a
world over which he reigned as a prince destined to be king.

His father was right. His performance had been remarkable.
China was a stroke of pure genius and he had done the research, studied the statistics and presented the information with
just the right combination of confidence and humility. He had
begun with the history—the fact that over twenty years ago
Germany's Volkswagen became the first foreign car manufacturer to enter the Chinese market, closely followed by General
Motors Corp and later Japanese companies such as Honda,
Suzuki and more recently Toyota.

And then he spoke of the problems—of how these foreign
manufacturers faced two major struggles. The first in the form
of stringent joint production quotas set by the Chinese government, which meant all foreign companies had to enter into
agreements with local car makers who had little experience at
running and maintaining large automobile manufacturing
plants. And the second a reflection of the local market itself—
and the fact that it was virtually nonexistent. Until recently,
fewer than ten in 1000 Chinese people of a driving age owned
a car and the prospects for a profitable local market looked
grim.

Next came the good news—the impressive actuality that
fresh research showed the rate of car purchases in China was
growing at twenty percent per annum, with the forecast for such
growth now stretching to the year 2020 and beyond. In other
words, Nagoshi Inc. would be entering the industry at a time
when manufacturers no longer had to export the great majority
of the automobiles made cheaply in their increasingly experienced Chinese plants.

And so the timing could not have been better. In fact, timing was the *key*, and it was on this point that Peter had taken a considered gamble by proposing something he was yet to discuss with his father. He suggested that to hesitate was a mistake, that they must announce this foray into the automobile industry *now*. The Guangdong plant had already produced twenty-five vibrantly colored prototypes of the Nagoshi "Dream" CC250—the company's first compact car—which would be shipped to motor shows all over the world as a public relations pre-runner to the automobile being released on the open market early next year.

"We must not allow this announcement to be foreshadowed," he had said, knowing his father would pick up on Peter's reference to the impending news of the arrest of his sister's suspected killer. "We must lead with this positive and allow other similarly fortunate announcements to provide closure on previous matters and consolidation of our new direction, progress and profit for the near future and beyond."

And his father, who had perhaps been somewhat taken aback by his son's daring at putting this suggestion to the board before discussing it with him first, had nodded in agreement, proving to Peter that his calculated risk was not so precarious after all.

Solidarity Global were a non-issue. He had spoken to Mr. Kwon that very afternoon, who had assured him the only contact the international do-gooders had made in the past week was a ludicrous but informative phone call from the pathetic American boy named Jones. According to Mr. Kwon, Jones said that SG's extensive study on Nagoshi Inc.'s Chinese operations would soon be released on their website—and the report would clear Nagoshi Inc. of any impropriety, describing their Chinese operation to be both "efficient and fair." But this boy, the same youth Peter knew had used his sister to try to undermine Nagoshi Inc.'s progress, claimed he did not accept the report's findings and was set on unveiling the company's injustices to the world. Jones said he knew the study was compiled under contrived circumstances and that he would make it his life's mission to prove it. *Good luck to him,* thought Peter. *Let him try.*

Jessica was a fool, for she had opened the gates to this disaster, not realizing the consequences of her actions. Somehow the

Jones boy had hoodwinked her with his rhetoric on the downtrodden unskilled and she had boasted of her father's dedication to just and reasonable management. She wanted to use Nagoshi Inc. as the prototype for honorable employment and in doing so had intruded into Peter's initiatives without asking his permission, and discovered what she was not meant to find. Her false face did not fool him. She was a Nagoshi in name but not in soul. She was making many mistakes, mostly due to her willingness to be seduced by the self-servedness of Western society and for this she, and her illegitimate unborn child, had paid the ultimate price. It was true that news of the child had unnerved him at first, but fate had its own path, and the demise of the bastard child was unavoidable once the course to eliminate its mother was set.

29

"Well done, Sara," said Nora Kelly, their Irish-born, fifty-something office assistant who was dedicated, hardworking and blessed with a sharp Gaelic wit that served to soften her prim façade with just the right amount of humor and heart. "It's a glowingly justifiable report," she added, looking over Sara's shoulder at the article on page five of this morning's *Tribune*. "To think, your first pro bono civil suit for this firm and you managed to settle for . . ."

"One point five million dollars," said Arthur from behind his antique mahogany desk. "Amazing, dear girl. Just amazing."

"It all happened so quickly," said a smiling Sara, now dropping the newspaper on the coffee table to pace around the office. Her adrenaline was pumping, the feeling of legal victory still fresh in her veins. "We didn't think Mr. Finch would settle but the man was apparently terrified of having to face his day in court. The one point five was really just a throwaway figure. I never dreamed he would accept."

Sara was referring to a man named Freddy Finch, the sleazy proprietor of a Mattapan restaurant and bar known as Tequila Mockingbird. Sara had represented a waitress named Aresha Sanchez and some of her fellow workers in a sexual harassment suit against Finch—who surprised them all by accepting the one point five million dollar proposal.

"Of course the jerk accepted," said David. "Even an idiot like Finch is smart enough to avoid facing Sara Davis in court. Am I right, Nora?"

"For once, lad," smiled the witty Irishwoman, who enjoyed nothing more than a verbal spar with the younger of her two "bosses." "You are 100 percent correct."

"So what next?" asked Arthur, getting them back on track.

This regular Friday morning meeting was a forum to summarize cases active and pending, giving them a chance to bounce ideas off one another.

"Next we oversee the distribution of the money," said Sara, now stopping in front of Arthur's desk, "the bulk of which will go to Aresha with the remainder to be divided among the other staff who had agreed to partake in the joint action." Sara was on a roll and it felt good.

"I do, however, have a list of potential clients' names sitting in a wad of message slips on my desk. I am afraid this morning's story has opened the floodgates to all and sundry who have a gripe against their boss. The problem will be sorting the wheat from the chaff. And Arthur . . ." she said before hesitating.

"What is it, Sara?" asked her casually dressed superior, who preferred open-necked shirts and khakis over the usual lawyer garb of dark gray suit and complementary tie.

"Well, I know you have been kind enough to . . . ah, give me a lot of leeway when it comes to pro bono causes. But I also know this is a business and I want to make sure I contribute financially."

"Sara," said Arthur, removing his wire-rimmed glasses to rub the red groove on the bridge of his nose, "the publicity you have given this firm this morning is worth its weight in gold—and I hope you know me well enough by now to understand my view of 'business' may not be the same as a lot of other attorneys' in this commercial driven metropolis. Besides," grinned Arthur, craning his neck to look at David who was sitting on the couch across the other side of the room, "David is the designated company cash cow. In fact, I am sure he is on the brink of signing his first multimillion-dollar client as we speak."

Sara turned to face David, but she saw that he wasn't listening. He had pulled the cover section off the coffee table and was now absorbed by a story on the *Tribune*'s front page.

"Perhaps if we offer him a bale of hay with his morning coffee we might get his attention," said Nora.

"What?" said David, looking up at the three faces now focused on him. "Sorry, I was just . . ."

"What is it?" asked Sara, now moving behind him to study what looked to be a major piece taking up most of the coveted page one.

"It's the Nagoshis. According to Marc's story, Nagoshi Inc. is about to announce a major foray into the automobile production business with their manufacturing plant based in China." He looked up at Sara, and she recalled their earlier discussion about Tony Bishop and his suspicions regarding the Nagoshi son. "Rigotti's report also says an arrest in the Jessica Nagoshi murder case is imminent. He even quotes a source at the DA's office who predicts they'll have a suspect in hand before the week is out."

"James Matheson," said Sara.

"Who?" asked Arthur, now obviously confused, and David took a moment to summarize what he knew about the case for Arthur and the equally as discreet Ms. Kelly.

"Dear Lord," said Nora. "Is that distasteful Mr. Katz trying to bully yet another young innocent?" This was not the first time they had been aware of the Kat's disregard for the truth in favor of a conviction and all the political kudos that went with it.

"Probably," said David. "But I'm not sure how he's going to pull it off. The last time I spoke to Joe he was on his way to Deane to question Matheson's friends. Maybe the kid's alibi didn't hold up after all."

"Whatever the case," said Arthur, and in that moment Sara knew her wise and caring boss had seen it too—the spark in David's eye, his need to right the wrongs, his determination to defend those being railroaded by a system set on finding someone to blame, "I understand you took a liking to the boy, David, but at this point at least, it is no concern of ours."

David nodded.

"But all this talk of Deane did remind me of one other matter," Arthur continued. "I expect to see you all at the President's Halloween Ball tomorrow night." The Deane School of Law function was a social must for the city's leading legal fraternity. "If I am going to suffer the evening trapped in a monkey suit and swapping anecdotes with a bunch of socially aware blue-chip barristers, then I expect you all to do the same."

David looked up at Sara again and she sensed that going to this ball—a "chore" he would have done anything to get out of a few weeks ago—was now something he felt compelled to do.

"We'll be there, Arthur," she said, just as Nora nodded her

confirmation before leaving the room to take a call from her desk immediately outside Arthur's office. "In fact, Jake is going too. His new bosses at Credit Suisse want to introduce him around. My little brother is being 'networked.'" She smiled. "Wonders will never cease."

"Good for him," said Arthur. "And good for me because I will probably stay no more than an hour before leaving you lot to fly our flag. I don't think I . . ."

"Sara," interrupted Nora, now standing at Arthur's door. "It's for you."

"Thanks, Nora, but if it's another disgruntled worker, tell them I will sort through my messages and call them back when I have had a chance to . . ."

"No, my dear. It's far more serious than that, I'm afraid. This young man says he is about to be arrested for murder—and he needs to talk to you *now*."

30

The Deane University School of Law library was an institution in itself. Founded in the late 1800s, it had opened its door with an impressive 1000 volumes, expanding its catalogue over two centuries to now boast a collection of 1.5 million books and manuscripts, 500,000 volume-equivalents on microform, and an impressive multimillion-dollar art collection to boot. It provided a warm, historically rich but ordered atmosphere in which to learn—and a ten-million-dollar-plus annual budget to maintain its status as one of the most up-to-date and respected places for academic legal research on the planet.

It also boasted a staff of over 100 personnel, all of whom James Matheson could have sworn were right this moment either peering at him, gossiping about him, or shaking their heads behind tall, book-laden petitions as they contemplated the walking, talking disappointment, tragedy, *murder suspect*, that was former "it" kid James Matheson. The grapevine had done its work. Everybody who was anybody, and even those who weren't, had heard the latest—that Matheson had been questioned by Boston homicide detectives in relation to the murder of corporate heir Jessica Nagoshi. They had also heard that barely hours ago the same said detectives met with Matheson's two best friends—peers they had no doubt would defend the popular Matheson to the death, unless (perhaps) it was in their best interest to do otherwise.

That was the thing about the law, thought James as he turned off his cell and took a seat at a poorly lit cubicle behind a shelving unit at the back of the main library hall. *It was impartial and just, to the point of being heartless and mercenary.*

It had been her idea to keep it quiet. She had told him her father, while rational and fair, would have frowned upon any distraction from her studies and her obligations as "Nagoshi chief executive in training." Her father, she had said, was a generous and understanding man, but he was also set on assuring his two children maintain focus on their destinies. He had had a plan for her and it was, at least according to Jessica, "good and true." But there were times when James wondered if such plans were not simply guises of control—and if Jessica, so completely unaware of the mesmerizing effect she had on people, would fall victim to such subtle domination without even realizing she was slipping into a trap. At the very least last night's drinking fest with his two best friends had been cathartic, but he could still feel the weight of the blame about him, and knew there were many hurdles to jump before people would see him again as the man he was destined to be.

"James."

He heard the voice before he saw her. Despite the fact she was two feet away and must have squeezed between two book docking trays to approach him from the narrow corner aisle. It was Jessica's friend Meredith Wentworth, the one who was with her at the Lincoln that night.

"Meredith," he said, managing a smile. "Sorry, I didn't see you there. I was absorbed in . . . ah . . ." He looked at the text in front of him, having no idea what it was about.

"Alternative Dispute Resolution," she read from the spine, coming to his rescue. "Enough to put anyone to sleep."

"I guess," he said, after which there was a long and awkward pause.

"Ah, listen, James," Meredith went on, hugging her own heavy texts to her chest, "I was just wondering if you . . . I mean, I didn't know if you were . . ."

"What is it, Meredith?" said James, bracing himself for someone to finally ask him the question he knew everyone was bursting to ask.

"I was wondering if you were going to the Halloween Ball tomorrow night," she said at last. "And if you were, if you could maybe use some company, that is if you were planning to go, of course, and if you haven't already asked somebody else, and wouldn't mind if I . . ."

"Meredith," he said, realizing what this kind young girl was doing and feeling more grateful than ever. She was making a

statement. As one of Jess's best friends. She wanted the world
to know that James Matheson was innocent and that her closest
friend, now cold in her grave, would have wanted her to stand
by him, no matter what.

"I . . ." he began. "I would be honored to take you, Meredith.
I mean, I kind of ditched the idea of going considering . . ."

"There is nothing to consider, James. I could sense how
happy Jess was before she . . . You were good for her, James.
You made her feel alive." And then she reached out to place her
smooth, pale-skinned hand on his shoulder. "You never know,
we might even enjoy ourselves."

"You think?" he asked, the grief now etched on his face.

"Well," she said, her own brow furrowing in sorrow. "I suppose we could try."

And James nodded. "Are you sure?" he asked at last.

"Sure." She nodded with the sweetest of smiles.

"Well, thanks, Meredith," he said.

And she shook her head. "Nothing to thank me for."

"Yes, there is, Meredith," he said, raising his own hand to
his shoulder to squeeze hers in a gesture of pure gratitude. "More
than you know."

31

"Peanut Butter the Jellyfish," Joe Mannix heard his fellow detective say. There was no mistaking it, as ludicrous as it may have sounded. But he knew he was meant to ask the question, and so . . . he did.

"What was that, Frank?" he said, sticking to the "routine."

"Peanut Butter the Jellyfish," said McKay, pointing at the small, orange clown fish in the New England Aquarium's Tropical Gallery. "That's where the concept of *Finding Nemo* came from. At least that's what some pissed-off dentist from Newark claims. The guy filed a suit against Disney and Pixar Animation claiming he wrote a story called *Peanut Butter the Jellyfish* in the nineties and pitched it to Disney who basically told him they weren't interested.

"Seven years later he takes his kids to the flicks to see what he claims is his story up there on the big screen, dentist character and all, except the big screen version turns New York into Sydney and Nemo into a clown fish as opposed to a jellyfish named . . .

"Peanut Butter," finished Joe.

"Exactly," nodded Frank. "Anyways, before this dentist submitted his story, Disney had him sign a two-page waiver that said he would only be entitled to $500 if he were to claim the company used his material without permission. Now the dentist has asked the court to void the waiver and give him a portion of the $340 million the movie made at the box office." Frank shook his head. "Just goes to show, Chief," he went on. "Not even little guys like Nemo here are above the law."

"Especially if their names used to be Peanut Butter and Jelly."

"Not Peanut Butter *and* Jelly, Chief. Just Peanut Butter who was a . . ."

"Jellyfish," said Joe. "I got it."

It had just gone noon. The air was thick and moist and heavy and the dimly lit circular corridors inside the historical aquarium were crowded with excited kids on field trips, flustered teachers trying to contain them, and determined tourists jostling their way to the front of the glass in an attempt to get the best shot possible of the nine foot great white that circled the tank like an angry submarine.

"Where's Jones?" asked Joe.

"He'll be here," said Frank.

"We need him, Frank. We need somebody to shed some light on exactly what was or wasn't going on between Matheson and the Nagoshi girl. Katz is breathing down my neck big time—and God knows what new bullshit he is concocting with the press while we are sitting on our asses here in the magical land of Atlantis." Joe was referring to this morning's article on the Nagoshi automobile initiative and the suggestion that a suspect in the Jessica Nagoshi case would soon be in custody. The impatient ADA was using public opinion to put pressure on Mannix to make an arrest, and while normally he wouldn't have given a rat's ass what the arrogant attorney did or didn't say, he had to admit that this time, he was feeling it.

"The Rousseau girl is up on some goddamned Swiss Alp and we'll be lucky to find her before the weekend, which will make it two whole days since I told Nagoshi we would . . ."

"Wait," interrupted Frank. "Here he comes. See down by the entrance near the penguin exhibit. It looks like he has somebody with him. In fact," said Frank, squinting into the distance as if to make sure his eyes were not playing tricks on him. "It looks like . . ."

"Sara," said Joe.

"Hi, Joe," said Sara, walking toward them, no doubt reading the surprise on both their faces.

"Sara, what are you . . . ?" Mannix began.

"Lieutenant, Detective," said the soapbox kid, shaking both of their hands with vigor. Jones was now surrounded by school kids in short pants and embroidered shirts and the thought went through Joe's head that if he had have been dressed like the rest of them he would have been corralled by a teacher before you could say . . .

"I gather you know Miss Davis," said Jones, interrupting Joe's thought. "I have just engaged her as my attorney."

"What?" said Frank. "What the hell for, kid? You are not under suspicion. All we wanted was a chat and some clarification of your earlier comments regarding James Matheson. We're not here to bust your balls, kid. We just want to . . ."

"I killed Jess Nagoshi," said the boy at last, leaving an astonished Joe and Frank rendered speechless. "That's right, Detectives, I am the reason she is dead. It is all my fault."

• • •

They took a seat by the window at a far corner of the Aquarium's second level café—Joe, Frank and Sara opting for coffees while a pale-faced Sawyer ordered a super-sized chocolate shake. It was raining, and the wind was forcing the downpour sideways, so that it smacked against the window with visible force, blurring the harbor view beyond and making Joe feel that he too must have looked like a fish in a tank to the jostling Friday afternoon pedestrians beyond.

Sara made it clear that she had had little time to confer with her client and that while she was willing to let him tell his story to the two detectives, she maintained the right to terminate this voluntary discussion if and when she saw fit. "My client has some information relating to events that may have led to the death of Jessica Nagoshi," she said. "And I am recommending he provide you with as much information as possible. However, if we reach a point where I feel the direction of questioning leaves my client vulnerable, where he might unwittingly violate his own fifth amendment rights, I shall recommend this interview be terminated immediately. In other words," said Sara, looking directly at Joe, "I've told Sawyer you can be trusted, Joe. He wants to help. And I know you won't take advantage of that."

Joe picked up his blue paper cup, an animated smiling shark now peeking between his wide, dark fingers. He sipped his coffee slowly, before replacing the cup on the table and facing Sara. "I understand your position, Sara, but the kid just told us he is guilty of murder. He's lucky we didn't cuff him right then and there in front of fifty elementary school kids and all manner of aquatic life beyond.

"So let me make *myself* clear. I will sit and listen and ask what I need to ask, but the minute I feel young Jones here is taking advantage of our generosity I will arrest the kid on suspicion of murder and drag him down to HQ before he has a chance to make a dent in his shake."

Sara was a friend and Joe didn't want to sound harsh, but this was a murder investigation, and no ordinary one at that. If this kid had anything to do with Jessica Nagoshi's death, he was gonna pay for it, friendly counsel or not. "So, here's your chance, kid," he said, turning to Sawyer. "Tell us everything you know and we'll do our best to protect you. But the minute I feel you're taking the piss I'll cut you down. You got it?"

"Yes, sir," said Jones, his complexion whitening by the minute. "And if it's okay with you, I'll start with China."

• • •

Sawyer Jones first noticed Jessica Nagoshi way back in November last year. She was second year pre-law, just like him, but their paths had not crossed to any great degree until they both opted to take on a subject known as international jurisprudence. It didn't take long for Sawyer to work out who she was—multinational heiress, corporate royalty—and while Sawyer had only just assumed the senior position of Solidarity Global Youth Director, he saw an opportunity to make his mark as leader of the group by taking the bold step of recruiting the daughter of the "enemy" as a dedicated one of their own.

"I cornered her after class one day," he said, looking across the table at a now transfixed Joe and Frank. "I was straight up, asked her if she wanted to have a coffee, learn more about the group. I promised her I had no sinister motives, but was interested in getting her perspective on SG's initiatives, given her upbringing as part of a corporate dynasty.

"At first she just looked at me," said Sawyer, now turning his pink plastic straw around the bubbly froth that sat on the top of his chocolate shake like milky spun cotton. "Her face a complete blank. But then she smiled and said one word—'*sure*'—as if hooking up with me to learn more about SG was like accepting an invite to a girls' night out.

"Anyway," he said moving on. "We had coffee the next morning. She said she was interested. She said she had great respect for what we were doing and shared her father's philosophy on workers' rights. She said her father had never compromised on his principles. She said he had rejected suggestions to downgrade the working conditions of indigenous workers in satellite plants, despite promises of increased output and profitability, because he was a man of integrity who was raised on the philosophies of veracity and truth.

"And eventually she said she thought it would be more than appropriate for her to become a member of SG and pulled out her wallet to pay the joining fee right there and then." Sawyer closed his eyes, feeling the momentary need to block out his surroundings, as if ashamed of what he had to say next, but knowing it had to be said.

"And that was when it started," he said, opening his eyes once again, "when I first dragged her in. That was when I took her hand and she slipped one slender foot over the edge of her grave—the other one soon to follow—as some time next summer she came up with her own 'brilliant idea.'"

Sawyer then explained how late last August Jessica called him from her home in New York, saying she wanted to help SG by providing a "prototype" for responsible employment practices. He told them how Jessica had elaborated on her father's latest initiative—a new business foray into China where the booming industrial power would play host to Nagoshi Inc.'s first automobile plant—a plant built on the principles of "productivity by fairness and egalitarianism."

"She was very excited about it," he said. "And so was I. She wanted to make her father's company—*her* company—a benchmark for others to follow and was willing to open up its operations to scrutiny of the highest order."

"So what did that mean?" asked Joe. "And how does this have any bearing on . . ."

Sawyer could see the stress in the tired-looking lieutenant's eyes and reminded himself that, despite the desire to cut to the chase, this was a discussion best conducted slowly, calmly, carefully. He would get to his point, he knew. But not until he had laid the groundwork for what he had to propose.

"Please, Lieutenant Mannix," said Sawyer. "I need to tell this my way. I promise it will all make sense eventually. Just allow me to . . ."

"Give him some space, Joe," interrupted Sara.

And Joe nodded, allowing Sawyer to go on.

"First up," he said, after taking a long, slow drink of his shake, "you have to understand that China is the key to all of this. The great Asian expanse is currently the largest maker of toys, clothing and consumer electronics in the world, and swiftly moving up the ladder in car production, computer manufacturing, biotechnology, aerospace, telecommunications and other sectors thanks to low-cost, high-tech factories.

"China is also where the world is investing. In 2004, for instance, the city of Shanghai alone attracted over $12 billion in direct foreign investment, roughly the same amount as all of Indonesia and Mexico put together. It is widely acknowledged that China's huge population is one of the greatest natural resources on the planet. Largely because hundreds of millions of peasants have migrated from rural to urban areas to find work, providing an unlimited, low-wage workforce to power China's economy—and that of its foreign investors.

"So where does Nagoshi come into all this?" Sawyer asked rhetorically, now aware he had to bring the conversation back on track. "You probably read in this morning's paper that the establishment of Nagoshi Inc.'s first automobile production plant in China is being hailed as a multibillion-dollar win/win for the consumer goods multinational, and the *Tribune* is not far wrong.

"Nagoshi Inc. has been smart enough to establish a plant in a place where wages are as low as twenty-five cents an hour, where lack of regulation allows companies to drop this pitiful wage even further, and where appearances can easily be manipulated by clever local foremen who swear by equality but are rewarded financially for practicing exploitation."

"Are you saying John Nagoshi is not the saint his daughter made him out to be?" asked Frank. "That his Chinese workers are doing their daily grind for little more than a piss in a pot?"

"No and yes," said Sawyer. "I actually believe Jess was right about her father. In fact, to this day I still do not think he knows what is actually going on behind those high brick walls in Guangdong. You see, China is her brother's initiative, and from what I can gather, he has 100 percent control."

Sawyer saw the lieutenant glance at his partner and guessed that perhaps this was not the first time Peter Nagoshi's name had come up in relation to matters of disquiet.

"So what gave you the idea that something was amiss?" asked Joe after a beat.

"Well," said Sawyer, almost draining his shake before moving on. "The minute Jess organized for a team of SG inspectors to visit the Nagoshis' Chinese plant, I heard the alarm bells ringing loudly in my ears. The plant manager was nervous, the SG reps delayed, the inspection day heavily monitored and the resultant report straight from the manual of good worker management 101."

"But that's a good thing, right?" asked Joe.

"Of course, if it were not for the fact that I received a call from a Mr. Lim Chow, one of the plant workers, who claimed conditions in the factory were now beyond appalling—that wages had dropped below the ten cents mark while hours had increased and personal benefits had been withdrawn."

"So," said Joe with a frustrated sigh, "I still don't get how this relates to . . ."

"Jess found out about the call," interrupted Sawyer. "In fact, she had just arrived back in town and happened to be in my office when the call came in. She spoke to Mr. Lim herself. She was beside herself, devastated. She mumbled something about her brother Peter—but stressed she was determined to set things right."

"So what did she do?" asked Mannix.

"She told Mr. Lim that she would arrange for his passage to America—so that he might meet with her father face-to-face. She told him her father knew nothing of this and that he too would be horrified. She told him that she and her father would put an end to the torture, that the foreman would be dismissed, that they would pay their workers compensation and assure them that they would never allow anything like this to happen to his people again."

"And did she?" asked Frank. "I mean, did this Lim jump on

the first flight from Shanghai and front the boss and shoot the shit and . . ."

"No," said Sawyer. "For Mr. Lim, a forty-nine-year-old father of six, was killed in a factory accident within twenty-four hours of making that call. And Jessica was dead another twenty-four hours after that."

. . .

Silence. Nothing, as the white noise that people made in busy places such as these merged into one low, monotone hum where words and activities around the now huddled group of four became slow, blurred, indecipherable.

"Kid," said Joe at last, now leaning low across the formica tabletop to look directly into Sawyer's eyes. "Are you telling us you think this thing in China . . . that Jessica's knowledge of Mr. Lim's accusations led to her murder."

"Yes . . . No . . . I'm not sure," said a now obviously confused Sawyer who pushed his empty paper cup out of the way so that he might place his elbows on the table and rest his shaking head in his hands. "But the timing was way off—or should I say spot on . . . don't you think?"

"Jesus," said Frank.

"The thing is, I have no proof," said Sawyer, lifting his head once again. "But I do believe it was either China or . . . or my advice on the other thing that got Jess killed. Either way it was my fault. Either way I had a hand in her death. Either way I will have to live with that knowledge for the rest of my . . ."

"*What?*" said Joe, not believing what he was hearing. "*Either way*, kid? You said '*either way.*'"

Joe looked about their table, quickly, quietly, before reaching across the scratched rectangular surface to grab Sawyer by the wrist—his large hand engulfing the boy's miniature lower limb, his grip causing Sawyer's blood to pool on either side of Mannix's broad, white-knuckled clench. Jones immediately began to wince under the pressure, and Joe saw the first sign of fear in his normally confident pale brown eyes.

"What the fuck does that mean, kid? Are you saying you have *two* theories on the cause of Jessica Nagoshi's death? Are you saying you have two fucking hypotheses—neither of which you have decided to share with the goddamned Boston Police until now?" Joe squeezed a little harder, causing Sawyer to let out the tiniest of yelps.

"*Joe!*" said Sara. "Stop this." She reached across to pull on Joe's sleeve. "He's only a kid, you're hurting him."

"No," said Joe. "I'm sorry, Sara, but Jones here is no kid. He may look like a teenager but he has to be at least . . . what . . . nineteen to be second year pre-law? He's an adult, Sara, an adult with legal representation on hand. He came to us, remember? If he has something to say he sure as hell better say it now, because I for one am getting sick of all this bullshit."

Jones looked at Joe, his face flush, his hands shaking, his mouth opening and closing, allowing nothing but the tiniest of squeaks to escape. And in that moment, just as Joe began to relax his grip, he could have sworn he saw something else in Sawyer's wide pale eyes—some sense of strategy, some indication that his Mensa brain was working overtime on exactly how to play this one out.

"You see that building across the other side of the Harbor, kid?" asked Joe, noticing the clouds had finally given way to a crisp afternoon sun. Jones did not respond.

"Look at it, turn your fucking head and look at it." Joe released his grasp on Jones' arm and lifted his hand to Sawyer's narrow boyish chin, forcing his head to the right. "You see it now?" he asked. "You see that big redbrick building with the fancy glass façade—the one with the group of kids playing on the freshly mowed lawn out front?"

Mannix watched as the boy's eyes refocused south, toward Fan Pier and the modern, medium height architectural "statement" that was John Joseph Moakley Courthouse.

"That may look like a museum to you or an art gallery or some lah-dee-dah office block where people come and go to 'brainstorm' and 'network' and make shitloads of easy fucking money day after day after day. But looks can be deceiving, kid—that there is the US Federal Courthouse of Massachusetts where criminals have to answer for their bullshit every single day of the year."

"I know what it is," said Jones, perhaps tired of being treated like an idiot.

"They come in thinking they are smart enough to manipulate the system," Joe went on, ignoring the kid's retort. "Confident they can ride the wave and come out pumping the air like a pack of goddamned invincibles. But they don't, Jones—come out, that is. More than likely their bullshit, and the ego that usually goes with it, has them locked up for good in some not so utopic rat-infested federal prison.

"Now your bullshit is of the State variety, granted, but it is bullshit nevertheless—withholding evidence, lying to the police, failing to report information vital to the progress of an internationally significant murder investigation. As Miss Davis here can tell you, kid, Suffolk County Jail ain't no playpen for young intellectuals—especially pretty ones the likes of you."

"For God's sake, Joe!" said Sara, starting to rise from her seat. "This meeting is over. You can't threaten my client like that. He came here of his own free will. He is willing to cooperate if you would just . . ."

"Sit down, Sara," said Frank.

But Sawyer and Mannix paid no attention; their eyes were locked in a silent bond of understanding. Mannix guessed the kid knew he had gone as far as he could—and as such realized it was now time to cut to the chase.

"The lieutenant is right," said Sawyer at last. "I am a coward who likes to think my exceptional intellectual ability makes me better than everyone else. Yes, Lieutenant, I believe there are two ways in which my friend Jessica may have lost her life and sadly, regrettably, I had a hand in them both.

"My motives for enticing her to join SG were selfish, and if it was China that got her killed then I am guilty by association, unwittingly maybe, but at fault nevertheless.

"Secondly, I have to admit, it was also I who started the whole disastrous scenario which is now playing out detail by detail, accurate or not, inside every café, dorm, library, corridor, lecture hall and study room of Deane University. *James Matheson killed Jessica Nagoshi*—it's all anyone can talk about."

Joe stole a glance at Frank.

"You see, Lieutenant," Jones went on, "it was me who convinced her to go out with him. She came to me just before summer break, to ask whether or not I thought she should take a chance and go for a guy who was perhaps not the obvious choice for the daughter of a Japanese-American dynasty. She said this boy was young, smart, idealistic, intuitive . . .

"And I told her to go for it . . . that love was all too rare in this callous, competitive universe that we young intellects are forced to exist in each and every day of our precious superior lives. I told her to tell the boy she wanted him, to belie the consequences and dive into the wonderful, dangerous quagmire that was inappropriate but unbridled devotion.

"Of course at the time I foolishly thought she was referring to somebody else. But she was talking about Matheson, you see. The one person everyone seems so sure was responsible for squeezing the life out of her with his own goddamned hands." Jones looked down at his own hands then, and quickly shuffled them under the table and into the hidden recesses of his lap.

"*Shit,*" said Joe at last, realizing what the kid was saying. "You thought Jessica was in love with *you*. You thought she was feeling you out, to see if you felt the same way."

"Not so smart after all, hey, Lieutenant," said Sawyer, his eyes now glistening with tears. "I told Jess to seek out James Matheson. She thanked me—kissed me even, and then left to meet him by the river. They spent the next four months sneaking here and there and I witnessed every last second of it."

"You followed them?" asked Frank.

"Let's just say I wanted to make sure she didn't get hurt," answered Sawyer, most likely not wanting to come off as the poor pathetic fuck that he actually was.

"You have proof they were together?" asked Joe.

"Yes, and just in case my word isn't good enough . . ." Jones looked to Sara then, who gave him the slightest of nods. "Why do you think I asked you here in the first place, Lieutenant?" he went on, lifting his arms to indicate their chaotic surroundings. "You think I spend my life frequenting commercial crap houses like this? These places are nothing but inhumane jailhouses for creatures confined to tanks that bear little or no resemblance to the great ocean expanses from which they were so cruelly abducted."

Jesus, thought Joe.

"No, Lieutenant," Jones went on. "We are here because this was where they came for one of their rendezvous—the last week of August, barely days before she died."

With that Sara reached into her handbag to lay something

square and plastic on the blue formica table. "New England Aquarium security camera CD-ROM recording, Saturday, August 26," she said. "James Matheson and Jessica Nagoshi, here, together, and judging by their body language, very much an item. It's yours, gentlemen," she said, handing it to Joe, "on one condition—that my client be given full immunity on any charges relating to his delay in providing this information to the police."

Joe took the disc, turning it over once, twice, three times in his large, thick hands.

"You need them together, Joe," said Sara at last. "And from what I can gather this is the only piece of evidence you have so far. I don't want to railroad the Matheson kid, Joe, but they were involved, and if Matheson says otherwise then he is a liar."

Joe looked at her then, his eyes flicking back to Jones briefly as if trying to gauge what his motives might be.

"So do we have a deal?" asked Sara, obviously anxious to secure her client's immunity.

"If the disc shows what you say it does," said Mannix at last, "Jones can have his immunity. But if I find out this kid is holding anything else back or, God forbid, lying about any and all of the above, I swear to God I will kick his ass to hell and back faster than he can say 'Save the goddamned Whales.' "

Sara looked at Sawyer who gave a short nod in response.

"Agreed," she said, shaking Joe's hand across the table. "You have his word on it, Joe, and you have my word on it too."

32

"He is just so refreshing, David," said Sara, taking a sip of her merlot, the subtle light of the table lamp casting shadows across her high cheekbones. "He is young and wealthy but unaffected by all the trappings that go along with that sort of existence. He is completely dedicated to helping people less fortunate than himself. He lives and breathes it, David. He is smart and intuitive and devoid of any of the usual pretense that goes along with being one of the Ivy League elite."

David said nothing. They were facing each other from either end of the sofa, she with her legs crossed "schoolgirl fashion" underneath her, he relaxed with a wineglass in his hand, socks on his feet and his beautiful, enthusiastic girlfriend sitting mere feet in front of him. He could not believe it was just over a year since Sara had agreed to move in with him—transforming his neat but characterless bachelor apartment into a home—the first real one he had known since he left Jersey all those years ago. Everything around him now "breathed" of Sara—the minimalist limestone-based lamp, the dark grain, low-set coffee table, the whitewashed walls, the black-and-white photography and the comfortable but stylish slate-colored lounge on which they now sat. And he loved every piece of it, because everything reminded him of . . .

"David . . . ?" she asked, smiling. "Are you listening to me? I know I am going on about this kid but he was kind of inspiring—a breath of fresh air in a generation supposedly reared in the ethos of self-advancement and personal satisfaction."

"He made an impression on you," he said at last, pulling one of her feet out from under her to massage it gently on his lap.

"Yeah," she said. "I guess he did."

David knew he wasn't showing the enthusiasm he should.

He knew Sara was on a high after the Sanchez ruling and the subsequent newspaper article, which was read by one Sawyer Jones who had immediately concluded Miss Sara Davis was the smart, determined, humanitarian lawyer for him. But he couldn't help but think this Jones was, if nothing else, a little on the dramatic side. He still wasn't sure why he engaged Sara as his attorney in the first place, given he had nothing to do with the Nagoshi girl's murder. For some reason this Jones seemed intent on implicating himself by association—and in the process managed to exonerate himself of the actual deed by suggesting two possible alternatives for Jessica's demise.

If David was a skeptic, he might even come to the conclusion that the kid was orchestrating this whole "woe is me" charade on purpose—to divert Joe and Sara and everyone else from the real course to the truth. That was Joe's gut feeling, or at least what he alluded to in his private call to David's office late this afternoon.

"Sara," he said at last.

"Yeah?" she said, taking another sip of her wine.

"This kid is smart, right?"

"Sure."

"His father is a lawyer and he's pre-law at Deane so you have to assume he is pretty clued up when it comes to judicial process."

"Don't worry, David, if you think I am taking this one on pro bono you're wrong. Sawyer has already offered to pay me. I told Arthur I wanted to contribute to the firm financially, and while I won't be asking Sawyer for a huge fee, it will be more than enough to cover my time and expenses."

"No," said David. "That's not what I meant. What I am saying is . . ." David paused then, knowing that as much as he and Sara were committed to a relationship based on honesty, it would really knock her confidence to know that he and Joe had been discussing her vulnerability mere hours before. He could see she was overwhelmed by this boy and feared that perhaps the kid could see it too—enough to take advantage of her and use her as a pawn to divert any possible suspicion on his part.

"This Jones was obviously in love with the Nagoshi girl—he admitted as much himself. He also knew she was in love with somebody else and no matter how strong and optimistic you are, at nineteen that kind of rejection has got to . . ."

"What are you saying, David?" she said, slowly retrieving her foot to curl it neatly back underneath her.

"Don't take this the wrong way, Sara," he said, knowing she probably already was—or more to the point, wasn't. "I am not suggesting he had anything to do with the girl's death but you have to admit, if you take a step back, that his story could be seen to be somewhat contrived."

"I don't believe this," she said, the previous energy and enthusiasm now completely drained from her face. "You spoke to Joe. He called you and the pair of you sat and gossiped and concluded that poor little Sara was naive enough to be tricked by a teenager who was playing me for a fool."

"No, Sara," said David, now sitting up straight and placing his wineglass on the coffee table. "That's not it. We just don't want you to . . ."

"So you *did* speak to Joe?"

"I . . . yes. But . . ."

"What is it, David?" she interrupted. "Is it the Matheson boy? I have no idea why you seem so convinced of his innocence, especially since you have only met with him a couple of times over coffee.

"Do you see yourself in him, David? Is that it? Because if that's the case, I just don't get it. He may be enthusiastic about his studies but his upbringing, his lifestyle . . . in many ways he is nothing like you, or at least not the David I know. He has lied to the police, surrounds himself with friends who are described as conceit personified and according to your good friend Joe is the number one suspect in the homicide of the year. Why can't you see it, David? Why is it so hard for you to believe that he did this?"

"Why is it so easy for you to believe that Sawyer Jones did not?" David asked, regretting his question the moment it came out of his mouth.

And he saw it then—the anger, the resentment, the hurt at his seeming determination to hijack Sara's night of victory and turn it into a blistering pit of self-doubt.

"I'm going to bed," she said at last.

And he wanted to say something to make it better, wanted to

turn back the clock and have them sitting here, peacefully, happily together. But in the end he said nothing. Because, if truth be told, he knew she was right. He did feel an affinity with James Matheson, he did "sense" that the kid was innocent of the heinous crime everyone was so keen to claim he committed, he did hope that Matheson was not about to become the third victim in a crime that already taken two innocent lives and above all else, if that was to be the case, more than anything he wanted to be the one to defend him.

Maybe he was frustrated. Maybe he missed the adrenaline of a seemingly unwinnable high-profile case—a rush he had not felt since defending Stuart Montgomery over a year ago. Maybe he was jealous of Sara's latest high, maybe he wished it was he who pulled off the 1.5 million dollar settlement and was dragged into a murder investigation unwittingly or not.

But he knew that wasn't the case. Admittedly he relished the chance of taking on Roger Katz again, but this had little to do with ego and more to do with his gut. What that would mean for Sara and her new client he did not know, but he sensed, if he got what he wished for, he was about to find out.

33

"Gabe, honestly, you look fine," said an exhausted Marie Mannix, pushing a stray blond lock away from her tired blue eyes. It was late and she was kneeling on her sons' bedroom floor surrounded by a myriad of Halloween costumes that had been worn and re-worn by the four Mannix boys for over a decade.

"I'll paint the lightning bolt on your head tomorrow night. Stephen said he'd lend you his old glasses, and if you carry the garden broom you'll be a dead ringer for . . ."

"But *everyone* goes as Harry Potter, Mom," said Gabriel, the third of the four Mannix sons. "And most of them have capes or Quiddich robes from Toys 'R' Us, not cutouts from their moms' old dresses."

"But the skirt looks just like a cape, Gabe, and . . ."

"Gabriel," said Mannix, who had heard the ongoing banter all the way from the downstairs living room of their much-loved if not slightly weatherbeaten West Roxbury Colonial and decided it was time for a Halloween reality check for his nine-year-old son. "Do you know how much those costumes cost?"

"No, sir," said a sheepish Gabe.

"They cost one million and twenty-five dollars," said six-year-old Michael who was happy to sit on his top bunk and watch the drama play out beneath him.

"Shut up, doofus," said Gabe.

"Gabriel!" said Joe, walking into the room. "You apologize to your little brother and hightail it into bed right now. At this rate you'll be grounded from trick-or-treating for the next twenty years. Your mom has been kind enough to make you a costume so the least you can say is 'thank you.'"

"I'm sorry, Dad," said an obviously overtired Gabe. "But Henry Bosco is always giving me shit for wearing Joseph or

Stevie's hand-me-downs, so what's he gonna say if he finds out I am wearing my mom's dress?"

"Don't say 'shit,' " said Marie Mannix, now clearing the bedroom floor of Halloween debris. "Your father's right. One more complaint and you can stay home while your brothers are out filling their bags with candy."

"Okay," said a stubborn Gabe at last, crawling into the lower bunk with a look of pure disgust on his olive-skinned face. "Thanks, Mom—but I'm still not wearing the dress."

"Up to you, Gabe," said Mannix. "Totally up to you."

"He'll get over it," said Joe as he turned out the younger boys' light before moving down the hall to check on his two older sons, Stephen and Joe Junior, who were sitting up in their own single beds playing some form of handheld computer game, which Joe was convinced was turning them slowly into zombies.

"Lights out in five minutes, boys," said Marie as she took her husband's hand and headed for the stairwell.

"Maybe I should have bought him the new costume," she said as she moved across the living room and into the kitchen to get Mannix a beer and pour herself a glass of Sangiovese. The room was still warm from the family's home-cooked dinner, the air thick with the comforting scents of tomatoes, garlic and Parmesan.

"Nah," said Joe. "Gabe's a good kid. He'll be okay. Back in my day all we needed was a sheet with two holes cut out and . . ."

"Back in *your day*," said his wife. "Stores weren't marketing Halloween to a generation of kids brought up on consumerism."

"Yeah," said Joe. "And we could roam free on the streets for hours without our parents fearing we might be abducted, assaulted, raped."

"They're going to be fine, Joe," she said, smiling at him as she shook her head.

He could not help but marvel at the woman who stood before him—her flaxen hair, pale eyes and rich olive skin still glowing with the youthfulness those of Northern Mediterranean descent seemed blessed with.

"Rough day?" she said, moving some draining dishes to the

side so that she might lean against the counter and face her husband head-on.

"I guess," he said.

"You'll work it out, Joe," she said taking his hand. "You always do."

"With this one I am not so sure," he said. "There is just too much riding on it. The pressure is building, Marie. Katz wants an arrest and I may not have the power to . . ."

"What does your instinct tell you?" she asked, looking directly into his eyes.

"That's half the problem. I can't seem to get a read on it. Things are happening too slow and too fast all at the same time."

She put down her glass of wine then, leaning forward to reach her arms around him. "Just don't let them railroad you, honey. It'll come. You just need time to think it through."

But she was interrupted by the shrill ringing of the telephone, the long piercing sound sending a shiver up Joe's spine. He was on edge, he knew.

Marie let go of him then, making some brief comment as to the lateness of the call before reaching to her far right to grab the old red wall phone from its cradle.

"Mannix residence," she said. And then a pause, until: "Yes, he's here. Can I ask who's calling?"

She looked up at her husband and Joe saw it in her eyes. Trouble, he knew. Trouble in the form of . . .

"It's ADA Katz," she said. "And he says he needs to speak to you—now."

34

There were five other men in the room, observed Joe Mannix as he perched himself on the edge of the low bookcase just inside the door. Or more specifically one man—John Nagoshi; two assholes—Roger Katz and the lawyer; and two boys who, despite their obvious attempts to appear humble, looked more like a matching set of spoiled brats than ever.

Nagoshi sat opposite the two boys in the same seat he had occupied at their last meeting. He was silent, calm, dignified, while Katz was still running the show up front and Gordon Westinghouse had spread himself out in the now single space, where Joe and Frank had squeezed previously, at the other end of the table.

"Right," said the impeccably dressed Katz, signaling for his sour-faced assistant Shelley to finish pouring the ice waters and leave.

"We all know why we are here so, out of respect to Mr. Nagoshi," he said, and Joe could have sworn he took a slight bow, "I suggest we get to it."

"Mr. Katz," said Mr. Westinghouse. "As you are aware, my son Heath and his friend Mr. H. Edgar Simpson have some information relevant to the murder of Jessica Nagoshi, which took place a little under two months ago on the night of Friday, September 11 of this year.

"Messrs Westinghouse and Simpson are willing to divulge such information but not until a reasonable set of circumstances can be met." Westinghouse paused there for effect, tapping his Mont Blanc pen on his leather-bound legal pad before moving on.

"You can appreciate their situation, Mr. Katz," he said with appropriate furrow in his tanned brow. "They have struggled with the American value of loyalty to a trusted friend versus a responsibility to behave as law-abiding citizens, and have honorably decided to do the right thing. They will give you the name of Miss Nagoshi's killer and the evidence to put him away, but not until we can come to some form of . . . arrangement."

"Mr. Westinghouse," said Joe, who had finally had enough. He stood from his corner perch—a perch he was designated by insinuation, considering there were now only five chairs and five glasses of ice water around Katz's cherrywood conference table. "Forgive me for being blunt, but these kids are after one thing and one thing only—the reward money. Now, money or no money, just the fact that they are here tells me your son and his, ah . . . companion have information that they have withheld from police.

"Myself and fellow homicide detective Frank McKay have been an active presence on their campus over the past two months and have made repeated public pleas via their university president for all students to come forward with any information they feel may assist us in our investigations.

"Further, we held a private meeting with the two young men less than one week ago during which they denied any knowledge as to their friend's possible involvement in Miss Nagoshi's death." Joe knew his voice was rising, but at this point he didn't give a damn. "Now, all of a sudden, they have information, coincidentally just as Mr. Nagoshi here confirms the speculation of the posting of a substantial reward. Well, I could be wrong, but in my line of work that adds up to obstruction of justice, and makes these two smart-ass kids a pair of bona fide criminals—"

"Lieutenant Mannix," said Katz, cutting him off with a stare that shot daggers across the room. "We understand your frustration at not being able to solve this case."

Joe took a breath.

"But in the end, all that matters is that we find the person responsible for this heinous crime and make sure justice is done. Mr. Nagoshi and his family have been through enough and Messrs Simpson and Westinghouse, despite their obvious initial hesitations, should be congratulated for coming forward to assist us.

Katz went on. "That being said—"

"That being said," interrupted Gordon Westinghouse, who obviously felt it was time to exercise his high-three-figure-an-hour clout. "The reward money *is* an issue, Mr. Katz. We are all adults here," he said, looking at Mannix in disdain for referring to his son and his friend as "*kids*." "And Mr. Nagoshi is a respected and experienced businessman who understands the importance of a mutually beneficial negotiation. So let's cut to the chase, shall we?"

And so they did.

And less than fifteen minutes later the deal had been struck.

"Now that that is agreed," Gordon Westinghouse went on, as he arched his back and expanded his chest in what Joe could only describe as an old-fashioned pruning of feathers, "my son and his friend are happy to continue this conversation on the principles of good faith. But we must have your word, Mr. Nagoshi, that the money, which I remind you is *not* refundable if the District Attorney's Office fails to follow through with a conviction, will be wired to the specified accounts in the Grand Caymans within the hour.

"Finally, my son and Mr. Simpson, who I remind you are protected by the aforementioned clause of confidentiality, will not divulge the said information unless the individual they identify be allowed to turn himself in by the end of the day. My son and Mr. Simpson feel it is the least they can do for the individual in question, so as to eliminate any unnecessary embarrassment on his part."

"What?" said Joe. "Unnecessary embarrassment? If these boys are right then the so-called person in question is a goddamned murderer. Now call me harsh, but to be honest, Mr. Westinghouse, whether or not the killer is embarrassed is the least of my concerns."

"I am sorry, Lieutenant," said H. Edgar, the first words he had spoken all morning. Simpson signaled to his friend's father that it was all right, he wanted to speak and was not going to offer anything to jeopardize their agreement.

"I am afraid this last request, while grounded in altruism, is not as unselfish as it first seems. You can understand our relationships with our fellow students at Deane are extremely important to us, and we do not want our peers to misunderstand the reasons for our providing you with the information needed to file charges against our friend."

"You worried this little snitching act might get you scratched off the 'A' list, kid?" asked Joe, now standing from his perch. "Is it just me or is this whole fucking scenario getting sicker by the minute?"

Joe locked eyes with John Nagoshi then, and felt an overwhelming embarrassment on behalf of the stoic Japanese businessman. His daughter was dead and here they were haggling over how to maintain the burgeoning health of these two young assholes' social status. It was beyond repulsive. Joe knew it, and judging by the look of pure despondency on John Nagoshi's face, the grieving father knew it too.

"You have our word," said Roger Katz then, ignoring Joe to speak directly with Gordon Westinghouse. "Our detectives will give the young man in question a small window of opportunity to hand himself in—say until 7 p.m. this evening."

"That will be fine," said the older Westinghouse, shifting his chin slightly to the left in a gesture of dismissal at Mannix's obviously "irrelevant" objections. "That being agreed, and as it is . . ." The Italian-suited attorney shifted his Tiffany cufflinked sleeve to examine his Rolex. ". . . almost noon, I suggest we proceed with Mr. Simpson and Mr. Westinghouse's statements. The young men will go on record here today so that you might secure an arrest and further agree to repeat their statements in front of a grand jury at your earliest convenience so that you might secure an indictment. Fair?" He looked to Katz.

"Indeed," said the obviously delighted ADA.

He nodded at the two boys then, H. Edgar taking his natural position as leader by lifting his ice water to his lips and taking the smallest of sips before clearing his throat as if ready to move on. Gordon Westinghouse gave Katz a nod and the ADA reached across the table to press the red "R" button on the rectangular recording device strategically placed in the middle of the conference room table.

"My name is Homer Edgar Simpson," H. Edgar began, his voice loud and crisp and strong and clear. "And I give this statement of my own free will at the offices of the Suffolk County District Attorney at 11:52 a.m. on Saturday, October 31 in the presence of my attorney, Mr. Gordon Westinghouse, Assistant District Attorney Roger Katz and Boston Police Homicide Unit Commander Lieutenant Joseph Mannix."

Jesus, thought Joe.

"Myself and my friend Heath Gordon Westinghouse are here to share information we feel relevant to the investigation into the death of Jessica Nagoshi. In other words, gentlemen," he said, and Joe could have sworn he was in the process of constricting the beginnings of a smile, "we know the identity of Jessica's killer and we have evidence to support such a claim."

The room went quiet then, as if H. Edgar wanted his moment in the sun to last as long as was humanly possible. The antique clock ticked, the air-conditioning hissed and the five people present seemed to hold their breath in anticipation of what was to come out of the Simpson kid's voice next.

"Who was it, son?" said Roger Katz at last, his words gushing forth in an eruption of uncontainable excitement. He was obviously unable to hold back with the question he had been dying to have answered for weeks.

And then Joe saw it, the corner of Simpson's lips lifting in an expression he could no longer suppress. "James Matheson," he said at last. "Our friend, James Matheson, killed Jess Nagoshi with his own bare hands."

"And you have proof?" interrupted Katz.

"Yes," answered Simpson.

"In the form of . . ." urged the ADA.

"A confession," said H. Edgar.

"A confession?" asked Katz, obviously savoring every word. "How? Matheson told you he . . . ?"

"As good as," said H. Edgar, now smiling quite unashamedly. "Admittedly he was slightly under the weather at the time, but the information came right from the horse's mouth, Mr. Katz."

"No," interrupted Joe, determined to put a stop to Katz's feeding frenzy before it got even further out of control. "A confession is not proof, Roger, it's hearsay. How do we know Simpson here is not lying? How do we know Matheson was not just shooting off his mouth during some emotional college drinking fest?"

But then he looked at Simpson, and he could see the boy had anticipated Joe's cynicism and was, as always, on the ready with a reply.

"He took her shoes," said Simpson, his eyes now focused on Joe, his expression pure delight at having dropped a bombshell on the detective's attempts to discredit him.

"He whacked her over the head, strangled her with his bare hands, laid her on a rock and took her shoes. Does that qualify as proof, Lieutenant?" He studied Joe then, relishing in the shock in his expression. "Yes," he said at last, his victory now complete. "Yes, I thought so."

35

The Grand Caymans

Grand Cayman Island Caribbean Trust and Banking Corporation financier Kitt Baptiste was a very happy man. He was one of those "glass half full" human beings who saw the light beyond every shadow, the rainbow beyond every storm and the good in everyone—even his new assistant Sonita De Paisa who, despite having received two weeks of intensive training, still found it difficult to grasp what Kitt thought to be the simplest of tasks.

"A beautiful day," said Kitt as he arrived at his office after attending a rather pleasant outdoor lunch meeting with representatives from Deutsche Financial and the Royal Bank of Canada.

"Yes, Mr. Baptiste," said Sonita with her now customary hopeful smile. She was a pleasant young woman, who tried her best, apologized for her shortcomings and thus—buoyed by her genuineness—Kitt had decided to give her the benefit of the doubt and stick with her until the penny dropped, which he knew it had to do . . . eventually.

Ah the joy of it, thought Kitt as he entered his office and looked out over his expansive Georgetown view. His lunchtime discussions had been most inspiring. According to German and Canadian research, the banks of Grand Cayman were finally getting the respect they deserved. Of course the world's top financial institutions had appreciated the idyllic Caribbean location as the fine, full-service international investment district that it was for years. But Kitt was at last getting the feeling that the general populace were finally seeing this exquisite strip of sand, surrounded by clear aqua waters, some 480 miles south of Miami, as more than just some glorified tax haven for greedy Western industrialists.

Of course it was that too—offering a banking system that carried no capital gains tax, corporation tax, withholding tax, property tax, payroll tax or income tax payable by employees to boot, which was also the reason why Cayman was now the fifth-largest financial center in the world, attracting international blue-chip corporations by the bucket load.

"Mr. Baptiste," said Sonita who had left her desk to tiptoe up to his door without making the slightest hint of a noise.

"Yes, Sonita," said Kitt with a smile, his bright white teeth gleaming against the richness of his dark mocha skin. "What is it? Come on in."

"It's the new American account, sir. I thought you would like to know the money has been wired."

"Good," said Kitt, taking delight in what seemed to be Sonita's expanding capabilities. "If you will forward the information to me I will make sure it is split into the three accounts as specified," he went on.

"No, sir."

"No, Sonita?"

"No, sir. You see a little over an hour ago, while you were at lunch, we received new instructions. It seems the gentlemen concerned only require a two account split—one in the name of Simpson, and the second in the name of Westinghouse. I have all the details here, sir, if you would like to oversee the transaction yourself."

"Yes, indeed," said Kitt, finding nothing unusual about this change in instruction. "If you would like to forward me the details of the transfer, I shall make sure all is in order."

"Certainly, Mr. Baptiste," said Sonita with the sweetest of smiles.

"And well done, Sonita. Well done, indeed."

• • •

Switzerland

They call it Glacier 3000, basically because that is exactly what it is—a crisp, flat, perfectly formed glacier floating some 3000 meters above sea level, doused in sunlight, covered in snow and acting as a platform from which you can take in one of the most breathtaking views on earth. Glacier 3000, also known as the Tsanfleuron Glacier, is located in the Les Diablerets or Lake Geneva Region of Switzerland, and as well as the year-round cross-country and on-piste skiing, offers all sorts of activities including snowboarding, hiking, and husky dogsled rides that are said to provide one of the greatest natural highs on the planet—both figuratively and literally.

And so, with another perfect autumn day almost put to rest, and the promise of sparkling blue skies and optimum skiing conditions predicted for the next week and beyond, Glacier Manager Urs Zubriggen was taken aback with his incredible fortune—a fortune that had grown even richer no less than ten seconds ago when a knock on his door revealed a young woman so sublime he almost dropped his locally brewed brandy on his brand new antique ivory Tabriz rug.

"Yes?" said Zubriggen before sucking in his modest middle-aged spread with one almighty intake of breath.

"Mr. Zubriggen?"

"Yes."

"I am sorry to bother you so late, but we just arrived at our chalet and there was a message for me there to contact you immediately."

"Ah," said Zubriggen, gesturing for the girl to come in from the cold. "Yes. Mademoiselle Rousseau, I presume," said Zubriggen, extending his arm.

"Yes, monsieur," she said, taking it and shaking it with the softest of palms. "Is anything the matter?"

"No, mademoiselle, nothing to worry about. I believe the police in Geneva have been asked by their compatriots in America to track you down, something about a version of accounts or the like. But they assure me there is no reason for concern on your part. They want your help, mademoiselle, and have stressed there is no need for distress."

"I see," said Barbara Rousseau. But Zubriggen could tell the girl was not convinced.

"From what I am told, mademoiselle, it is a matter to be cleared up over the telephone. You don't even need to leave the resort," he smiled. "Can I offer you a drink?"

"No, thank you, monsieur," said Barbara, and Zubriggen

sensed by the tone in her voice that this girl could also most likely smell a come-on from a mile away.

"But if you do not mind, I would like to use your telephone," she said.

"Of course," said Zubriggen, being realistic enough to know when a *beauté* was out of his league.

"Come, this way," he said, finally allowing himself to release the breath he had been holding since he answered the door. "I have the number right here. A Sergeant Donders. He gave me his work and private numbers so I am sure he will not mind the lateness of the hour."

"Thank you, monsieur," said Barbara, walking into Zubriggen's living room to pick up the receiver and make the call.

Zubriggen moved to the kitchen, just far enough away to give the girl space but close enough to get the gist of her conversation. The girl reached Donders almost immediately, and moments later seemed to be connected to another party in the US. Zubriggen moved toward the coffee machine, just beyond the living room annex, straining his ears to ascertain as much as he could of the exchange.

"Lieutenant Mannix," she said. "This is Barbara Rousseau. I believe you have been trying to reach me and I . . .

"I am so sorry. We have been skiing in areas beyond telecommunications range.

"Of course I do not mind, Lieutenant. Ask away.

"Deane University, that is right. I was there for two years and left for Paris at the beginning of the semester.

"Yes, I heard about it, of course. Jessica was a lovely girl. I am so sorry.

"Yes, whatever I can do to help."

Zubriggen listened as Barbara continued to answer the American's questions with a series of definite yesses and nos. And then the girl said nothing for a very long time, and Zubriggen stood there watching her, entranced. He was completely absorbed by her beautiful face and could almost feel her pain when her flawless complexion began to color and her perfect features began to distort in expressions of confusion, and distress, and perhaps a trace of anger.

"No, Lieutenant. Absolutely not. The thing is . . . to be honest, I was sort of interested. James is, well . . . you know, he has a lot going for him. But he had been drinking and seemed a little distracted so in the end I went home to pack. My flight left the next morning and I still had much to do so . . .

"If by friends you mean Heath Westinghouse and his red-haired constant companion then yes, they saw us talking. You have to understand how a place like Deane works, Lieutenant—it is like a small, exclusive club and the law school even more so. Everyone likes to know everybody else's business—a little . . . what is the English translation? Incestuous? No?

"Yes, I think that James left with Heath and the shorter friend, but then . . . actually he must have come back because I believe I saw him out the front of the club just as I left to hail a taxi.

"Alone? Yes, I think so.

"No, I saw Jessica earlier but not with James.

"Of course I shall provide a statement if that is what you need, Lieutenant. I shall be back in Paris the day after tomorrow and Sergeant Donders said you have my numbers so . . .

"No need to thank me, Lieutenant. But, before you go, I feel I have to say . . ." Barbara hesitated then, and Zubriggen heard her take a breath, before clearing her throat and moving on. "James is a gentleman, Lieutenant, and while I do not know the details, I feel it only fair to tell you that I find this news surprising. James would be the last person I would suspect of being capable of anything such as this.

"But if you are asking me if I was with him that evening—during the same hours that Jessica was killed, then the answer is a definite 'no.' I have nothing against James, Lieutenant, but if he is using me as his alibi, then I am afraid he is not the person I thought him to be."

• • •

"*Shit,*" said Joe, hanging up the phone.

"Jesus," said Frank who had listened to the exchange on speaker.

"Shut the door, Frank," said Joe, now racing behind his birch laminate desk to pick up his office issue phone.

This was an unusual request in itself, given Joe Mannix never shut his office door to his hardworking homicide team beyond. In fact, McKay had a hard time budging the frosted glass paneled door from its permanent resting place of "open."

The carpet seemed to have grown up around it and McKay had to use both of his hands to yank it from its stubborn two-inch groove.

"What time is it?" asked Joe.

"Six forty-five," said Frank, glancing at his Timex.

"No way this kid is handing himself in," said Joe, searching for a number in his notebook.

"No. No, I guess not."

"Damn it," said Joe, rifling through the pages. "Where is his goddamned number?"

"Whose number, Chief?"

"Nagoshi's. I need to stop the transfer of that reward money. Those kids played us for fools, Frank, and now they are two million dollars richer."

"Maybe they didn't know Rousseau would . . ."

"Of course they knew. They can't have it both ways, Frank. They say Matheson killed Jessica and if that's what they believe, then they had to know that his alibi—the same one they gave to us in the first place—was a total fabrication."

"You think they knew we'd have trouble reaching the French girl?"

"Trouble enough for them to score themselves a quick two mill."

"Jesus, Chief. That sounds like a stretch even for them. And besides, it was Nagoshi's idea to give the money away. You can't blame yourself for . . ."

"Sure I can. I should have stood up to Katz. I should have forced Nagoshi to give us more time. I should have waited until we spoke to Barbara Rousseau and then we might have nailed the Matheson kid without the help of his two so-called friends."

"But they have a confession."

"So they say."

"They are risking their precious social status by going down this road," countered Frank.

"Yeah—and they can spend all their lonely nights counting all that money."

"They knew about the shoes, Chief."

And there it was. They knew about the shoes—and whatever else they were, Joe knew this one fact made them privy to information that no one else had access to.

Joe put down the phone.

"It's almost seven, boss, the money's gone," said Frank, his tone one of pure consolation. "As hard as it is, we have to put those two assholes on the backburner for the moment, and do the job we set out to do from the get-go."

Joe said nothing, just rested his knuckles on his paper-strewn desk, looked down at his feet and nodded.

"We need to go find Matheson, Chief, and arrest his lying ass before he has a chance to disappear. We need to go out and get him, boss, and we need to do it now."

36

The next time he saw her was from behind.

She was standing still, her black glossy hair pouring straight down her long narrow back like a slick of the darkest satin.

He approached her slowly, his shoes making that customary *click* that seemed to be handed out at the door when you entered any major international art gallery—New York's Metropolitan Museum of Art, better known as "The Met," was obviously no exception.

He found her in the Robert Lehman wing, a pyramidal structure of glass and limestone that was decorated more like a Central Park mansion than a display center for some of the world's most famous European masterpieces—an observation she later told him was actually quite astute, given that this extraordinary two-story triangular adjunct was designed to evoke the ambience of Lehman's own house on West Fifty-fourth.

"Have you been here before?" she asked without turning around, making him wonder how she managed to distinguish his footfalls among the sea of others.

"Ah . . . yeah," said James, stopping short. She still did not turn so he answered her question from behind. "Once, as a kid. My father brought me to New York for a weekend not long before I moved to Sydney with my mother. It was like he would not let me go until America was imprinted on my soul—and he is a banker so to him, America and New York are one and the same."

"He appreciates art?" she asked.

"He appreciates its value," he answered. "I remember he

made me stand in front of this one painting—a Van Gogh I think it was—something with a field and trees and . . ."

"*Wheat Field with Cypresses*," she said, still facing forward.

"Yeah, that was it. He told me some guy had bought it for almost $80 million and then lent it to the Met for the world to share. He said art was the most colorful money in the world, and one of the safest long-term investments available in a volatile marketplace."

She laughed then as she turned suddenly to take his hands and kiss him on the cheek. "A real philanthropist, your dad," she said.

"My father is all for the voluntary promotion of human welfare, as long as his welfare is catered to first."

"Does that make you sad?" she said, a look of pure curiosity on her face.

"No. Should it?"

"Probably," she said, turning back to the painting that had been the focus of her attention just prior to his arrival.

"I like it," he said, looking at the smallish portrait of a pretty nude girl with long red hair.

"Why?" she asked.

"I don't know, because it's nice to look at."

"The best answer yet," she said, still focusing on the painting before her. "It's called *Young Girl Bathing* and it's a Renoir—1892. Do you see what she's doing?"

"Well," said James, moving closer to the rectangular artwork before him. "She's bathing I guess—by some river."

"Yes, but more than that. See how her eyes are focused downward, on her feet?"

"You can't see her feet, the picture ends at her calves and . . ."

"First up, James, it's not a picture it's a painting and you don't need to actually see her feet to know they are in the water. She is looking at them, probably running her toes in and out of the polished pebbles that line the riverbed. The water is cool and clear and reflecting the hundreds of shades of reds and greens and ochres that Renoir uses here," she pointed. "She feels free and content and at one with the world. She's lucky, don't you think?"

"Yeah, I guess she is."

They stood there then, a foot apart, hands by their sides, staring straight ahead at the lucky nineteenth-century French girl with the contented smile and cooling feet.

"You know," Jessica said at last, "Renoir was once asked what he tried to achieve with his art. What makes it special, what gives it life, what allows it to grow beyond the flat surface of the canvas and move those who stand here—like us—as humble, admirers of his talent."

"And what did he say?" said James, drawing his eyes away from the masterpiece before him to take in the even more exquisite vision at his side.

"He said: 'The work of art must seize upon you, wrap you up in itself and carry you away. It is the means by which the artist conveys his passion. It is the current which he puts forth, which sweeps you along in his passion.'"

"You do that to me," he said, the words spoken before he even had a chance to consider how she might take this simple, powerful admission.

She looked at him then, her eyes bright, her head tilted slightly to the left as if examining him with a new sense of curiosity. And then she did something that he would never have anticipated. She did something that perhaps was the most erotic, exhilarating interaction he had ever encountered with another human being in his whole entire life. She leaned forward, and reached up, so that her full, red lips were mere millimeters from his ear. And then she took a long slow breath, exhaling sweetly before stretching her perfect narrow neck that fraction further to whisper. "I want to feel what she feels, James," she said, referring to the girl in the painting. "I want to be cool and fresh and free and lucky. I want you to bathe with me, James."

And just as she said this, she retreated slowly, her lower lip tracing the line of the edge of his ear.

"Where?" was all he could think of to say.

"Where else, silly?" she said as if she found the question ridiculous.

"This is New York, James. We are going to the Plaza."

· · ·

And so, as James Matheson realized the water had run cold, as he registered the sting the now icy flow was delivering to his freshly shaven face, he lifted his hand to turn off the faucet. He grabbed a towel and stepped from the shower, his skin on fire despite the cold, his eyes having trouble focusing on the living area of his pool house apartment at the back of his father's Brookline home—his own little corner of Ivy League comfort.

"Jess," he said aloud in some pointless attempt to call her from beyond. But that was not to be and he was still alone, knowing this entire evening would be defined by loneliness and misery and the countless feigned attempts not to mention the unmentionable.

And he would smile and shake their hands and they would smile and shake his back and then he would move on and they would congregate again and wait until he was just beyond ear-shot before they returned to the subject on everyone's "must discuss" list this evening. And then they would feel all noble for not embarrassing him and he would pretend not to hear their faintly disguised whispers—which in the end may have been weak enough to be swallowed by the evening's festive ambience, but strong enough to tear at his slowly diminishing reserve.

He looked at his OMEGA Seamaster. It was almost seven. He had to leave within minutes if he was to be at Meredith's on time. He could not let her down. She was Jess's friend. She had asked him out of respect for Jess and so it was the least he could do.

Minutes later he was straightening his bow tie, securing his cuff links and removing his dinner suit jacket from the dry cleaning plastic before throwing it over his shoulder and moving out the door. And as he left his living room and walked around the pool toward the garage he found himself stopping once again, this time staring at the mosaic-tiled expanse of his own backyard swimming pool. And then he closed his eyes and turned before the water took him back again, to another time when pictures were paintings, the world had color and the girl with the long dark hair swept him away in a current of passion, just as Renoir had described.

37

"Wow," said David Cavanaugh when his girlfriend emerged from their bedroom at the far end of the apartment. "You look amazing."

And she did. The dress code for the Deane School of Law's highly anticipated Halloween Ball was listed on the gilt-edged invitations as "black as night," and to David, Sara's long, fitted, sequined gown looked like the best dream he had ever had. She walked toward him then, holding her dark sapphire pendant at either end of its chain before turning around so that he might fasten the clasp at her neck.

"Sara," he said, securing the clip before bending to kiss her. "I am so sorry—for last night. You have every right to represent the Jones kid and I shouldn't have spoiled what was a perfect evening."

She turned to place her long manicured finger on his lips. "Shhh. David, you weren't the only one at fault. I shouldn't have been so defensive. Besides, I think fifty apologies in twenty-four hours are enough. Not to mention the fact that you . . ."

". . . spent at least half of those hours in bed with the most beautiful attorney in Boston," he said, kissing her again.

"Boston's a small city, David," she smiled.

"Hmm, you're right, let's throw in Cambridge for the bargain."

She punched him in the arm then. "You might have at least expanded the parameters to the state border," she laughed.

"But from what I hear, there's a really cute tax attorney in Chicopee . . ."

"You wanna break that fine ice you're skating on, Cavanaugh?" she asked, taking a step back to place both hands on her hips.

"No, ma'am," he said. "Massachusetts and beyond."

"Flattery will get you everywhere," she said, before stepping forward again and reaching up to kiss him.

"I hope so." And then he held her tight, kissing her again, this time slowly, until time stood still and the previous night's argument became a distant memory.

It felt good, burying the hatchet. Last night he had fallen asleep on the couch before waking at 3 a.m. and feeling like a right ass for ruining Sara's evening. Moments later he was moving down his apartment corridor toward the bedroom where he found a similarly wide awake Sara to whom he apologized for his bullheaded behavior and promised never to act like such a selfish schmuck again. In all honesty he was still concerned about her involvement with Jones, and Joe's suspicions that the kid wasn't totally up-front. But this *wasn't his case* and Jones *wasn't his client* and Sara was a big girl who was smart and experienced enough to make her own choices. Besides, he had certainly represented some less than savory characters in his past—so how bad could a nineteen-year-old college geek be?

"We should go," she said, pulling away to straighten his bow tie before taking a step back to place her hands on her hips once again as if sizing him up for approval.

"Well?" he said.

"You'll do." She smiled.

"Geez, is that the best you can do?" he asked, grabbing his jacket from the back of the sofa.

"You want more I suggest you call your tax attorney friend in Chicopee."

. . .

In the early 1900s, the then twenty-year-old Deane University issued an invitation to all its architecture graduates, past and present, to come up with a plan for the university's first Great Hall. The graduates were issued numbers so that they might submit their designs anonymously—assuring impartiality in choice by a board who, even then, were driven by prestige, politics and power.

The choice was unanimous, in the form of an American Gothic cathedral-style masterpiece submitted by entrant No. 7 who, as it turned out, was the son of the chairman of the board of trustees. While it was widely acknowledged that No. 7 had been a particularly average student, it was also rumored that his father knew of a talented but impoverished designer who had been willing to assist his son in his submission and accept cash rather than kudos as his payment.

If nothing else this cozy arrangement, which saw the university construct one of the most magnificent Gothic structures the nation had ever seen, lent itself to the wonderful myth that the Hall was now haunted by the ghost of its true creator—an unknown genius who sold his soul so that his dream might become a reality, so that his work might be enjoyed for generations of young students to come, and more important, so that his family might have food on the table.

And so, just as David Cavanaugh pulled up at the front of the white gravel circular drive, his Land Cruiser easing to a stop in the slow moving parade of vehicles being met by valet attendants dressed completely in black, Jake Davis warned him and Sara of the unexplained noises and self-shutting doors and the mysterious moaning and baffling vibrations that were said to rock the towering structure from its foundations to its spire.

"You're full of shit, Jake," said David, putting the car into park.

"I know," said Sara's brother. "But it's a good story, and it's Halloween so . . ."

"So we're not kids anymore and you can no longer frighten me with your pathetic little brother scare tactics," said Sara.

"Boo!" yelled Jake so loudly in Sara's ear that she practically leapt from the car.

"For God's sake, Jake." She smiled.

And then the three of them looked up to behold the breathtaking sight before them. The impressive stone and gray slate structure stood high and mighty, set apart from the world around it by a luminous outline of thousands of tiny fairy lights strung high and stretched taut from ground to rooftop, eave to eave.

The front steps—of a rustic, well-worn sandstone—were now covered in a thick carpet of white rose petals, some lifting in the cool evening breeze, caught in the paths of upward tilting spotlights that cast flickering shadows on the lofty Gothic edifice above them. Centered on the steps was a long white carpet, bordered by black rope balustrades, behind which jostled scores of reporters and photographers snapping the who's who of Boston as they moved toward the grand entranceway like the glamorous movie stars of old.

In fact, if David had not been so mesmerized by the spectacle before him he would have hurried up the smooth white walkway in an attempt to avoid the press who eventually recognized him and called out to say: "Mr. Cavanaugh, Mr. Cavanaugh, looking forward to the night ahead?"

"Sure," answered an embarrassed David who tended to forget that last year's Montgomery case had turned him into the local legal icon.

"Mr. Cavanaugh," called a reporter from Channel 4. "What's your next big case? Who's your next client?"

"Ah . . ." said David. "Actually, it's my partner here who's getting all the good cases these days. Maybe I can take it easy for a while," he joked.

The group now focused on Sara who was rapidly building a profile of her own after the seven-figure Sanchez settlement. "Miss Davis, Miss Davis . . ."

But luckily they were almost at the top of the stairs, Sara now dragging David by the elbow, Jake complaining he was the only anonymous one of the three.

Their conversation was cut short at the hand-carved double wooden doors, where they stood back in awe at the sight of scores of suspended strips of billowing see-through fabrics— the finest of black silks falling in consecutive layered rows across the main foyer, wafting around the mesmerized partygoers, caressing their frames, slowly lifting and falling in a breeze created by discreet heating fans, and promising light, activity and more surprises at the main stairwell and beyond.

"Unbelievable," said David as he took Sara by the hand.

"It's incredible," she said, as the final piece of silk gave way to reveal the giant marble staircase that was a breathtaking revelation in itself. And there it was before them, what must have been tens of thousands of silver votive candles lined up row upon row on the white marble steps. The tiny candles were set in perfectly aligned rows, enabling the awestruck guests to walk upward without unsettling their flames—their wicks giving off an almost sparkler effect of pure white light, along with a subtle scent of roses that wafted through the air in waves.

They walked slowly upward, beckoned by the music of the mini-orchestra now playing Vivaldi in the main Great Hall. The silver light on the stairwell finally gave way to a burst of color as they took the rise over the landing to behold what could only be described as a sort of Roman-themed extravaganza—the lofty eighty-five-foot-high ceilings now covered in temporary frescoes, the length of the Hall divided by faux marble columns and archways—just like a Roman palazzo with tented lounges, custom-built terraces and a fifteen-foot-high gray marble fountain that had been constructed at the front of the room.

Potted lemon, lime and orange trees lined the venue, bordering a space that now held over one hundred white-clothed circular tables of ten, each with sparkling silver flatware, crystal drinking glasses and jet black placemats offset by centerpieces of full-blown white roses that let off a scent that was sweet without being overpowering. The black-clad orchestra in the far right-hand corner was balanced by a massive vine-covered bar to the left where champagne was flowing, imported spirits were being selected and red and white Italian wines were being poured and ushered around the expansive hall by scores of eager waiters and waitresses dressed completely in white.

It was, without question, the most amazing sight David had ever seen. In fact, he and Sara were so taken aback by the spectacle before them that they failed to see the man approach them from the left. A tall, olive-skinned man in a $5,000 Armani suit and teeth so white they appeared to the part of the black and white décor extraordinaire.

"Counselor," said Roger Katz, extending his manicured hand to David.

"Roger," said David through gritted teeth.

"Miss Davis," said Katz, now taking her hand and raising it to his lips, his eyes absorbing her from head to toe, making David angrier by the minute. "You look stunning as usual. And I read about your recent little victory, by the way. Well done! She's beautiful and blessed with beginner's luck, hey, Cavanaugh?" He smirked, now turning back to David. "You're a lucky man, Counselor."

"I was," said David. "Up until about a minute ago."

"Roger," interrupted Sara before David could go any further, "this is my brother Jake."

Katz turned to shake Jake's hand. "Not another lawyer in the mix?" he said, the sarcasm flowing just as fast as the water that gushed in the huge marble fountain at the front of the room.

"No, sir," said Jake. "I work for Credit Suisse."

"Ah," said Katz, and David could not help but wonder why the ADA was so damned amicable tonight—a quality that, at least on Katz, always made him nervous.

"Well, it's a pleasure, Jake. But I must say, I would never have picked you two for siblings. Well, obviously. But I did read somewhere, did I not, Miss Davis, that you were adopted?"

David had had enough. "Forgive us, Roger, but I can see my boss and his secretary at the front. We're a little late and I want to check in."

"Of course," said Katz. "Don't worry, Counselor, I am sure you'll make partner one of these days and won't have to raise your hand for roll call." Katz raised his right hand in mock schoolboy fashion, his monogrammed cuff links catching the light of the crystal chandeliers.

But David didn't respond, just took Sara's hand and walked as quickly as possible toward the bar at the front of the room.

"Jesus," said Sara.

"What a wanker," said Jake.

"I need a drink," said David.

38

Roger Katz could not contain himself. He was floating in fucking bliss!

It was almost as if the universe had aligned itself, as if everything he had ever wanted was slipping into place and feeling every bit as rich as the black label whiskey that now slid down his throat like liquid velvet, warming his ambitions and firing his desire to make the most of every single second of it . . . right down to kicking Cavanaugh's middle-class ass in front of his dark-skinned girlfriend and her Benetton commercial brother.

Cheers!

Moments before he spotted Cavanaugh and his United Nations companions, he had hung up a call from his so-called boss Loretta Scaturro—the MIA DA who, as luck would have it, "could not see herself returning before the end of the year."

Better still, Attorney General Sweeney was expected at this shindig momentarily, giving Katz the perfect opportunity to mention the extension of Scaturro's embarrassingly long leave before updating him on the progress of his now "firing" prosecution of the Jessica Nagoshi case.

McKay had promised to alert him by seven if there was a problem at hand, and given it was almost eight, and given the stars were fucking fixed over his goddamned head this evening, and given he felt so freaking good and looked even better, he saw nothing but success in his future—a success that would begin with the wall-to-wall coverage of Matheson's arrest in tomorrow's papers and grow with the Nagoshis' eternal gratitude (although Katz would be sensitive enough not to bring up the issue of district attorney campaign donations until at least the beginning of the trial), and consolidate itself with his victory in one of the most high-profile cases this state—hell, this country—had ever seen.

And then, as if another sun had decided to slide into his perfect procession of personal endowments this evening, Katz saw John Nagoshi enter at the back of the hall—his son at his right, his lawyer at his left, the Japanese-American now the center of attention as he shook hands and bowed to the many similarly bobbing sycophants around him. Seriously, he didn't understand how those people managed to avoid banging heads—the trivial thought had popped into his head like a happy little aside. Katz had had to duck and weave at least twice at their past few meetings and the ridiculous social custom seemed, at least to him, to appear both comical and . . . a touch effeminate. Still, tonight was his night and he would bow if he had to, he thought as he swallowed the last of his aged double malt in a flourish. It was a small price to pay.

. . .

"Anyway," said Heath Westinghouse, now downing his fourth imported beer in the past half hour, "so then Wes corners me after lunch and asks me what my intentions are. He said Charity's designated fat ugly friend told him I had cut his grass—that I had moved in on Charity before they broke up.

"So then I told the jerk to go fuck himself, and that if I was as fucking ugly as him I would count myself lucky to have slept with someone as hot as Charity in the first place."

H. Edgar took a breath. Westinghouse was getting drunker by the moment—slipping into that moronic freshman vernacular that was, in all honesty, incredibly immature and way beneath him.

"So then . . ." Westinghouse went on after finishing his beer, his right arm gesturing at his stunning date across the other side of the hall who had been "mingling" with the VIPs for most of the evening so far. "Then he says he didn't give a crap because Charity was nothing more than a puck fuck, lacrosstitute." Terms H. Edgar knew referred to girls who only slept with guys on the hockey or lacrosse teams. "And then I said he was nothing but a full of shit asshole who . . ."

"Jesus, Westinghouse," said H. Edgar, who was now getting more than a little worried about his friend's hastened state of inebriation. He knew Westinghouse was hyped after today's rather intense negotiations, but he didn't think his friend would be stupid enough to get pissed in front of this loaded crowd—no pun intended—especially one that included their beloved benefactor John Nagoshi and the goddamned ADA.

"Tone it down, will you? There is nothing to worry about. By now James is in custody and, with any luck, will be released by morning. The money is in the bank, Barbara will confirm his alibi and we'll be sitting pretty. Just don't blow this by acting like a lush."

H. Edgar paused then to shake hands with one of his father's retired corporate friends before leading Westinghouse off to the side of the bar and looking him directly in the eye.

"Look around you, Westinghouse. This room is filled with opportunities. These are not the people you party with but the people you impress. 'Puck fuck, lacrosstitute'—what the hell is that? You are selling yourself short, Westinghouse. Now act your age and sober the fuck up before ADA Katz comes to shake your hand for being the fine upstanding citizen that you are. Don't embarrass me, Westinghouse. Pull yourself together."

And then he saw it, if only for a second, the slightest slither of anger in his blue-eyed friend's expression. It was there, and then it was gone.

"I know what you're saying, H. Edgar. But I gotta tell you. This doesn't sit right. It's clever, brilliant, fucking genius even, but something inside me says . . ."

"Shut up, Westinghouse," interrupted H. Edgar. "Katz is on his way over. Just do up your jacket, focus on standing straight and let me do the talking."

• • •

"I hate to admit it," said Arthur, now fidgeting with the bow tie around his crisp collared shirt, "but this isn't too bad. If they had mentioned the Australian beer on the invitation I might have been more enthusiastic from the outset."

"If they had mentioned Katz was gonna be treating this shindig like his own personal push for DA party, I would have gone to Melbourne for the original," said a smiling David who, in the very least, had calmed down enough to see the humor in the blatant campaign of self-promotion Katz was currently conducting from one end of the room to the other.

"Hey," said Jake, obviously following David's line of vision. "That's them—with the ADA," he said.

"That's who?" asked Sara, accepting champagne from Nora who had taken two cold glasses from a passing waiter.

"James Matheson's two creepy friends."

"Katz and Matheson's friends?" said David. "I wonder why he . . . ?"

"David," said a voice from behind.

"Tony," said David, turning to shake the hand of his fellow Boston College grad. "You know Arthur, Nora, Sara, and this is Sara's brother Jake Davis." There were handshakes all around.

"If your eyes were daggers, the Kat would have just lost one of his nine lives," said Tony Bishop, patting his friend on the back, and David was happy to see his friend was looking a lot more like himself than he had a few weeks ago.

"Have you been watching him?" grinned Tony. "He's been working the room like a teenage boy at a supermodel convention."

"Yeah," said David, with a furrow in his brow.

"Who are the kids?" asked Bishop.

"Law students," replied David.

"Then why is he wasting his time with—?"

"The Kat never wastes his time," interrupted David.

"Yeah, well," said Bishop, accepting a beer from yet another passing waiter. "Ten bucks says the Ivy League twosome are about to be dumped for the much bigger fish that just swam in the doorway."

The group all turned toward the back of the room.

"The attorney general has arrived, ladies and gentlemen and . . . Jesus, watch him go," said Tony just as Roger Katz swung about as if a sixth sense had him "smell out" a bigger opportunity some fifty yards south. "You gotta hand it to him. The guy is slick. He couldn't have made that maneuver faster if he had been driving at NASCAR.

"Looks like he and Sweeney are tight too," he said, as Katz reached the AG in record time and shook his hand with fervor—Katz leaning in to whisper something into Sweeney's ear and prompting both of them to nod in agreement.

"He's up to something," said David, now watching the AG

introduce the Kat to a series of VIPs from the AG's office beside him.

"Who gives a . . . ," said Tony, taking a long drink of his beer. "As long as it has nothing to do with you. Right, my friend?" Bishop smiled. But David was focused on Katz and his overzealous mingling with the AG's entourage.

"David?" said Sara, her brow now also showing the slightest trace of concern.

"Ah, yeah. Sorry," said David, turning to face the group again.

"Is anything . . . ?" she began.

"No." He smiled, putting his arm around her shoulder. "What do you say to another champagne? Mrs. Kelly?" he asked, including Nora.

"Don't mind if I do. Thank you, lad," said Nora.

"Come on, Bishop," he said, grabbing Tony by the arm. "You can accompany me to the bar."

39

"Jesus," said Joe Mannix, pounding his fist on the steering wheel as he hit yet another red light. "This traffic sucks."

"Take it easy, boss," said McKay. "As my wife always says: 'With time and patience, the mulberry leaf becomes satin.'"

"What the fuck is that supposed to mean?" asked an obviously frustrated Mannix as he took a left off 128 into Worcester.

"No idea," said Frank. "Just sounded like the right thing to say at a time like this."

"Skivvies and satin, McKay. I'm beginning to worry about you."

"No need, Chief," said Frank who, Joe noticed, had started his own beat of nervous tapping on the car door armrest. "Besides, we're almost there. If the Wentworth girl's mother is right, they should be only a few minutes ahead of us, and our uniform backup is about the same behind us."

Joe said nothing, taking another sharp corner on Oakland along the main stretch leading to Deane's historic front gates. The traffic started to slow, as some of the later limousine arrivals reduced their speed to enter the grounds of the historic university.

"We're about to cause a shit storm in a teacup, Frank," said Mannix at last.

"Yeah," said McKay, his left leg now joining in the rhythmic routine with his tapping right hand. "That we are, Chief. The ADA sure as hell won't be happy. But somehow, I ain't got a problem with that."

"Me neither, Frank," said Mannix, turning to his friend. "Me neither."

• • •

"That's him there," said Tony Bishop, now standing with David behind a vine-covered trellis just left of the crowded bar. The announcement had been made that dinner was about to be served so the obviously thirsty guests were now "stocking up" before taking their seats at the extravagantly adorned tables.

"Where?" asked David, straining to pick out Peter Nagoshi from a crowded group of multinational businessmen and attorneys.

"There, behind my boss, Gareth Coolidge."

Luckily David knew Coolidge by sight and could just make out the dark-haired young man behind him. Bishop turned to David then, a look of earnestness on his face.

"Look, David," began Tony. "I was kinda tired the last time we talked, jumped to some wrong conclusions. I heard on the grapevine that an arrest in the Nagoshi case is imminent and that the perp *isn't* Peter Nagoshi. He's a hard one to read, DC, and I just got it wrong."

"Maybe not," said David, his eyes still fixed on the young Japanese businessman.

"What do you mean?" asked Tony.

David turned his attention back to his friend, a new sense of urgency in his voice.

"Look Tony, you know that when we talk like this I know that you . . ."

"Of course," said Tony, his own voice now low and curious.

"Then what would you say if I told you we might have come across some new information that supports your original assessment of the Nagoshi son? Would it shock you to know you may have been closer than you think with your reservations about Peter Nagoshi and his handling of Nagoshi Inc.'s operations in China?"

"Well, probably not but . . . Jesus, DC, I am the Nagoshis' lawyer so maybe you shouldn't be . . ."

"No, Tony. You can't have it both ways. You are the one who came to me with this in the first place. You are the one who suggested the son would do anything to guarantee his own future—and now Sara has a client who backs up your suspicions with bona fide proof."

"Shit," said Tony. "But this can't be right. This whole bloody room is talking about this so-called imminent arrest. Some are saying the guy is already in custody, which would explain why the Kat is so goddamned cocky this evening."

"Since when has Katz allowed the truth to get in the way of his own personal advancement?" David stopped then, taking a breath before going on. "I got a bad feeling about this one, Tony. I think some poor innocent college kid is about to get a taste of the Kat's version of justice while your client is adding another executive title to his high-powered last name."

"Shit," repeated Tony.

"Oh no," said David, just as his friend turned toward him, no doubt reading the new expression of surprise on his face.

"What is it now?" asked Tony, following David's train of vision back toward the main entrance of the hall.

"He's here," said David, now talking over the echoing beep of a sound system microphone, which had apparently been switched on somewhere in the main presentation area in the center of the room.

"What? Who's here?" said Tony, raising his voice over the din.

"The sacrificial lamb. His name is James Matheson and my guess is he is about to be thrown to the lions."

• • •

But there was no time to act. Dean Johns was now standing at the main podium under an elevated latticed gazebo painted in the freshest white and draped with thick green vines carrying heavy bunches of blood red Montepulciano grapes in the center of the hall.

The dean proceeded to officially welcome one and all to this "fine Halloween extravaganza" before making some joke about the clever function organizers who had managed to "pull off a sophisticated All Hallow's Eve without a single pumpkin in sight."

"We thought it best to give the blessed orange fruit a rest," said Johns, standing broad and tall and resplendent. "And yes, ladies and gentlemen, you heard me correctly. I have not had too much vino—at least not yet. The pumpkin is a fruit and not a vegetable and I promise you that is the last lesson this aged academic will bore you with this evening.

"I also promise there will be no more speeches until you good people in this fine Great Hall are fed! So without further ado, ladies and gentleman, I welcome you to your tables."

And within seconds a series of bright red pin spots appeared to explode from the ceiling, casting perfectly centered, soft pink spotlights on the hundred circular tables below.

And seconds after that, Heath Westinghouse looked to the back of the hall to see one of his two best friends proceed toward the middle of the room.

And seconds after that Roger Katz saw him too.

• • •

"H. Edgar," said Westinghouse, his face now lit up in the widest of smiles. "You are a legend."

"What?" said Simpson. "What do you mean?"

"It's James," said Westinghouse, pointing toward his friend. "He's here already. He must have been questioned and released. Barbara must have given them his goddamned alibi and now he is home sweet home and we have a tidy 700 K to celebrate with. You did it, man. I swear to God you are one brilliant son of a bitch."

But Simpson obviously wasn't listening, for all he could manage was, "Fuck."

• • •

"Hey, you two, where's our champagne?" asked Sara, as she and Arthur and Nora were taking their seats at a crimson lit table to the right of the main gazebo.

"Ah . . ." said David, and he could see she read the anxiety in his and Tony's expressions. "Sorry, Sara, but . . . where's Jake?"

"He's sitting with his colleagues at the Credit Suisse table," said a now obviously confused Sara as she pointed toward the back of the hall. "But why do you . . . ?"

"Matheson's here," he said.

"*What?* But the rumors," she began. "Why on earth would he expose himself to . . . ?"

"He has to be crazy," said Tony. "Or stupid."

"Or out to prove a point," finished David. "Whatever the case, Katz is on the warpath and if Jake is a friend, he'll get him out of here now."

"David," said Sara, her expression now pure frustration, "*if* the kid is innocent, I feel for him. But *he's not your client.*"

"I know," said David, looking her directly in the eye. "But think about it, Sara, it was *your* client who brought up the China thing—and Tony here is the Nagoshis' lawyer, and he believes that . . ."

David stopped then, not wanting to jeopardize Tony's legal obligation to attorney-client privilege any more than he had to. But a reluctant Tony finally gave a nod, and Sara looked back toward David in surprise.

"The only evidence Sawyer Jones provided against Matheson was that he was dating the girl," David went on. "He followed them everywhere, Sara, and never once saw a single ounce of animosity between them.

"But do you think Katz will even consider the Chinese angle if it means pissing off the Nagoshis? Do you think a privileged kid like Matheson has any chance of a fair trial with the entire city gunning for payback? Are you willing to sit by and let Katz destroy yet another innocent life just because he is . . ."

"No," she interrupted then, looking to Arthur and Nora who had been close enough to hear their exchange. "Go," she said after a beat.

"Move quickly, lad," said Nora.

"Get Jake to pull him out the back way," said Arthur.

"And David," said Sara, taking his hand. "You go with them. James Matheson idolizes you, and something tells me he's going to need . . ."

But it was too late. The group looked up to see Roger Katz striding toward James Matheson like a torpedo locked on a target. And worse still, the other now-seated guests at Katz's table, including AG Sweeney and the Nagoshis, were following the ADA with their eyes.

David saw Peter Nagoshi's smooth, unlined face contract in an expression of pure anger. And then he saw him shove back his chair, rise to his feet and turn from the table to take long swift strides after the ADA, with speed and determination, toward the back of the room.

* * *

"What is it?" said Dean Johns who had no sooner left the podium before being summoned by one of the function organizers to meet the two Boston detectives at the top of the Great Hall entranceway.

"We are here to make an arrest, Dean," said Mannix. "And as much as we hate to spoil your little shindig, I am afraid we have a warrant and are ready to move in."

"What?" said an obviously horrified Johns. "Lieutenant Mannix, I appreciate you have a job to do, but surely this can be orchestrated without upsetting our guests. You have no idea how many high-powered . . ."

"High power this," said Frank, waving the warrant in front of the dean's now red face. "I'm sorry, Dean, but I really don't think you want to go down in history as the first Law School Chief to be arrested for obstruction of justice."

"Well, no, but . . ." said the Dean. "I still think there is a way to do this without . . ."

But Johns was cut short. For the next thing they knew the bloodcurdling scream of a young girl rang out through the high-ceilinged edifice like a siren preceding an almighty catastrophe.

"What the hell was that?" asked McKay.

"The party's started without us, Frank," said Joe, breaking into a run.

"Radio for the uniforms to get in here. I need backup now."

• • •

Minutes earlier, just as Mannix and McKay were "negotiating" with Dean Johns at the top of the Great Hall stairs, Roger Katz was undertaking some rather frantic negotiations of his own, trying to talk James Matheson into accompanying him out of the hall for a private and extremely urgent conversation.

"What?" said James, his eyes now darting back and forward across the pink-hued audience around him. "With all due respect, Mr. Katz," he said, lowering his voice, "we were invited to this function, and we just want to sit down and eat our dinner and . . ."

"This is ridiculous," said an obviously angry Meredith Wentworth turning to the ADA in disgust. "You have no right to accost us like this. James hasn't done anything wrong."

But then Katz felt an almighty force from behind. As if a strong invisible wind with smooth, weightless hands had lifted him up and to the side, removing him from the huddle and clearing its path so that it might confront its target with potent precision.

Peter Nagoshi did not hesitate. He swung about in what Katz could only describe as a circular whooshing motion, lifting both of his arms high and wide until they cut sharply down—one connecting with James Matheson's left cheek, the other slicing into his right shoulder, sending him spiraling down toward the Great Hall floor.

For once in his life Katz was completely unsure as to how to react. One part of his brain told him to restrain Nagoshi, another suggested he should join in the fray to show the corporate son exactly whose side he was on, and a third, perhaps that portion that represented his true self, urged him to take one gigantic step backward so as not to get injured, so as to protect his perfect face and so as to avoid the embarrassment of getting his ass kicked by a twenty-something kid.

In the end he took option three, which was just as well because tonight was his night and by hell or high water those lucky stars of his were determined to shine for as long as they were needed—for in that second, just as the girl screamed and the police entered the Great Hall at the top of the main entryway, James Matheson got to his feet and smashed Peter Nagoshi square between the eyes. It was a powerful punch, with a clear intent to do major damage, and it was thrown with such anger, such force that Katz almost tumbled in the fallout.

And there he saw it, the boy's green eyes alive with the purest of rage, his hands clenched, his chest heaving, his inner beast exposed with such terrifying intensity that those at the tables around him stood and ran and cowered at the sight of the black-suited, bloodied-cheeked maniac before them. Katz saw in James Matheson a potential killer, and the rest of the one thousand strong crowd, well, they saw it too.

• • •

"James," said Jake Davis, reaching him first, pulling Matheson who was now advancing on a collapsed, semiconscious Peter Nagoshi once again, back and to the side. "Enough," he said, perhaps trying to get the boy to refocus.

David set himself in the center of the fray, acting as a physical barrier between Matheson and Nagoshi, and as it turned out, a mere foot away from ADA Katz who, David could have sworn, swallowed a smile before setting an expression of outrage and authority on his chameleon-like face.

"Cavanaugh!" declared Katz, now pushing back his dinner suit sleeves as if he were the man ready to control this unholy calamity. "Move back. This has nothing to do with you."

"Fuck off, Roger," said David, just as a further commotion broke out from behind in the form of four uniformed police officers who were now pulling the boy David assumed was Heath Westinghouse away from Matheson so that Frank McKay might cuff him from behind.

"Leave him alone," yelled Westinghouse. David also saw the look of pure disgust on Joe's face as his detective friend entered the huddle and moved to stand directly in front of Matheson.

"What the hell did you expect?" said Joe through gritted teeth to the tall athletic kid. "What is it they say, Westinghouse?" asked Joe of the boy. "Be careful what you wish for?" He then shook his head, before turning his attention back to the bloody-faced Matheson.

"James Matheson, you are under arrest for the murder of Jessica Nagoshi. You have the right to remain silent. Anything you say can be used against you in a court of law."

Joe said this while facing Matheson but also managed a quick sideways glance to his right, catching David's eye and nodding ever so slightly before continuing with the job he obviously knew he had to do. "You have the right to have an attorney present now and during any future questioning. If you cannot afford an attorney, one will be appointed to you free of charge."

David looked at Matheson. He was obviously in a daze. But then, just as Frank McKay pulled on his cuffs, just as the police officers started to move back to allow passage of their latest Mirandized perp, Matheson looked up, his now glistening eyes meeting David's with a desperate plea for help.

"Please," he mouthed almost imperceptibly.

And that one simple word said everything, prompting David to nod at Matheson before moving forward to say, "My name is David Cavanaugh and I represent Mr. Matheson. He has no comment to make until he has consulted with his attorney."

He then took two swift steps forward to lean into Matheson and reinforce his directive by whispering, "Don't say anything. I'll meet you at headquarters."

And with that Mannix nodded and McKay took the lead in ushering the newly arrested suspect back out the Great Hall entrance. David stood there, stock-still, watching them go as if caught in a time warp where his ominous predictions had finally come true.

And then she was in front of him, taking his hand, looking deep into his eyes before asking the question he knew she had to ask. "Are you sure about this?" asked Sara, to which he replied a straightforward "Yes." And then he squeezed her hand before moving back to his table. He retrieved his jacket and nodded at his boss. He grabbed Jake's elbow in thanks and looked at Tony Bishop who just stood there and shook his head in a gesture of inevitable fatality. Seconds later, he was moving again, walking, striding, then running toward the back of the room, like a man on an impossible mission, about to attempt the rescue from hell.

40

"Spill it," said David, barging into Mannix's office at the Roxbury headquarters of the Boston PD.

"Listen, David. The kid is still in processing, we haven't even sat down with him yet."

"Which you wouldn't do until I was in the room in any case," said David.

Joe just looked at him and David took a breath.

"Look, Joe, I am not here to bust your balls, but at the very least my client deserves to know how this came down. He wasn't even given the chance to confer with you guys before you marched in guns blazing and arrested him in front of his entire academic and professional fraternity. You think the kid has any kind of future after tonight's mini-spectacular? Guilty or not, Matheson's name is now dirt in this city, thanks to a massive overreaction from the ADA and the police who were obviously doing his bidding."

Joe said nothing, but David, who knew he had pushed too far, could see the anger rising in his friend's face. Joe pushed past him to the door, yanking it from its resting place and slamming it so hard that the reverberation of the frosted glass echoed through the low-ceilinged Homicide Unit like a train through a tunnel.

"Where the hell do you get off?" asked Joe, now moving back toward his desk to meet David eye to eye. "You're a friend, David, and I know it's your job to act in the best interests of your client so I can forgive your frustration at how tonight went down. But if you ever accuse me of doing Katz's bidding again I swear I will kick your ass out of here so fast you won't know what hit you."

David started to say something but Mannix wasn't finished.

"You're a good guy, David, but one day you're gonna have to realize that things don't always play out the way you want them to. Katz is a prick, granted. In fact, this case is surrounded by pricks all with their own fucking agendas. But don't you see, I have no agenda bar finding the perp who strangled that young pregnant girl."

David nodded at his friend before leaning back to rest on the edge of his desk. "I'm sorry," he said after a time.

Now Joe nodded.

"I need to know what you have against him," said David after a pause. "And I want your take on it."

"No."

"What?"

"No, David. I'll tell you the facts, but that's where I stop. I've been trying to get a take on this pit of shit for close to two months and all I've come away with is the stench of lies and self-interest."

Joe stopped then, moving to the back of his office where he sat on the edge of his small two-seater sofa, his expression one of pure fatigue.

"All I will say is that you have your work cut out for you. In fact, you are the only friend Matheson has right now. His enemies are influential and powerful and determined to make an example of him. Did he do it? That's for you and Katz to argue, and for a jury of twelve to decide. As for me, I'm done."

They said nothing then, their eyes downcast, two men understanding nothing and everything, exhausted by a system that sucked people in and spat them out of a machine driven by politics as much as justice.

"You're not, Joe," said David at last.

"I'm not what," said Joe, looking up.

"Done. You're not done—and you know it."

Joe said nothing, his bloodshot eyes now blinking in a gesture of recognition.

"I hate you, Cavanaugh," he said after a pause.

"I know."

• • •

It was 1:45 a.m. James Matheson had just finished giving a detailed statement to Mannix and McKay, in which they covered the major issues of the investigation. First up, and most important, he admitted to, and showed remorse for, lying about his relationship with Jessica Nagoshi—but he vowed he was innocent of her murder.

He told them he had seen her that night at the Lincoln but had left the Club shortly after his friends and gone home alone. He denied actually lying about partaking in a sexual rendez-vous with Barbara Rousseau, but did agree he "falsely alluded to the possibility of sexual activity with her," and "made no attempt to dispel his friends' assumptions otherwise," largely to "satisfy their curiosity" and deflect them from discovering the "true nature of his growing relationship with Jessica."

He explained it was Jessica's idea to keep their connection quiet, that her father "discouraged extracurricular affiliations." He expressed regret for the untruths he had communicated in a desire to respect Jessica's privacy. He confirmed he did own a pair of Nikes, size 11, but once again was aware of numerous other students at Deane who owned the same style of shoe. He denied ever being in the Nagoshi greenhouse, explaining Jessica thought a visit to her home would be unwise.

Finally, he denied having "confessed" to his friends Simpson and Westinghouse. He had no idea why either of them would concoct such a story, but assumed they must have misconstrued a conversation he had with them at the Deane University bar, better known as The Fringe, the night before last. They invited him to meet them and he had gotten rotten drunk, and while he was not sure exactly what he said, he believed he may have told them of his guilt at not being able to save Jessica Nagoshi's life.

As for the shoes—he had no idea.

Bottom line, he gave one of the most legally "perfect" post-arrest statements David had ever heard in all his years of practicing law. His answers were short and to the point, polite but direct, and devoid of the telltale hesitations that littered the depositions of liars. It was a statement that, while guided by David's direction, gave testament to Matheson's expansive legal knowledge and, more importantly, to his innocence.

• • •

By 2:30 a.m., David had been talking for close to an hour. And for that entire time Matheson sat still and focused, his bloodied dress shirt rolled up to his elbows, which supported his upper body as he leaned on the stainless-steel interview room table before him.

He looked disheveled, drained and yet determined to take in every word his attorney delivered—which David did calmly, slowly, realizing that while his client was doing his best to maintain some sort of control, it would not take much to push him over the edge.

"You did well, James," he said at last, and James nodded. "Now the police will need time to compile your statement along with their other evidence, before making a full report to the ADA."

"The man tried to force us outside," said James. "He was rude to Meredith. He thinks he is God."

"Among other things. But don't worry about Katz. You leave him to me."

As much as David wanted to protect his client, he also knew, given James' legal nous and serious circumstances, there was no point in denying that the ADA would be able to build a very solid case against him. Katz had established probable cause for the arrest and now, David knew, would be working his ambitious butt off to secure the next step in his meticulously charted route, in the form of a grand jury indictment that would confirm his client's route to trial.

Even circumstantial evidence like James' ability to use a kayak oar, or his close proximity to the victim on the night of her death, was enough to take to a grand jury, which, no doubt, Katz would be doing within days. Add James' lies, Simpson and Westinghouse's testimonies and the denial of alibi from Barbara Rousseau, and David had no doubt the ADA would have his precious indictment before the week was out.

"There is little point in trying to reason with the ADA," David explained. "And even if we wanted to plea, Katz would not consider it. Katz hates to plea at the best of times, especially when he is guaranteed the ring leader's position in a high-profile case such as this. He is in this for the long haul, James, and we will be giving him hell, every step of the way.

"All you have to do is keep your head down. Show the same respect for our system of justice as you did in this interview room tonight, restrict your visitors to immediate family and whatever you do, do not, I repeat, do *not* have any communication with your two so-called friends."

And there it was—the stab that cut the deepest. It was the suggestion of Westinghouse's and Simpson's betrayal that had obviously hurt James the most. David knew his client was clinging to the idea that his drunken ravings at the university bar had been misconstrued by his two best friends, and convincing him otherwise was going to take some doing.

"It's not like they need the money," said James. "I must have said something on Thursday to make them think I was somehow involved. I can remember talking about her—it was a relief, you know, to get it off my chest. But as for a confession . . . ? Why didn't they come to me first, David? If they asked I would have told them."

"I'm sorry, James," said David. "But sometimes it's better to know the truth about what your supposed buddies are capable of."

They sat there for a moment, taking it all in, until James asked the one question David knew he could not answer.

"How did this happen?" he asked at last, his simple question bouncing hard and hollow off the cold cinderblock walls.

"There's no one answer to that, James," replied David. "Sometimes one wrong turn sets us on a course we never anticipated." And that was the truth of it, David knew, the harsh, horrible truth that lives can be shattered with the blink of an eye if those are the cards that fate has dealt you.

"This is all a mistake," said James, his eyes now glistening with tears, his swollen face making that sad but unavoidable transition from optimist to realist, boy to man. "Just a few months ago I honestly believed I was the luckiest person on earth and . . . I was. I had a real future, and I'm not just talking about the money or the career. I loved Jess, David, more than I have ever loved anyone or anything in my entire life. She was so smart, so intuitive—so different from anyone I have ever met before."

David nodded. "I know it is hard, James, but right now I need you to think in the now rather than in the past—or in the future. I promise you I will do everything I can to help you reclaim your life. On that you have my word."

James managed the slightest of half-smiles in gratitude.

"You need to get some rest," said David at last. "Try to sleep. I'll be back by nine."

James nodded. "The detective said I could use the private holding cell."

"Mannix is a good guy. He appreciated you being so cooperative—in processing, giving your statement, providing your DNA." And then David saw the confusion in James' eyes, as if a new question had just entered his obviously overcrowded brain.

"Why did they do that?" he asked. "I understand their taking my prints, but from what I've been told, there was no DNA left at the scene."

David looked at him then, and realized he did not know. But then again, if she did not tell him, how could he? The police did not elaborate on why they required the DNA sample, and his friends had not given this second piece of "privileged" information as part of their traitorous testimonies.

"James," he began, "I am so sorry."

"What?" asked Matheson. "What is it?"

"Jessica was pregnant, James, and chances are the baby she was carrying was yours."

"Oh God," he said with an almighty intake of breath, holding it, and then releasing it with a long, silent shudder.

"I didn't know," he went on as the tears started to roll unevenly down his cheeks, traces of dark dried blood making for tiny obstacles in their rocky path toward the metallic table before him.

"She didn't . . ." He went on as his body started to shake, his head now resting in his hands, which were clenched into tight contorted fists.

"My life is over, David," he said, looking up at last, barely managing to speak through the sobs that wracked his entire being with grief. "They are both gone. No matter what they do to me, David, nothing could be worse than this."

41

David, Sara and James had been at it all day, or rather James had been at it while David and Sara sat back and listened. They wanted to spend these early hours getting to know James better and so allowed their client to speak freely without interruption. James spoke of his unusual but loving upbringing, of his mom and dad's unique relationship, his move to Australia and his return back home to Boston. He told them he had spoken to both of his parents who were now en route from overseas locations and similarly devoted to assisting his attorneys in whatever way possible. He talked of his time at Deane, about his friendship with Westinghouse and Simpson, about his studies, his sport, his career plans and finally about Jessica Nagoshi.

As far as David and Sara could tell, James and Jessica's relationship, although grounded in lifestyles of privilege, was a basically normal one for two young lovers set on keeping their growing attraction discreet. They did typical things like walking, swimming and studying together, and venturing to standard student haunts like art galleries and museums. James told them about their rendezvous in New York early last June, and how they first made love at the Plaza which, while definitely not the usual "hookup" location for new college lovers, did not seem terribly out of the ordinary, given Jessica's New York base and her father's more than substantial fortune.

The defense scored an early break in the form of the morning's news reports which, David had to admit, were fairly unbiased given the spectacular nature of the arrest and the identity of the poster boy suspect. Luckily photographs were limited—thanks largely to last night's ban on press inside the venue. In fact, the only images used were some yearbook photos and a long-lens shot of James being shepherded into an unmarked police car, parked some yards from the media who had been moved back by Mannix's efficient uniformed backup. They were even more grateful that Joe had been able to keep the news of Jessica's pregnancy out of these early reports, a coup Mannix managed despite what would have been some heavy-duty pressure from the ADA, who no doubt was determined to paint James as a callous, cold-blooded killer from the outset. All in all, not a bad start, but they knew this was not going to be easy, and so were determined to take it one step at a time.

Sara left on her own errand at three, after which David began by describing to James the protocol for tomorrow morning's arraignment, stressing that, as James no doubt knew from his studies, arraignments are procedures of record rather than argument. He was just beginning to approach the subject of bail when he was interrupted by a knock on the door, marking the presence of a casually attired Mannix who poked his head around the frame to look directly at David.

"Got a minute?" he asked.

"Sure," said David before nodding at James and following Joe to the adjoining room.

"It's Sunday, Joe. You should be at home with Marie and the kids," David began as he shut the interview room door behind him.

"I should also be sailing a yacht around the Caribbean, but that ain't happening any time soon either."

David released a small laugh as the two men turned toward the one-way mirror, watching an obviously exhausted James Matheson fidgeting in the room next door.

"Something's up," said Joe.

David turned to look at his detective friend.

"I just got word the Kat has been down at the ME's office all day," Mannix went on.

"That's easy," said David. "He is probably pissed as all hell Gus won't have the paternity test results until tomorrow afternoon, and even madder at you for managing to keep the news of Jessica's pregnancy out of the morning papers."

"No."

"No?"

"If he wanted the pregnancy in, it would have been in. A newsworthy leak like that would have hit the front page with one phone call. I don't know about you, but I've never known the Kat to sit on protocol."

"Me neither," said David, his brow now furrowed in confusion.

"Then ten minutes ago it got even more interesting," Joe went on. "I got a call from John Nagoshi. He wanted to thank me, and asked me to pass on his thanks again to ADA Katz."

"What for?"

"Apparently we made a joint decision to continue to withhold the public release of the pregnancy until we confirmed paternity. Katz told Nagoshi that he and I appreciated he was a man who has his children's best interests at heart. He said we agreed it would be best to protect Jessica's memory, or more to the point, her reputation, by limiting the public's knowledge of any possible sexual partners she may have had over the past few months. Katz told Nagoshi he didn't want the media speculating on Jessica's sexual promiscuity. He told him we decided not to speak of the unborn child until Matheson was confirmed as the father."

"But why would he do that?" asked David, thinking on his feet. "The Kat should be busting his balls to get the pregnancy into evidence, and tomorrow's arraignment would have been perfect—public, high profile."

Joe nodded.

"Even if he doesn't have the results," David went on, "Katz could still table it in court tomorrow. It might play better if James is the father, but regardless of whose baby it was, the ADA could still play the 'boy murders pregnant girl' card and wring it for all it is worth."

"Right again."

"So what is he up to?"

Joe shrugged. "Not protecting Nagoshi's sensibilities. That much is for sure."

David nodded, the slight twinge of a headache now creeping into his temples.

"Well, thanks for the heads-up," he said after a time.

And Joe nodded.

They stood there for the moment, listening to the shallow hum of the air-conditioning unit, watching James who sat like a specimen in a cage—young, primed, genetically blessed.

"This kid worth it?" asked Joe at last.

"I think so," said David.

"You going this one alone?"

"No. Sara's been here all day, but she left a little while ago to sort things out, clear her decks."

"Jones?"

"Yeah, Jones. She hoped we might be able to hold on to both but . . ."

Joe nodded. "Not necessarily a bad thing," he said.

"No argument there. Besides, Sawyer Jones doesn't need a lawyer. If anything Katz will be crawling all over him to try to woo him as a witness for the prosecution."

"Conflict of interest."

"No matter which way you look at it."

Mannix nodded again. "That kid creeps me out."

"Well, as of tomorrow he will be officially off our books," said David. "I'm going to need all the help I can get on this one, Joe—Sara, Arthur, Nora and . . ."

"I'm not here to help, David."

"Could have fooled me."

42

In the Commonwealth of Massachusetts all potential defendants charged with a crime are entitled to a speedy arraignment within forty-eight hours of their arrest. In most cases their first court appearance usually occurs within the first twenty-four hours—unless the offender is apprehended over the weekend, in which case he has to sit tight until Monday comes around. The arraignment itself is not intended as a forum to hear evidence, rather to establish the basics. The defendant and his lawyer appear before a judge who reads the charge and informs the defendant of his constitutional rights and the possible penalties involved. The judge then asks the defendant to enter a plea, of guilty or not guilty, before opening the floor to the two main opponents who, more often than not, come out fighting, this first round of fisticuffs dedicated to the issue of bail.

"Your Honor," said Roger Katz now parading in front of the packed Suffolk County Superior Courtroom number seventeen. The atmosphere was taut with anticipation, the only disappointment so far coming in the form of a "no-show" from John Nagoshi and his son, Peter who, according to this morning's news reports, was still recovering in Massachusetts General following an emergency nasal reconstruction. Seventeen was one of the smaller courtrooms in the Superior Court building at Three Pemberton Square, and David had no doubt Judge Isaac Stein had requested it specifically, so as to restrict the voyeurs, limit the press and maintain control of a case that had already triggered a national media frenzy.

"The Commonwealth vehemently opposes bail in this case for a number of reasons." Katz raised his perfectly manicured hand to reveal a crisp white cuff, linked by gold monogrammed cuff links, under his charcoal Armani suit. "First of all, the violent nature of this crime, the brutal means by which Mr. Matheson bludgeoned and manually strangled . . ."

"Objection." David was up. It was the fourth time he had got to his feet in the past ten minutes, which was extremely unusual in arraignments. "Mr. Matheson has not been convicted of any crime and therefore I would ask the Assistant District Attorney to use the word 'alleged' when referring to the crime of which my client has been so wrongly accused."

Stein rolled his eyes. David could tell the rigid but fair judge was ruing the day he drew this legal short straw.

"He's right, Mr. Katz. Watch your language—and get to the point."

"Yes, Your Honor," said Katz, stealing a quick sideways glance at defense counsel. "As I was about to say, the heinous nature of this crime—warranting the charge of first-degree murder, indicates the level of atrocity of which the defendant is capable."

"Judge!" yelled David.

"I know, Mr. Cavanaugh, he did it again," said Stein, waving David away. "Mr. Katz, I repeat, this defendant, like all others in this fine country, is innocent until proven guilty. Do I make myself clear?"

"Yes, Your Honor," said Katz with a look of humility on his face, a look David knew hid the beginnings of a smile. The Kat was obviously determined to make sure his awestruck audience left this morning's proceedings with no doubt who the real killer was, and if that meant getting a rap over the knuckles for the odd misuse of language, then so be it.

"Mr. Matheson openly admits lying to police in the course of this investigation," Katz went on, "and has the monetary resources to flee the country. He has a large number of international ties with foreign associates, including a close relative in Australia."

David was on his feet again. "Your Honor, my client's Australian connection is not a foreign associate but his mother—who, I might add, is on her way to Boston as we speak. Mr. Matheson currently resides with his father at the family home in Brookline, and his father, respected merchant banker Jed Matheson, is also currently on his way back from a conference in South Africa. My client has no previous record, has been nothing but cooperative with police, and is more than willing to surrender his passport in the event that . . ."

"Bail is denied," said Stein, his pale hazel eyes under a bushy canopy of pepper-colored brows now focused on David, obviously ready for further objection.

"Your Honor . . ." David began.

"No, I am sorry, Mr. Cavanaugh, but Mr. Katz is right. The very nature of the crime makes bail impossible—foreign associates or not." This was, David knew, a consolatory dig at the ADA, but denial of bail was denial of bail, compensatory jibe or not.

"In regards to possible penalties," Judge Stein began.

"Your Honor," Katz interrupted, causing Stein, who had obviously had enough of the endless disruptions at this morning's proceedings, to sit even taller in his seat and glare over his bifocals at the now advancing ADA. "Before we proceed to possible penalties, I would ask the court's permission to readdress the nature of the charge."

"I do not understand," said Stein, his voice now raising a notch. "Murder one is as good as you get, Mr. Katz, so unless you want me to consider reducing the charge?"

"No, Your Honor. I was actually proposing an increase in the number of homicide charges—from one to two."

And that did it. A terrified James said "No" as he grabbed David's arm under the table. The gallery erupted in a gasp of disbelief. The media scribbled madly onto palm-held notebooks, the judge lifted his gavel and slammed it once, twice, three times, just as a horrified David finally realized exactly what the ADA was up to.

"Objection!" he yelled, now rising to his feet, aware of his shuddering client beside him. "Your Honor, this is nothing short of preposterous. The court has no record of a second homicide."

"Your Honor," said Katz, "this is the first court appearance in regards to this case. Mr. Matheson was only arrested on Saturday. There has been no opportunity to table this charge earlier—a charge that required sensitivity from the Boston Police and further investigation by the District Attorney's office."

"Get to the point, Mr. Katz," said an impatient Stein, waving David back to his seat.

Katz nodded, before taking two swift steps so as to align

himself in front of the judge, dead center in the middle of the now captivated room.

"As you are aware, Your Honor, sometimes, in the interest of apprehending an offender, the police and the District Attorney's office withhold certain details of a crime from the media and as a consequence from the greater public as a whole. This has been the case in regards to the Jessica Nagoshi homicide— or more specifically double homicide, considering the nature of the information withheld."

Shit, said David to himself. He knew Katz was determined to play this card—but had totally underestimated his intent.

"In short, Your Honor," a jubilant Katz went on, "Jessica Nagoshi was pregnant at the time of her death, the unborn child inside her—a boy," said Katz, obviously trying to leach as much pathos as possible from the now horrified crowd. "And when the defendant murdered the mother he destroyed the unborn child's life as well. It was a double homicide—or, more specifically, a homicide and a feticide. There is no question."

The air seemed to suck from the room as the crowd reacted in a simultaneous intake of breath, the resulting exhale releasing itself in sighs of disbelief.

"Your Honor," screamed David, who rose so quickly that he knocked his heavy wooden chair backward onto the parquetry floor behind him. "This is insane. There is no law that defines a standard approach to feticide in this state. There is no precedent . . ."

"On the contrary," said Katz. "Look at the highly publicized Peterson case. Scott Peterson was convicted of double murder for killing his wife and his unborn child." Katz was referring to the extremely high profile 2002 homicide of Laci Peterson and her unborn son, Connor. "The jury convicted Peterson of two counts of capital murder with 'special circumstances,' and sentenced Peterson to death."

"That was in California," objected David. "And the fetus was eight months old."

"Massachusetts 1989," Katz pressed on over the din. *"Commonwealth v. Lawrence.* A man was convicted for the murder of a sixteen-year-old girl and the involuntary manslaughter of her unborn child."

"The fetus was twenty-seven weeks," said David.

"*Commonwealth v. Cass*, 1984." Katz was determined. "A Massachusetts court extended the vehicular homicide statute to include a viable fetus."

"My point exactly," countered David. "A thirteen-week-old fetus is a long way from being defined as *viable*. The law defines fetal viability as the period when an unborn child reaches a stage where it can survive outside of the mother's body—and that's at twenty-three weeks at best. There is no way a fetus of thirteen weeks would . . ."

"Mr. Cavanaugh is correct," said Katz in rebuke. "But there are no specific laws preventing a state judiciary from considering a nonviable fetus as a human being as well."

"This is *insane*," yelled David.

"*Enough!*" shouted Stein. The judge was losing control of his courtroom, a fact, David knew, that would have the respected adjudicator seething with anger.

"If prosecution and defense counsel cannot conduct themselves with the necessary decorum I shall have them both removed for contempt," he said. "And if the gallery continues to interrupt these proceedings with verbal outbursts of impropriety I shall call for their removal as well."

The crowd reacted immediately, obviously chastened by Stein's heated rebuke, but determined not to lose their precious front row seats.

"Your Honor," said Katz, his voice now lowering a notch. "I realize this is a new area but the laws of Massachusetts have always had a high regard for the potentiality of human life. Thirteen weeks is early, granted, but a Minnesota court recently ruled in the case of a twenty-seven-day-old embryo—a mere two inches in length—that the question of 'viability' is irrelevant to criminal liability under the statute. Instead, the court found that viability here requires only that the genetically human embryo be a living organism that is growing into a human being.

"In other words, Judge, are we to disregard Jessica Nagoshi's unborn son just because he was murdered ten weeks before he became so-called 'viable'? Are we to label John Nagoshi's grandson as irrelevant just because his potential life was extinguished before he made it to the hallowed twenty-three weeks?" Katz shook his head then, before looking up again and delivering his final kick. "I think not. Because if we do, Your Honor, we are telling the people of this fine state that innocent victims like this unborn child are not really victims at all—indeed that they never existed. But this boy *did* exist, he *did* live and he should not be denied justice simply because he never got to see the sun."

"Jesus!" said David, not realizing he had uttered this last objection aloud.

"My chambers," said Stein, rising quickly to his feet before flipping his billowing black robe over the back of the chair behind him. *"Now!"*

■ ■ ■

David turned quickly to his ashen-faced client, instructing him to drink a glass of water and sit tight until he returned. He then followed Katz toward the corner of the courtroom, the Kat stepping aside to allow David to exit the room before him.

"After you, Counselor," he smiled.

"Get fucked, Roger," said David under his breath.

Minutes later they were standing in Judge Isaac Stein's chambers, the elderly arbitrator now having removed his robe, which lay draped over a nearby dark green leather sofa.

"What the hell was that?" boomed Stein at last as he paced restlessly behind his black walnut desk. The judge was a tall man who needed no robe to assert his authority in the Superior Court or beyond.

"That, Judge," David began, "was a case of the ADA showing a blatant disrespect for the general laws of Massachusetts and for the courtroom over which you preside. It was a reprehensible, pathetic attempt to incite media and public frenzy over a case that already runs the risk of being swayed by the powerful force that is public opinion.

"His claims are ridiculous, his grandstanding unforgivable. There is no way on earth, in a state that upholds the principles of *Roe v. Wade*, that the court should consider the termination of this fetus' existence as feticide."

David was referring to the groundbreaking 1973 US Supreme Court decision that ruled most laws against abortion violated a constitutional right to privacy. The decision overturned all state laws outlawing or restricting abortion, thereby becoming one of the most controversial cases in Supreme Court history.

"As for the cases Mr. Katz referenced in court, all were in regard to viable fetuses of twenty-three weeks or more and—"

"This case has nothing to do with *Roe v. Wade*," interrupted Katz, "which by the way is being challenged by what new studies reveal to be as many as thirty-four of the fifty states. Feticide law differs greatly from abortion cases in that the issue of a woman's choice is not in play.

"We are talking about murder, Judge," said Katz, taking a step forward in an effort to make his point. "The brutal death of an unborn boy who, if James Matheson had not interfered, would have, in all probability, grown to adult manhood."

"Your Honor," countered a now furious David. "For every case Mr. Katz quotes on the viability of feticide, I can refer to ten more that rule a child cannot be termed a human being until it is born alive or, in the very least 'viable.' My client has not only had to suffer the injustice of being wrongly accused of his girlfriend's murder, but now has had to sit through the ADA's selfishly motivated mantra to use what is more than likely my client's unborn child as a bargaining chip to secure the maximum sentence."

"I can understand Mr. Cavanaugh's distress," said Katz. "But in all honesty, this is not about severity of sentence nor about protecting the defendant's sensibilities. It is about justice."

"Ambition, more like it," said David.

"Shut up, the both of you," said Stein. The judge moved in front of his desk, pushing various papers out of his way so that he might perch himself on the front edge to stare the two men directly in the eye.

"What are you after, Mr. Katz?" he asked after a time. "One count of murder for the girl, and involuntary manslaughter for the unborn child?"

"No, Your Honor. The Commonwealth calls for two counts of murder one—with the penalty being two life sentences to be served consecutively."

"*What? That is insane,*" insisted David. "Murder one requires premeditation. My client only found out about this pregnancy yesterday. In fact, I was the one who told him."

"Matheson is a top-notch law student. He knows how to play the game," countered the Kat.

"Not everyone who studies law sees it as a stepping-stone to self-gratification, Roger."

"All right, gentlemen," said Stein, his arms now raised in mock surrender, signaling he had had enough. "Let's get a few things straight, shall we?" The judge took a breath, and exhaled with a sigh before moving on. "Firstly, if either of you ever use my courtroom, or my chambers for that matter, as a boxing ring again, I shall send you both to the county lockup. Do I make myself clear?"

"Yes, Your Honor," said Katz, as David nodded.

"And Mr. Katz, you hijack my courtroom again with the high jinks just demonstrated and I will demand another prosecutor be assigned to the case."

"I apologize, Judge," said Katz. "But my interests were only ever grounded in a desire to . . ."

"Secondly, Mr. Cavanaugh," said Stein, obviously now deciding it was time to do some interrupting of his own. "I agree with your argument that viability is the major issue here. Thirteen weeks is early, Mr. Katz," he said, turning to the ADA. "You are entering uncharted territory here and, worse still, inviting a frenetic free-for-all for anyone with any sort of opinion on the issue of fetal personhood.

"I . . . ," Katz began.

"Shut up, Mr. Katz. I have not finished."

"That being said," the judge went on, "despite my feelings on the issue . . ." Stein stole a quick glance at David. "The law requires me to in the very least consider the double charge of murder, on the basis that this trial, if indeed one comes to fruition, appears before a panel of twelve unbiased jurors."

"Judge," a now furious David begun.

"No, Mr. Cavanaugh, you must allow me to finish. With this consideration, Mr. Katz," said Stein, focusing on the ADA once again, "comes the stipulation that the jury must have the fall-back charge of involuntary manslaughter in regards to the unborn child—and the appropriate lesser penalty that accompanies it.

"In short, it will be up to you, Mr. Katz, to convince the jury that the defendant committed two crimes, both with malice aforethought, on the night of September 11. And it will be up to you, Mr. Cavanaugh," he said, turning back to David, "to convince the same lucky dozen that your client is guilty of nothing more than falling in love with the wrong girl."

"Your Honor, *please*," David begged.

"I am sorry, Mr. Cavanaugh, but that is my decision. Now get out, both of you, and leave an old man to ponder the travesty of his lot. Playing judge is one thing," he said as he shook his head, "but playing God—well, that is entirely another."

43

"Dear God," said Sara as she perched herself on the edge of Arthur's sofa. She, Arthur and Nora were now staring at the television at the far end of Arthur's corner office, mesmerized by the news flash being beamed live from outside the Suffolk County Superior Court.

"Yes, Anita," said the attractive female reporter with the serious expression now in a live two-way with her equally as striking studio anchor. "Assistant District Attorney Roger Katz has called for a second charge—of feticide—against Deane Law student James Matheson. And while the latter half of arraignment proceedings occurred in the judge's private chambers, it is believed the ADA will be asking for the maximum charge of murder one.

"It is also believed the ADA will be asking for the maximum penalty of two consecutive life terms, which means if convicted, twenty-two-year-old Matheson will be spending the rest of his life in jail." The screen split then, so that Katrina might share the limelight with the similarly grave-faced Anita.

"So the next step will be to await the judge's decision," said Anita.

"Yes, in fact," said Katrina, flipping her shoulder-length blond locks to the side as she read from a note being handed to her from her on-site producer, "we are being told the ADA is about to exit the court building behind us here." She gestured. "And has agreed to make a statement. He, ah . . . here he comes now."

Katrina turned with a flurry of similarly coiffed on-air reporters and more casually dressed journalists to shove and hustle toward the now emerging ADA. Katz advanced, chest out, head high, with an expression that spoke of the seriousness

of his business, the burden of the task ahead, and yet his undeniable determination to seek justice, no matter what the cost.

"Ladies and gentlemen," he said, his raised hands now calling
for silence. "You have no doubt heard of the Commonwealth's
intention to call for the introduction of a second charge of murder in the Nagoshi case. This second charge refers to the feticide of an unborn boy whose life was extinguished the moment
James Matheson brutally bludgeoned and strangled the child's
mother to death."

Katz paused then, allowing the din to diminish to an almost
eerie calm.

"I am pleased to say that Judge Stein has agreed with the
District Attorney's Office that two crimes were committed on
the night of September 11, and moments ago formally charged
the defendant with double counts of murder one."

The crowd let out a gasp, a mix of horror, surprise and, on the
media's part, plain old-fashioned exuberance at the promise of a
guaranteed ratings and circulation bonanza for months to come.

"The District Attorney's Office is devoted to convicting
criminals," Katz went on when the noise subsided, "no matter
what their background or circumstance, and this case is a perfect example of our determination to secure justice.

"I can assure you that James Matheson, despite his obvious
life advantages, will meet with the full force of the law and I
will do everything in my power to secure both convictions and
hopefully, in the process, provide the Nagoshi family with
some semblance of peace. That is all. Thank you."

"Good Lord," said Nora.

"Katz is out for blood," said Arthur.

"Matheson's," added Sara. "And David's as well."

⋅ ⋅ ⋅

John Nagoshi lifted his eyes from the television and stared
across the expanse of his open-plan Wellesley living room. Peter sat stony faced on the cream-colored sofa, his cheeks still
swollen, his nose covered in a bandaged splint that reached down
toward his mouth, making him look somewhat like a grey-
hound wearing an oversized muzzle. He adjusted his position
so that he might return his father's glance, his neck obviously
still stiff and swollen from Saturday evening's altercation. "Did
he tell you of this?" he asked, his voice thick and nasally.

"No," said John Nagoshi. "In fact, Mr. Katz promised he would keep the pregnancy quiet until paternity was resolved."

"Then he is a liar."

"Yes."

They both said nothing.

"Still, my father," said Peter at last. "Perhaps it is for the best. No matter how he was conceived, your grandson deserves to be acknowledged, and if this secures a purposeful sentence for Matheson . . ."

Nagoshi took a breath at Peter's distaste at the child's conception, his mind casting back to his son's outburst in Katz's conference room last week.

"It is not the result that concerns me, *segare*," said Nagoshi, knowing there was little he could do to change Peter's disapproval of his sister's affair. "But the motivation behind it. True peace cannot be achieved without sincerity; egotism is the primary cause of human anguish."

"This is not just about *wa*, Father," said Peter, referring to the Japanese term for harmony. "Do not forget the examples of our Samurai forefathers. *Adauchi* brought them peace."

"No, *segare*," said Nagoshi with a new passion. "*Adauchi* does not bring peace. Vendetta and revenge only bring sadness of heart and further retribution. A true man knows that revenge is best dealt with by forgetting it."

"Forgive me, Father, but they are hollow words spoken by men of little courage."

Nagoshi took another breath, his son's harsh perspective sending a slip of fear and foreboding down his spine. There were times when Nagoshi looked at his son only to see a stranger, and this troubling sensation was more frequent of late.

"Be careful, *segare*," he said at last. "This is not what your sister would want."

"Then she should not have chosen the path she chose, and started this disaster in the first place."

■ ■ ■

"He's here," said Sara when she saw him open the outer office door.

"Come on in, lad," said Arthur.

"I'll get you a coffee," said Nora.

"David, I don't believe this," began Sara as David moved

into Arthur's office, throwing his briefcase on the sofa. "It is not possible. He can't get away with it."

"Yes he *can*, Sara," said an obviously furious David, now tugging off his overcoat and pacing the room. "In fact, he just did."

"I can't believe Stein allowed it," said Arthur.

"Katz was very convincing," said David, stopping short in front of Arthur's desk. "It was my fault. I wasn't prepared. I should have seen this coming."

"How?" asked Sara, now joining them to form a huddle of three. "This is totally out of left field."

"No," countered David. "Joe told me Katz had been with the ME all day yesterday. I thought he was hassling Gus for paternity results, but obviously he was after an age of the fetus. I underestimated him."

"Well," said Arthur, obviously trying to calm his troubled prodigy. "What's done is done. We need to regroup, focus, fight this thing on all fronts."

"But that's just it, isn't it?" asked David, who nodded at an obviously concerned Nora as she placed his coffee on the desk before them, and joined the now tightly knit group of four. "Katz will have every associate in his office on this case and we are—well," he said, gesturing at his three colleagues, "this is basically it. We not only have to clear James of Jessica's murder but we also have to tackle the even more sensitive issue of feticide, an issue that will see us branded heathens by every pro-lifer in the county. And even if the jury finds James not guilty of the premeditated murder of his own son, they have the much more palatable charge of involuntary manslaughter to fall back on.

"No, Arthur," he said after a breath. "This is a lose/lose for us—and more importantly for James—no matter which way you come at it."

"David," said Arthur, "I know it sounds impossible but giving up is not an option."

"Giving up?" said David then. "I'm not giving up, Arthur. In fact, if anything, I know the worse it gets the harder we have to fight. We cannot afford to lose this one, Arthur. We are that kid's only hope and there is no way I am going to let him down."

Sara looked at him then, realizing just how attached to this case David was. They had been through some difficult battles before, risked their reputations, their relationship and even their lives. But she had to agree, the seeming hopelessness of this latest effort did make the thought of victory close to unfathomable—and she was terrified what she was about to say would make matters even worse.

· · ·

"David is right," said Nora, at last getting David to take a seat. "We can do this. Call me old-fashioned but I still believe if a group of people believe in something, and work hard to . . ."

"Thanks, Nora," said David, taking her hand and squeezing it. "But I am afraid faith will only get us so far."

"Then we'll clear the decks," said Arthur, now moving behind his desk to sit as well, Sara perching herself on a corner. "We'll make it our single priority. Sara can co-chair, I will work on precedent. Nora will keep track of discovery and assist us in the filing of motions. We can do this David. I am sure of it."

"David," said Sara at last. "I am so sorry that I wasn't there with you this morning."

"It's okay," he said, turning toward her, her very presence fueling him with hope. "I am sorry you had to bump the Jones kid. But in all honesty he really doesn't need a lawyer. A shrink maybe, but not an attorney."

"I didn't," she said, looking him straight in the eye.

"You didn't what?" he asked, confused.

"Bump him. In fact, I reaffirmed our representation, just a few hours ago."

"What?" said David, his voice rising a notch.

"What do you mean, Sara?" asked Arthur.

"Look," she said. "I know this sounds crazy but I think the kid can help us. You said it yourself, David. He was the one who gave merit to your China theory."

"He also gave the cops their first ironclad piece of evidence that James and Jessica were a couple," argued David.

"Maybe," she countered, taking a step back. "But he never suggested James was violent toward Jessica. In fact, he is a witness to their affection, not their animosity."

David shook his head.

"Listen, David," Sara went on. "By retaining Sawyer we keep him away from the ADA. Katz will have to subpoena him to appear and at the very least we can prepare him for what the Kat has in store. The kid is smart," she added. "He can help us

investigate the China angle, he can attest to Jessica's high regard for James and James' affection in return. He is willing to
help us, David. In fact, he even suggested it."

David looked to Arthur before turning back to Sara once
again.

"Sara," he said, trying to remain calm. "Did you ever think he
is retaining you so that he can keep a close handle on this case? I
am not suggesting he did anything wrong," he said, reading the
look of anger now rising on her face. "Just that he was in love
with this girl and, given that, his views might be somewhat . . ."

"I *can* read my own clients, David," she said.

"All right, let's all calm down," said Arthur at last. "Sara is
right on at least one point," he said, turning to David. "The
Jones boy could be an asset. His ties to Solidarity Global will
give us better access to the Nagoshis' plant in China. And
keeping him away from Katz is a priority."

David looked at them both. He was so tired and confused
and frustrated and angry—and yet in their eyes he saw a genuine desire to help, which made him consider that perhaps it was
he who was jumping to conclusions.

"Okay," he said at last. "But the kid can't become a drain on
our resources, Sara. I am going to need you here with me, 24/7."

"An offer any lass would find hard to refuse," said Nora, and
in that moment David was thankful for Mrs. Kelly and her perfectly timed considerations.

"I'll be here," said Sara at last, just as the telephone rang,
prompting Nora to move around Arthur's desk and pick up the
central extension. "And don't worry, I won't allow Sawyer to
take up all my time. He'll be an asset, David, not a problem. I
promise."

"Excuse me, Sara," said Nora, cupping the receiver in her
hand. "It's for you. I'll transfer it to your office if you like?"

"No. It's okay," said Sara, moving around the desk. "I'll just
take it here and be as quick as I can. Who is it Nora?" she
asked, taking the handpiece.

Nora hesitated. "I'm sorry, lass," she said at last. "It's Sawyer Jones and he says he needs to see you—urgently."

44

"Fuck," said Heath Westinghouse, fidgeting in his seat like a three-year-old who needed to use the little boys' room. He had just signed off on a call from his father, the short but direct conversation making him even more agitated.

"Calm down, Westinghouse," said Simpson, now sitting across from his friend in a discreet corner table of the Deane Law School café.

"How am I supposed to do that? Tomorrow, H. Edgar, they want us in front of the grand jury. *Tomorrow."*

"We promised we'd testify," said Simpson. "It was part of the deal."

"Well I'm not doing it. We've caused enough trouble."

"Shut up, Westinghouse," said Simpson, who was now aware of a small group of first years staring at them from a nearby table. "Refusing won't do any good. The ADA will just issue a subpoena."

"Well, at least that way it will look like we were forced to testify against our friend."

"Yeah," said H. Edgar. "They twisted our arms to the tune of two million."

"Fuck." Westinghouse finished his double strength megamug of coffee in one gulp, slamming the cup on the table before lowering his voice and going on.

"How the hell did this happen, H. Edgar? I thought you had all bases covered."

"I did," said Simpson, leaning into his friend. "But there must have been a breakdown in communication—a misunderstanding."

"Fucking A there was a misunderstanding. I misunderstood you when you said James would walk. Now he's rotting in some filthy prison cell with a motherfucking team of butt-humping bandits. Thanks to us, the whole country thinks he killed his girlfriend—and his kid as well."

H. Edgar knew this was coming, but was getting slightly agitated by his friend's heightened state of anxiety. He needed to appease him, calm him down, if they were to get through this, reputations intact.

"All right, Westinghouse, you want a pound of my flesh, fine. But let me remind you that we are in this together and experience should tell you I am your only lifeline out of this mess."

Westinghouse shook his head, his face still flush with frustration.

"I have no idea why James didn't play to the script," H. Edgar went on. "Maybe he got cold feet, maybe he couldn't bring himself to hand himself in, maybe he tried to stop us but couldn't contact us in time. Who the fuck knows? The point is, what's done is done. James is where he is, and we have to look after ourselves."

"Are you suggesting we rat him out?"

"Fuck, Heath, wake up to yourself. We *already* ratted him out," said Simpson. "This was a three-way deal and he is the one who failed to deliver. Don't forget, Westinghouse, James was the one who lied about Barbara in the first place."

"So he didn't fuck the French girl. Who hasn't lied about sex at one time or another?"

"It was stupid," said H. Edgar. "And if anyone is responsible for being in the predicament James is in, it is James. You have to stop this, Westinghouse. You start to panic and our stories fall apart, and then the cops will come after us for perverting the course of justice."

"You said we were safe," said Westinghouse.

"We were, until James stuffed it up."

They sat there then, H. Edgar giving his friend time to digest the seriousness of their situation. Simpson sensed he would have to calm his friend just that notch further before setting him on the desired path and steering him in the right direction.

"So what the hell do we do?" said Westinghouse at last, opening the door just as H. Edgar knew he would.

"We stick to our original statements. We testify. We give them what we know, and maybe even . . ."

"But I don't know anything, H. Edgar," said Westinghouse, interrupting a new thought that had begun to rise in Simpson's superior brain. "Only what you told me, and what James said when he was seriously loaded the other night. None of this makes sense."

"Then count yourself lucky, Westinghouse, because ignorance, as they say, is bliss." And then he saw it again, that look that he glimpsed briefly the other night at the Halloween Ball, that flash of anger that lingered, perhaps a little longer this time, before disappearing again.

"They'll say we betrayed him," said Westinghouse at last.

"No, no they won't, Westinghouse. There is no reason why the payment of the reward should be made public. That was also part of the deal."

"But they'll assume . . ."

"That we struggled with our inner conscience," interrupted Simpson, "that we spent close to two whole days wondering what the hell was the right thing to do. But in the end we decided that we could not live with ourselves if we did not speak up. A girl is dead, Westinghouse—and, as it turns out, her innocent unborn child as well."

"Be careful, H. Edgar," said Westinghouse, his eyes showing a spark of that now more familiar intensity. "For a moment there it sounded like you actually cared."

"Good," said his red-haired friend. "Because that, Westinghouse, is exactly how I intended it to sound."

45

He was in the "dirty room." At least that was what the locals here at Nashua Street Suffolk County Jail called it, the room before processing and searching, after which you became "clean." He was wearing his "arraignment" suit. The newly dry-cleaned, conservative Italian suit that David had collected from his law school locker, still in its plastic, after a summer of interning at Westinghouse, Lloyd and Greene. It still had that lemon-ish smell of the dry-cleaning fluid. A sweet citrus scent that seemed to be leaching from him second by second only to be replaced by the strong stench of antiseptic, which, despite its eye-watering power, could not quite mask the underlying stink of vomit and urine and sweat. He was beginning to realize just how much of a favor Lieutenant Mannix had done him— allowing him to stay that one extra night in Boston PD lockup. For some reason the temporary small gray cell in Roxbury felt closer to the real world, while this whitewashed hellhole spoke of guilt and permanence—even though he knew that if convicted he would be transferred to another, even more horrifying maximum security institution where young men like him were sucked in, chewed upon, swallowed, digested and crapped out the other end until someone else came along and sucked them in all over again.

Processing was slow. The jail workers were bored and disinterested, never once making eye contact. He figured this was because they either feared catching whatever criminal germs that he carried or more likely because they just didn't give a fuck.

They took his details, fingerprinted him. They made him strip. He was weighed and examined by a doctor. Then he was taken to the "clean room" where some robotic stick figure with sunken cheeks and soulless eyes searched every orifice of his body—slowly, mechanically, like he had followed this routine a million times before with the same senseless aim of coming up empty.

His suit was taken away. And with it the scent of freedom. He was given new clothes. A shapeless red top, matching cotton pants two sizes too big and a pair of dirty white flip-flops. Flip-flops.

"It's cold," he said to the pale-skinned skeleton, the first voluntary words he had spoken since he had arrived at the jail some two hours ago. "I saw other inmates wearing sneakers. Why do I have to wear these?"

"Because you're up on six," said the man, looking everywhere but at James. "Maximum security. The homicide floor."

"So you are making me wear these for my own protection— so I can slap somebody to death?" said James, feeling the burning sensation of injustice rising deep within his gut.

"It's not you we're worried about," said the praying mantis. "Sneakers grip the floor a lot better than sandals."

"What? I don't get it," said James, now somehow obsessed with this seemingly ridiculous detail.

"You will when you see a fight breaks out and understand how important floor grip is. Serious injuries have been reduced by almost thirty-five percent since we swapped the sneakers for flip-flops."

"These flip-flops are supposed to protect me from major injury, simply because whoever decides to beat the crap out of me can't grip the floor?" asked James, the words somehow foreign as they spewed from his mouth.

"No," said the man with a half-smile, his cool hazel eyes meeting James' for the very first time. "But they have been known to make the difference between just fucked up and dead."

46

The minute David turned off Beacon and onto Harvard Avenue, eventually finding Brown (thanks to the bored looking camera crews camped on the sidewalk), he got the sense that the Matheson home was going to be something special—and it didn't take long for him to realize that James Matheson didn't live in a house, he lived on an estate, or more specifically, a picturesque portion of it. He gave his credentials to a private security guard at the front entranceway and turned into the drive—a long, narrow gray-graveled pathway, bordered by perfectly trimmed hedges and "lollipop" manicured figs. At the end of the driveway were two large whitewashed wrought iron gates, which opened automatically a good ten seconds before David reached the intercom at which he had intended to announce his arrival.

Security cameras, he thought.

He passed through the gates and followed the drive north, the greenery eventually giving way to reveal a massive cream-painted Colonial, with white-accented window borders and miniature balconies with flowering window boxes and impressive hand-carved, whitewashed double doors. Even more impressive were the two people standing on the front sandstone steps, obviously awaiting his arrival. The couple—the man's long arm extending comfortably across the woman's shoulders—were nothing short of perfect. In fact, standing there as they did now, David could have sworn they were in some surreal commercial for the virtues of blue-blood America—he with his pepper-colored hair, tanned features and toned physique and she with her naturally thick dark locks, green cashmere twinset and Katharine Hepburn pants.

David put his foot slowly on the brake, feeling the strange

need to bring his Land Cruiser to a gradual stop, careful not to disturb the evenly distributed gravel, which, for some reason, he suspected would upset the harmony of this perfectly arranged environment.

"Mr. Cavanaugh," said the man who approached him with his arm outstretched as David got out of his car. "Jed Matheson—and this is my wife, Diane."

"Mr. Cavanaugh," said the strikingly beautiful green-eyed woman. "We cannot tell you how much we appreciate everything you are doing for our son."

"To be honest with you, Mrs. Matheson," said David, shaking the woman's smooth and slender hand. "I thought you and your husband might have had other preferences when it came to an attorney, so I suppose I am the one who is flattered by your confidence."

"Nonsense," said Jed Matheson, now steering David toward the house. "We're aware of your record, Mr. Cavanaugh, and it is nothing short of impressive. You are right when you suggest that I know a lot of lawyers, but not too many who represent those accused of . . ."

Jed Matheson obviously could not bring himself to say the word.

"First up," said David, feeling a need to put this amiable couple at ease, "you can call me David. And secondly, I can totally understand why you have had little or no dealings with criminal attorneys. Finally, I am just as determined as you are to clear your son's name. James is a good kid, Mr. and Mrs. Matheson, and I will do everything I can to make this go away."

David spent the next half hour in the Mathesons' sitting room, a high-ceilinged, neutrally decorated space with cozy cream and beige striped sofas and matching thick pile rugs. He was drinking tea, a strong English blend, with a side tray of freshly baked macaroons sitting on a blue and white Wedgwood platter placed slightly left of center on the antique white oak coffee table before him.

"I appreciate your willingness to help," said David who had just listened to the pair give a detailed summation of the first twenty-two years of their only child's life. "It is obvious James is a very talented young man."

"He is a blessing, David," said Diane Matheson. "And has

never given us one ounce of trouble. Admittedly there were the usual teenage dramas, but nothing out of the ordinary."

"I understand," said David. "But we'll need to talk about those incidences in more detail even if they seem trivial. James is obviously a good kid, but that just means the ADA will dig even deeper to unearth whatever he can and then, undoubtedly, try to put his own spin on it." David saw a slight furrow in Diane Matheson's brow as she nodded and replaced her teacup on its matching china saucer.

"I don't want to scare you, Diane," he said. "But there is no point in my sugarcoating things. James made a few mistakes with his handling of his situation, mistakes that, among other things, have left him in an extremely serious position. So now we have to be as thorough as we can, and speaking of thorough . . ." He leaned forward on his seat, wanting them to focus on what he was about to say. He wanted to prepare them for what was no doubt going to be one of the most harrowing afternoons of their life—the formal police search of their much loved family home.

"In about half an hour the police will arrive. Lieutenant Joe Mannix is a good man—direct but fair, so I have every faith he will instruct his men to carry out the search with every respect for your property. They will have a warrant so there is no point in being antagonistic. In fact, the more cooperative you are the better. You don't have to serve them coffee and cake, but you do need to make them feel free to turn this place upside down if they want to."

Jed Matheson shook his head.

"I know, Jed," said David. "This is not going to be easy, but believe me, there is no other way to play it."

Diane Matheson nodded, taking a breath, straightening her back as if she was more than willing to take this on if it meant being of help to her son.

"So they will want to search the entire property," said Jed at last. "Even though James lived largely in the pool house."

"Yes," answered David. "James may have spent most of the time in his own quarters but he still used this house as his home. Having said that, and if it's okay with you, I'd like to have a quick look at James' residence before the police arrive. It might give me a better take on the aims of their search."

"Certainly," said Matheson rising to his feet, his lemon
V-neck sweater sitting comfortably on his fit fifty-something
frame, his single pleat pants falling comfortably into place.

"Diane, why don't you get the key and I'll walk David down
the south entrance toward the pool. And then," he said, looking
David directly in the eye, "my wife and I shall leave you to it.
Some things are best undertaken solo, am I right, David?" he
said with a look of calm determination on his face.

"Ah, yes sir," said David, not knowing what else to say. He
could have been wrong, but he was pretty sure the man had just
invited him to confiscate anything he might have regarded as
"evidence to the negative" from his son's private pool house.

David then got the sense that Jed Matheson had probably
done a good search of his own over the past twenty-four hours—
but was most likely unsure of exactly what to look for. The man
believed in his son's innocence, David was sure of that, but he
was also aware that a successful merchant banker like Jed
Matheson was probably no stranger to the practices of manipulation and subterfuge. He wanted to cover all of his bases in the
event the police found anything that might be misconstrued as
evidence against his son. And he wanted David to help him.

"Jed, I know you have James' best interests at heart. But,
you have to understand, I cannot . . ."

"My son has every faith in you, David, as do Diane and I,"
interrupted Matheson, patting David squarely on the shoulder
as he steered him toward the glass bifold doors and out onto the
limestone-paved courtyard. "We know you will do *everything*
in your power to help our son. You said it yourself, David, James
is innocent, so let's show those bastards what we are made of
and get this done."

47

"This is Mannix," said Joe as he picked up his direct extension in his Boston PD Office.

The phone had rung just as he and Frank were heading out the door and normally he would have let it go. But he knew the ADA would be calling with any news on this morning's grand jury hearing, and while the thought of talking to Roger Katz turned his stomach at the best of times, he was anxious for an update.

"Joe," said the friendly voice. And Joe had to admit the call from FBI Boston Field Office Special Agent in Charge Leo King was still a welcome alternative.

"Simba," said Mannix. "What's up?"

"Oh, you know, the usual. Mickey just won some major art award at school. Some drawing of a cricket. I'm actually gonna take time out at lunch to attend some special elementary school award-giving ceremony." Leo and his wife, Janet Leung King, had eleven-year-old twin daughters, Elena and Michela, both of whom were the apples of their father's eye.

"Good for her, and even better for you," said Joe. "In fact, if it's a free for all, I'm happy to ditch the Matheson search and come along as part of the Michela King fan club."

"Sounds like you've got a day ahead of you."

"You could say that," said Joe. "So I'm praying you're calling to add some sunshine to my otherwise gray existence."

"Sorry, Joe," he said. "No such luck. The guys at Quantico came back with their print analysis and I'm afraid it's not good news."

"None of the three prints match Matheson?"

"Two are a definite no—the one on the glass near the greenhouse doorway and the one on the flower. The prints belong to the same person, but they're not a match with your perp."

Mannix had taken David's advice and got the Crime Response Unit to test the orchid for prints. The team came up with one juicy impression, an almost perfect replica of somebody's right thumb.

"They ran the two prints through CJIS but didn't find a match," said King, referring to the FBI's Criminal Justice Information Service Unit's latent print database, which contains the world's largest repository of fingerprint records. "Even tried to match the plant with the gardener but it was a no-go all round. In other words, whoever they belong to is record-free. We're checking further, with other international bodies, but at this stage . . ."

"And the third?" asked Joe, realizing he probably should be disappointed, but registering nothing but acceptance, almost as if he had been expecting the prints to be a dead end from the start.

"The third print," Simba went on, "the one on the rock where the Nagoshi girl was placed . . . I am afraid that one was pretty much unreadable. It was really only a half print to begin with, and the rock was porous and flaky. The lab ran it through the IAFIS over a dozen times, the best they could come up with was a possible match for both comparisons."

The IAFIS was the FBI's Integrated Automated Fingerprint Identification System—a primarily ten-print system that can digitally capture ten-print images and perform several functions, including enhancement and improvement of image quality, comparison of latent fingerprints against suspect ten-print records retrieved from the criminal fingerprint repository and determination if a prior arrest record exists.

"By the way," said King. "Why did you give me *two* prints to test against? I know one was Matheson's but who . . ."

"It was mine."

"What?"

"I knew the print was foggy. I just wanted to make sure we had a fair comparison."

"So you submit your own print," said King. "And when the lab comes back with the same result for both, you know there is no way it'll stand up in court."

"Pretty much—or in this case, the confirmation that it is just as likely that I topped the Nagoshi girl as the kid we sent to the lockup."

Joe had said too much. He realized he was allowing his growing suspicions to seep into his role as lead homicide detective on the case. It was a mistake, and he regretted it the minute it came out of his mouth.

"Whoa," said King. "Did I just hear you right because I thought you said . . ."

"I gotta go, Simba," interrupted Joe. "I'll get our guys to bag the kid's shoes so you can compare them to the impression left at the scene."

"Ah . . . okay," said King. "But make sure they bag them with any dirt intact. I'll tell the lab to run them through Materials Analysis—that way you'll get a full geologic, mineralogic, metallurgical and elemental report, which we can match to the material under the print."

"No stone left unturned, hey, Simba?" said Joe.

"I guess not," King hesitated before going on. "And Joe?"

"Yeah."

"If you ever need someone to shoot the breeze with . . ."

"I gotcha, Simba. And thanks."

48

James Matheson's pool house looked like something out of *Vogue Living*. The front-facing wall, which bordered the aqua mosaic tiled pool, was made up of a line of whitewashed glass bifold doors, which were now drawn back, their canvas roman blinds pulled up to their extremities to reveal the three room "apartment" within.

David, who was now alone following Jed and Diane's departure back to the main house, stepped into the living area where the slightly weathered pale timber floors were covered by a massive natural fiber rug. The furniture was a mixture of comfy cream couches and wicker chairs, with a weathered coffee table supporting a stone textured vase that exploded with blue and white hydrangeas. There were pale green throws and blue and white cushions and similarly colored wall art, including a pair of old semi-stripped green-painted wooden oars that sat above the western windows—all of which was reflected in a huge framed mirror on the far side of the room.

Next came the bedroom, which was basically an extension of the feel of the picture-perfect living area beyond, the neatly arranged shelves stacked with law texts, the bed made up in a masculine blue, the stand-alone wardrobe stocked with freshly ironed shirts and chinos and the simple white desk supporting more texts and neatly organized assignments in progress. In fact, the only barren space in the entire room was the rectangular area at the center of the desk, which was no doubt where James would normally place his Titanium laptop, which David knew had already been confiscated from his Law School locker at Deane.

David poked his head into the equally pristine bathroom, all white tiles with a limestone floor and perfectly rolled Egyptian cotton towels, and was overcome with the strange sensation that he had walked onto a movie set, a world where summers were long, pool parties were civilized and jugs of Pimm's and lemonade, complete with mint and cucumber, were served at dusk. It was a scene where the entire cast was straight from a Ralph Lauren commercial, all buff and tanned and fit—the American college dream. Truth be told, James *was* a living, breathing example of such a dream. He was smart, rich, healthy, likable. He had good-looking friends, supportive parents, straight "A" grades and, at least up until the last few months, a future filled with nothing but promise.

But David could not help but think that perhaps this would be James' greatest obstacle. Many would assume he was smug and conceited. One look at this house, where the decorations alone cost more than your average college kid's first apartment, and people were bound to jump to conclusions. Even David found the order of this young man's home somewhat disconcerting, but he knew that this was how the privileged few lived, with housekeepers and pool cleaners and staff to service their every need. And besides, he thought, within the hour this designer's showcase would not be so pristine, despite the cops' feigned attempts to leave things in order.

He was wasting time. He had to focus. He checked the obvious places first—drawers, cupboards, rubbish bins, keepsake boxes, wardrobe floors. He found James' shoes—including a pair of Nikes—at the bottom of the wardrobe, aligned and clean with not a trace of dirt beneath them. David knew these would be the first pieces to be taken into evidence, after which they would be analyzed to within an inch of their lives by the world's most competent forensic experts.

He glanced over James' assignment notes, flicked through some texts, lifted up some cushions until finally he found himself staring at the carefully arranged walnut-framed black-and-whites on the far side of James' bedroom wall. There were shots of James as a child, sandwiched between his two flawless parents, an older one of his mother and father's wedding, a few of the three of them skiing on some family winter vacation and another of a teenage James and his mother in scuba gear, perhaps taken on the Great Barrier Reef. There were a series of action shots, of James powering down the pool, kayaking on the Charles, and one from his school years winning a rowing race in some Sydney regatta. And the more recent shots—of James and his college friends, a variety of young men and women all smiling and laughing with perfect hair and perfect bodies and no doubt even more perfect brains.

And then he saw them, a shot of the three. James took center stage, his arms draped casually around the shoulders of the two young men on either side of him—Heath Westinghouse to his left, all tanned skin and white teeth; H. Edgar Simpson to his right, shorter, thinner but with a look of pure arrogance on his pale, spotted face.

And then, just as he started to turn away, two things caught his eye simultaneously. The first was in the form of the corner of a yellow Post-it Note that had been stuck behind the picture of the three, and the second, a red flashing dot reflected in the glass surface of the framed photograph before him—it was coming from the bedside table, beyond the portable telephone and the ivory colored lamp.

He stopped.

He could hear them now—a convoy of police cars making their way toward the main house. The crunching of gravel was loud and getting louder and the urgency of it grated on him. He did not have much time. He pulled the photo from the wall and peeled the yellow note from the back of the frame. *Cabot 312* it said. Nothing more, nothing less.

He put the note in his pocket before turning to the source of the flashing. He heard a car door slam, and then another and another, and found himself diving for the gadget that sat hidden beyond the bedside paraphernalia. He would have to hurry. It would not look good being found in James' apartment just minutes before the prior arranged search—a search Mannix had kindly coordinated with David as a courtesy to his friend and the accused boy's parents.

It was an old-fashioned answering machine and according to the light indicated James had five new messages. He picked it up, fiddled with the buttons but, realizing he was running out of time, cut to the chase and pushed the eject button so that the machine might release the miniature tape inside. The machine obeyed, slowly, carefully, lifting its little plastic hinged door to reveal the cassette inside. David could have sworn he heard it creaking, a little further, a little further, until . . . nothing. The tape had been removed. Someone had lifted what was obviously some vitally important information from James Matheson's answering machine—and David was pretty sure he knew exactly who it was.

49

Forty minutes. He had been in there for over forty minutes. Sara looked at her watch again. It had been a gift from David, a family heirloom that once belonged to his grandmother. It made her think of him and that now familiar twinge of guilt rose in her stomach, sending a wave of bile toward her throat. She knew he was at the Matheson house, and she knew she should be there with him. At the very least she could have helped him console the parents. Explain the process of the search, share a cup of coffee with James' mother.

But here she was, sitting motionless outside a Suffolk Country Superior Court grand jury hearing room, waiting for *her* client to emerge from screwing *his* client to the wall, and hopefully giving her some take on where Katz was going with this whole bloody mess. Truth be told, she was beginning to think she should have "bumped" young Sawyer Jones after all.

She looked around her, at the cold stone walls and dark wooden benches, at the gray-painted ceilings and dusty overhead lights. The corridor was reasonably quiet, the odd pedestrian making their presence known moments before they turned the corner into the main thoroughfare with the click of their shoes on the green tiled floor. In fact, she heard them now, a group of approaching feet, six to be exact, belonging to three suited men, two young, one older. They stopped at the far end of the passageway, the older man, obviously a lawyer, gesturing toward a bench where they all took a seat and leaned forward into a huddle.

Westinghouse and Simpson, she knew. They were here to give their testimony. Katz would be following Sawyer's confirmation of James and Jessica's relationship with the two friends' account of the critical confession. It was the perfect strategy.

One, two, three. He would begin with James' lies and finish with his emotional admission of guilt.

There were twenty-three jurors in that room and all Katz needed was the go-ahead from twelve. There was no doubt about it, the ADA would have his indictment within the hour, she said to herself as the door finally opened and her slightly flushed client emerged. Roger Katz had caught his fish—hook, line and sinker.

Sara got to her feet, starting to approach Sawyer, but stopped dead in her tracks when he lifted his left hand, ever so slightly, indicating her to move back and away. She shifted her feet quickly, and reversed into a water cooler recess in the wall, tilting her head forward slightly to see Katz now materializing behind her client, moving out into the corridor, shaking Sawyer's narrow hand before turning his back on the young student to greet the three obviously more important people coming toward him.

The group of four stood in a tight circle, Sawyer now ignored and off to the side where he fished into his pocket, retrieved his cell phone and appeared to be turning it on so he could check for messages. He was slow and deliberate, measured and thoughtful as he stared at the phone, pressing the odd button every few seconds or so.

He was also close enough to hear what they were saying, Sara was sure of it—and then she knew that retaining Sawyer Jones as her client had not been such a bad idea after all.

50

"So?" said David as Joe Mannix emerged from the now crowded pool house. The blue skies overhead were rapidly being replaced by a thick layer of dark rain clouds, the wind now whipping up from the northwest—a sharp, bitter chill that went straight through David's light wool suit jacket, biting into his skin.

"So I feel like I just emerged from the pages of some fancy interior design catalog."

"I know what you mean—but that wasn't what I was asking."

"We're done," said Joe. "The crew is cleaning up."

"That wasn't what I meant either," interrupted David, removing his sunglasses to look his detective friend in the eye.

"Jesus, David. You know the rules," said Joe. "We've bagged everything we see as a potential piece of evidence. It'll be sent to the lab for analysis and . . ."

"BP Crime or FBI?"

David knew most pieces of evidence recovered during the course of a murder investigation were analyzed by Boston PD's respected Crime Lab Unit. But this case was different. Katz would want the added credibility of having the FBI on board and Mannix would most likely agree—not because he did not think his own guys were good enough, but because he would want the security of the backup, because he wouldn't want Katz crying foul if something went awry and because Leo King was a friend.

"Both," said Mannix, confirming David's guess. "Leo called this morning," he added quickly, perhaps knowing that while he could not discuss the results of the search with his attorney friend, he could give him a heads-up on the FBI test results. "You got lucky."

"None of the prints match my client," said David, a new wave of hope banishing the chill.

"Two no-gos and one inconclusive."

"And the two no-gos?"

"No idea."

"Well, it could have been worse," said David, who despite the good news was disappointed the prints could not be matched with another possible perpetrator.

"I gather you got the paternity results," said Mannix, lifting his jacket hood over his head. The rain was beginning to fall, the first small droplets landing on the pool and sending tiny concentric circles dancing across its glossy aqua surface.

"Yeah. Gus called last night," said David. *"Shit,"* he added, "I have to tell the Mathesons."

"I'll leave you to it," Mannix nodded, looking back toward his men who were almost ready to leave. "No word from Sara?"

Neither of them had heard any news as to the progress of this morning's hearing and both were anxious to get some word.

"Nothing."

"Oh well," said Joe. "I'll catch you."

"Sure," said David, still dissatisfied at having learned nothing from the search. "But you'll call, right?"

"When I can," said Joe, obviously determined to play this by the book.

• • •

Jed Matheson was holding an umbrella over David's head, walking him back to his car. The man was quiet, contemplative, David having explained he was unable to garner any additional information regarding the results of the search.

"Jed," said David at last. "There's something I have to tell you—you and Diane—about . . ."

"You have the results of the paternity test," guessed Jed Matheson, turning to face David.

"Yes."

Matheson said nothing, just waited for David to go on.

"It was your grandson, Jed. I'm sorry."

Matheson nodded and in that moment the tall, handsome, fifty-something looked for all the world like an old man with a broken heart.

"You will save him, won't you, David?" he asked at last, his gray eyes glossing over with tears. "For I am afraid Diane and I could not go on without . . ."

"I'll prove he didn't do this, Jed," said David, hoping beyond all hope that he could follow through on his promise.

"All right, then," said Jed, taking a breath before shifting his umbrella to his left hand and placing his right in his pocket, then retrieving it again to shake David's outstretched hand.

"And you know . . ." he said. David felt it immediately. Matheson was squashing something into his palm. "I will do anything to help my son."

David released Matheson's grip and, to his own surprise, curled his fingers around the hard flat object, making no attempt to look at it before opening his car door and climbing inside.

"I understand," he said shutting the door behind him. "I'll be in touch."

"Yes," said Jed Matheson. "I expect you will."

51

Tony Bishop was nervous as all hell. And it wasn't because this special meeting included his boss and firm partner Gareth Coolidge. It was the two men across from them that saw his heart now up a beat, or more specifically one of them, in the form of Peter Nagoshi.

Bishop had gone to his boss first thing this morning. The Nagoshis were contacted and asked to attend a meeting on the stately twenty-ninth floor Financial District offices of Williams, Coolidge and Harrison at their earliest convenience. They had decided to hold this little gathering in the more contained setting of Coolidge's harborview office. Smaller than the firm conference room, it offered an intimacy perhaps more appropriate to delivering the extremely sensitive information they had to share. And so here they were, grouped around the small meeting table, backed by the extensive views across the now-deep gray waters that met the horizon in a blur of offshore rain.

Tony glanced around the table—at Peter looking like some Hannibal Lecter impersonator with a large white bandage across the middle of his face, at the normally expressionless John Nagoshi who was perhaps also showing the slightest signs of uneasiness, and at Gareth Coolidge, the coolest attorney Tony had ever known, now carrying the beginnings of circular sweat rings under the arms of his pristinely pressed Brooks Brothers shirt.

"We have a problem," Tony began after Coolidge gave him the nod. "This morning I received a call from Terrance Tan, one of the senior attorneys at our office in Singapore. Mr. Tan is Chinese with an extensive history in Chinese business law

and he has been assisting me with the legalities of the establishment of your operations in Guangdong."

Tony took a sip of the ice cold water before him, stealing a
quick glance at Peter Nagoshi, whose dark brown eyes were set
on him with a new intensity.

"Mr. Tan told me he heard a rumor. No," added Tony, knowing there was no way to sugarcoat this thing. "Not a rumor,
more confirmation that Tsohuang Manufacturing were about to
release a new compact car, 'The Apple,' to the local market—a
car that, according to Mr. Tan, is an exact replica of the Nagoshi 'Dream' CC250."

"What?" said Peter, sitting forward in his seat.

"'The Apple,'" Tony went on, needing to get this all out
before he had to deal with what he knew would be the Nagoshis'
anger, "is not only visually identical to the 'Dream,' but according to Mr. Tan's contacts, also contains numerous identical
parts and components. It will be released to the Chinese market
within the month, flooding local car dealers with vehicles
priced at seventy-five percent of what you planned to charge."

And then he saw it—the utter devastation on their faces.
Despite the fact that Peter's features were largely concealed,
the visible portions were now distorted in an expression of
rage. Tony found himself placing his palms on the edge of the
table, as if bracing himself in preparation for the possibility
that the younger Nagoshi might leap across the table and . . .

"How did this happen?" asked John Nagoshi at last. His tone
even, his voice showing only the slightest trace of a quiver.

"All too easily, I am afraid," said Gareth Coolidge, speaking
for the first time.

"John," he went on, leaning over the table. "You knew in
order to base this plant in Guangdong, you would have to enter
into a joint agreement with a Chinese manufacturer—fifty percent is as much as the Chinese government will allow foreign
operators, and that leaves you open to all sorts of confidentiality risks. I am not saying your Shanghai Holding's partners
were at fault," Coolidge went on. "But they have joint ventures
with other foreign automobile manufacturers, who in turn have
joint ventures with other Chinese companies—including out-
fits like Tsohuang. I am afraid technology theft is a rampant

reality in China, John, so much so that it is becoming almost impossible for foreign companies to keep secrets from global competitors."

Coolidge paused, obviously leaving an opening for Nagoshi to ask another question.

"These are not answers, Mr. Coolidge," said Peter, obviously miffed that their attorney saw fit to address his father directly, effectively excluding him from a conversation on China—*his* China, his undeniable success! "I hear what you are saying but it does not equal reason. Plans for each part of the Nagoshi 'Dream' have been kept separate, individual, so that this might be prevented. We have gone to the greatest lengths to assure our security," he said, his nasally voice now rising a notch. "Even the prototypes have been kept under lock and key, and constantly guarded by security workers."

"Yes," said Tony. "But there were other prototypes, initial testing models, which were left on the plant floor. You have to understand, Peter, that the Chinese are masters at reverse engineering. They do not need plans. All they need is access to the finished product, or close enough to it, and they work backward part by part. And then they start from scratch, building an identical copy, socket for socket, plug for plug."

"Are you saying one of our workers is responsible for sharing our knowledge?" Peter's fist hit the table, causing the ice in their crystal tumblers to chink in a musical scream of protest. "Because I can assure you our employees are loyal, dedicated . . ."

"Happy? Yes, so I hear." Tony could not help himself. Peter Nagoshi was an arrogant son of a bitch and Tony was sick of his egotistical demands and holier-than-thou attitude, especially considering he may well be responsible for the most unspeakable of crimes.

"Look," said Coolidge at last, perhaps feeling the need to throw a little water on what was becoming a very heated discussion. "I know this is hard to hear but if you recall, Peter, I did warn you of these potential problems when you decided to base the plant in China."

Tony noted a slight twitch in John Nagoshi's left eye. Perhaps Coolidge's warnings were not passed on from son to father—from subordinate to chief.

"You saved costs, sure," Coolidge continued. "But the reality is, there is no way to protect your technology on the great Asian continent. Honda, General Motors, Volkswagen, Toyota, Nissan and many others have been bitten by piracy of their logos, parts, trademarks, technologies—and, like Nagoshi Inc.—even entire cars."

"What is our legal recourse?" asked John Nagoshi, his voice low and tempered.

"The Chinese are setting up tribunals to hear the foreign manufacturers' disputes," responded Coolidge. "But in all honesty, a true judicial system monitoring technology theft is years, maybe decades away." Coolidge looked to Bishop.

"They are making too much money, Mr. Nagoshi," said Tony, taking his superior's lead. "Billions of dollars to be exact. The problem isn't going to go away. Rip-offs like Tsohuang's 'Apple' will be overproduced in a country where the people are keen to buy but the streets are narrow and already congested with vehicles. We hate to be the bearer of bad tidings, but our job is to tell you everything we know and give you the best advice we can."

"Which is?" Peter countered. "Tell me, Mr. Coolidge, Mr. Bishop, what do you advise?"

Tony looked at his boss and nodded, letting him know that he was willing to be the one to see this thing through. He had been the one to stumble across the technology theft in the first place, after all—when he was doing some private investigations of his own.

"You have a few options," Tony began. "You can tweak the 'Dream' and class it more upmarket, or you can leave it as it is and reduce the price."

Peter shook his head, incredulous.

"But in all honesty, our advice would be to move your automobile manufacturing operations onto Japanese soil. That way, at least you will own the plant one hundred percent and the risk of another copycat usurper would be reduced to a minimum. Costs would be higher, granted, but once you reestablish yourself, six to twelve months down the track you . . ."

"Father, this is outrageous," yelled Peter. "We do not need to listen to the false words of . . ."

But John Nagoshi raised his hand, calling for his son's silence in no uncertain terms.

"You think we should cut our losses?" John Nagoshi asked Tony at last.

"Yes, sir," Tony replied, looking the older Nagoshi directly in the eye. "Our advice is—*my* advice is—you have to get out, and you have to get out now."

52

"Call home," she said, moving the salt and pepper shakers aside so that she might push her cell phone across the surface of the lime green tabletop toward him.

Sara had texted him just as he was leaving the Mathesons', the tiny cassette tape Jed had given him now packed safely in a side pocket of his brown leather briefcase. She asked him to meet her at Myrtle's for a late lunch so that she might fill him in on the goings-on at this morning's hearing and he might do the same in regards to his news of the search.

"Sara," he began. "I am just getting over the news that our innocent client is headed for trial and you are asking me to call our apartment when the only two people who live there are . . . well . . . sitting right *here*?"

"I know the indictment is bad news, but in all honestly it is no surprise," she said. "There was no way Katz wasn't going to convince at least twelve of them that he had evidence enough to warrant the criminal charges. It was just a formality."

She was right. It was a blow but it wasn't unexpected. What was, however, was Sara's strange insistence that he call home. But given he was feeling like crap, the cold and drizzle just visible beyond Mick McGee's now steamy glass windows only adding to his somewhat depressed demeanor, he figured he had nothing to lose. So he dialed the number.

He heard the ring and then the click of their answering machine as it kicked into gear. Then he heard Sara's voice asking him to leave a message, as the real Sara took his hand and squeezed it. "Retrieve our messages," she said.

He pressed the three-digit code to bring up their voicemail and was told there were two new messages—the first from his mom in Jersey asking if he and Sara could make it home for

Thanksgiving, and the second a message of sorts from the most unlikely of callers—Suffolk County Assistant District Attorney Roger Katz.

"Listen to me," said Katz, his voice direct and low. *"We don't have much time so you have to focus and take this in as quickly as possible."*

"All right," said a second voice, younger, but just as confident.

"You have done this state a fine service, H. Edgar. The new information is just what the Commonwealth needs but—and please do not take this the wrong way—I do not want you to talk of it this morning, in front of the grand jury."

"What new information?" asked a confused second voice, another young man David guessed could only be Heath Westinghouse.

"It's something I remembered this morning, Westinghouse," said Simpson, a sliver of impatience in his voice. *"I haven't had a chance to tell you about it.*

"I don't understand," Simpson went on, obviously turning his attention back to Katz. *"I thought that was why we were here—to provide as much information as possible."*

"Yes," interrupted Katz. *"But I am sure a savvy young legal mind such as yours knows that occasionally a prosecutor sees the benefits of, shall we say, rationing the goods. I have the indictment in the bag, gentlemen, and I intend to save this lovely little bombshell for trial."*

There was a pause then, a static hum as, David gathered, the two boys were taking this in.

"I'm not sure about this, Katz," said a new voice, an older man with a tone of authority.

"This is all aboveboard, Gordon. At the very least it gives us time to verify H. Edgar's information."

The man, who David guessed to be Westinghouse's father, failed to reply.

"All right," said Katz after a beat. *"You're up first, Heath, and I'll close with H. Edgar. And don't worry, everything will be fine. There will be no surprises, just straight as we rehearsed."*

There was another pause then and David sensed that perhaps Katz was not getting the positive affirmation he desired from his prized witness number one.

"You are doing the right thing, Heath. You are a fine student and will make an even finer attorney. I know Matheson was your friend but believe me when I tell you he was a wolf in sheep's clothing. This may be difficult, but it is also your duty as a potential officer of the court. One thing is for sure, you and Mr. Simpson have made lifelong friends in the Suffolk County District Attorney's Office, for you are young men of honor and the people of the Commonwealth of Massachusetts shall be eternally in your debt."

. . .

"Jesus, Sara," David began, lowering his voice, the two of them now leaning into each other, feeling somehow "safe" in this huddle of unknown conspiracies. "How did you . . . ?"

"Sawyer recorded it," Sara began. "He was brilliant, David, he just waltzed out of that grand jury hearing room and stood a foot to Katz's right. He was smart enough to think of calling my number and, well, needless to say Katz had no idea he was sharing his very private conversation with the lead defense counsel and his co-chair.

"The good news is we know he is up to something," Sara went on. "But the bad news is . . ."

"We have no idea what it is," finished David.

"Exactly," she said, picking up her spoon to stir the soup Mick had delivered moments ago.

"So we have to assume Simpson and Westinghouse's testimonies were basically a relay of what they told Joe," added David. "But that Simpson has something else, some *bombshell* that, judging by Katz's excitement, could be devastating to our client."

"I'm afraid so," said Sara. "We have to fight this, David. The ADA has a legal obligation to provide us with all evidence discovered in the course of his investigations, and if he is guilty of a failure to disclose, then we can demand the evidence be precluded from trial."

"But we don't even know what it is, Sara. And worse still, we found out about it via means of an illegal recording of a private conversation."

"This is no time to have a go at Sawyer, David," she said, pulling back a little.

"I wasn't," he said, taking her hand and pulling her close

again. "I'm grateful, believe me. The kid is kinda freaky but he's damn smart. It's just that now we are between a rock and a hard place—we can't go to Stein with it, and we can't stroll on up and ask the Kat what the hell he has in his illegal bag of tricks."

"Then we have to go to . . ."

"One of the boys," finished David.

"Westinghouse," she countered.

"No. He may not be the ringleader, Sara. By the sound of things," he said, gesturing at her cell, "Simpson is still pulling his strings."

"Who then?" she asked, their soup still ignored.

"The only other person who can help us," he said before bending down to retrieve the small cassette from his briefcase. He took the tiny plastic tape from a side pocket and placed it in front of her.

"What's that?" she asked at last.

"I'm guessing it's a tape from James' home answering machine."

"What is it with today and secret recordings?" she said, looking up at him again. "David, tell me you didn't lift that from the search." said Sara, pointing at the cassette, the uneasiness in her expression obvious.

"Not me, his father. He retrieved it before the cops had a chance to . . ."

"What's on it?" she interrupted.

"I don't know. I haven't had a chance to find out. But I was going to suggest we head back to the office and use Nora's dictaphone. Then . . ." He looked at his watch, it was almost four. "First thing tomorrow we take it to the one person who will hopefully be able to shed some light on both of our recorded mysteries."

"James," she said at last. "He was the third musketeer, he knows how Simpson thinks."

"And he has nothing to lose," finished David. "Grab your coat, Sara. Something tells me that whatever it is, we have to get on top of this thing before it blows up in our faces."

• • •

Two hours later Roger Katz did something he had not done in his entire career—he left the office early. Well, six o'clock may not seem early to some, but it was to him. Hell, he was rarely out of his workplace by nine—a fact his incompetent assistant Shelley could attest to, given she was forbidden to leave until he had officially called it a night.

But the past two days had been so glorious, so fucking *triumphant* that he needed some way to release the incredible rush of adrenalin that surged through him like a drug. He pictured porky Shelley doing her own little dance of freedom as she replaced her scuffed heels with her dirty sneakers and headed out the door early with a rare smile on her fat freckled face, which, come to think of it, was not a vision he needed in his blissfully ecstatic mind on this fine November evening, and so he banished it before it had a chance to take form and spoil . . . there, it was gone!

Was the fulfillment of ambition better than sex? *Definitely!* Many men, he knew, might find this admission emasculating, many more would consider it an indication of his assumed "poor performance" in bed, but Katz had every faith in his "performance" and knew men who made such postulations were insecure beings who saw a few seconds of Neanderthal pleasure as the ultimate in human highs. Those men were not capable of realizing the true ecstasy of the ultimate career accomplishment, and never would be.

He was headed for the gym, his red Corvette now weaving down Beacon, the roof down despite the cold, the body shining from its weekly wax and Beyoncé singing "Survivor" on the radio. How appropriate! Come to think of it, that Sara Davis looked a little like the Beyoncé chick, which made for a much more pleasant vision than Shelley, and so he settled on that for a while.

The past forty-eight hours had started well and gone from good, to better, to *fan-fucking-tastic!* First, there was his brilliant craftwork in persuading Judge Stein to introduce not one but two charges of murder, then there was the mastery of his work in convincing the grand jury to issue the indictment, and then that wonderful "Ace in the Hole" delivered by young H. Edgar Simpson. The kid was an arrogant son of a bitch, but he liked the way his mind worked, probably because it operated in a fashion not unlike his own.

Simpson had the reward, but some time in the past two days

he had realized that his career prospects, his social standing, were much more important than the money which, to a trust fund baby like him, would be nothing more than spare change in any case.

Simpson had realized (a realization carefully reinforced by Katz), that James Matheson, his beloved college comrade, *had* to be found guilty if Simpson were to survive. For if found innocent, both H. Edgar and his puppet Westinghouse would be branded as personal and professional lepers—the Judases who got it *wrong*! And so in order to assure a conviction, Simpson had been doing some detective work of his own, work that resulted in him coming up with a little gem that would shock that holier-than-thou Cavanaugh to his Irish-American roots and secure his client the ultimate of sentences.

No doubt about it, this day was a winner! A triumph made all the sweeter a mere hour ago when AG Sweeney called to offer his own personal congrats.

"Well done, Roger," he had said. *"The feticide charge, the indictment—you are a credit to your office, Mr. Assistant District Attorney, and to the legal fraternity of Massachusetts as a whole. Men like you are a walking, talking argument against those who claim that justice can be bought. In fact, I just got off the phone to some friends at the AG's office in DC—they are tired of the criticism that money can buy an acquittal and you, my friend, are now their poster boy for egalitarian justice. They are watching this case carefully, Roger, as am I, and so far you have been nothing short of impressive."*

It was true, the Attorney General had copped some flack in recent years over a string of high-profile criminal cases where rich and powerful defendants with fat wallets and expensive attorneys had walked. Which was another reason why this case was so important to him—it gave him a chance to launch his "justice for one, justice for all" policy, a slogan he planned to use in next year's election for Suffolk County DA. Regardless of whether he believed it or not, it was a damned fine catchphrase and one he could well ride all the way to DC.

And so, he would hit his exclusive Copley Square Health Club, pump some iron and just as his toned arms were reaching that edge between push and pain, he would position himself on the treadmill directly behind the front row of ever-present white "Beyoncé-esque" bootie that gyrated in tiny Lycra shorts for the appreciative audience of lawyers, bankers and other corporate types in the rows behind. Like everything else in this fine democracy, this was commercialism at its best. The girls displayed their merchandise, the boys decided to buy, and before you knew it those tight little butts were seated in luxury European convertibles with Tiffany diamonds on their fingers and Amex Blacks in their purses.

Yes, life was good, and while Katz did not need the added satisfaction of scoring some flawless ass this evening, he was more than happy to window-shop with the best of them, knowing that today was a day of victory, and the best was yet to come.

53

Beep. Click. Shuffle. Pause.

"James," the recording began. *"It's me, Heath. It's Saturday. About, um . . . four,"* the voice went on in a half whisper. *"I am just about to put on my penguin suit for this Halloween thing and . . .*

"Are you there? Pick up if you are, man. I know we are not supposed to talk, but . . . I didn't see you yesterday and I was hoping you got home okay after Thursday night because you were pretty wasted and . . .

"You are probably out—turning yourself in. God! How crazy does that sound? H. Edgar would kill me if he knew I was calling.

"Look, I know you got this covered, James. And I am probably worrying for nothing. The money is in the bank and H. Edgar says he has everything under control."

A pause. A breath.

"Anyway, I guess after today it will all be over and we can celebrate. And then you have to tell me how you found out about the shoes, man. That sure as hell clinched the deal for H. Edgar . . . I mean for us.

"Anyway, I'll be seeing you."

Pause. Shuffle. *Click. Beep, beep, beep.*

"Jesus," said David at last. He looked across at Arthur, who had cracked some icy cold longneck bottles of his favorite Aussie beer and was sitting gobsmacked, a mustache of the bitter white foam sitting untouched on the stubble above his upper lip.

"I don't believe this," said Sara. "Westinghouse thought James knew about their little scheme from the get go. H. Edgar lied to him from the outset. The boy is pathological."

"So it appears," said Arthur, using the back of his right hand to wipe the froth before standing from his chair. "So we need to slow things down a little," he said, as he started to pace the room. "Backtrack and put ourselves into Simpson's head."

"Okay," began David, now looking up at his boss. "When John Nagoshi posted the reward, Simpson saw an opportunity. He somehow found out James was seeing the girl on the quiet and knew the police would want to question him."

"So," Sara went on, "he brings Westinghouse on board. He tells him that while they know James is innocent, and Barbara Rousseau's alibi will prove it, they have a window of opportunity to make some money."

"Exactly," said Arthur. "But he lies to Westinghouse, assuring him James knows of their little scam. He sets up the night at the university bar, gets Matheson drunk and . . ."

"When James starts telling them about Jessica, Simpson manipulates it into some form of confession," finished David.

"Wait," said Sara, now rising from the couch. "If this was about the money, why did Simpson involve Westinghouse at all? Why concoct a lie for two when it would have been easier to go it alone and take the entire reward for himself."

"He needed him," offered David, picking up on her train of thought. "Westinghouse and James were too tight. If H. Edgar went out on his own Westinghouse would have sided with James. This way he divides and conquers."

"You're right," said Sara. "After that night at the bar, he tells Westinghouse to stay away from James, and given Westinghouse believes Rousseau will come through with the alibi, he thinks they will all be 'home and hosed' by Saturday night, after James hands himself in and the French girl clears his name."

"Which is why they negotiated a deal based on an arrest, not on a conviction," added Arthur.

"Okay," said David. "But what are Simpson's motives? I mean, we all agree it couldn't *just* be about the money. Why would a kid worth tens of millions of dollars go to all this trouble to sell his best friend up the river?"

"Maybe it's an ego thing?" suggested Sara. "Joe says the kid is arrogance personified. Maybe he concocted this whole thing so that he could prove to himself and others just how clever he is."

"Which explains everything apart from the shoes, lass," said Nora, making them all stop in their tracks. "How did young Mr. Simpson know about the girl's missing shoes?"

David looked around him, his colleagues equally as chagrined. It was the most obvious question of all—how Simpson came to know about the shoes, how he planted the idea in Westinghouse's head that it was James who had spoken of them in the first place—but one they had forgotten to ponder in their rush to discover the truth. But when he thought about it, when the fog cleared and Nora's simple query rang crisply and candidly in his mind, David realized there was only one answer to her all important question, and as Sara's eyes lit up, he knew she saw it too.

"I don't believe it," said Sara.

"There is only one way he could have known, Nora," said David at last. "This was never about the reward money—at least not from H. Edgar Simpson's point of view."

"Well I'll be . . ." said Arthur at last.

"He killed her," said David. "H. Edgar Simpson killed Jessica Nagoshi and then cleverly framed one of his best friends for her murder, making a million profit in the process."

"It explains Sawyer's recording," said Sara. "Simpson has obviously concocted some new evidence for Katz, to steer everyone even further away from the true killer, to make sure his friend is convicted for a murder he committed himself."

"He has no alibi," added Arthur as they continued to tag team it around the room. "Westinghouse dropped him home before the Nagoshi girl was killed. He could easily have gone out again without anyone knowing."

"I need to talk to Joe," said David. "If we are right, H. Edgar Simpson has to be one of the cleverest sons of bitches I have ever come across. It was all one big smoke screen, one brilliantly conceived plot to throw us off the game and crucify our client in his stead."

"Dear Lord," said Nora. "A dimple on the chin, the devil within," she added, quoting an old Gaelic proverb.

54

It hit him—just like that, the irony of it all. Three days ago—only three days ago—he was sitting in Deane's grand historical library, taking solace in the scholarly ambience of it all. He was burying his head in books, and while at the time he felt "imprisoned" by the gossip and innuendo that surrounded him, it was nothing like this—nothing like this at all.

The Suffolk County Jail library was small, a cramped corner enclave that dedicated more space to Stephen King paperbacks, which sat dog-eared and soiled at the top end of the room, than law journals and legal references. He lifted his head, something he had learned over the past twenty-four hours was not the most advisable of movements, toward the only other inmate in the room—a huge black building of a man with a mop of unkempt dreadlocks and pockmarked skin. The man, who he had learned over the course of the day from another prisoner on "badassmothafucka" level 6, was better known as "The Drill." But James had not asked about the pseudonym's origins, largely because he was afraid of what the answer might be.

The Drill was reading—slowly, carefully—his choice of genre not crime or horror or war or even shoot-'em-up, knock-'em-down kick-ass western. The Drill was reading a children's book, or more to the point, mispronouncing every second word in it. It was one of James' childhood favorites—*Danny the Champion of the World* by Roald Dahl.

"What the fuck you lookin' at?" It was The Drill. He broke off from his stilted verse, his voice now thick with animosity.

"Nothing," said James, averting his gaze.

"You got a problem with my reading?"

"No. I . . . ah . . . I love that book. I read it when I was a kid and . . ." *Stupid thing to say, stupid!*

"I'm reading it to my kid," said The Drill, luckily not picking up on the inference. And then James noticed the recorder in front of him. "I speak into this. They send my boy the tape."

"Wow," said James, struck by the incredible ingenuity and simultaneous sadness of it all. "A bedtime story," he added, not knowing what else to say. "What's his name?"

"Who?" said The Drill, the gravel turned down a notch or two.

"Your kid?"

"Danny, of course," he said, pointing to the cover of the book. "He's eight."

James nodded. "I'm sure he'll get a kick out of it," he said. "You know—having it read to him by his dad."

The Drill nodded, a look of pride spreading across his broad black face—a look almost immediately replaced by an expression of pure wretchedness, and regret, and sorrow.

"If he likes Roald Dahl," James went on, trying to ease his discomfort, "you should read him *Charlie and the Chocolate Factory* next."

"What the fuck for?" asked The Drill, a look of intensity returning to his eyes. "Don't you listen? His name is Danny, you fuckin' fruit, not Charlie."

"Sure, sorry," replied James, putting his head back down. But he could feel The Drill still staring at him and so James glanced up to see a fresh look of curiosity on his face.

"You know what these pheasants are?" asked The Drill at last, pointing to the illustration of the bird before him, pronouncing "pheasants" with a "p"—like "peasants."

"You say 'pheasants'—like the word starts with the letter 'f,' not 'p,' and they're birds, kinda like chickens. They serve them in fancy restaurants."

James expected to see some form of appreciation in The Drill's eyes, but to his horror saw the exact opposite. He had thought he was having his first meaningful conversation, some sharing of experience with another human being in a similar fucked up situation, but those eyes told him he was wrong. The next thing he knew, The Drill was on his feet. He moved so swiftly for a man of his bulk that James barely had time to lift his arms in defense before he felt the sharp, searing sting of

The Drill's right hand slapping him upward, diagonally, across the right-hand side of his face.

"The next time you tell me how to read I'll rip your fucking head off," he said, James barely able to hear him above the hot, thumping beat of his heart. "If I say it's 'p' then it's 'p,' you pucking frick."

And then The Drill smiled at his own joke.

"God help me," said James at last.

And then he began to cry.

55

Kwon Si was in a most unfortunate predicament. It had been a difficult day. Production was at an all time high but his men were tired and hungry and increasingly ill at ease. He was counting the moments before he might leave this place of disquiet and seek refuge in the comfort of his home, until this evening's call brought a most unsettling communication that was, while unexpected, almost inevitable given the recent escalation of restlessness amongst his exhausted employees. He could almost feel the handpiece of the telephone vibrate as he shifted it away from his ear, cowering from the lifeless piece of plastic that seemed to shake with the spirit of a man who was located some thousands of miles away in a city where the sun was only just starting to rise.

"How did this happen," yelled Peter Nagoshi down the phone.

"I told you, Mr. Nagoshi. I do not know."

"It is your duty to know," countered the voice. "You are the manager. I do not accept your denial."

Kwon hesitated then, wondering if perhaps, at least on this occasion, honesty was the safest option. "There has been some unrest. Work continues, but the men are burdened."

"What unrest?" asked Peter.

"Some talk, some expressions of displeasure regarding the working conditions, the pay."

"If a man complains I want you to fire him, Mr. Kwon. The workers are amoebas and easily replaced."

Even Kwon, who was all for pleasing management in the interests of personal advancement, took offense at this latest observation. His men were hard workers, and they toiled under difficult conditions for a mere pittance.

"It is not just the working conditions, Mr. Nagoshi. There

have been some questions regarding Mr. Lim and his untimely death."

"The man was stupid enough to electrocute himself, Mr. Kwon. I am sure the only reason he had not managed to do this to himself at home was because his hovel most likely has no electricity."

Kwon cringed. "His brother is one of the workers devoted to engine development," he said. "He is educated and he is angry. He has many friends—those willing to listen to his suspicions that Mr. Lim was taken before his time. The family are Taoists. They follow the art of *wu wei,* which is to let nature take its course, and there is some suggestion Mr. Lim's course was ended by unnatural means."

"Ancient Chinese superstition. I will hear no more of this. Insubordination will be met with loss of jobs. Do I make myself clear?"

"Yes," said Kwon at last. There was a pause, as Mr. Kwon prepared himself for his orders.

"You must find out who betrayed us and relieve them of their employ," Peter Nagoshi began. "And then . . . then you must triple your efforts, Mr. Kwon. The only way to salvage this disastrous situation is to bring our deadline forward and further reduce the cost of production. If we can cut our bottom line we can release the 'Dream' early and at a cheaper price. Then we can, as the Americans like to say, head our competitors off at the passage."

"What passage, Mr. Nagoshi?" asked Kwon.

"It is a stupid Hollywoodism, Mr. Kwon. Something to do with cowboys and Indians."

Kwon said nothing.

"Are you listening, Mr. Kwon?" pushed Nagoshi.

"Yes, sir. We shall do our best, but my men are exhausted. We will need some time to . . ."

"You have a week, Mr. Kwon, after that the plant shall exist no more. I can only delay my father so far. His lawyers have his ear and they fill it with the weakness of panic. If you do not succeed he will move my plant to Japan. Your men will die breaking their backs in the slime of their stinking rice fields and you shall, well, to be honest, Mr. Kwon, I could not care what you should do."

"I understand," said Kwon, feeling the rise of resentment in his throat.

"Good."

Seconds later a weary Kwon hung up the phone and rose from his dirty plastic chair, scraping its scratched metal legs across the harsh concrete floor. His perch high above the factory floor used to give him a feeling of satisfaction. He felt big despite his small stature, clever despite his having left school at age ten, and perhaps more importantly, responsible for a troop of dedicated workers toiling toward a common goal.

But more and more over the past months, his eagle-eye view of the world had started to sour. His muscles had begun to shrink as his brow was beaten by a man half his age with all the compassion of a cobra. But Mr. Kwon was not stupid. He had learned much from his hardworking parents, about honor amidst oppression, and strength in the shadow of tyranny.

He moved toward the window to look down upon the factory floor beneath him. There were sixty, perhaps seventy, men still sweating, still toiling, a physical eternity since their arrival some thirteen hours ago. Many were thin and tired, their grease-covered bodies heavy with burden. They were too young and too old, too pale, too weak. And in that moment Kwon Si knew what he had to do.

He found the number in his personal diary. Something had made him write it down all those months ago when the false sun of greed had blinded him to the oncoming storm. He reached to his left to pick up the phone, clearing his throat as he extended his narrow pointer finger to punch in the thirteen digit figure.

To his surprise, the voice answered immediately. It was young and foggy as if it had been pulled from sleep by a secret ready to reveal itself at last.

"Mr. Jones," said Kwon.

"This is Sawyer Jones."

"My name is Kwon Si. I am calling from Guangdong. I work for . . ."

"I know who you work for," said the boy, now awake. "How can I help you, Mr. Kwon?"

"I . . ." Kwon hesitated. "I need to speak with you and your comrades at Solidarity Global, about my . . . about our situation here."

"It's all right Mr. Kwon. I understand your predicament, and I realize how hard it must have been for you to make this call. But I think perhaps you are a man of honor, Mr. Kwon, and believe me when I tell you we will help you in any way that we can."

And then there was a pause.

"Are you at work, Mr. Kwon?"

"Yes."

"Are you alone?"

"Yes."

"You need to go home, Mr. Kwon, and I shall call you there."

"Do you think this phone might be . . . ?"

"Perhaps. It has happened before."

"Oh . . . I . . . This is not safe for me or my workers."

"Give me your home number, Mr. Kwon. Go home and then we shall talk."

"Yes."

"But," Jones started, obviously anxious to ask one further question before the shield of secrecy was set. "One more thing, Mr. Kwon, I need you to think about the question I am going to ask you and I need you to answer me a simple yes or no. Do you understand?"

"Yes."

"I need to ask about one of your men, or rather a man who used to work for you." Jones stopped there, obviously not wanting to compromise Kwon's situation any further.

"Accidents are not always as they seem, Mr. Jones," answered Kwon as cryptically as he could, given his limited grasp of English nuances and overall fear for his safety. "A flame went out before it reached the end of its wick, Mr. Jones, and now there are many questions as to who blew out the candle."

"I understand, Mr. Kwon," said Jones. "I want you to get in your car and . . ."

"I have no car."

"What?"

"You see the irony," said Kwon. "I manage an automobile

plant and I have no automobile. I cannot afford one, Mr. Jones I have a wife and five children."

"So how do you get home, and how long does it take?"

"I walk, Mr. Jones, and it takes me a little under an hour and a half."

"Give me your number," said Jones, and Kwon could hear the shuffle as the young American obviously sought out a pen and some paper. "I shall call you in exactly ninety minutes. I promise."

56

Breakfast in the Mannix house was pure bedlam. It reminded David of his youth—as one of three scruffy-haired kids clanging plates and spilling juice and arguing over who would get the plastic toy at the bottom of the Cheerios packet, all in the manic confines of the Cavanaughs' tiny Newark kitchen.

They had tried to reach Joe last night, but it had been Marie Mannix's birthday and part of Joe's present to her was his promise to turn off his cell phone while he took her out to their favorite Italian local. And so David left a message and early this morning was woken with an invitation to join Frank McKay at the Mannix household for this frenetic family feast.

David dived across the table, beating Gabriel to the fast diminishing box of Frosted Flakes.

"Aha," said David.

"No way," smiled nine-year-old Gabe.

"You can have the Raisin Bran," laughed David.

"Raisin Bran sucks," said Gabe.

"Yeah, Raisin Bran sucks," repeated his younger brother Michael, causing Marie to kick the dishwasher door shut with her foot while reaching across the table and grabbing the Frosted Flakes from David's hand and passing them to Frank.

"Frank gets the Flakes for being so polite," she smiled. "And the rest of you . . ."

"We know," said David. "Raisin Bran."

Fifteen minutes later Marie had managed to pack the four boys into the family SUV, leaving Joe, Frank and David to clean up the kitchen and catch a few moments of privacy before the chaos of the day began. David knew he would have to be careful, not because he did not trust the two men currently stacking plates in the cupboards beside him, but because he *did* trust them, and respect them, and wanted to avoid jamming them into a professional corner at all costs.

"Coffee?" asked Joe at last, shutting the pantry door.

"Sure," said David.

"And I'll make myself a tea," said Frank. "Two bags, if that's okay, Chief. Something tells me whatever Cavanaugh has to say to us this morning calls for the strong stuff."

"Knock yourself out," said Joe, tossing Frank two generic brand tea bags before turning back to David. "All right, David. Let's hear it."

And so he began, starting with his chat with the Mathesons, Jed's parting gift following yesterday's police search, and finally getting to Sawyer Jones' recording of Katz's confidential conversation. He told them of the content of both recordings—of Westinghouse's lament, and of Roger Katz's gratitude to Simpson for delivering some evidence the prosecutor had intended "saving for trial."

"He's a criminal," said David. "The ADA is under a legal obligation to disclose any evidence relating to . . ."

"Hold on," interrupted Joe as he rose from his seat. The kettle was boiling and had started to scream. "You know as well as I do that the two pieces of evidence you just described were obtained illegally. And any evidence you discover as a result of such findings are fruit from the poisonous tree—inadmissible."

Joe was right. According to Massachusetts law, the "exclusionary rule" prohibits the use in criminal proceedings of any evidence obtained illegally.

"I know," said David. "And I'm not looking for any favors, Joe. But I am asking you guys to hang up your badges for a few moments so I can tell you the theory that goes along with those recordings. And then, if you think I'm crazy or clutching at straws, you can kick me out or better still ring the ADA and tell him I was as good as standing next to him outside his precious grand jury hearing when he conspired to entrap my client."

Joe gave him a half smile. "That thing with recording the Kat—illegal as all hell but . . ."

"I know," grinned David. "Inspired, wasn't it?"

And Joe nodded.

David smiled. "Okay," he said at last. "Let me give it to you straight."

. . .

"Don't worry, Sawyer," said Sara as she turned left off Baker and onto Spring and headed south toward Joe's house in West Roxbury. As soon as Sawyer had hung up the call a half hour earlier, she had jumped in her car and headed to Wellesley, thanking God for the light early morning traffic and the fact that David was already at Joe's.

"You did the right thing in calling me. We'll make it to Joe's in time. I promise."

Sawyer looked at his watch. "I know. It's just that . . . I don't think Lieutenant Mannix is one of my biggest fans."

"Joe's a good guy, Sawyer. He can be trusted. This is not a time to play coy. If you are going to have a conversation with Mr. Kwon I want someone like Mannix in the room."

Sawyer didn't seem convinced.

"Listen to me, Sawyer, recording ADA Katz's conversation yesterday was a stroke of genius, but as valuable as that information may be, it was recorded illegally which means we cannot use it in court. So now we have to cover our bases. *Shit!*" she added, banging her palm on the steering wheel as she caught a red on Center Street. "Joe should be able to record the call to Mr. Kwon—legally. He can also help you phrase your questions, get as much information as possible without . . ."

"Scaring poor Mr. Kwon half to death," finished Sawyer, shaking his head, his mop of hair moving with him before finally settling in a mass on his forehead. "He didn't volunteer to be a witness in a murder investigation, Sara," he said, lifting his hand to shove the mop back in frustration. "The man is terrified. He came to me for help."

Sara stole a look at the jittery young man beside her as she turned onto Joe's tree-lined street. He looked so pale, so childlike. And in that moment she felt a sliver of guilt steal into her stomach—guilt for using this kid and his altruistic motives for solving their case.

"Look, Sawyer," she said as she pulled into Joe's red paved driveway, stopping short of a red BMX bike that stood at a diagonal to the whitewashed garage door. "I know this feels like we are using Mr. Kwon's misfortune for our gain. But don't you see? Mr. Kwon, Mr. Lim, Jessica, even James, if you are right about this China thing, then they all could be victims of the same evil—Peter Nagoshi."

Sawyer nodded, but it was a halfhearted effort, and so she turned to take his hand, feeling an overwhelming need to comfort him, just as she had done for her own little brother hundreds of times, what now seemed like just as many years ago.

And when she did, when she reached out to touch him, he took her hand so swiftly, so completely that it took her by surprise. And in that moment she saw in his eyes complete sadness, complete loneliness, an all-consuming hunger for affection. She felt his pulse beneath his skin as his hot clammy hands held to hers, and he lifted his eyes to say: "I am not as confident as most people think, Sara."

She squeezed his hand. "That's okay, Sawyer. Neither am I. But maybe with the two of us put together?" she smiled.

Sawyer took a deep breath and released his grip, slowly, deliberately, before sitting up in his seat and placing his hand on the door handle. "I'm ready," he said. "I can do this, Sara."

"I know, Sawyer. I know."

57

Joe did not know what to make of it. His coffee was bitter, cold—in fact, he had not taken a sip since David uttered the words: "We think H. Edgar Simpson murdered Jessica Nagoshi."

Mannix looked across at McKay, expecting him to be just as shocked, but oddly enough Joe saw no indication of surprise in his partner's eyes. On the contrary he saw an expression of resolution, like Frank had suspected the arrogant son of a bitch from the get-go.

"David," Joe began, "I am not saying your argument doesn't have merit, but it seems to me you are giving this kid too much credit. You're saying a young man barely into his twenties perpetrated the almost perfect crime."

"The fucker's smart, Chief," said Frank.

"But, hopefully, not smart enough," said David, obviously relieved the two men did not discount his theory outright.

Joe shook his head. "It just seems so contrived, so tidy. I mean, the kid gets to walk *and* a reward for his troubles?"

"And, perhaps more importantly, the personal kudos of pulling it off," said David.

Joe paused there, taking it all in, shifting his chair slightly to his left, away from the early morning glare that now flooded through the eastern windows, casting long, tall shadows across the gray laminate floor.

"There are too many unanswered questions," he went on at last. "Like how did a kid like Simpson manage to clobber the girl with such force—using both of his scrawny Ivy League never-seen-a-day's-work-in-his-entire-life arms in the process?"

"If the kid was angry enough, he could do it and more," said

David. "You've seen it a hundred times, Joe, what the power of rage can do to an average sized killer."

"Witnesses told us he was drunk," countered Joe, "barely walking when he left the Lincoln."

"That was at one," said David, balancing his argument once more. "And Gus estimated Jessica's time of death as three. He had two hours to sober up, to let the adrenaline of fury seethe through his veins."

"How did he get from Chestnut Hill to Wellesley?"

"A taxi dropped him a few blocks away, or maybe he was sober enough to drive? We can check on the cab thing, and see if anyone saw a car matching the description of whatever Simpson drives in the vicinity of the Nagoshi estate."

"He left no physical evidence," said Joe, grabbing his mug for another sip of the cold caffeine.

"Didn't he?" asked David, leaning in to the table now. "You said Leo's FBI pals came back with two unidentified prints. Maybe they belong to Simpson? Maybe they put him right there at the crime scene? Maybe Simpson has a pair of size eleven Nikes that do the same?"

"Somehow I don't think so," said Frank. "If this murder was premeditated the kid would have been wearing gloves—and he would have ditched the shoes. Simpson is too smart for that."

"Unless he was still a little hazy," argued David. "And angry enough to let the details slip."

There was silence then, as David looked to Joe, perhaps hoping for some sign that what he was proposing was possible.

"Look, Joe, just think about this for a second," David went on. "I may not have been in the room when Leo's profiler gave his report but my guess is it went something like this: young, white male—angry, emotional."

"But controlled and organized," added Frank, who *had* read Special Agent Jacobs' report, "to the point of being meticulous."

Joe was starting to see it then—starting to see *him,* Simpson, sliding into Jacobs' hypothetical perpetrator's shoes.

"The crime scene was clean, boss," said Frank, now rolling up his shirtsleeves and resting his elbows on the table. "Which Jacobs' suggested mirrored the perp's personality. And Simpson is one tidy little fucker. His clothes ironed within an inch of their country club lives, not one hair out of place on his Howdy Doody head. Jacobs said the offender would be sanitary, neat . . ."

"Confident, adaptable, intelligent," finished Joe, now quoting from Jacobs' report.

Joe looked at David then, and saw that his friend was convinced of the Simpson kid's guilt—and that alone told Joe this was worth investigating further. David's argument was a reasonable one, after all. Joe had done his best to punch holes in David's theory, a strategy he utilized more for David's sake than anyone else's. But no matter what Joe threw up, David's answers had been sound, logical—and, more to the point, one hundred percent arguable in a criminal court of law.

Bottom line, if David was right, Simpson was literally laughing all the way to the bank, while his "friend" was wearing a red monkey suit up at the Hotel County Lockup. And that wasn't something Mannix could live with, not now, not ever.

"Okay," he said at last. "The kid is a possibility." He noticed David's shoulders relax a little. "But your theory has one big fat hole in the form of motive. Your client was her lover—and lover quarrels have been known to lead to violence. But why in the hell would H. Edgar kill the girl? Why would he murder his best friend's lover in a fit of uncontrollable rage?"

"I've thought about that," said David, now sitting back in his chair. "In fact, I have thought of nothing else for the past twelve hours. And the way I figure it, there are two possible theories, both of which amount to probable cause."

"All right, Cavanaugh," said Frank at last, scooping the dregs of sugar out of the bottom of his Buzz Lightyear mug with a too-big dessert spoon. "Don't leave us hanging here. Tell us why the young genius risked his oh-so-brilliant future by bludgeoning a young girl to death? Why did he do it, David? Why did he squeeze that girl's neck until it snapped like a twig in a vice?"

"Because he was jealous, Frank, because he wanted what James had—Jessica Nagoshi, bright, beautiful and connected."

"So he pops the girl because—if he can't have her, no one can?" said Frank, obviously not agreeing with the theory.

"I see where you are going here, David," said Joe. "But to be honest I just don't buy it. I've seen a lot of lovesick perps in my time and believe me, this Simpson kid is not one of them. I'd be willing to bet the kid never dated a girl in his whole superior life. So if your first motive is jealousy I . . ."

"No—*both* my motives are jealousy," corrected David, looking his friend straight in the eye. And then Joe saw it, crisp and clear, as the fog that surrounded Jessica Nagoshi's murder lifted like the condensation in that stinking greenhouse, all those weeks ago.

"You think Simpson is in love with Matheson," he said at last. "You think he killed Jessica because he wanted the boy to himself."

David gave the slightest of nods.

"Fuck," said Joe.

"I know," said David.

"Homer is a homo," said Frank, looking up at his boss. "Now *that* I can see."

• • •

The rap on the door was hard and fast, the sharp successive knocks acting like little punctuation marks to Frank's final comment.

"Marie?" asked Frank.

"No. She has her key," said Joe, wondering who the hell it might be. He moved down the corridor toward the door, David and Frank standing from their seats and following him out into the green carpeted hallway out of some instinctive back up re-action.

Joe looked through the peephole and released the tension in his shoulders. He opened the door quickly to stare at the un-likely pair before him.

"Sara," he said in surprise. "David didn't tell me you were coming."

"That's because he didn't know," she replied.

"Lieutenant," said Sawyer, to which Joe responded *"Jones,"* more in recognition than in welcome.

"Sara," said David, now moving down the hallway. "What's wrong. Are you . . . ?"

"David, I want you to meet Sawyer Jones," she said, moving aside so that the two might shake hands.

"Mr. Cavanaugh," said Sawyer, taking David's hand, and

Mannix noticed the kid squeezed so hard that the blood drained completely from David's fingers.

"What's going on here?" asked David, releasing his hand and shaking it slightly before looking at Sara.

"Can we come in?" she asked, holding up her hand as if to say she would explain things in a moment. "We don't have much time."

"Sure," said Joe, reading the urgency in her voice as he stepped back to allow them into the hall. "Come on into the kitchen. I was just about to make some fresh coffee."

"I'm sorry, Joe," said Sara, grabbing his arm. "There's no time. Sawyer has to make a phone call and we need you and Frank," she said, nodding at McKay, "listening in as witnesses."

"I'm sorry," she said again, this time looking toward a now obviously confused David. "I was going to call ahead but I left my cell in the apartment and there was no time. About an hour and a half ago a Mr. Kwon Si, foreman of the Nagoshis' automobile plant in China, contacted Sawyer regarding his situation at the Guangdong factory." The three men said nothing so Sara went on.

"We believe—I mean, Sawyer and I think that Mr. Kwon wants to discuss the working conditions of his employees and more specifically . . . the recent death of Mr. Lim."

"Shit," said Frank, making the connection.

"Hold on," said David, determined to catch up. "Lim—isn't he the man who . . ."

"That's right," she said. "Mr. Lim died in a factory accident the day after he called Sawyer and asked for Solidarity Global's help. He was the same man who spoke to Jessica Nagoshi the morning before she died."

"You think this Kwon is going to rat on the Nagoshi kid?" said Joe at last, cutting to the chase. "You think he'll link Peter Nagoshi to this Lim's death, and to . . ."

"Yes, Lieutenant, I do," said Jones looking at Sara, and in that moment Joe got a sense that the kid drew a great deal of strength from her support. "I have spoken with the downtrodden many times, Lieutenant, and have become pretty good at gauging when they have had enough—when they *need* to tell the truth.

"Mr. Kwon knows more than he was able to say in our brief conversation this morning. But I believe—no, I *know*, that I can get him to tell me everything he knows, about Peter Nagoshi, about Mr. Lim, and perhaps even about Jess."

No one said anything for several long moments.

"What time did you say you'd call?" asked Joe at last.

"Eight a.m. our time," answered Sawyer.

Joe looked at his watch. It was 7:56 a.m.

"Come with me," he said, grabbing Jones by the arm and pulling him inside. "Frank, call George in audio and get him to open a record on my home line." Frank nodded.

"We have three minutes, kid, so for once in your life I need you to sit down, shut up and listen. If what you say is true, my guess is we may only have one shot at this. Understand?"

"Yes, Lieutenant," said Jones, and once again Joe got the sense this bravado was for Sara's benefit. "You can trust me, Lieutenant. Just tell me what you want me to do."

58

Heath Westinghouse hung up his cell. It had been a stupid idea.

What was I thinking? he said to himself as he drained his extra strong espresso in the corner of the Law School common room, a cranny he now seemed to be coveting, a good thirty feet from the center of the room where he and his two best friends used to hold court. *Did I honestly think that I could just call James at his new residence and shoot the breeze about— oh, I don't know—how I ratted him out to the cops and fucked his life over?*

But that's what he had done—well, actually he was guilty on both counts, fucking his friend over and then being stupid enough call Suffolk County Jail and ask to speak to James like he was still living a few miles east. His question had been met with a sigh by some bored telephone operator before she offered a response that went something like: *"I am sorry, sir, we do not permit detainees to leave their cells and just wander over to the phone willy-nilly,"* which had been followed by some spiel about visiting hours, a derogatory laugh and the long slow beep of a hang-up. It was a jail not a fucking resort. What a bloody idiot.

The truth was, his latest conversation with H. Edgar had made him sick to his stomach. So much so that he made up some bullshit about having a private meeting with Professor Novak so as to avoid going to a Corporate Finance tutorial with him this morning. First up, he had no idea that H. Edgar was gonna pull that "new evidence" stunt to the ADA yesterday and he was seriously pissed that his friend had not given him a heads-up in advance. Heath had no idea what H. Edgar was talking about, and now that Katz had told Simpson he wasn't to speak of it, H. Edgar had yet another excuse to keep Heath in the dark. Finally, and worst of all, H. Edgar had sat here, across from him, mere moments ago and uttered the unimaginable—that *James had done it*! That he had killed Jessica Nagoshi. That he had fooled them all along. That he had *used* them in some pathetic attempt to try to get himself off. And that Heath had better wise up and accept the fact their best friend was a fucking Menendez brother in disguise.

But no matter which way Heath looked at it, it just didn't make sense. Why the hell would James ask them to turn him in if he was guilty? He wouldn't, of course. So now Heath was thinking that maybe something else had been going down from the beginning, and maybe, just maybe, James wasn't the only one being played in this confusing little game of "piggy in the middle." Heath shook his head, trying to clear the fog. Lately, with James out of the picture, he had got the feeling the whole university had started to look at him differently. And the view they were consuming wasn't exactly one you'd run on the cover of a *Forbes* 500 issue. And so maybe it was time he started looking after his own backyard, and after James' as well, considering he was in no position to tend it himself.

If the mountain can't come to Mohammad, then Mohammad needs to get his fucking shoes on, he said to himself then. The operator at County lockup had told him visiting hours were Sundays at two—and so, this coming weekend, he would go and see James and find out the truth for himself.

59

It was cold out. David knew this because as he sat in Joe's now crowded living room, the Jones kid directly across from him in front of the north-facing window, he could see the slightest trace of icicles forming at the corners of the glass outside, framing Sawyer's head like some sort of crystal blue halo.

"Don't be nervous," said David, at last feeling the need to say something after Sara had left the room to get Sawyer a coffee, and Joe and Frank had formed a last minute cop-to-cop huddle in the corner of the room. "You're a smart kid, Sawyer, and Mr. Kwon obviously trusts you."

It was a lame attempt at reassurance, but the best he could come up with.

"Sara told me you only represent people who you think are innocent," said Sawyer, the statement catching David by surprise.

"Ah, yeah," said David, not knowing what else to say.

"How do you know?" asked Sawyer, his eyes now wide and inquiring, the blue light behind him now bouncing off his shiny young face.

"Well," said David, looking directly into his big brown eyes, "I guess I trust my instincts. I weigh up what my client tells me against the prosecution's evidence and, in the end, I go with my gut."

"Doesn't sound like legal logic to me," said Sawyer, his face now relaxing into a smile.

"Me neither," said David, smiling in return.

David knew how Sara felt about this kid, and despite Mannix's reservations, was relieved to find himself thinking that perhaps Sara might have been right after all. Maybe Jones really was genuine in his attempt to help others, and the overconfident façade described by Joe was just that—an identity he had given himself to prevent being singled out for less appealing reasons.

David guessed that young Sawyer Jones had known he was different pretty much since he was able to communicate. And he had more than likely chosen his own "arrogant crusader" persona so as not to be labeled with some less socially acceptable moniker like "intellectual freak" or "annoying geek." He had also noticed the way he looked at Sara, and guessed that the last time Sawyer got close to having a girlfriend was when he held hands with his cousin in his backyard sandpit.

"It's time," said Mannix, appearing above Sawyer with the telephone. "Just do exactly as we discussed. Keep it slow and easy. You'll be on speaker so if Frank or I think of anything else you should ask, we'll write the question on this pad." Joe signaled at the notebook beside the phone.

"Remember, you are under a legal obligation to tell Mr. Kwon the conversation is being taped, but you must stress the recording will not leave the possession of the Boston PD. In other words, you have to make sure he knows the Nagoshis will never learn of this conversation and our only aim is to protect him and his workers—and to find out who was responsible for Mr. Lim's death." Joe took a breath, perhaps wondering if Jones was up to this. "You got it, kid?"

"Yeah," said Jones, now glancing up at Sara who had returned from the kitchen to place an encouraging hand on his shoulder. "I got it."

And then Sara took a seat next to David as Sawyer dialed the number and Joe and Frank hovered above him. They heard the line ring and a man pick up and Sawyer take a long, deep breath . . . to begin.

. . .

"Mr. Kwon," he said.

"Yes," said the clipped, accented tone in reply.

"Thank you for agreeing to take my call. I understand how difficult this is for you, but I can assure you, I only want to help you, Mr. Kwon, you and your employees."

Kwon said nothing so Sawyer took a breath.

"Mr. Kwon, I need to tell you something before we begin and I need you to know that what I am about to explain has been organized in your best interests—for your protection."

"I do not understand," said Kwon, and Sawyer could already hear the hesitancy in the Chinese manager's voice. Sawyer knew he needed to keep him on the line, not just for the police but because this man had come to him for help. If he lost him now, after months of trying to emancipate the Nagoshi workers in Guangdong, he would never be able to forgive himself.

"The police are here, Mr. Kwon, the Boston police. I am afraid they fear that what has been occurring at your plant—and perhaps even the circumstances around Mr. Lim's death—may also be related to the death of Mr. Nagoshi's daughter." Sawyer could almost feel Kwon recoil, so he pushed on, trying to keep the connection alive.

"Please, Mr. Kwon, you have to understand, if two lives have been lost, if this is the way Peter Nagoshi operates, then this is just the beginning. You owe it to your workers, to yourself and your family, Mr. Kwon, to be honest, to clear your conscience, to tell the truth as you know it. We will make sure you are safe, for as it stands, if what you began to tell me this morning is true, you have little choice."

There was a pause.

"I . . ." began Kwon, obviously still unsure.

And so then Sawyer said the only thing he could say, the only thing that would scare Kwon enough to keep him on the line, and tell them all what they needed to know. "Peter Nagoshi may have killed his sister, Mr. Kwon, and if you do not believe me when I tell you this, I shall be happy to hand you over to Boston's Chief of Homicide who shall spare no details in describing the grisly details of her death.

"So think, Mr. Kwon, ask yourself in all honesty, if you think Peter Nagoshi would lose one second of sleep if your blood or that of your workers were added to the smears already present on his young and ambitious hands. No, sir, I am afraid every second you procrastinate you are taking another step down the road of no return. You have come this far, Mr. Kwon, do not make the wrong decision now."

And then there was silence, deathly silence as Sawyer closed his eyes and swallowed the bile that had risen in his throat, half of him hoping what he had just said was enough to reach the terrified Chinese foreman, and the other praying God would forgive him for using this poor man in this game of deception and lies.

"All right," said Kwon at last, and Sawyer felt the strange sensation of relief and anticipation and guilt wash over him all at the very same time.

"I will talk to you, Mr. Jones. I will even urge my coworkers to do the same. But you must not betray us, for Guangdong is a long way from Boston, and I fear that Peter Nagoshi is a man who lives in many places, and is ready to destroy all who stand in his way."

• • •

While all in the room were hoping Mr. Kwon would shed some light on Peter Nagoshi's operations in China, while all were praying the anxious Chinese overseer would help them make a link between Peter's business activities and his sister's death, none of them were prepared for the extent of Mr. Kwon's revelations as to the magnitude of the Nagoshi son's ambition, and the lengths he would go to assure his own success.

Were the Nagoshi workers underpaid? Yes. Were they overworked? Without question. Were they intimidated, downtrodden, abused even? Most certainly. Mr. Kwon told Sawyer how the Guangdong operation had been Peter's "offspring" from the very beginning, how he had built the plant under his father's directive but then, left to his own devices, cut costs, extended working hours, demanded significant lifts in production and set harsh, unreasonable deadlines regarding the production of the new Nagoshi "Dream." He then told them of the death of Mr. Lim, following rumors he had started to complain, first to his fellow workers and then to outside groups such as Solidarity Global.

"Late one night, not long before Mr. Lim's death, Peter Nagoshi asked me about Mr. Lim," Mr. Kwon had told Sawyer. "He asked if he was a *bèi pàn*—a traitor. I told him he was one of the older workers, a respected elder who had expressed some concern for the tiredness of his comrades." Days later, Kwon explained, Mr. Lim's brother, Mr. Lim the younger, concerned his older sibling had not yet returned from work, went back to the plant late, to find his brother dead, in the corner of the plant's extensive pit—electrocuted by the main switch of the generator.

"There is a cleaning tub in the back workroom, where the men wash parts to remove grease and residue," Kwon had said.

"Mr. Lim often worked at the tub, cleaning parts for the mechanics. The pit itself contains many electrical devices, on shelves in and around the main floor. But the safety switch on the main generator was always in place to prevent any accident from occurring."

Mr. Kwon went on to explain that when Mr. Lim was found, literally fried by the massive surge of voltage, his tarred body slumped over the water tank, a drill was discovered at the base of the large oval-shaped tub.

"The drill was connected to the main power source," Kwon had continued. "And the source was operational, as the safety switch on the main generator had been disabled."

"Is it easy to disable the switch?" Sawyer had asked.

"Yes and no. You would have to walk out to the main power board to accomplish this task," Kwon had answered. "But once there, it is literally a flick. You see?"

"Yes," Sawyer had said, looking up at the four stunned faces above him. "We see."

And so, Kwon had explained, the rumors had begun. The tales of a *yāo* or devil in their midst, the same *yāo* who was working them to the bone and robbing their children of the food they were promised when they left their paddy fields to toil for the Westerner with the Asian face.

Finally Sawyer had asked Mr. Kwon—why now? Why had Mr. Kwon made the decision to step forward and tell what he knew? And Mr. Kwon told him how Peter Nagoshi's worst fears had been realized, that the "Dream" was no longer a much anticipated industry secret but a victim of technological theft.

"He believes one of my workers sold the specifications for the 'Dream' to a competitor, and—to be truthful with you Mr. Jones—he is mostly likely correct. But that is what you get when you treat men like dogs.

"And so now we are out of time, Mr. Jones," Kwon continued, his voice low and resolute. "We cannot save this plant and, deep down, I believe Peter Nagoshi knows this also. He is not a man to discriminate, Mr. Jones. If he does not discover who sabotaged his 'Dream,' figuratively and literally, he will not hesitate to act on the principles of widespread retribution."

Kwon had paused there, before taking a breath to share one final observation.

"And so, Mr. Jones, if you tell me Peter Nagoshi's sister stood in his way, and that he killed her as punishment for the inconvenience, then in all honesty, my eyes do not blink. I will help you if I can, Mr. Jones, but I ask that you move quickly, for I fear that time is not on our side and the darkness of reprisal continues to creep across our souls, slowly, surely, each and every second of each and every day."

• • •

The air in the room was thick, heavy, stifling. Joe moved to the window, raising it just a notch—the gap wide enough to cool the tension with a welcome icy breeze but narrow enough to prevent the whipping November sleet from entering the cluttered space that was the Mannix family living room.

"One thing's for sure," said Joe as soon as Sawyer had agreed to leave the room. "That kid is one for the books.

"I told you he was on our side, Joe," said Sara.

"Well, I wouldn't want him as an enemy," said Frank.

"So what next?" said David, bringing them back on course. "I know we should be grateful, having two viable suspects instead of one but . . ."

"Three," interrupted Joe, knowing it had to be said. "I'm sorry, David, but you can't overlook the fact that Matheson is still top of the suspect list, at least in the eyes of the law. We may know what we know, or at least what we think we know, but we can't forget the evidence against your client was enough to convince a judge of probable cause, and a grand jury of voting in favor of issuing an indictment."

Joe saw the disappointment on his friend's face, a disappointment tinged with the knowledge that what he said was true. "I'm not saying these new theories don't make sense," he went on. "But at this stage that is all they are—theories. Whereas your client is the one with his name on the rap sheet and the ADA is determined to make it stick."

David nodded, the cool air now whipping across the room, lifting his sandy-colored hair off his hot, shiny brow.

"You're right, Joe, but in the very least you have to admit that after today we have a whole new field to play on. No matter which way you look at it, Simpson is a bona fide suspect, with an intellect superior enough to pull it off.

"And then we have Peter Nagoshi, who . . ." David paused, a recent memory now forcing its way into his consciousness. "It was some form of martial arts," he said at last.

"Come again?" said Sara.

"The night of the Halloween Ball, when Nagoshi attacked James." David stood to lift his two arms in the air. *"Whoosh,"* he said. *"Whoosh, whoosh,"* he repeated, this time bringing his two arms down simultaneously at forty-five degree angles. "Remember?" he asked the group in front of him. "One blow to James' shoulder, the other to his cheek?"

"Two blows from different arms at opposite angles with equal force," Frank began, "in the shape of an 'X,' just like the indentations on Jessica Nagoshi's head. The guy has a temper, Chief. You remember what he was like when we told him about his sister's pregnancy. Burst out of his seat, yelled something in Japanese . . ."

"What was it he yelled again?" asked Joe, now wondering if this small detail might tell them something.

"Um . . . ," said Frank, now pulling at his forehead as if trying to draw the memory into his consciousness. "It was . . . Bita, Bato or . . ."

But Joe was already on his feet, grabbing the phone to call work and ask for a Japanese-American officer named Karl Sumi—who was on the line within seconds.

"Are you sure?" Joe asked after a pause, having inquired what the word might mean—before thanking Sumi and signing off and facing his friends once again.

"Baita," he said then. "When we told him his sister was pregnant, Peter Nagoshi got to his feet and yelled '*Baita*.'"

"So what does it mean?" asked Sara. "Is it some form of Japanese expletive?"

"Not exactly," said Joe. *"Baita* means prostitute—in other words, Peter Nagoshi was calling his sister a whore."

Joe lifted his head and turned to Frank. "We need to find out if Peter Nagoshi practices some sort of kick-ass karate, Frank. And we need to do it now."

Frank nodded, making a note in his notebook before looking up again.

"Okay," said David at last. "This is all progress but we cannot afford to get ahead of ourselves. None of this means anything without proof. Katz is a man on a mission and once he has his eye on the prize . . ."

"So if we are in this, we are in this together," said Joe, looking directly at David, needing to make the point. "You, me, Frank, Sara and even young POTUS-in-waiting out there," he added, gesturing toward the kitchen where Sawyer had been banished to make a fresh pot of coffee. "That means we take this slowly, carefully and keep each other informed."

"I know what you are saying, Joe," said David. "And I appreciate your offer to help. But as far as the ADA is concerned, this case is closed and any investigation you undertake will put your job in jeopardy. I was the one who lit this fire in the first place and . . ."

"No, David," interrupted Mannix, knowing where this was going. "All you did was identify the kid in a sketch," he said, trying to alleviate his friend's misplaced feelings of guilt. "Me and Frank, we're the ones who built the case against Matheson—his lies set the ball rolling and then all the little things started to add up. We did what we had to do, but that doesn't mean we sign out just because our report is filed and stamped.

"Simpson, Nagoshi . . . none of this stuff was ever meant to be discovered. But you and Sara and Jones out there found it. I will help you, David, because I could not live with myself if I didn't. And because this *is* our job," he said, gesturing at Frank. "This is what we do."

• • •

Moments later they were on their feet, the beginnings of a strategy in place. David knew that investigating Simpson and Nagoshi was not going to be easy—and his first priority was buying the team some time. While they did not want to see their client incarcerated any longer than necessary, they were more afraid of the consequences of going to trial without the evidence to back up their claims—claims that could ultimately identify the real killer and set their client free. Earlier in the week Katz had filed a motion for a speedy trial—no doubt motivated by the fear that DA Scaturro might return from leave and crash his perfect party for one. And while David had not disputed the motion at first, he was now determined to slow things down by filing a counter motion before the day was out.

"I need to see Stein," he said. "I want to voice my objections personally. That way, at the very least, I can gauge his views on timing and maybe get a feel for his preference for this year or the next."

Sara was off to see James. They had yet to discuss Westinghouse's "loaded" recording with their client and, as hard as it would be, she also needed to tell him about their latest suspicions regarding Peter Nagoshi and his friend, H. Edgar Simpson.

"This isn't going to be easy," she said. "No matter how low those boys stoop, James seems reluctant to see them for the traitors that they are."

"I know," said David. "But somehow we have to make him see just how much is at stake."

"Frank," said Joe at last. "Grab your jacket. You, me and young Mr. Jones here are heading out to Deane. Sawyer is gonna help us recover some evidence."

Sawyer, who had only just been summoned from his "holding cell" in the kitchen, looked more confused than ever. "*What* evidence? I thought this was about China? Why would I need to go to Deane?"

"We'll explain on the way," said Mannix, throwing the kid his sweater.

"It's all right, Sawyer," said Sara, slinging her handbag over her shoulder. "Just go with Joe. This is important."

"I . . . okay," said Sawyer, throwing on his oversized cable knit.

"Call me," said David, as Mannix went to retrieve his keys from a side table just inside the living room door.

"Same," said Joe in return.

"And Joe," said David, as they reached the front door, ready to brace themselves against the wind, to head down three different roads, having no idea where they would take them, "I just wanted to say . . ."

"No need," said Joe, pulling the door open to face a rush of leaves that swirled around their feet before sucking up toward their faces in a whirlwind of late morning chill. "Besides, since when did I require gratitude for an opportunity to kick the Kat?"

60

He was sitting in a closet. Well, not so much a closet as a maintenance room—a filthy four-by-four dust bucket that moaned with the cranks of an ancient heating system, which, having now examined its disgusting buildup dust and grime, H. Edgar decided was probably feeding the privileged students of Deane a decent dose of bacteria along with its decidedly dank hot air.

He was losing Westinghouse. He could sense it. His friend had avoided him all day, skipping lectures and failing to show at the university café for lunch. He was feeling shaky and needed a moment to think, away from the suspicious glances and poorly concealed whispers of his fellow students—and worse still—Deane's esteemed academia.

It was Katz who had convinced him to take a different tack. He had suggested that it was Simpson's good fortune that a man such as himself was leading the prosecution, because he was the best and could guarantee a conviction. He alluded to the fact that any lesser prosecutor might not have the balls to see this one through—to take on a rich kid like James, wealthy and connected, and nail his blue-blooded ass to the wall. And H. Edgar knew what he was saying, that a win for James would be social and career suicide for him and Westinghouse, as James would be seen as the innocent victor and he and Westinghouse as the two greedy bastards who sold their friend out for a measly mill apiece.

But while Katz was busy trying to keep H. Edgar on board he had not realized his argument was, in effect, doing the exact opposite. For H. Edgar was the prototype of wealthy, intellectually gifted, young America and any attack on James' "kind" was also an attack on his own. Worse still, H. Edgar knew he could not do this alone. What if Westinghouse decided to spill the beans? He certainly appeared to be reconsidering his role in all of this, and there was no doubt in H. Edgar's mind that his usually pliable friend was slowly drifting back into the camp that wanted to establish James' innocence.

And so . . . what to do? How was he to salvage his reputation, regain Westinghouse's trust, and reestablish their superiority in the process?

He needed to re-form the three, reunite them in a single cause, and place them ahead of Katz and every other fucking inferior who wrongly believed they could stamp out the power of the invincible young elite.

Think, he told himself as he took a short sharp breath, swearing he could feel the dirty particles of dust scratching at his trachea as they surged downward to swarm in his lungs like a pack of hungry bees.

And then it came to him, crisp and sweet and clear as a sunny winter's day. For if there was one fact H. Edgar knew to be true, if there was one cliché that superseded its delegation to formula, it was the adage that "Every man had his price"—or in this case, *"every woman."*

Yes, he said to himself, the idea was utter brilliance. Simpson's train had sped out of control, no doubt about it, but all he had to do now was pull the lever into reverse and send it right back to the beginning, exactly where he intended it to be.

■ ■ ■

Sara almost did not recognize him when he walked into the room. The right-hand side of his face looked like it had disappeared in a shadow, like he had painted it a dark shade of purple almost directly down the middle. His right cheek stuck out in a puckered stretch of flesh, his weeping pale green eye barely visible in a gully between the cheek and a protruding forehead. His brow was distorted at a misshapen angle that curved downward like a "V" as if pointing at the destruction below.

"Oh, my God," said Sara, rising from her gray vinyl chair to help him to his seat. "James, I . . . What the hell happened?"

James attempted a smile, which, considering the distension on the right-hand side of his face, looked more like a scowl than a shot at bravado.

"I had a run-in with Danny's dad." His words were almost

lost in their effort to negotiate the puffiness on the right side of his lips.

"I don't understand," said Sara, pulling out his seat and pouring him a glass of lukewarm water from the jug on the small metal table between them.

"Danny's old man objected to a little phonetics lesson I stupidly undertook in some misguided attempt to make a friend," he said. "Danny's dad is called The Drill. He didn't know that 'p' and 'h' put together make the sound of the letter 'f,' " he said, his teeth now slipping off his fat lower lip. "And I didn't know that Ivy League law student and big illiterate delinquent put together would make, well . . . this," he said, gesturing at his face.

"Oh, James, I am so sorry," she said, reaching across the table to take his hand. "Have you seen a doctor?"

"Yes. He gave me some aspirin. They said they were going to admit me to the infirmary. But I have to wait until a bed is cleared so . . ."

"Well, we'll report it," she said, scrambling for some piece of action that might make this situation "better." "This Drill will be reprimanded. If necessary we'll try to get you moved."

But James said nothing.

It was cold. The large rectangular whitewashed cinder blocks that made up the walls in the tiny visiting room made Sara feel like she was in an igloo—trapped in a blizzard a million miles from nowhere, where logic went out the window and reason came in the form of powerful uneducated criminals with names like "The Drill."

"Sara," James began. And then, within seconds, Sara felt his hand grow cold and wet with chill. "I need you to get me out of here," he said as he relaxed his grip. His one "good" eye seemed to be rolling into the back of his head. "Please . . . I am begging you. I cannot do this, Sara, I . . . ."

His body began to slouch as his head rolled to the right, the swelling seemingly forcing it down toward the table.

"James!" yelled Sara, getting to her feet.

And then James Matheson fainted, his body slipping off the chair like a dead man released from the confines of a noose.

• • •

David found him in the cafeteria.

He was sitting with his back to the main entranceway, his

long spine aligned with the back of the tall wooden chair upon which he sat, his long arms, elbows at right angles, negotiating the mountain of lunch before him.

"Mr. Cavanaugh," he said, and David wondered how the hell Judge Isaac Stein knew someone was approaching him from behind, or more to the point, how he knew it was him.

"Judge," said David, taking a breath.

Somehow, on the way to Government Center, David had convinced himself not to go in all guns blazing. He knew he had to fight tooth and nail for an extended preparation period and he also knew he could not tell the judge why. But more importantly he knew that Stein was not the type of man to be influenced by the raw, sentimental arguments of attorneys overcome with emotion. He demanded calm and logic, backed by a sound legal argument.

"Do you mind?" said David, gesturing at the seat across from the Superior Court stalwart.

"Be my guest," said Stein, pointing his fork at the chair.

"That looks very . . . ah . . . green," said David, nodding at the huge bowl of "leaves" before the obviously unenthusiastic judge.

"A garden salad," said Stein. "Which I suppose is an accurate description, given it undoubtedly came from a garden and there are no clauses in the legal definition of salad to preclude the insertion of weeds.

"My wife has me on a diet, Counselor," said the tall, thin Stein. "Not for the usual reasons, of course, but for my cholesterol—300 milligrams per deciliter of blood, at least 60 milligrams over what is apparently considered acceptable."

David nodded. "What about the pie?" he asked, as Stein pushed the greens aside and replaced them with a dessert, which he dragged into place with a fresh sense of satisfaction.

"Lemon meringue," said Stein, scooping a large fluff of white from the top of the cloudlike flan. "It's made from lemons, and lemons are grown in . . ."

"Gardens," finished David.

"My argument exactly," said the judge before lifting his gaze from his plate to look David squarely in the eye. "What is this about, Counselor?" he asked after a pause.

"The ADA's motion, Judge."

"Which one, Mr. Cavanaugh? I believe the industrious Mr.

Katz has filed several over the past two days. Sometimes, in the dark of night, I have this image of all these hardworking little elves working around the clock at the DA's office, preparing motions, issuing notices . . ."

"With Roger cracking the whip," added David sarcastically.

To which the judge just smiled.

"I need some time, Judge, to see this one through. It's already November and with this new, second charge . . ."

"The death of the child requires no further investigation, David. Sadly this is more a matter of legal semantics than anything else. Personhood, viability . . . the poor child is famous before he was even born, and his name, or lack thereof, will go down in history as precedent one way or the other."

"It's not just the feticide, Judge. You know the ADA has a personal agenda with this one, with Scaturro on leave and elections due next year."

"Ah . . . now there you go again," interrupted Stein, "always seeking an opinion from a man whose job depends on neutrality."

"He is railroading us, Judge, he wants to use this trial to launch his campaign for DA. This is not about the truth, it is about winning at all costs."

"And that's it?" asked Stein. "Your counter motion to a request for a speedy trial is based entirely on the ADA's supposed ambitions?"

David paused. He had too much respect for the man in front of him to lie, but too much riding on their secret investigations to tell him the truth.

"I see," said the judge when David failed to elaborate. "Son, I like to think I know you better than most, and therefore trust that what you have put to me today is not just some veiled attempt to buy some time so that you might clutch at some very thin straws."

David went to open his mouth, but Stein raised his fork, signaling that he was not finished.

"My eyes may not be as good as they used to be, but ironically, I have found that as the years of experience weigh upon you, your ability to see is replaced by your ability to *see*. Do you understand?" he asked.

David nodded, urging the judge to go on.

"ADA Katz is a man hell-bent on getting ahead, and on the surface, there is nothing wrong with that. However," he went on, "my elderly sense of vision allows me to look beyond the obvious and perhaps see things that bring a sour taste to my mouth."

The judge was at least acknowledging Katz's motives, and for this alone, David was grateful.

"But," Stein continued, "I am, as you know, a judge of the Suffolk County Superior Court and, as such, cannot even consider a counter motion based on the opinions of two like-minded men who sit here, surrounded by various garden foods, agreeing on matters of conscience. What you or I think of ADA Katz is of no consequence. What matters is that the path I carve allows *both* sides to follow the letter of the law in regards to the process of justice—for if I fail in that, I do a monstrous disservice to you, to your client, and most of all to myself."

David looked at him, knowing what he was saying was true.

"Judge . . ." David began at last, realizing the only way to play this was straight down the line. "The truth is, we—"

But he was interrupted by the rumble of his cell, which he had placed on the table between them after muting it to vibrate so that its shrill might not intrude upon this all-important conversation. He reached across the table, determined to shut it off. But before doing so, he saw the incoming number, which sent a new sense of concern through his now exhausted body. It was Sara, who should be with James. Sara who would not be interrupting his meeting with Stein unless something untoward had happened, something unexpected and urgent and . . .

"I'm sorry, Judge. It's my co-counsel. She's with our client and wouldn't be calling unless . . ."

Stein nodded, gesturing for him to pick up the call.

The conversation was largely one way as David, head down, shoulders collapsed, was forced to confront the latest nightmare in this escalating journey of horrors. He looked up at Stein, the judge's expression now one of deep grooves of unease. His wizened face a canvas of gullies and ridges carved by decades in a chair that carried the weight of justice and the destinies of the thousands of lives that had stood in judgment before him. David realized that no matter how much time they thought they needed, their client was crying out for someone to help him, and it was their job, their *duty*, to do so as quickly as possible. He whispered something to Sara, hung up the phone and placed it once again in the middle of the table before looking up to Stein once again.

"There will be no counter motion, Judge. If Katz wants his speedy trial, as far as we are concerned, he can have it."

"But I thought you . . . ," a confused Stein began, only to be met by a slight shake of David's head as he lifted his forefinger to his lips in a plea for silence.

And then, as if on cue, his cell vibrated again. David snatched it from the table, pressed several buttons and then, slowly, carefully rotated the phone so that the screen sat mere inches from the elderly Judge's nose.

"Is that close enough?" asked David.

"Dear God," said Stein at last, first squinting, then leaning in, then instinctively pulling away from the shocking image before him.

"Another inmate," said David.

"Is he . . . ?"

"All right?" finished David. "For now."

And then David removed the phone as Stein rested back in his seat, his face an ashen shade of gray.

"Judge?"

"All right, Mr. Cavanaugh," said Stein at last. "You've made your point. I will give Mr. Katz's motion my immediate attention."

And despite it all, David nodded in gratitude.

61

Sawyer was nervous as all hell. Nervous—but exhilarated, excited, buzzed. He felt like that girl on the TV show, the one where the CIA conscripted a university student to become an undercover agent and the girl lived this double life as an average college kid on one hand and a kick-ass super sleuth on the other. And then his mind went off on another tangent where he imagined himself as Matt Damon's character in the Jason Bourne films—with twenty passports and fifty different forms of currency hidden away in some hard-to-find safety deposit box where . . .

Cut it out, he said to himself, chopping this chain of unrealistic internal banter before his lack of focus threatened to distract him from the all-important task at hand. And so he took a breath, reorganizing his thoughts to take in the scene before him.

The law school common room was a large rectangular space, cluttered with plush, comfortable lounges covered in what looked to be some sort of rich red velvet. He moved diagonally from the front entranceway, negotiating the couches and various coffee tables along the way, trying to look as casual as possible, walking slowly but with purpose toward the bulletin board where he started to peruse the mess of colorful posts. Once there, he took the opportunity to shift some of the obscured Solidarity Global brochures to the front of the board, moving a "bike for sale" Post-it and a "shared accommodation wanted" ad carefully to the side. Then he shifted his feet, before turning slowly, deliberately, diverting his eyes left toward the red-haired young man who sat next to the fireplace at the far right-hand corner of the room, his head lowered in concentration above a pile of heavy texts.

He looked at his watch. 2:55 p.m. He was sure Simpson was due in Professor Elliot's elective on professional responsibility at three. And if that was the case, he should be gathering his books by now. He should be glancing at his own timepiece, shaking his head and realizing he had less than five minutes to . . .

Simpson looked up toward the antique clock just above the mantelpiece. He shut his texts, closed his laptop, took another sip of his water and gathered his notes before running his hand across his slick ginger hair and getting to his feet. He ignored everyone around him, which was not unusual considering the room was now almost full of first years. And then he picked up his books and the . . .

Shit, said Sawyer to himself. *He wasn't meant to take the glass! Why the hell would he do that?* The glasses were meant to be left on the tables so the students who worked part-time cleaning the common room for some measly handful of change could collect them at the end of each day and take them to the cafeteria to be cleaned in the industrial-sized dishwasher.

But then he saw Simpson shake his head, as if he had realized he had picked up the glass by mistake. And then he let it drop on the nearest table—on its *side* for God's sake—with no regard for the poor sods who would have to clean up the mess in his wake.

Simpson walked toward the exit. Sawyer waited by the bulletin board. Simpson pushed his way out the door. Sawyer gave a sigh of relief.

And then Sawyer "Undercover" Jones did some breezing of his own. Well, not so much breezing, but definitely some fancy footwork, in and out of the furniture toward that upturned water glass, which sat on the now wet coffee table just ripe for the taking.

And then he went to retrieve the pen—the one Lieutenant Mannix had given him, stressing he was not to touch the glass no matter what. He was meant to scoop it up—like a hoop on a stick, but he had . . . *Shit, where the hell was that pen?* It wasn't in his pocket. Where he had put it? It must have fallen out, but when, where?

And so, knowing opportunities such as these only came along every once in a while, and telling himself that Jason Bourne would think on his feet without hesitating, Sawyer inserted his thumb into the glass like a hook and lifted it from the table, immediately dropping it into the plastic evidence bag provided by Detective Frank McKay.

He took a breath. He felt his heart finally starting to slow, and then he smiled ever so slightly as he gave himself a mental pat on the back and headed out the back way toward the main quadrangle. He was meant to meet them by the doughnut stand, just outside the main gates, where no doubt McKay would be devouring his umpteenth Krispy Kreme as he and Mannix waited with anticipation for their "deputy" to deliver them the evidence.

And he would—deliver it, of course, with all the humility he could muster. All the time knowing they could not have done this without him, and feeling damned fine about the whole thing, now that it was done.

62

The water fell down her back in a cascade of miniature rivulets, her long brown hair now drawn straight against the force. She turned to face him, her aqua eyes now blinking against the stream, and he wrapped his arm around her waist, pulling her close, kissing her deeply.

"David, I . . ."

"Shhh," he said, kissing her again, this time lifting her up so that she might wrap her legs around him. He turned his back on the water, moving forward so that she might rest her back against the cool tiles of the shower recess. And then they made love slowly, deliberately—their hearts beating as one, their breaths long and deep until any trace of the past twenty-four hours was a vague and distant memory.

And finally, as he released her, David made a promise to himself that he would never forget that this was what life was about—the ability to love and be loved, to have faith in a future and someone to share it all with.

* * *

Hours later the moonlight was drifting through their bedroom window—on, off, on, off, as it sneaked its way between the intermittent clouds that surged across the midnight sky as if determined to get somewhere by morning. Sara lay awake, nestled into David's shoulder, his breathing slow and regular, telling her that he was most likely asleep, or close enough to it.

"David," she said in a whisper, not knowing exactly why she felt the need to talk about this tonight, especially after the day that they had had, and considering the grueling months she knew were sure to follow. "David, are you awake?"

"Yeah," he said, although he sounded anything but. "What

is it?" he asked, as he shifted slightly, pulling her even closer to him, his arm now wrapped around her shoulders.

"I was thinking," she began, not knowing exactly how this was going to come out. "No, not so much thinking, more like questioning what this all means—to us, and what we believe."

"Come again?" he asked, tilting his head so that he might look into her eyes.

"Well, to be honest, it has been on my mind since the arraignment, since Katz raised the whole feticide issue, the argument of when a pregnancy becomes valid, when a promise becomes a person and when an unborn child becomes a life."

"What are you trying to say, Sara?" he asked, and she could see his brow furrow in the muted white light.

"I don't know, it's just that . . . I know our client is innocent and I know Katz's grandstanding is ultimately just that. But I can't help but think that two weeks, ten, thirteen, twenty-three—to that child's parents, in this case James and Jessica, that potential life became a person the minute they made love."

David said nothing, but she sensed the trace of a nod.

"I am not saying I agree with Katz legally, but morally, personally . . . I mean, if my mother had disregarded me before I became 'viable,' if she had chosen to abort me instead of adopting me out . . ."

"Sara," he said at last, now rising up onto his elbow to look her direct in the eye. "It's all right to feel angry, confused. Hell, if we didn't question this issue, what kind of potential parents would we be?"

He stopped there and she wondered if he had meant to say what he had. They had never discussed the issue of children before, at least not like this; alone, exposed, in an atmosphere that demanded openness and sincerity and truth.

"But don't you see," he went on. "As sad as this might be, the reality is, the minute we make that child legally viable, the minute we allow our own sensibilities to enter that courtroom, we hand Katz his double homicide on a platter. This child should not be used as a bargaining chip. To me that is even more reprehensible than fighting to dismiss the charge."

He took a breath before going on.

"I'm a Catholic, Sara, born and raised, and I value human

life as much as the next guy. But I am also an attorney, hired to save a young man's life, and if that means fighting the feticide tooth and nail then that is exactly what I'll do."

And she nodded, knowing he was right and feeling the sting of his candor, both at the same time.

"And if it was me?" she said at last, asking the one question she knew he would not want to hear. "If it was me and our baby who were murdered in that greenhouse—me and your potential son who lost their lives in a brutal double massacre."

"Then I would walk to my dresser, pull out my gun and shoot the person responsible until he died twice over—once for you and once for . . ." His voice began to falter and for some inexplicable reason, she loved him all the more for it.

"I am sorry," she said at last, the tears now falling freely down her face.

"Don't be," he said. "That's why I love you—and why, despite it all, you give me a reason to cherish this crazy world we live in."

63

"Quantico, Virginia, is in Prince William County, twenty-three miles north-northeast of Fredericksburg near Dumfries and Stafford along Highway 619," Frank began. "It is totally surrounded by Marine Corps Base Quantico and the Potomac River. It is located south of the mouth of Quantico Creek on the Potomac and, as of the 2004 census, had a population of 561."

"And if you don't give it a rest, Frank," said Joe, peering through the rain-soaked windscreen, "I will leave you here to make it an even 562."

"The FBI Academy is located on the Marine Corps Base," continued a now grinning Frank, raising his eyebrows above his bifocals and extending his arm so that the brochure was now even farther away from his pink, flushed face. "The 385-acre Facility provides the security, privacy and safe environment necessary to carry out the diverse training and operations functions for which the FBI is responsible."

"Safe." Joe laughed. "I'm sure it was until about a year ago when Leigh torpedoed the place with her presence. Simba says she spent the first eighteen weeks of training correcting her superiors and the next six months trying to get her head across every damned unit on the base."

"I thought all new agents were recruited to field offices immediately after training?"

"They are," said Joe. "But according to Leo, when she topped her academy class and asked if she could spend the next six months learning how the FBI lab techs and profilers work, her Special Agent in Charge found it impossible to say 'no.'"

"Imagine," said Frank with a chuckle. "Someone finding it hard to say 'no' to Susan. Just didn't have the balls to stand up to her, is all."

"And we did?" countered Joe.

"Absolutely," smiled Frank.

They had just turned into the Academy's western gate and were approaching the third and final security checkpoint, the first two having been manned by the Marines and this final one by the FBI Police. Joe and Frank pulled out their IDs while the officer checked their names on the visitors' sheet and within minutes they were told to park at the main reception stop. Agent Leigh would drive down from the main facility to pick them up.

Joe held tightly to his briefcase, which contained the glass Sawyer had retrieved from the Deane Law School Common Room. For some reason he had become very protective of this lone piece of evidence, so much so that he had physically opened his case and checked on it three times in the past six hours.

"Don't worry, boss," said Frank, as if reading his mind. "Susan said she could pull some strings in Latent Prints. Get it rushed through on the quiet."

Joe nodded.

"And Agent Jacobs is all lined up. Simba called him personally and asked him to meet us under the radar."

"We have to be careful we don't mention Simpson or Nagoshi by name," reminded Joe. "Jacobs is stand up but I don't want to place him in the middle of things."

"So we just allude to our two suspects via character rather than name," said Frank.

"Exactly, and if either of their profiles fit, well, at least we know we are on the right track."

Half an hour later, Simpson's prints had been rushed to the Latent Print Unit to be compared to the two unidentified prints from the Nagoshi greenhouse, and Joe and Frank were getting an impromptu but extremely informative tour of the new FBI laboratory facility from their ex-fellow detective, now FBI Agent Susan Leigh.

Leigh was obviously genuinely excited about showing her ex-boss and partner around her new "home" and was, as usual, a walking encyclopedia of information.

"This place is amazing," she said. "The lab, which is only six years old, by the way, takes up almost 500,000 square feet over four floors, three of which are dedicated to specialized laboratories and offices for the scientists and technicians who work here. All laboratory areas are separate to offices to avoid evidence contamination—they even have special biovestibules that act as airlocks between the two work spaces, where the technicians change in and out of their examination gear."

"So what kind of stuff are we talking here?" asked Frank. "I mean, apart from the obvious."

"Some serious shit, McKay," said the enthusiastic Leigh, falling back into the comfortable cop to cop vernacular. "This place conducts over a million examinations a year with over fifteen units following different areas of expertise. There are the obvious ones, like latent prints and DNA analysis but there are other units who look solely after chemistry, computer analysis, explosives, firearms, audiovisual, hazardous materials, minerology, questioned documents, photographic and racketeering."

They stopped in front of a glass display showing a range of guns and other armaments, everything from homemade pistols to rocket launchers.

"See that there," said Susan, pointing at a small handgun that sat snug inside a rather thick book. "The perp carved out the pages in the shape of the weapon so that the pistol was a tight fit. Then he walked into a bank, book in hand, and proceeded to rob the joint."

"How much did he score before he got popped?" asked Frank.

"Not enough," said Susan with a half smile on her face. "Here," she said gesturing to them both. "Lean forward. Take a closer look at the book."

Frank and Joe moved closer to the glass to get a better view. It was a thick, hard cover version of an old novel, the pages fibrous and yellowed with age.

"Jesus," said Joe. "Is that what I think it is?"

"Yep," smiled Susan at her ex-chief's astute observation. "Margaret Mitchell's *Gone With the Wind*—first edition, May 1936. Basically, we worked out that this big thinker would have had to have robbed ten banks to get the book's worth back again. The idiot hacked his payroll to pieces and spent the rest of his life paying for it."

"Obviously a budding rocket scientist in the making," said McKay.

"Aren't they all?" said Susan.

They had made the decision on the way down to tell Susan as much as possible without compromising her position as a federal law enforcement officer. They trusted their ex-coworker 100 percent, but were also determined not to place her in a position where she felt obliged to inform her superiors of the nature of their investigations.

"So," said Leigh once they were seated in a windowless meeting room on the third floor of the sprawling facility. "How much can you spill?"

"Not much, except to say the prints, and the matter we want to discuss with Special Agent Jacobs, are related to an ongoing investigation."

"Ongoing, huh?" said Susan with a half-smile. "I thought the Nagoshi case was closed."

"It's nothing for you to worry about, Susan," said Joe. "Just dotting our 'I's, crossing our 'T's."

"Damn it," she replied, her dark brown eyes now alight with interest. "And here I was getting all excited at the prospect of being asked to help you both with some covert little gem—something that might rub that asshole Katz the wrong way."

Joe smiled before stealing a glance at Frank who gave him the slightest of nods. "You enter at your own risk, Susan," he said at last.

"Then let me the hell in."

• • •

Sara sat down beside him and took a breath. This was not going to be easy. They had decided to tell James everything, not just because it was his life they were dealing with, and not just because they needed to ask him questions relating to their two alternative hypotheses, but also because they knew he had a bright legal mind, and could well be of assistance as they built their case for trial. They would have liked to have waited until he was out of the infirmary, but they had effectively strangled their preparation time the minute they had decided to agree to Katz's motion for a speedy trial, and now had to live with the consequences.

And so Sara started with Peter Nagoshi, and Mr. Kwon and Mr. Lim, and the human rights atrocity that was Nagoshi Inc.'s automobile plant in Guangdong. James sat up in his bed, listening to it all—silent, still, apart from his right hand, which seemed to twitch involuntarily every few seconds or so.

"I don't believe this," he said at last. "For starters, Jess rarely mentioned her brother. I sensed they weren't close but she never criticized him openly, apart from making the odd jibe at his conservatism and obsession with work."

Sara frowned. This was a blow in itself. They were hoping Jessica had relayed some form of concern regarding her brother's ambition and determination to usurp her as future company CEO. They thought perhaps she might have told James about China and her fears that Peter was going behind their father's back. But then again, she only spoke to Mr. Lim mere hours before her death, so she probably didn't get the opportunity to . . .

"Jess would have been pissed," said James, interrupting her thoughts. "She hated that sort of thing. She often spoke of her father's humanitarianism and, if she found out, I am sure she would have been determined to fix things."

There was a pause.

"So she knew?" he asked after a time. "About what was going on in China?"

"She found out the night before she died."

"Oh," he said, nodding his head. "Did he kill her?" he asked at last.

"Perhaps. In fact, we believe it was either Peter or . . . ," Sara hesitated, not knowing exactly how to tell him.

"Or who?" said James, his voice rising a little.

"Or your friend H. Edgar Simpson."

James was speechless, the color now draining from his face completely.

"This is crazy," he managed. "You cannot be serious. What are you guys trying to do, Sara? Jess's brother, H. Edgar? Are my chances that slim? Is my situation that dire that already, months before trial, you are leaning toward a last resort 'Plan B'?"

Sara knew what James was asking and, in all honesty, she could not blame him. "Plan B" was a term used when desperate defense lawyers, with no real proof of their client's innocence, play the only card they have left—throwing up a series of alternative scenarios, or more specifically, possible perpetrators, in an effort to establish reasonable doubt. Truth be told, no matter how despairing, it was a viable strategy, but they knew that in order to maintain at least some form of credibility they needed to narrow their field of potential alternatives to one—which was why Sara was so determined to push on, in the hope that James might assist them in identifying the real killer in their midst.

"Think about it, James," she began. "Why did H. Edgar turn you in in the first place? And you need to look beyond the motive of greed."

"It was all a game. He thought Barbara would come through with an alibi."

"Did he?" she interrupted. "Then why didn't he recant his testimony after you were arrested?" Sara took a breath, now looking her client directly in the eye. "We believe H. Edgar had another motive for lying about your confession, James. The reward money, the 'game' as you call it, definitely appealed to his sense of superiority, and certainly helped get Westinghouse on board. But we have further evidence, we have *proof*, that H. Edgar has provided the ADA with fresh, far-reaching evidence against you, and is intent on revealing it at trial. He is not your friend, James. In fact, he is . . ."

"No," said James, interrupting her. "H. Edgar is a mercenary bastard, but I can't believe he would go as far as you suggest."

"He sold you out, James, and convinced your other best friend to do the same."

"Heath wouldn't do this either. Unless, perhaps . . . H. Edgar convinced him that I . . ."

"That you killed her? Which is probably what he did."

Sara took his shaking hand in hers. She wanted to comfort him, to stress that he was not alone. But selfishly, the twitching was also upsetting her, as it emphasized James' frailty, weakness, vulnerability.

"I am sorry, James, but we believe H. Edgar manipulated Westinghouse for his own personal gain and, perhaps more to the point, to divert the blame away from himself."

James shifted in his narrow hospital bed, wincing as he lifted his shoulders up off the hard rectangular pillows that were propped behind him like two thick tablets of rock.

"But why would he want to hurt Jess? He didn't even know her. H. Edgar never does anything without intent. He is the most focused person I know."

Sara knew she had to tell him about David's theory.

"We think he was in love with you, James."

"What?" said James, lurching forward, the two pillows now falling to the floor with a thud. The nurse in the corner looked around, but Sara signaled that all was okay and quickly returned the heavy, blood-stained blocks to their place behind James' back.

"Did you ever get the sense that he . . . ?" she began.

"No!" said James, and Sara could see that James was wrongly taking this "theory" as some form of assault on his own sexuality. "H. Edgar is straight. Whenever Heath and I were talking about girls he would . . ."

"Join in?"

"Yes."

"But have you ever *seen* him with a girl, James? Has he ever had a girlfriend, or even a one-night stand for that matter?"

"I . . . He must have . . . I don't know. I guess we just assumed he liked to keep those things to himself. H. Edgar is one arrogant son of a bitch, Sara, and Heath and I always figured he saw most of the girls at Deane as somewhat below him."

"The girls at Deane are some of the prettiest, wealthiest, most connected and intelligent young women in the country," countered Sara.

"Well, sure but . . ."

"So H. Edgar was holding out for a Kennedy princess with a Nobel Prize? I don't think so, James." Sara didn't want to be blunt, but she also knew she had to push the point. Simpson's sexuality was key to their argument, and if by any chance Joe managed to place him in that greenhouse, it gave them motive to Joe's opportunity, the means being a long thick garden hoe and a pair of strong young hands driven by resentment, jealousy and rage.

James shook his head.

"Look," said Sara at last. "I know this is a shock, and if you tell me there is no way on God's earth that he is gay, then I will trust your judgment. But if there is *any* chance James, any small doubt in your mind then . . ."

They were interrupted by a guard at the end of the long narrow room, entering with Diane Matheson who nodded her thanks and began to walk down the side wall toward them.

"James?" said Sara at once, determined to finish this conversation before Diane reached them.

"Look, I . . . I never really thought about it."

"*Think*, James. Open your mind and at least consider the possibility. Could H. Edgar be gay, James? Is it at all possible?"

"I . . . Yes. Yes, it is possible," he said at last.

And Sara breathed a sigh of relief.

■ ■ ■

Diane Matheson was a mess—a green-eyed, designer-clad, beautiful mess.

Sara had dragged her from the jail at midday, telling her James needed to get some sleep before he was released from the prison infirmary and sent back into the general population.

They had found a quiet riverside café not far from North Station, which overlooked the Charles across Bunker Hill Bridge and beyond. The morning drizzle had finally passed, the sun was now warming the icy ground and making the puddles shimmer.

"He's going to be all right, Diane," she said after their sandwiches had arrived. "He's a strong boy with plenty of good people to support him."

"Not in there he isn't," countered Diane, and Sara nodded, knowing there was no point in trying to hide the truth.

"I know this is hard, but as I explained, it looks like we are headed for an early trial and . . ."

"So they can't kill him," she said.

"No," Sara said, knowing this was the one lie she had to tell. "So that we can get him home, to you and Jed, as quickly as possible." She took a sip of her ice water before going on.

"We need your help, both yours and Jed's, to come up with a list of character witnesses who can tell the court the truth about your son. We need teachers and coaches and family and friends, elders and peers who can paint the real picture, and prove to the jury that there is no way on earth that your son is capable of the charge they have made against him."

"Charg*es*," bit Diane, not so much in anger but out of frustration and grief and fear.

"Charges," confirmed Sara, realizing this woman was too astute for sugarcoated platitudes. Sara reached across the table then, taking Diane's hand. "We have to focus here, Diane—on the trial, the witnesses. It's okay to be worried—hell, it's down-right necessary. But you have to find a way to use that energy to help us get this done. Do you understand?"

"Yes," said Diane, swallowing hard. She then proceeded to pick up her black Prada bag and unlock its clasp before reaching inside to retrieve a piece of pale blue notepaper.

"The list," she said, unfolding the sheet of stationery. "Many of them are in Sydney but they will come if you need them. They are teachers and principals and coaches and the like. Family doctors and local priests and councilmen and more. The list contains forty names, but I can add to it if necessary."

Sara smiled, taking the page from Diane's slender hand. "That's terrific, Diane," she said. "And if it's okay with you, we'll take some time going through them, one by one."

Diane nodded—a short, sharp, definite sign of agreement.

"Considering the nature of the charges," Sara went on, "we're going to need to focus on James' peers. I need young men and women, just like his current friends. Kids who studied with him, spent their weekends with him, partied with him and most importantly dated him. These are the witnesses who will make the biggest impression given they mirror the characters in our scenario here, his fellow law students, his friends, his . . ."

"Girlfriends like Jessica Nagoshi," said Diane as if needing to say the name herself.

"Yes," said Sara with a nod.

And Diane managed a nod in return, but this time slower, less enthusiastic, as if the very mention of Jessica's name had drained what little hope she held for the future of her only child.

"Is that okay, Diane?" asked Sara with a smile, squeezing Diane's hand in encouragement, needing to keep her on track.

"Yes," Diane managed, taking a breath before releasing it slowly with just the slightest of shudders. "I am sorry, Sara. I'm fine, really." She smiled, squeezing Sara's hand in return. "Let's get to it."

64

David was furious! Livid! This was the last thing he needed. Jed Matheson's call had come out of the blue, an unexpected knock that, truth be told, David should have anticipated the moment his client was arrested.

They were going to expel him. Deane University was abandoning their star pupil and the minute the news hit the press, David knew every potential juror in the state would be given one more reason to nail his innocent client to the wall.

"This is outrageous," said David, perched on the edge of a purple upholstered chair in Dean Johns' similarly hued office. "You have no grounds to expel my client. James Matheson is an excellent student and accomplished athlete who has been a credit to your university and all the principles it claims to uphold."

"But that is exactly my point, Mr. Cavanaugh. *Has been.* Past tense. I am afraid the controversy now surrounding Mr. Matheson is . . ."

"None of his own doing," countered David. "James is innocent, Dean. If you wish to expel anyone perhaps you should be looking a little closer at his two so-called friends—H. Edgar Simpson and Heath Westinghouse who . . ."

"Whose father is a respected member of our board of trustees," said the Dean, his honesty taking David aback.

"So you admit this decision has been influenced by the board?"

"I admit no such thing, Mr. Cavanaugh," said Johns. "I was simply making an observation regarding the relationship between one of our better students and a respected member of our board."

Johns was quick, thought David, and why shouldn't he be?

He had practiced law in some of the country's finest establishments before turning his hand to academia several years ago.

"Come off it, Dean," said David. "You and your precious board are trying to protect the university's reputation and all the kudos and financial benefits that go with it. But you represent a school of law in the state of Massachusetts, and I am afraid that means that as well as teaching the law you have to abide by it."

"He is late with a payment."

"What?"

"A fee installment, Mr. Cavanaugh. I am afraid James' swim fees were due last week and as the payment deadline has expired we . . ."

"Swim fees, for Christ's sake? How much are they, Dean?" asked a now exasperated David pulling his wallet from his top shirt pocket. "Tell me the figure and I'll hand it over to you right here, right now."

"I am afraid it is too late for that, Mr. Cavanaugh. I have checked with our lawyers and this is all aboveboard."

"And let me guess, your lawyers just happen to be . . ."

"Westinghouse, Lloyd and Greene. A matter of coincidence—nothing more. Besides, according to the district attorney's office, Mr. Matheson will be incarcerated at least until the end of the year, which means I am afraid he will miss numerous compulsory classes and exams that are necessary for him to pass the bar. Our places are limited, Mr. Cavanaugh, we have hundreds of inquiries every day and . . ."

"What?" said David at last, missing everything the dean had said after "district attorney's office" and "incarcerated at least until the end of the year." "You spoke to ADA Katz?"

"Briefly," said Johns. "But I can assure you that the decision is ours entirely."

"When did he call you?" asked David, hoping the dean would give away the fact that it was Katz who had called *him*.

"This morning," said the Dean. "But this is all beside the point. As I explained we . . ."

"Bullshit," said David at last, finally rising from his chair. "Katz started talking consequences for the university and you made the decision to pull the pin on my client within minutes of hanging up the phone.

"You screwed him, Dean—you and your goddamned board. You have abandoned one of your own, the very law grad you and your fellow academics should be proud to list as a future alumnus. You have shattered his family and participated in a charade that will no doubt contribute to the burgeoning lies being peddled by an ambitious ADA.

"When I was a kid, I actually dreamed of being able to afford attending a law school like Deane and now my former aspirations have exploded, in one almighty surge of disgust."

David looked at the now rising dean and saw the slightest trace of remorse on his round, flushed face.

"I am sorry, Mr. Cavanaugh. It is just that . . . the board they . . ."

"Are a greedy bunch of snobs who are so intent on preserving this university's blue-blood earning potential that they are willing to sacrifice one of their own." David took a deep breath, determined to say one last thing before he left this lavender lair that now reeked of the sickly scent of betrayal.

"I will win this thing, Dean, and when I do, I will make sure James Matheson gets his chance to graduate law at an institution with far worthier principles than your own. But if I fail, if by any small possibility I do not do the job he deserves, you and your blessed board can rest assured that his blood will fall decidedly on your hands."

■ ■ ■

The traffic was thick, dense, sluggish. It had taken him mere minutes to race back to his car, loop onto the Worcester Turnpike and relish a relatively smooth ride before hitting Huntington and the early evening traffic. It was Friday, and the roads were clogged with workers desperate to either head in or out of one of the world's most compact cities as the sun finally gave way to a determined twilight, the air cool, the taillights blinding.

It took him almost forty minutes to make it to Government Center, where he parked illegally without bothering to lock his Land Cruiser. He ran down City Hall Plaza past Scollay Square and into Sudbury Street—negotiating the various construction site blockades and dodging the "face-down" pedestrians heading for the various T stations at Government Center, Park Street and Downtown Crossing. Finally, he turned into the narrow Bulfinch Place where he entered the first building on the block. He picked up his pace and ran through the lobby, calling for the elevator while watching the lethargic light dial mark its slow descent to the ground floor.

He moved in the second the doors opened, forgoing the usual decorum of allowing the existing passengers to exit first. And then he counted the seconds until the elevator rose one floor, two, three, four, realizing that his anger, if anything, had not subsided but multiplied over the past hour—reason now completely forgotten, retribution his only goal.

"Where is he?" he asked as he entered the main reception of the Suffolk County District Attorney's Office.

"I am sorry, sir," said the counter clerk, looking up from her desk. "It's after seven, our offices are closed and . . ."

"Never mind," said David, ignoring the girl's protests as he bounded down the hallway past various empty laminate desks and dark, windowless offices.

The place looked deserted, which David knew was rare for the DA's office even at this late hour on a Friday evening. But then he heard them, the congregation down the corridor. Friday night drinks or the like—Katz no doubt lording it over his troops like some godforsaken aristocrat rewarding his slaves with the pleasure of his company, dishing out the advice with no end of references to his stellar expertise.

He reached the end of the gray carpeted passageway, Katz's secretary still glued to her desk—too low on the ladder to warrant an invite, but high enough to require that she stay late to take her more superior colleagues' messages.

"Is Katz in there?" asked David, the girl's wide eyes telling him she knew exactly who he was.

"I . . . This is a private function and . . ."

"*Is he in there?*" David repeated, and in that second he could have sworn the young girl gave the very slightest of smiles.

"Sure," she said, lowering her voice. "In fact, he is entertaining the attorney general."

And then the girl did something completely unexpected. She stood from her chair, negotiating her rather substantial bulk back from behind her desk, and gestured toward the closed conference room door, beyond which David could hear the civil joviality of Friday night backslapping playing out like some sycophantic lovefest.

"Stuff it," she said at last, standing back to let him pass. "My boss is an asshole, Mr. Cavanaugh, in case you haven't already noticed. You're the last person he'd be expecting to be seeing this evening so . . . let's shake this party up a little, shall we?" She pointed to the door. "Be my guest."

65

"Shit," said Joe, crouching low to look over the bald technician's shoulder.

The light in the laboratory was low and had an eerie green tinge to it. The room buzzed with the dull hum of high-tech machinery, the requisite cool temperature adding to the feeling of sterility and detachment. Joe considered the two images before him, his heart sinking at what he saw. The print on the left looked nothing like the one on the right. It was not a match. H. Edgar Simpson was not in the Nagoshis' greenhouse—or if he was, he left no evidence to prove it.

"As you can see," said the technician, who Susan had introduced as an Agent Wicks, "the print on the left, the one from the greenhouse, has a number of large loops and whorls.

"You have to realize we only get 'accidentals' like this—meaning a clean print showing the complete loops and the whorls—about five percent of the time so at least we had something reasonable to work with.

"As for the one on the right—from the drinking glass you supplied—well, admittedly it's not as clear, but Blind Freddy could tell you this one comes from a completely different individual. The ridges arch and curve differently, the loops exit to the left, whereas in the first print they exit to the right.

"I could do some point comparison but, and forgive the pun, there really isn't any point. They're apples and oranges, ladies and gentlemen."

"Shit," said Frank. "This case will not cut us a break."

He was right. Joe felt like they had been walking backward the minute they had arrived in Quantico—Ned Jacobs blowing their profiler ideas out of the water, Susan's technician buddy dashing their hopes of placing Simpson at the crime scene with one flick of his "ninety-eight percent accuracy rate" screen.

"Look," said Susan, after thanking Wicks and directing her two obviously disappointed friends back out of the laboratory. "It's not all bad. The prints aren't a match, but that doesn't mean Simpson wasn't in that greenhouse. You keep telling me how smart the kid is—so maybe he was careful, wore gloves or . . ."

"It doesn't make any difference," said Joe, stepping back so Susan could exit the heavy lab door first. "No evidence is still no evidence, and Jacobs is set on his sexual attraction theory so . . ."

While profiler Jacobs had agreed the killer's organized, controlling approach to the murder could fit someone of either Peter Nagoshi or H. Edgar Simpson's personality, he was still convinced the killer had some sort of sexual attraction to Jessica. He said the shoes were the key, as many perpetrators saw their victim's feet as extremely erotic.

"The feet are incredibly sensual—but safe," he had explained. "Removing her shoes was a particularly clean way to assert his control over her. He did not need to rape her, to risk revealing his identity by leaving his DNA at the scene. But still he managed to commit this crime in the way that he needed to commit it. No, I am afraid my assessment stands, gentlemen. The killer was attracted to her—no doubt in my mind."

And so Jacobs had effectively destroyed both of their theories in one sweeping observation.

• • •

The scene was just as David expected—small groups of mostly males congregating in clusters—talking, drinking, smiling. The large conference room table had been pushed aside to create a wide open space in which to mingle. The curtains were wide open, revealing the city lights below. The men were basically clones of one another—dark suits, short hair, their ages in that appropriate margin that spread comfortably above or below the respectable watershed that was middle age. The women were dressed much the same, their suit skirts ending just above the knee, long enough to scream credibility and short enough to win the eye of an ever-appreciative ADA.

And there he was, all genuine interest and ingratiating

smiles. He was chatting with Sweeney and his entourage, his dark brown suit screaming fine Italian wool, his shoes so damned shiny they must have required a set of high-powered double As just to maintain the wattage.

David moved forward, ignoring the stares from the few suits who had already looked across to see him bounding across the floor. And then Katz glanced upward, no doubt distracted by the peripheral image of a man torpedoing across the room toward him.

"Cavanaugh," said Katz at once, and in that moment David saw three emotions shift quickly across his expression—alarm, anger, and then, perhaps, a determination to swallow his panic and "strut his stuff" in front of the powerful, influential supporter beside him.

"What an unexpected surprise," he said, turning toward David, a sort of half smile, half grimace on his perfectly chiseled face.

"We need to talk," said David. "We can do it here, in front of your fearless leader, or you can choose to step outside."

"I'm sorry, Mr. Cavanaugh," Katz began. "But I am afraid this is a private function."

"Your choice, Katz," interrupted David, "because to be honest I don't give a crap who hears what I have to say."

"Excuse me," said Sweeney, now moving into their space. "Mr. Cavanaugh," he said, extending his hand on instinct, before quickly withdrawing it at David's glare. "Counselor, I have heard great things about you and your work, but I am afraid this behavior is completely unacceptable."

"So sue me," said David, turning toward the AG.

"For God's sake," said Sweeney, his face now flush with color. "Roger, call security."

Katz was obviously in a bind: on one hand he needed to obey Sweeney; on the other, he did not want to look like a pussy in front of his entire staff, who were now viewing the exchange with great interest. So in the end he compromised. He leaned into David's ear and whispered, *"Outside, now,"* before straightening his tie and directing David toward the back of the room.

The silence was deafening, the suits lost in some mesmerizing game of people tennis—except there were two balls in play and both had been lobbed straight to the back of the court and, sadly, out of bounds.

The minute they were out the door Katz let loose, no doubt realizing he had a small window of opportunity to show his wares before the slow moving air pump closed the door with a hiss.

"What the hell do you think you are doing, Cavanaugh? How dare you waltz in here uninvited. Shelley, call security. I want Mr. Cavanaugh here arrested for trespassing."

"No chance," said David, noticing Shelley had not moved an inch. "The DA's office is open to all citizens of this fine state and I am, whether you like it or not, Roger, one of those fine goddamned taxpayers. You fucked with me today, Roger. You screwed with my client. You had him expelled from Deane knowing full well how that would play out in the press."

The door shut with an almost inaudible *click* and Katz took a quick step back. "So, you heard about my little call to Dean Johns? An extremely insightful administrator, if ever there was one."

"You are one sick fuck, Katz," said David, his heart now pumping in triple time.

"Really? Then why do I feel so healthy, Cavanaugh? I am sitting pretty with a long career and a life full of promise ahead of me. Which is more than I can say for you, or your client who . . ."

"There is no way you will win this, Roger. James Matheson is innocent and the court will know the truth. One day you are going to have to face what you do to these people, count the lives you have ruined and be accountable for them. What you did today was a perversion of justice, plain and simple. So, while racing toward this speedy trial you requested, you better make sure you prepare a speech for Stein as to why you effectively tainted a statewide jury pool by interfering with . . ."

"You're not filing a counter motion?" interrupted an obviously confused Katz.

"Why would I? James is innocent. We want to make sure he is home for Christmas."

"And so you shall," smiled the Kat. "Christmas 2999. Of course he will be well into his hundreds and his eyesight might not be as great as it is right now, but in the very least he'll enjoy seeing in the new millennium and sipping the odd glass of cider."

David took a breath before looking straight into his enemy's dark brown eyes, seeing nothing but arrogance and over-confidence and greed. He took a step forward—slowly, carefully, until he was face-to-face with the shiny-faced ADA, Katz's stance now unsure, his breath hot and sour and tinged with the slightest trace of fear.

"Are you listening to me, Roger?" David asked, his voice barely over a whisper. "You need to listen to me because what I am about to say is going to change your life.

"I am going to win this thing, you pathetic excuse for an attorney, and sink your precious future in the process. I am going to cut you down and wring you out and leave you bloodied and bare and wishing you never took me on in the first place.

"I am nothing if not determined, Roger—even you can give me that. And so know," he said, "know, in here," he said again, this time pushing his right fist hard against Katz's chest, "that it is my mission to expose you, to humiliate you—personally, professionally, publicly—for your criminal manipulation of the law and the oath you swore to uphold. Your total disregard for humanity is beyond evil, Roger, and I will not rest until you get what you deserve."

Just then they were interrupted by a figure approaching from down the hall, and David, whose eyes did not leave the ADA's, presumed it was the security guards ready to remove him from the premises. But it could not be the guards, he thought, at least not yet, as Shelley had not lifted a finger to summon them.

It was a waiter, carrying a fresh tray of drinks. And as he eyed the pair, obviously sensing the tension and making a rather wide circle around them in an effort to reach the conference room door unscathed, David called *"Wait!"* before grabbing the man's arm and reaching across to grab an icy cold beer from his tray.

"Humph," said Katz, taking a swallow, momentarily relieved to have David leave the confines of his precious personal space. "What do you plan to do, tough guy?" he asked, finding a new surge of confidence as he took another step back. "You gonna throw a drink in my face? Don't worry, I've had more than a few whores respond in exactly the same way when they have been disappointed by my rejection."

David said nothing, merely lifted the drink to his lips and took several deep swallows, allowing the cold amber liquid to cool his parched throat. He drained the glass within seconds before placing the empty tumbler back on the tray, nodding to the waiter in thanks and turning to Katz.

"You're an asshole, Roger," he said, after which he pulled back his arm and closed his fist, his punch connecting with Katz's right cheek before the Kat even knew what hit him.

And then he turned to Katz's assistant, totally disregarding the now flailing ADA who lay in a heap on the worn hallway floor.

"Shelley," said David, rubbing his fist. "Thanks for the invite. It's been a pleasure."

"Any time," said Shelley with a smile, diverting her eyes from her "beloved" boss to the man who stood triumphant before her.

66

"I'm sorry, H. Edgar," said Alison Westinghouse. "But I am sure I heard him correctly. He said he was going to visit his best friend and clear the air. Now, I know that you are his closest friend, so I just assumed you two had had some sort of spat, which is completely understandable given the pressure you poor boys have been under, and that he was going to meet you to make amends.

"Perhaps he is stuck in traffic," Alison Westinghouse went on. "Although I assumed he was meeting you at home so he should be there by now. Do you think we should be concerned?"

"No," snapped Simpson, his brain now working double-time. "I mean, I am sure he is fine, Mrs. Westinghouse. It must be the traffic. The Red Sox are playing at Fenway so . . ."

"Oh, I see."

"You're right," he lied. "We did have a disagreement. Nothing huge. Like you said, this has been a stressful time and well . . . Heath has been a rock, Mrs. Westinghouse. I am lucky to call him my friend."

"And he thinks the same way about you, H. Edgar. You two must stick together now given . . ."

"Yes, ma'am," said Simpson, now desperate to get off the phone. "I'll see you then."

"Of course, H. Edgar. You know you are welcome any time."

"Thanks, Mrs. Westinghouse." And then he hung up the phone. H. Edgar stood stock-still in the hallway of his parents' grandiose Chestnut Hill mansion, the Persian rug thick beneath his feet, the corridor walls covered in original landscapes, and the only heir to this monstrous Brahman haul now fearing that life as he knew it was over—or at least in its agonizing death throes.

No, he said to himself, realizing what his friend was about to do. *"No,"* he said aloud, knowing that if he did not act, his brilliant strategy of damage control would be sabotaged before it even got a chance to get off the ground.

He took a breath, closed his eyes and opened them again, now looking up to see the keys to his mother's BMW X5 hanging on a hook above the marble-topped side table. He leapt forward, snatching them off the wall before running for the door and, once outside, turning left toward the estate's expansive six-car garage.

He looked at his Rolex. 1:52 p.m. Westinghouse was at least twenty minutes ahead of him so there was no time to waste. He unlocked the SUV and jumped up into the leather upholstered driver's seat before turning on the ignition, releasing the hand brake and screeching down the circular drive, kicking up a tornado of polished white pebbles in his wake.

* * *

Heath Westinghouse was sick to his stomach. In fact, he had felt the nausea rise in his esophagus the minute he walked into Suffolk County Jail. Everything about this place said "puke." The smell was so sickly he swore he could see the airborne germs bumping heads with the chemically toxic antiseptics that saturated the air like napalm. The guards were so fat that the guns in their belts looked like leather-holstered penises, standing at attention to their bulbous waists. The walls were so white he felt sure they were painted daily, with years of in-ground grime left to fester underneath. And the population was so black that he . . . well, needless to say, this was *not* a scenario he was used to.

Heath closed his eyes and shook his head rapidly from side to side as if attempting to rid it of all the concerns (prejudices) and worries (fears) that were forcing their way to the forefront of his brain. He was here to see James, to sort things out, clear the air, apologize for being responsible for their sending him to this fucking hole that . . . But one quick reminder of the significance of his surroundings and the wave was back again, this time rising as far as his throat, forcing him to swallow his very own vomit. And then he felt it—a welcome sigh of relief—at the sound of the doorknob twisting before him. His friend was here—James, his smart as all hell, athletically gifted friend who, in the very least, would appreciate his discomfort.

"Fuck," he said as James entered the room. "Jesus fucking Christ, man. Shit! What did they do to you? You look like . . . Shit. Jesus. Fuck!"

James said nothing, just moved in slowly to take the seat across from him in the small, white, cinder block room.

"I am so sorry, man," said Heath, shaking his head, diverting his eyes, looking everywhere, anywhere but at the distorted human being before him.

"I am not supposed to be talking to you," said a weary James.

"I . . ." Heath began. "I know. I mean, we are obviously supposed to be the enemy. But James, we never thought it would come to this. H. Edgar told me you were cool, and the money was split and . . . Why did you lie about Barbara?"

"So this is why you are here?" said James, shaking his head ever so slightly.

Heath winced at the sight of his friend's swollen black eye, which puckered as his head moved from side to side.

"You want to bang me up for lying about getting laid?" asked James. "Well, I'm sorry, Westinghouse, but as you can see, somebody already beat you to it."

Heath nodded. He had not cried in years, but that was what he was doing now—slowly, silently, the tears tracking down his smooth, tanned cheeks.

"James," he began. "I don't understand any of this, man. H. Edgar says you are guilty."

"I know," said James at last, his own tears now leaking from the corner of his one good eye. "And to be honest with you, I am almost past caring." James stopped there, as Heath leaned in across the table, desperate to comfort his close friend but unsure as to how, given James' horrendous injuries and the oversized asshole standing guard by the door.

"You know," James went on, now mere inches from his friend, "sometimes, at night, I imagine what it would be like to join them. To let go, to give in. And then I close my eyes and shut out the world, and then I see them, Heath. I see Jess and my son, smiling, relieved, *grateful* that I have finally worked out exactly where I belong."

"*No,*" said Heath, now gripping James' wrist, causing the overweight uniform to take a step forward. "Enough is enough, James. You cannot forget what you had and what you *will* have again. Jessica is gone, and that is a really awful thing, but if she loved you like you say she did, she would not want this for you. I will talk to H. Edgar. I will . . ."

. . .

H. Edgar saw the guard tap on the door and push it open, revealing the two young forms seated at the small metallic table in the middle of the tiny windowless room.

"Seems you're popular today, Matheson," said the guard. "Visitor number two which means Mr. Baywatch here has gotta hit the road. Only one visitor at a time, them's the rules."

H. Edgar entered to see Westinghouse's mouth agape—his blue eyes shot with blood, his complexion flush, his cheeks wet. And then the other inhabitant, almost unrecognizable in his red, shapeless prison garb, turned to face H. Edgar, eye to eye. Simpson gasped, the very sight of his "genetically perfect" friend, sending a strange intense heat through his entire body and squeezing his heart in a vice. But then he took a breath, collecting himself, controlling his thoughts and reminding himself why he was here. This was all about survival, *his* survival, nothing more, nothing less.

"H. Edgar," said Westinghouse, rising quickly from his chair, its metal legs screeching in protest as it scraped across the cold, polished floor. "We need to do something, man. Look at him. We need to . . ."

"One of you has got to take a hike," interrupted the guard. "You have exactly three minutes before visiting time is over."

"Westinghouse," said H. Edgar calmly, "I need to speak with James."

"Not unless you promise to . . ." Heath began.

"It's okay," interrupted James, turning back to his fair-haired friend. "Give him his minute."

And Westinghouse nodded, standing to maneuver his way out of the now crowded room. "I've got your back, James," he said to James before facing H. Edgar at the door. "You'd better be here to make this right," he added.

But H. Edgar said nothing, just stared at his tall friend as he passed by and into the corridor beyond.

And so there they stood.

Two of the inseparable band of three.

Two feet and a million miles apart.

"You did this to yourself," said H. Edgar at last.

"Fuck you, H. Edgar," said James. "You know exactly how this went down and from what I hear, you are about to give the ADA another nail to hammer into my coffin."

H. Edgar took a breath, wondering how James could possibly know about his new piece of so-called evidence. "It wasn't meant to happen like this."

"Really?" asked James. "Are you trying to tell me you screwed up because if that's the case then why am I the one wearing the red cotton clown suit?"

"You know who I am, James," said H. Edgar. "I have never professed to be anything different."

"And I cannot help who I fall in love with."

H. Edgar felt that now familiar rush of heat again, and waited for it to subside—the two of them standing there, saying nothing, but knowing that no matter what happened, they would never be friends again. And then Simpson took the slightest of steps forward, his shoes squeaking loudly against the gray concrete floor.

"Stay away from me," said James, the back of his legs now flush against the square metallic table. And H. Edgar stopped, realizing just how much damage had been done.

"All right," he said, "I'm leaving, but I want you to remember that what I am about to do has nothing to do with you. I am a rare beast, James, who will always survive against the odds. So when this is over, I do not want your thanks."

"I do not want your help, H. Edgar."

"Maybe not, but you need it."

"Then I choose to refuse your fucking generous offer."

"Then I choose to refuse your refusal."

James said nothing, and so H. Edgar turned to leave.

"You know your problem, Simpson?" said James at last. "You can't see past your own fucking nose. The world does not live or die by the beat of H. Edgar Simpson's drum."

"Perhaps not, but as I am about to save your skin, Matheson, I suggest you swallow your goddamned pride and allow me to do exactly what I do best."

67

Three weeks later—Thanksgiving

They were only three hours into a five-and-a-half-hour drive and already they were running two hours late. Sara had taken an early "Happy Thanksgiving" call from Sawyer who had just happened to mention that his parents were on some skiing vacation in Canada and that he planned a quiet day, on his own, sitting in his dorm, eating turkey takeout from the Deane cafeteria.

"He is all alone," Sara had said at 8 a.m. just as they were getting into the car. "I mean, turkey takeout . . . ?"

"Turkey is turkey, Sara," David had replied.

But then she gave him that smile—that wide-eyed, innocent, impossible to refuse expression that had inevitably resulted in them driving to Wellesley to meet Sawyer for a cafeteria-cooked Thanksgiving breakfast of processed turkey and a too-dry cranberry sauce on two burned pieces of rye. And it was as if the kid, who Sara had grown increasingly fond of over the past month (which wasn't such a stretch considering Sawyer seemed to spend every spare moment either at the office or popping into their apartment), had been treated to the breakfast of kings—his bright face alight with an expression of pure joy and appreciation.

Two days. They had given themselves two days to drive to Newark and see the family before heading back to Boston and the approaching Matheson trial. The past three weeks had been tough and forced them to take a difficult but necessary reality check as to what they had and what they did not, where they were headed and where they could not afford to go.

Ironically, the only good news came in the form of a victory for Katz. The ADA had won his motion for a speedy trial, the date now set for early December, a mere week and a half away. Judge Stein had argued that if the ADA wanted his fast track to justice, then this was the only window available. Any later in the year and the courts would be closed for Christmas and the trial, if not resolved, would be dragged into the New Year. From Stein's point of view, and ironically, the defense's as well, any lengthening of the period in which the media could exploit the "sexy" Matheson case was a negative. The judge was already concerned about finding an unbiased jury and stressed his ruling was based on a desire to "curtail an environment where gossip was rife and speculation the flavor of the day." In other words they had ten days to pull it all together which, at this point in time, seemed close to impossible.

China was a nightmare. They had managed to talk Mr. Kwon into working his people double-time, a request they hated to make. But keeping the plant operational was the only way they could continue investigating Peter Nagoshi's possible role in Mr. Lim's death.

FBI Agent Susan Leigh had been a blessing. She had spoken to her FBI colleagues in Beijing who were currently undertaking a series of secret investigations into the Guangdong operation with the help of Mr. Kwon and his colleagues. There was even talk of organizing the secret passage of Mr. Lim's brother to the US so that, if necessary, he might testify at trial.

However, a fundamental problem came in the form of the very nature of the workers' suspicions. For while they felt sure Peter Nagoshi was linked to the older Mr. Lim's death, their "proof" was in the form of intuition rather than fact. As Taoists they believed that people were good by nature, but they also believed that the ghosts of those who once lived evil lives could be born again, and from what David could gather, the Lims and their friends believed Nagoshi to be a sort of reincarnated devil, most likely a colorful take on the truth, but not one that would hold up in court.

Their next tack was to investigate Peter Nagoshi's martial arts training, and once again Susan had come through. Her discreet investigations had revealed that Nagoshi was indeed a

master at the Japanese martial art of Bujinkan. But this posed a
problem in itself, given that Bujinkan was not motivated by violence or aggression.

The ancient Japanese martial art was in fact based on the
principles of patience, self-control and dedication. Worse still,
its mantra spoke of a "foundation in peace" and a path to the
immovable heart or *fudoshin*. In other words they knew it
would be extremely difficult to claim Nagoshi's dedication to
Bujinkan could have been utilized to slaughter his only sister
with his own bare hands, especially when the art's philosophy
was based on respect and a dedication to the well-being of
others.

And so progress on this front had been slow, or more to the
point, close to nonexistent. It had been hindered by the distance
of miles, the barriers of philosophical and religious differences
and the bona fide restrictions of fear. Worse still, their investigations had been mired by the need for secrecy, for they had no
doubt that if Peter Nagoshi got wind of what they were up to,
despite his dedication to the Chinese operation, the plant would
most likely disappear, and any potential evidence against him
right along with it.

H. Edgar Simpson seemed impenetrable. James told them of
his two friends' visits and Simpson's strange promise that he
would set things right. But they all suspected, especially since
they had no evidence to the contrary, that a scorned H. Edgar
was simply telling James what he wanted to hear. By all accounts, Simpson and Westinghouse were still firmly in Katz's
camp and they had no reason to believe this would change. And
to top it all off, Joe had found no evidence of Simpson being
near the Nagoshi estate on the night of Jessica's murder. For
starters, Simpson did not own his own car and a canvasing of
taxi activity on the night had turned up nothing.

The prints had come up negative as had any attempt they
had made, with Sawyer's help, to try to establish the nature of
H. Edgar's sexuality. If the kid was gay they had no proof of it.
In fact, if anything the young man appeared to be asexual. David had argued his asexuality could well be a result of sexual
confusion or, more to the point denial, only to be countered by
the informed Sawyer, who explained asexuality was a legiti-
mate sexual orientation in itself, a word used to define people

who lack sexual attraction or otherwise find sexual behavior unappealing.

And so, with no new evidence, physical or circumstantial, at their disposal, they had decided there was only one way to play it—or rather two, simultaneously. And ironically, it had been James who had come up with the double attack plan that they had eventually decided to follow.

First up, if they could not establish who did kill Jessica Nagoshi, then they had to establish who *didn't*. They would use all the evidence Katz had against their client and manipulate it to paint the real picture—that James was a victim, a young man of high character set up out of greed, that he was guilty of one thing and one thing only—falling in love and conceiving a child with the girl he intended to marry.

Secondly, once they had painted James as an unlikely culprit, they needed to hand the jury someone else in his stead. In other words it was a "Plan B" with a twist. This was where it became a little tricky, for they knew they could not afford to appear desperate and disorganized to a savvy jury of twelve. If they threw up two separate alternatives, with little or no proof to support either claim, they could well shoot themselves in the foot by watering down their defense with what would appear to be fantastical finger-pointing. And so they would pick one alternative, one target at which to fire—a target, at least at this stage, they decided would have to be H. Edgar Simpson.

The reasons were fairly simple and largely based on the difficulty they knew they would face if they set out to accuse a respected young executive of killing his sister. Despite his social shortcomings, Peter Nagoshi was highly regarded in the international business world and any slight on him—who had been painted in the press as a familial victim saddened by the loss of his only sibling—may result in the defense being branded heartless desperadoes.

Simpson was another matter however. For starters he reeked of arrogance and moneyed superiority—qualities David knew, despite any efforts on Simpson's behalf, would be evident to a jury from the moment he took the stand. The boy had no alibi and he was a ruthless conspirator who had manipulated a police investigation to suit his own needs, while all the time focusing on securing his half of the much coveted reward. While

David knew it was "not about the money," he also knew that the majority of the jury would only ever have dreamed of possessing such an amount, and this alone should plant the seed of doubt in their minds, and paint the already wealthy Simpson as the mercenary Judas that he was.

They would hold off on bringing up his questionable sexuality unless they had proof, or more to the point, were desperate enough to do so. And they were hoping beyond all hope that whatever evidentiary "gem" Simpson had promised Katz on that fated recording could be proven to be fabricated, or at the very least, circumstantial.

And so it would come down to that—one friend set against the other with Westinghouse painted as the pathetic pawn in Simpson's malevolent game. While they knew Westinghouse was an important part of the picture, and still considered the possibility of approaching him in secret, they also knew this could backfire as anything they said to Westinghouse could well be relayed back to Katz. And if Katz knew they were gunning for Simpson, their entire strategy could crumble before they even had a chance to get it off the ground. This was James' life they were playing with, and no matter what else, they had to proceed with caution.

And so they would put their efforts into showing their client to be the hardworking, good-natured, well-intentioned young man that he was, and his greedy, traitorous "friend" to be a covetous criminal with no regard for the principles of loyalty or, more importantly, the law. How far they would go to paint him as the real killer was something yet to be determined. It would be decided at trial, as they gauged their own process, as they evaluated Katz's chances and studied the jury's response.

None of this was perfect—in fact, it was so far from iron-clad that it made David sick to his stomach every time he thought about it. But it was all they had, at least for the time being. And as Nora had so profoundly reminded them: "A trout in the pot is better than a salmon in the sea."

68

"I swear to God, Mom," said the dark-haired Lisa Cavanaugh as she swallowed the last morsel of homemade apple pie, "I have not eaten like this in . . . well, since the last time I was home." And she smiled then, before resting back in her seat and undoing the top button of her jeans.

"What, you gonna belch for us now?" said her older brother Sean, only half joking.

"Maybe," she smiled, her bright green eyes alight with amusement. "Unless DC here beats me to it. He seems to have had his 'eloquent sufficiency' as well," she said, gesturing at David beside her while mocking her oldest brother's tendency to play the "head of the house" all at the very same time.

"I don't know about eloquent sufficiency," said David, grinning at his sister. "But I will tell you I am well and truly stuffed," smiled David.

"Well, despite your lack of table manners I am pleased," smiled his mother. "Because you have lost a little weight."

Lisa was right, dinner had been delicious, from the starter of French onion soup to the main of herb-roasted turkey with cranberry and orange relish, to the sides of candied sweet potato and the finale of Patty Cavanaugh's homemade apple pie.

"Come to think of it, you are looking a little scrawny, DC," said Sean. "But then I guess that happens when you sit behind a desk all day."

"Leave him alone, Sean," said Sean's wife, Teresa, nudging her husband in the ribs.

"Come on, Tess. He's a lawyer. They are supposed to be good at handling the truth. All I am saying is, if he were working on the docks like me, or like Pop did before us . . ."

David had to hand it to him, although at least Sean had

managed to contain himself until *after* dinner before bringing up the eternal sticking point that sat between them like a festering sore. Somehow David's decision to leave Jersey and move to Boston to study law had always been viewed by Sean as a betrayal. A betrayal that intensified when their father died seven years ago, leaving Sean to manage the business alone. Did David feel guilty about it? Sure, especially since his little sister, Lisa, followed him to Boston to study nursing. He knew Sean and his family filled his mother's life with love and activity—and for this David was grateful. But while Sean's words still cut into his sense of culpability, he knew the decision he had made was the right one. He was doing what he needed to do, whether Sean approved or not.

"Come on, Sean," said David, swallowing his frustration and attempting to make light of the matter for his mother's sake. "If I was doing all that physical work, day in, day out, well, I would be a walking Mr. Universe." He managed a smile.

"Over my dead body," said Sara, taking a sip of her wine, her look telling him she admired his decision not to "bite." "I, for one, can't stand that Mr. Universe look."

"Me neither," said Lisa, finishing her beer. "In fact," she hesitated, waiting for her mom to leave the room to take some plates to the kitchen. "I once dated this 'roid freak who, well . . . let's just say his muscle was all stacked above the belt."

"Jesus, Lisa," said Sean. "The kids!" He tilted his head sideways to indicate his three children who were now sprawled on the living room floor.

"They didn't hear me, idiot," said Lisa.

"No, but I did," said Patty, now standing in the doorway.

"Busted," said David.

"Shit," said Lisa with a huge grin on her pretty, narrow face.

Half an hour later, the dinnerware stacked neatly in the dishwasher, the entire Cavanaugh clan was gathered in the living room of their old Newark duplex, watching David's oldest nephew, eleven-year-old Seamus, kick the butts of his two younger siblings in a Simpson's trivia game.

"Milhouse's last name is Muntz," said ten-year-old Katie.

"Wrong. It's Van Houten." Seamus smiled. "Nelson's last name is Muntz and Martin's last name is Prince."

"Okay, smart guy," returned Katie. "So what is Sideshow Bob's real name?"

"It's Robert Underdunk Terwilliger," answered Seamus.

"Geez," said Katie. "He's right!"

And so it went, the kids on the floor and the adults on the couches, and David felt somehow sad that once again he felt "old," sitting here looking down at his brother's carefree offspring.

"So how's the case going," asked his mom at last. "How is that poor boy coping?"

"As well as can be expected, Mom," said David. "He's feeling the pressure a week before trial. He's had a lot to deal with in the past three months—losing his girl, his child, being betrayed by his two best friends."

"His poor parents," said Patty.

"They're good people," said Sara.

"The thing is," began David. "This boy is normal, despite his privilege. He is smart and understanding and sees the good in people. He deserves a future, and not just because the one he had was so full of promise. He deserves it because he is just a good kid who has a vision of how to make things better.

"And besides all that," added David after a pause, "ADA Katz is using this case to kick off his campaign for DA. He is keeping company with the attorney general, who has most likely been showering him with promises of advancement if he manages to nail the Ivy League kid with the good looks and the big bank account."

"They want to convict him because he is wealthy?" said his mother.

"The government believes they have received unfair criticism. It seems the general consensus is that the richer you are, the easier it is to get an acquittal. And Katz, being the asshole that he is, sees this as an opportunity to . . ."

"I disagree," said Sean at last.

"What?" asked David.

"Not about your ADA, he sounds like a right prick, but as far as the government is concerned. The criticism is by no means unfair, DC. The statistics are clear—the wealthier the defendant, the more likely they walk. What is it they say? 'America has the best criminal justice system that money can buy'?"

"You think James will get an easier ride just because his parents are wealthy?" asked Sara.

"Sure," said Sean. "Most prisoners report incomes of less than $8,000 a year, and while these bastards are serving time for petty crimes, corporate criminals are getting pats on the back or serving limited sentences in prisons that resemble five star hotels."

"That's not exactly true, Sean," said Sara. "The last decade has seen a marked increase in accounting and corporate infractions, fraud in health care, government procurement, bankruptcy. And there is no such thing as a luxury prison. They simply don't exist."

Sean looked at Sara then, obviously ready with his argument in rebuke, but considering she was a guest and a girl, David guessed his old-fashioned brother would eventually decide his energies were better spent sparring with the target he had been practicing on for years.

"For God's sake, DC," he said, turning to David just as David knew he would. "The reality is that in America there exist two systems of criminal justice—one for the wealthy, who get kid-glove investigations, lackluster prosecutions, drug treatment, light sentences and easy, if any, prison time; and the other, for the poor, with tough policing, aggressive prosecution, harsh sentences and hard time.

"My point is that if your client were poor or black, he'd be represented by some goddamned public defender with zero chance of ever seeing the sunlight again."

David's heart was beating double-time, his blood beginning to boil. In fact, if it hadn't been for the look of concern on his mother's face, he would have stood up then and there and resorted to the more common form of justice used many a time by the two Cavanaugh boys.

"You're right," said David at last. "Sometimes connected people do get it easy but don't you see, Sean, that is exactly why my client is in so much trouble. The government, the taxpayers—people like *you*—are sick and tired of watching the wealthy walk. And that's why James has found himself the un-

witting whipping boy for ambitious assholes like Roger Katz."
David shook his head.

"The thing is," he said after a pause, "it doesn't matter how
rich James is. This isn't about his six-figure bank balance or his
Ivy League education, this is about whether he killed a girl or
not.

"He is innocent, Sean. He didn't do this, and no matter who
he is or how much he owns, it is my duty to give him the best
defense I possibly can."

Sean nodded, perhaps realizing David's job wasn't so black
and white after all. "This kid lost his future family?" he said.

"Yes," answered David.

"The girl he loved and his unborn son."

"Yes."

"Then maybe you should hand him back his life so that he
might have the chance to start over."

And David nodded. "I'll do my best."

69

In the state of Massachusetts, jurors are chosen from census lists, in a system that is said to be more democratic than selecting from registered voters, as most states do. The system also removes the numerous grounds for exemption from juror service. Even judges and lawyers and government officials exempt in other states are now required to serve. It is generally believed the elimination of these exemptions provides defendants with jury pools comprised of people more representative of the community from which they are drawn. So, in theory, the system is fairer. Prospective jurors are selected at random from the lists of residents supplied to the Office of Jury Commissioner by each of the 351 cities and towns within the state. But whether jurors are qualified to serve is unknown until they respond to the summons.

In the case of the Matheson trial, close to 450 summonses—a larger number than usual given the high-profile nature of the case—had been dispatched with each individual asked to attend court and begin by filling out a lengthy questionnaire. They were asked about their views on the Ivy League system and the associated opportunities that go with it, on interracial relationships, on the right to life versus abortion issue and what they had heard or read about the case to date. Close to half of these potential jurors would be excused for medical, financial or other personal reasons and others would be eliminated by Judge Isaac Stein who would have the first chance to consider their questionnaires and quiz them individually.

The first two days would be spent narrowing the pool down to about fifty, and the rest of the week reducing that number to twelve jurors and four alternates—with both the defense and the state allowed three peremptory challenges.

James Matheson would be present in court throughout the entire process. David would be tag teaming it with Sara and Arthur as he dipped in and out of court to prepare for the following week at trial. Both sides would savor their peremptory strikes and both would work with experienced jury specialists in order to create their "perfect dozen," a feat that, at least on this cloudy Sunday afternoon, seemed close to impossible.

"I'm sorry, guys," said jury specialist Phyllis Vecchio. "But what I said stands. You have no perfect juror. Your case sucks. When it comes to this jury, the Commonwealth are gonna kick ass. All you can do is try to avoid the selection of their ideal jurist, which . . . is basically anyone with a vagina or a penis."

"Jesus, Phyll," said Arthur. Vecchio was fifty-seven and weighed at least one hundred and ninety pounds. She was a cherry-topped fireball who had been working with Arthur for years, and they were used to her straightforwardness—and the potty mouth that went along with it.

"I'm sorry, Arthur, but you're paying me for my opinion so I ain't gonna shortchange you with a soft sell. Believe it or not, I can think of plenty of better ways to spend my Sunday afternoon than shooting the breeze with you and your fine young friends here in your poorly heated office. So since I am here, and charging you double-time by the way, I figure it would be a disservice to feed you a load of crap."

David shook his head, and the big-hearted Phyll, perhaps in an attempt to paint a slightly better picture than she had first portrayed, sat back in her chair and went on.

"Here's the thing," she began. "That fucker Katz will be looking for women—preferably older, from socioeconomic groups on the lower end of the scale. He's gonna want to appeal to their sense of resentment, their anger at the rich kid with the movie star looks who thinks he can get away with anything—including murder. But men are good too—working-class men who have toiled all their lives to earn a fraction of your client's school fees. He'll want men who are fathers and women who are mothers, both of whom will recoil at the brutality of the killing itself."

Phyllis took a breath—there was more.

"Minorities also work for the prosecution, blacks and Latinos whose chances of attending a university like Deane are somewhere between zero and zip. And Katz won't say no to young women either—girls who are sick of hot-looking kids like your client who lie about getting laid and have the power to stroke their pussy with one hand and squeeze their pretty little necks with the other."

"James is innocent, Phyll," said a now frustrated David, cringing at Phyll's analogy.

"Sure," said Phyll. "But everyone who's read a paper or seen the news in the past few months would probably beg to differ."

"Shit," said Sara.

"I know, honey, it sucks," said Phyll, taking a Coke from Nora and downing it in one guzzle. "And so in all honesty, all I can suggest is this. Keep 'em young and preferably male—and rich and college educated at that. Go for the good-looking ones over the geeks and save your peremptory strikes for your enemy number one."

"For God's sake, Phyll," said David. "You have just described enough potential enemies to populate a country, and we only have three bullets in the barrel. How the hell are we supposed to know which potential juror to strike, when your criteria for veto seems to be anyone with two legs?"

"Easy," interrupted Phyll, leaning forward in her seat, "because identifying enemy number one is a no-brainer. The minute a potential juror expresses a pro-life opinion, the moment you get a sense that he or she is determined to use this trial to exercise their views on the rights of an unborn child, then, and only then, do you get out that gun and fire."

70

"Mr. Cavanaugh," boomed Judge Stein from the front of the courtroom, "may I remind you that it is already Wednesday and so far we have only two confirmed members of the jury. You are the ones who agreed to the motion for a speedy trial, Counselor, but at this rate, I fear . . ."

"One minute, Your Honor," said David, barely lifting his head out of their huddle. They were determined to savor their three yet to be used peremptory challenges, but this one was tough.

Her name was Carol Cahill and she was a thirty-two-year-old computer analyst from the South End. She was small and unassuming, her narrow shoulders drooping at such a degree that every few seconds or so, she would tug at the neck of her dark cashmere cardigan as if terrified it would slip to reveal the crisp white shirt underneath. She was nervous and self-conscious and slumped so far down in her seat that she was practically disappearing behind the witness partition before their very eyes.

"Lose her," said Phyllis who had agreed to spend the week with them playing the contentious game of jury chess.

"No," argued Sara. "She is as close to good as we are going to get. She's smart, single, college educated. She comes from a wealthy family and she is *not* a right-to-lifer. She admitted to having an abortion in her youth, for God's sake. I mean, I know she is nervous, but using one of our strikes against her—come on!"

"Sara," said Phyll, who had a master's degree in psychology, "listen to what you just described—a smart, rich-as-all-hell, independent woman with a fancy college degree. On paper she looks great. But now ask yourself why she is like she is? Why is this seemingly fortunate soul perched before us like a fragile little bird, a mere shadow defeated by everything life has been kind enough to serve her up for breakfast.

"She regrets it, Sara, each and every day of her pathetic little life. She sees *herself* as a murderer. She killed her own unborn kid and will never recover." Phyll took a breath. "So, you guys do what you want. It's your goddamned funeral, or more to the point, your client's. But I swear, you keep this one in and you'll regret it. She cannot save her own child but she can certainly punish your client for taking somebody else's. She is a guilty verdict waiting to happen, troops. I'd stake my life on it."

David looked at Arthur and Sara who nodded in agreement. "We move to strike juror number thirty-six, Your Honor, for reasons of emotional distress," said David at last.

Stein looked at them over his glasses. Katz practically did backflips at the prosecution's table across the aisle.

"Thank you for your time, Ms. Cahill," said the judge at last. "You are free to go."

And with that Carol Cahill took flight from that witness box faster than David could blink. Like a woman running for her life—or the little that was left of it.

■ ■ ■

It was snowing. Temperatures had dipped into the low thirties with forecasters predicting accumulations of up to eight inches in Greater Boston by the time the storm was expected to move out to sea sometime late tonight.

David, Joe and Sara sat looking out the window from the warmth of the high-rise apartment. The thick wet flurries whipping against the glass, the large flakes appearing like a sea of oversized stars as they caught the reflection of the city lights and made their zigzag journey to the busy streets below.

"It's beautiful," said Sara, moving the stacks of case file papers to the side of the coffee table so that she might lean back into David's arms and lift her feet onto the freshly cleared space.

"Sure it looks nice," said Joe. "Until it gets so bad you need your own helicopter to get from A to B."

"This gonna get worse?" asked David.

"Not in the near future. The bureau predicts clear skies to-morrow but the commissioner sent out a memo today saying the next two weeks are looking pretty nasty. The uniforms were already going over their state of emergency protocols—which means no parking along designated major arteries, hospital closures, school closures and all the chaos that goes with it.

"A few winters ago, on Christmas Eve," Joe went on, placing his feet on the coffee table as well, "I attended a case where a five-year-old kid got into his daddy's snow-covered car and decided to play cops and robbers. He put the key in the ignition and ran the car for a coupla hours. But since the exhaust was buried under two foot of snow, he managed to poison himself with the carbon monoxide and . . ."

"Oh God," said Sara.

"Merry Christmas," said David.

"And a Happy New Year," said Joe.

They were depressed. There was no other word for it. Seven of the jury had been confirmed—four women and three men—and five of the seven were married with kids, and all three of the men were working-class.

They still intended to target H. Edgar Simpson, but they knew the evidence against him was weak. Worse still, they had no idea as to the nature of Katz's ace in the hole, which, if as good as the Kat seemed to think, could well blow them out of the water before they had a chance to point the finger at anyone—let alone the witness who delivered the case to the Commonwealth, hook, line and sinker.

The papers before them, including the horrific photographs of a deceased Jessica Nagoshi, were like graphic reminders of their impending defeat, taunting them with what they could see, and more to the point what they couldn't—what had to be there, but wasn't; what they knew, but could not prove.

David lifted his arm from around Sara's shoulder and leaned forward to pick up one of the shots—a close-up of Jessica's face and neck, her skin gray, her lips blue, her neck extended at an ungodly angle, circled by the marks of an unidentified monster.

"This is Katz's ticket right here," he said holding up the macabre image. "I can tell you exactly what he is going to do. He is going to blow up a shot of a smiling, healthy Jessica and juxtapose it with *this*," he said, shaking the gruesome portrait in his hand. "The thing is," he went on, "I look at this and I want to kill the bastard who did this too."

Sara put her hand on his back, and Joe nodded.

"If Simpson or Nagoshi did this, David," said Joe, "I promise you that Frank and I won't stop until we find the evidence against them."

"I know," said David, still mesmerized by the photograph. "But I . . ."

And then he saw it. Just like that. It was there, or rather it wasn't. He picked up another shot taken from behind, in a desperate need to confirm what he thought he saw. How could he have been so stupid? How could he have missed it?

"Jesus!" he said at last.

"What is it?" asked Sara, leaning forward to look at the images in David's hand.

"Can you stand up, Sara?" he said as he pointed to the middle of the room. "And can you put your hair up? And turn around. Thanks."

"Ah . . . okay," she said, grabbing an elastic band from the table to twist up her hair before moving around the coffee table and turning her back on David to face Joe.

"Don't move," he said before running to the kitchen and rifling through the top shelf of the narrow refrigerator. He moved to the sink beyond Sara and Joe's line of vision before returning to the living room, his hands out before him.

David's next move took Sara by surprise. He moved forward, quickly, and grabbed her long narrow neck with his large hands. "Ouch," said Sara.

"Sorry, but I . . ." David removed his hands, the purple grape juice he had poured all over them, leaving their mark on Sara's neck. He asked Sara to turn around to face him while Joe moved to the side table to switch on a lamp before jumping over the coffee table and standing next to David.

"Shit," said Joe as David held the images of Jessica Nagoshi up next to Sara's face.

"What?" said an obviously frustrated Sara, not able to see what was now so clear to the other two in the room.

"I can explain . . . it's just . . . can you turn around?" said David. "Slowly."

And she did—as David looked at Joe.

"Matheson didn't do it," said Joe.

"It is a physical impossibility," said David.

"Does this mean we can prove our client is innocent?" asked Sara.

And then David smiled. "Beyond all reasonable doubt."

71

"No," said Boston City Medical Examiner Gustav Svenson. Gus was a man of few words and David knew he would reject his first question outright.

"Wait, Gus. Hear me out."

"Yes," said the blond, six-foot-four Swede. "But before I hear, I repeat what I said many weeks ago when you ask me the same question."

David nodded, knowing he had to play this Gus' way.

"I refer you to *Journal of Forensic Sciences*, Volume 51, Issue 2, dated March 2006, pages 381 to 385," Svenson began. "Using techniques adopted from forensic odontology, a study was conducted that tested whether researchers could match the correct hands to fingermarks left on the neck of a simulated strangulation victim.

"Blue paint was applied to the fingers of twenty-one men, who then grasped the neck of a dummy and applied pressure similar to that necessary to achieve strangulation. The dummy's neck was constructed so that it had same compliance and consistency as a human neck with human skin."

David turned his hands in a circular motion, willing Gus to speed it up.

"When fingers pressed into latex-like material, an imprint remained. The blue paint on the fingers of participants preserved the prints. The imprints on the dummy's neck and participants' hands were photographed, and all images were uploaded on a computer, sorted by imprints and hands."

"Okay, Gus," said David, now shaking his head as he took a seat on Gus' white laboratory stool. "You told me this two months ago, when I asked if we could lift prints from the girl's neck. But now I am asking something different. Now I want to know if . . ."

"Ah . . . ," said Gus, holding up a finger. "I am not finished."

David shook his head before dipping his hand as if to say: "Go right ahead."

"Researchers were unable to make any correct match of a participant's hand with the imprints left on a dummy's neck. The study found that the matching of hands to finger marks is difficult and inconclusive."

"*But,*" countered David, lifting up a finger, "in four cases they matched the imprint with several hands, meaning they were able to eliminate certain hands simply because of their size."

Gus shook his head. "So you are not trying to find a print?"

"*No!*" said David.

"Then why not say this before?" said Gus in earnest. "Tell me what you want."

Gus was a good man. Forthright and fair. And while he lived and died by the boundaries of logic and science, he was also open to new possibilities especially, David suspected, if it meant reminding Roger Katz of an ME's professional responsibility as an independent analyst with no legal bias or predisposed opinions.

Gus had too much class to voice his own opinion of the demanding ADA, but David was aware of the Kat's repeated attempts to get Gus to sway his way, and his tendency to blame Gus and his fellow examiners for setbacks or losses at trial. And so while David knew Gus would not bend the rules on his behalf, he believed he may agree to lean on the side of restraint when it came to providing information the ADA should be seeking individually. In other words he was hoping that what he was about to propose would remain in this laboratory. Giving David his own ace in the hole, guaranteed to trump whatever Katz had up his sleeve, hands down.

David began by showing Gus the shot of Jessica Nagoshi and describing the impromptu experiment he undertook in his own living room late the night before. He highlighted the finger marks on the front of Jessica's neck, which led the ME to conclude the girl was strangled from behind, before showing him the second image of the murdered girl from the back.

"I do not understand," said Gus. "What point is it you wish to make? My information is correct, the girl was attacked from behind. If strangled from the front the thumb impressions would be at the front of the neck, like so," Gus held out his hands to form a circle as if grasping David's neck front on.

"I don't disagree," said David. "But if strangled from behind you would get the opposite—finger impressions on the front and thumb impressions on the *back*."

"Yes. Fingers front just as the image shows, and the other one, from behind, it . . ." But then Gus saw it.

"The thumbs," said Gus with an intake of breath. "They are not there. They should be at the back of the neck, here." He pointed at the second shot.

"That's what I thought," said David, hoping to lead the ME where he needed him to go.

"But they are at the side," Gus went on. "Here," he pointed again. "They do not reach far enough around to . . ."

"My client's hands are the same size as mine, Gus," said David, now standing in front of the ME, holding up his hands for Gus to see. "They are large, thick, broad. But the hands that did this," he said gesturing at the images, "they are . . ."

"Small, slender, slim," said Gus.

"And so . . ." David began, needing to hear it again, needing to know that this was the ME's official medical assessment, the same assessment he would be willing to back up in court, for each and every member of their "imperfect" jury to hear. ". . . just to clarify, it is your learned professional opinion that . . ."

"That the hands that killed your victim are below average size," finished Gus, still staring at the two shots before him. "A man with larger hands would have extended his thumbs to the top of the spinal column at the base of the back of the neck. I am sorry, David," he said, lowering his eyes. "I should have found this sooner."

"No, Gus," said David, unable to suppress the beginnings of a smile. "It's not your fault."

"Of course there are discrepancies," Svenson went on. "This is not an exact science. It is conjecture based on what we observe. But not everything is a mystery, David. In most cases the truth is there for us, plain and clear, as long as we are willing to see."

• • •

Roger Katz was in his element. Ten down and two to go. It could not have gone better. The jury so far was a prosecutor's dream—six women and four men, the majority public school educated, blue-collar workers with kids ranging from ages two to twenty. Two of the ten were black, one Hispanic and even better, praise God, one of Japanese descent!

It was as it should be, he pondered as he sat high and mighty at his desk on the right-hand side of the courtroom, waiting for Stein to return from their late luncheon adjournment. He had, as fortune would have it, realized at a very early age that opportunity was there for the taking; it was a perfectly straight road from *here* to *there* as long as you weren't stupid enough to get diverted along the way. But that is what happened, time and time again, as millions upon millions of supposedly intelligent moralistic morons slowed their own path by meandering off course to assist those less fortunate. Morons like Cavanaugh and his pro bono princess girlfriend, and their poorly groomed boss who, even now, was stooped in a huddle with Katz's prized kill.

He smiled. His right eye still smarted from Cavanaugh's pathetic muscle flexing blow some weeks ago—an attack to which he did not retaliate because he was focused enough to realize that any physical retribution would be below him. As AG Sweeney had so aptly put it in a private conversation later that evening, "You are a smart man, Roger, who will not be drawn into the brutish Neanderthal games of desperate attorneys like Cavanaugh. Your victory will be won in the courtroom, not the boxing ring. And that, my friend, will be the greatest victory of all."

And so, as Stein entered the room, the clerk calling for order, Katz turned his head to smile at Sara "Beyoncé" Davis. The look she returned was nothing short of abusive but he found even that amusing, or more to the point, stimulating, which, considering his mood, was just icing on the cake.

"Juror number fifty-two," said Stein, cutting to the chase, Katz now on his feet ready to move another one of his little toy soldiers into his growing battalion of twelve.

"Thank you, Your Honor," he said with a flourish, knowing that the best was yet to come.

. . .

Later that afternoon, Roger Katz made his first mistake, or
rather two mistakes in a row. He used his last peremptory strike
to veto a thirty-year-old electrical engineer and MIT grad
named Michael Davenport. Tall, slim, with slick fair hair and
fashionable glasses, Davenport looked like a walking, talking
prototype for the defense—handsome, college educated, a state
water polo champion with a furniture magnate father. In fact,
he looked so perfect that Katz had obviously made the decision
to strike him before he even took the stand, producing Davenport's questionnaire and telling Stein he wanted to use his third
and final challenge to remove this juror on the grounds that he
had a cousin who had once attended Deane. The fact that the
cousin was now forty-five and would have graduated when
Matheson and his friends were still in diapers was obviously
not a consideration. However, Katz did manage to convince the
judge that his objections were valid, and within seconds Mr.
Davenport was walking out the back door and on his way back
to his $150K a year career. And Phyllis Vecchio could not help
but smile.

"What a buffoon!" She grinned. "Katz had this guy pegged
for a strike from the get-go, but he is so bloody sure of himself
that he failed to see it."

"See what?" asked Arthur.

"The obvious dummy," said Phyll, rolling her eyes in mock
frustration. "Davenport works for Apex Electronics. In fact, he
got a promotion a few months ago and is now head of their
Electrical Engineering and Computer Science Division. Apex
are on the verge of signing a major new client, to supply them
with state of the art computer parts and technology for a new
generation of notebooks and PCs."

"Nagoshi Inc.!" guessed Arthur.

"In one," said Phyll. "In fact, according to my research, this
deal will make Nagoshi their second biggest contractor."

Sara smiled. "How the hell do you know this stuff, Phyll?"

"It's what I do, kid." Phyll rubbed her long acrylic fingernails
on her hot pink blouse in a gesture of self-praise. "It's what I
do."

Seconds later the judge called a young man named Josh Bergin. Bergin was twenty-one and listed his profession as "pro-

fessional student." He was a somewhat scruffy but good-looking kid, with long light brown hair and an earring in his right lobe. He was tall, with a three-day growth and piercing pale blue eyes, and could well have passed as a member of some Seattle-based grunge band from the '90s.

"Welcome, Mr. Bergin," said Katz. "Thank you for your time here today. I see you list your occupation as 'professional student.' Well, I am sure you are a young man with an insatiable quest for knowledge, so tell us, where do you do most of your studying?"

The question, aimed at discovering which so-called educational institution would welcome such a young man as Bergin, was dripping with the insinuation that Bergin spent more time trolling live music venues than hitting the books, and Sara guessed Bergin sensed this too.

"The Hark," he said. "And Starbucks, when I need a double espresso as a pre-finals pick-me-up."

Bergin smiled, the courtroom shared a chuckle, and Sara, who realized the young man's answer had gone completely over the ADA's head, looked at Phyll before breaking into a wide grin herself.

"And you are studying . . . ?"

"At the moment I am doing an extra course in positive psychology. It is aimed at teaching people how to be happy."

This was an oversimplification and Sara knew it. She had read about this course, it was actually one of the most sought after degrees in the country. It looked at the benefits of positive thinking and the power of optimism in the workplace.

"Working for you, is it, Mr. Bergin?"

"I'm doing okay." The young man smiled, and Sara could not help but smile with him.

"Tell me, Mr. Bergin . . ." Katz glanced at his Rolex before moving on. "Do you have a problem with the concept of another student being capable of murder?"

"No."

"Have you read about this case, heard the news reports?"

"Some."

"Do you think, that despite what you may have read or heard, that you could still make an unbiased assessment of the case based on the information presented at trial?"

"Sure," said Bergin, flicking the hair from his brow.

"Thank you, Mr. Bergin. I have no problem with this juror, Your Honor," said Katz, before turning his back on Bergin and swaggering back to his desk.

"Ms. Davis?" said Stein.

"One moment, Your Honor." Sara turned to Phyll. "The Hark," she said in a whisper. "Bergin is studying law—at Harvard no less!"

She was right. "The Hark" was the colloquial name for Harkness Common, the prestigious law school's café cum socializing and study area where students would hang out, hook up or find a quiet corner to read.

"I read about the positive psychology class in the *Tribune*," she went on. "It's now the most popular course at Harvard. Law students can take it as an extra subject. Apparently employers see it as a plus—the power of positive thought and all that."

"Right," said Phyll. "And Bergin may live in a rented apartment in Somerville, but his parents own a three-story brownstone on Beacon Hill."

"And I suppose that paint-stained shirt is designer too?" asked Arthur.

"It's Ralph Lauren's 'Rugby' line," said Phyll. "Ralph swapped his polo player for a skull and crossbones insignia and *voila*! A whole new market."

Sara squeezed Phyll's arm in gratitude before turning back to Stein. "We have no objection to this juror, Your Honor," she said. And with that, Josh Bergin was promptly confirmed as juror number twelve.

Moments later, Stein called for an end to the day's proceedings, reaffirming that the four alternates would be selected and sworn in tomorrow—Friday—after which they, and the official twelve, would be asked to return to court first thing Monday for trial instructions and opening statements.

As the room began to clear, Sara took James' hand and looked at his now healing face to say the one thing she had been desperately wanting to say for months. With David on his way back from the ME's office, and Bergin secured as their one glimmer of hope among a team of Commonwealth clones, she felt a welcome surge of optimism that all was not lost after all.

"This has been a good day, James," she said, squeezing his

hand, which, she was pleased to see, had finally stopped shaking. "The bruising patterns," she began, having filled James in on David's discovery during luncheon recess. "And now juror number twelve."

"He is one in a dozen, Sara," said an obviously still terrified James, glancing at the security guards approaching from behind, and clasping her hand even tighter as if begging her not to let go.

"One. Yes," said Sara, now feeling an all-encompassing need to hold him tight and protect him from the world, as she had her own little brother for so many years.

"I don't like those odds, Sara," said James. "In fact, they scare the hell out of me."

"I know," she said, pulling him in close. "But you are a student of the law, James, and as such have to remember one all-important thing. This isn't about odds, it's about reasonable doubt. And as that is the case, James, one is all we need."

72

"Thanks, Mick," said Sara, grabbing a fresh apple, carrot and wheatgrass juice from Myrtle's cheery proprietor.

"My pleasure," said Mick, handing David a more conservative orange and pineapple. "When this is all over I'm holding a little shindig here for you all—a victory celebration after hours. No alcohol, of course, given my license doesn't allow it, at least none that isn't approved by the law abiding Lieutenant Mannix." He grinned.

"Thanks for the encouragement, Mick," said a grateful David.

"Pleasure," said Mick. "And the juice is on the house."

They left Myrtle's and headed outside, planning to drink their juices slowly as they walked home to shower and change and head to the office for a long weekend of pre-trial preparation. David was just about to run through his ideas for his opening statement, a speech he would base on James' good character, when Sara's cell rang, prompting her to hand David her juice and retrieve her phone from her sweatshirt pocket.

"Hello," she said, and David waited as she walked silently beside him, obviously listening intently to the early morning caller on the other end of the line.

"The important thing is that they are off the ground by the end of the week," she said. "We figure Katz's witnesses will take at least four days and if that's the case we . . ."

"Friday, that's right. But the flight from Australia is close to a day and we want to avoid them being jetlagged.

"But surely, if it's a respected law firm they will understand if Flinn has to delay his start. It would only be a matter of days after all. What about Buntine?

"He would have to get to Perth then, or Darwin. Does Qantas even fly out of Darwin for the US?

"Okay, I understand the problems. But what are you suggesting, Diane?

"Yes. If it comes down to it, but it would be much better for us—for James—if they were here in person.

"Okay. It's cutting it fine but . . . Diane, do you think it would be better if we spoke to these boys direct, or at the very least to Flinn, who is contactable at this point.

"Yes, I know you know these boys. But keep us posted."

And then Sara hung up before turning to David to say: "We have a problem."

. . .

Two hours later they were back in the office and Sara was repeating their "problem" to Arthur and Nora.

"As we know, James had two best friends in Sydney—Lawson Flinn and Sterling Buntine. According to Diane they were inseparable at school—same classes, same sporting teams, same leisure activities and so forth.

"Lawson is in his second to final year of law at Adelaide University. He moved there from Sydney to be close to his fiancé who is the daughter of the premier of South Australia. According to Diane he has just accepted a summer internship at some seriously impressive law firm and starts this week, making it hard for him to get away."

Arthur shook his head and Sara stole a glance at David. This was unsettling news and they knew it, and unfortunately it only got worse.

"Buntine has been a little harder to track down. He was a boarder at high school, his family being wealthy landowners from the Northern Territory."

"Now that is the real Outback," said Nora.

"Exactly," said Sara, "which also means that, according to Diane, he has been extremely difficult to find. Apparently he has been jackarooing in the Kimberleys."

"But that's mid-north Western Australia," said Arthur. "Literally the middle of nowhere. How are we supposed to locate this boy? And more to the point, why didn't Diane Matheson flag these problems sooner."

David and Sara had asked themselves the very same question.

"She's stressed, Arthur," said Sara. "In all fairness to her she has lined up, organized and paid for the passage of three of James' school and sports teachers, including the principal of his highly regarded senior school. They arrive on Tuesday in more than enough time to give testimony."

Arthur nodded, before saying what David knew he was about to say. "But the friends are the key. You stressed this yourselves."

For some reason they felt like two admonished schoolchildren. The trial started in less than forty-eight hours and two of their key character witnesses had gone AWOL.

"Minding" Diane Matheson had been Sara's job, but David knew he should have been riding his client's mother too. It was too big a detail to miss, and a slip they could live to regret.

"If worse comes to worse, Diane said Flinn had promised to write a statement to be read in court. He is a lawyer so he knows what he is doing. He also said that if Buntine was unable to make it in time, he would organize for his statement to be taken in Western Australia. Apparently Flinn has contacted the Port Hedland Police in an attempt to track his friend down so . . ."

They sat there in silence, taking it all in.

"Who else have we got?" asked Arthur at last.

"One teacher, one swim coach and the principal from Sydney," David began. "The Reverend Luke Mitchell from Brookline who christened James and has watched him grow from a boy to a man, Jessica's best friend Meredith Wentworth and . . ."

"Still no one from the Deane faculty," finished Arthur.

There was no avoiding it. The lack of character witnesses from Deane was a major hole in their case. David had no doubt that Dean Johns and his blessed board had made it quite clear to the university as a whole that James was not to be supported. But even so, they had hoped someone would come forward on his behalf.

The problem was, David knew, that this was not so much a case of academic or administrative bullying; the cruel fact was that most of James' tutors and coaches, and even his fellow students at Deane, had a valid reason for refusing to testify on their client's behalf—they thought he was guilty, and that was the biggest blow of all.

Just then there was a rap on the door, and an energetic Sawyer came bounding into the room, almost knocking over an umbrella stand and tripping on a box of case files in the process.

"Whoops," he said, all arms and legs as he regained his balance and looked up at them all. "I thought this was meant to be a good day," he said, reading the despair clearly written on their faces.

"Well, time for a pick-me-up, folks," he grinned, as he flopped onto the office sofa next to Sara. "And as I am feeling particularly generous today, my good news will be delivered in twos."

"All right, kid," said David at last, rising from his chair to move to Arthur's beer fridge in the far corner of the room. David opened the door and grabbed a close-to-freezing Coke before tossing it across the room to Sawyer. "Don't keep us waiting. What have you got?"

Sawyer popped the Coke and took a long, slow drink. He wiped brown fizz from his top lip with the back of his hand, and offered a beaming smile before going on.

"First up, Mr. Lim the younger has arrived. I dropped him at the Regency Plaza where he is currently enjoying his first hot bath in over a year. He understands he may not be needed at trial but, considering his own suspicions, is willing to hang around, just in case."

This kid really *was* part of their team, thought David, and in lots of ways had more than earned his place among them.

"Secondly, you'll be pleased to know that I have been following your friend Simpson for the past twenty-four hours."

"You checked out his hands," smiled David.

"I sure did. Which was not easy, I might add, given he never removes his camel cashmere gloves. Which is understandable given I overheard him telling Westinghouse he bought them at Saks for 250 bucks a pair."

This was interesting in itself, thought David. Simpson and Westinghouse were talking—and obviously on friendly terms. They were still in Katz's camp, he knew, and to be honest, he was not surprised.

"Come on, Sawyer," said Sara, punching the kid in the arm. "Cut to the chase."

"Okay, okay," said Sawyer, obviously enjoying the attention. "Well, let me put it this way," he said, holding up his own set of narrow hands. "If we were in a small hand competition then H. Edgar would win hands down, no pun intended."

"Are you sure?" asked Sara.

"Saw them with my own eyes, but stopped short of asking to inspect his manicure." Sawyer grinned.

David looked at Arthur. "It doesn't prove he did it but it doesn't rule him out either. You did good, kid," he said, turning back to Sawyer.

"All part of the service," said a now beaming Sawyer. "Now, tell me, what else do you need me to do?"

73

The room smelled of snow. Well, not snow exactly but everything that had been walked into the room with it—fallen leaves and street grime and a million other city smells that gave the odorless white ice a pungent scent of its own.

It was cold outside and hot inside—the clerk having jacked up the heaters in Boston Superior Courtroom number nine to compensate for the below-zero temps outside, obviously not realizing that they were indeed *indoors* and jammed into a space now bursting with bodies and the bundles of discarded overcoats and scarves that came with them. The place looked like Grand Central Station before the holidays, thought David as he surveyed the room around him, and the people like travelers set on a journey of hope or catastrophe, depending on where they were headed and who they were expecting to see.

Katz was on his feet—pacing, head down. He had swapped his usual dark-hued suit for one of a deep taupe, a shade which, every now and again, when the sallow beam of the overhanging pendulums reflected off the snow-bordered windows, gave off a tinge of gold, creating the illusion of an aura. He had decided to forgo his usual palm-pumping, confident as all hell, bring it on persona for a more subtle "I am humbled to be chosen as the Commonwealth's representative to seek truth and justice in these very important proceedings" façade, which he had obviously thought would win him more points with the press, and more importantly, with the jury, who were now being shepherded into the room.

And there they were—the merry band of twelve and their four bridesmaids. Tall, short, fat, thin, male, female, young, old, black, white, Asian, Hispanic and sadly, from David's perspective, all already staring across the room at his client, with the glint of accusation in their eyes.

"They hate me already," whispered James—his clean-shaven young face now back to its former perfection—as he leaned toward David.

"No," said David, turning to his client. "They are just curious. People always have a morbid fascination with anyone whose image has been splashed across the media for weeks on end. They need to look at you, take you in, make you *real* in their universe. Before long they will get to know you as you really are, and by the time this trial is over, their eyes will show regret and remorse and anger that you have been put through all that you have."

•   •   •

Moments later the judge entered the room, his heavy footfalls resounding off the worn cedar floor. He took his seat, flipping his long black robe over the back of his chair, before donning his worse-for-wear wire-rim glasses and surveying the anxious crowd before him. He said nothing, just turned his head slowly from left to right, right to left, nodding separately at Katz and his associates, and David and his team, before lifting both his arms simultaneously to point at the boxed gathering of people at the far left- and far right-hand sides of the room.

"It is no coincidence that you are seated where you are," he began. "The good people of the media to my right, the generous people of the jury to my left. For just like the representatives of the Commonwealth," he said, gesturing at Katz, "and the defense," he went on, pointing at David, "you hold a great responsibility in these proceedings."

Stein adjusted himself so that he might turn to his right and address the already mesmerized members of the press.

"To the ladies and gentlemen of the media, I ask that you promise to uphold the principles of your profession and to report accurately and fairly without any trace of bias, abandon any personal opinions and serve the people of this great state, indeed this great nation, with accurate and impartial representation of the events that are about to take place."

Stein hesitated, various members of the press nodding in agreement, the room resting on his every word, before shifting slightly and maneuvering himself to his left.

"To the members of the jury, first and foremost, I want to

thank you for your unselfish determination to serve this court today, and in coming days as this trial progresses. I know I do not need to reinforce that this proceeding—our entire system of criminal justice—is based on one all-important principle: that if the defendant is to be found guilty, he or she must be found so beyond *all reasonable doubt.*

"Now," Stein paused then to lean toward them that few inches further, "I shall not insult your intelligence by embarking on a lengthy diatribe regarding the definition of reasonable doubt. We have all watched enough legal shows on TV to grasp the concept of that." He smiled, and the jury smiled with him. "But I shall say that any decision you reach must be justified *unquestionably,* and without the tiniest shadow of uncertainty.

"Secondly, ladies and gentlemen, I must stress that any determination you make must be based on the facts presented in this room and this room alone. You are not to be swayed by the reports of the good people to my right," he said, pointing over his shoulder to the press. "For despite their best efforts, they have been known to stray.

"Thirdly, you must promise, I repeat, you must *promise* this court, and more to the point yourselves, that any decision you make must be yours and yours alone. I know you are part of a group and groups tend to work as teams and I encourage you to discuss matters freely and openly during your deliberations but . . . I implore you to remember that the very nature of our system of justice is based on the rights of the individual and it is your right—your *duty*—to make decisions independently and not because they appear to be the most popular position of the day."

David wondered if this last remark was for his benefit. Stein was not stupid; he knew the jury was stacked toward the Commonwealth and perhaps this was his way of telling each and every one of the twelve that they should not be swayed by the majority.

"Finally," said the judge, swiveling on his chair once again to face the front of the crowd, "I want to express my condolences to both the Nagoshis and the Mathesons," he said as he nodded to the two men sitting behind Katz and to the impeccably dressed Jed and Diane Matheson behind the defense table. "Parenting is, no doubt, the most difficult job any human being can undertake, and I acknowledge your feelings of loss and deep-seated concern."

Stein took a breath then, before straightening the papers before him, pushing his glasses back up his nose and looking up at the crowd with a new expression of intent.

"I believe we are ready to begin, Mr. Katz," he said, his former tone now replaced by one of authority and purpose. "So if the Commonwealth is ready to deliver their opening statement . . ."

"Of course, Your Honor," said Katz, springing to his feet.

And so, it began.

* * *

"Ladies and gentleman," Katz started, buttoning his jacket and moving around the table to pace slowly toward the jury. "I want to be honest with you," he said, looking down, shaking his head. "I have been working on this opening statement for some weeks. In fact, up until last night I was pretty happy with it—thinking I had it down pat." Katz lifted his hands and gave the jury a slight, confessional smile as if to say, "Call me the clichéd conscientious prosecutor because that's exactly who I am."

"But for some reason, late last night, something occurred to me, not just about my part in this trial, but the job we are all here to do." He nodded then, taking yet another step toward them. "Justice is a positive force and, selfishly, one of the main reasons I love my job so much. I *do* get a sense of satisfaction every time I remove a violent perpetrator from the streets, I *do* feel proud every time I secure a conviction against an offender who has violated the rights of others, and I *do* feel admiration for every juror who does their duty and finds a guilty man to be so, no matter how difficult that may be.

"And then I considered this case, this defendant, and in all honesty I felt sad." Katz shrugged and nodded again. "That's right, ladies and gentlemen, it seems like such a basic, simple word but there is really no better way to describe it. It struck me, when I considered the defendant, James Matheson," he said, turning to gesture at James, the jury's eyes following his direction, "that this is one of the saddest cases I have ever had to prosecute.

"Of course," he went on, taking another small step forward, "my sorrow, my grief, stems from a number of sources. First of all, it is felt for Jessica Nagoshi who, let us not forget, was the one who experienced the *incredible* pain associated with such a brutal killing—the blows to the head, the manual strangulation, and most likely the knowledge that as the life was leaving her lungs, it was also leaving those of her unborn child, whose silent screams would never be heard.

"Secondly, it comes for the Nagoshis, who will mourn the loss of their beautiful, energetic, enthusiastic, intelligent, humanitarian daughter and sister, and their unborn grandson and nephew, each and every day of their lives.

"But finally, and perhaps surprisingly, it also comes for the loss of the defendant, or more specifically, for what he represents."

"What the fuck is he doing?" whispered David, leaning into Arthur's ear.

"I'm not sure, but it's making me nervous," returned his boss.

"You see, James Matheson, at least by all appearances, is a smart, amiable, friendly, trustworthy, talented young man," Katz said, slowly counting off James' attributes on his long manicured fingers. "He comes from a good family, has plenty of firm friends and is admired by all who know him as someone who is reliable, dedicated and a generally nice guy to hang out with. He is good-looking and athletic, attentive and interested, and has the well-earned reputation of a young man unafraid of hard work to achieve his own highly set goals.

"Now, the defense will bring before you a number of people who will describe these attributes in detail, and I feel it only fair to say that everything they tell you will most likely be true."

"Fuck," said David in a whisper, finally realizing what the ADA was doing.

"And *that*, ladies and gentlemen, is what I find so distressing." Katz was right in front of them now, his hands clasping the wooden bar before him so that his upper body was literally over the bar—on their side, part of their team.

"Part of me wants to believe James Matheson is innocent, and part of you will too. But the sad fact is, this young man with so many outwardly wonderful characteristics, this young man, the epitome of the American Dream, is a murderer plain and simple.

"However," he said, straightening again, looking each and every juror in the eye, "I can promise you that, no matter what my feelings of regret, no matter how difficult it may be to shatter the reputation of a young man with so much to live for, no matter how upsetting it will be to know that James' upstanding parents are learning the true nature of their son for the very first time, I will present the truth about the defendant—for Jessica, for her unborn child, for the Nagoshis, and most of all for the system of justice that this country represents.

"And so," he said taking a breath, his face giving off the slightest trace of a sheen, "when you see that the evidence is irrefutable, when you realize that Mr. Matheson is the only viable suspect, when you hear that he lied to the police, that he concocted an alibi, that he confessed to his friends, and that he fathered a child who he killed in cold blood . . . you will have *no choice* but to swallow your sorrow and do your duty as well. For any less would make a mockery of this court, and fail to uphold the principles that we, as Americans, hold dear."

• • •

David was in shock. Katz had taken his entire opening statement, based almost exclusively on James' good character and turned it against him. It was a disaster. They were losing their case before they even had a chance to begin.

"David," whispered Sara. "You have to take a recess, we have to regroup. We . . ."

"No," he said, realizing that now, as Katz had taken his seat, the entire jury were staring directly at him. "We call for a break we look weak. Katz has left us with only one way out and we have no choice but to take it." He was starting to sweat.

"How? David, please."

"David," said Arthur just as David rose to his feet. "Sara's right. You need to think about this, you need to . . ."

But it was too late. David was up. Sara clasped James' hand under the desk and the jury sat frozen in anticipation. The press had stopped scribbling, and the crowd held their breath. David glanced briefly up at the judge who, he could have sworn, gave him the slightest nod of encouragement before moving forward, swiftly, toward the twelve men and women on the other side of the room.

"Mr. Katz is right," he said, beginning on the same spot it had taken Katz ten minutes to reach. "James Matheson is a person I am proud to call friend, and I will not take any more of your time repeating the positive attributes the ADA so rightly bestowed upon him.

"Mr. Katz is right. Murder is the ultimate tragedy and all of us, most significantly my client, would give anything to reverse the clock and return Jessica Nagoshi to her family.

"Mr. Katz is correct when he says that satisfaction and sorrow come as two equal and opposing by-products of our profession, and Mr. Katz is right again when he says it is your duty to convict the true killer no matter how privileged or promising he may be."

David paused there, his heart beating triple time. He knew it sounded to the jury like he was giving in, like he was conceding his client had made the ultimate "mistake." But this was right where he wanted them, in a state of confusion, uncertain as to what he was about to say next and on the edge of their seats, ready and willing to hear every single word.

But as they sat there, staring at him, he did something none of them could have anticipated. He turned his back on them. He turned and stopped and looked directly at his client, his green eyes locking with James' in some unspoken promise of truth. And in that moment it was as if all else in the room had disappeared, as James nodded in thanks and David refocused, turning back to the jury quickly, decidedly, with a new edge of determination in his voice.

"James Matheson did not kill Jessica Nagoshi. He loved her, and he would have loved the child that he also lost at the hand of a so-far unidentified monster. Mr. Katz talked of sorrow, of loss and pain and regret, but unfortunately nobody—nobody—knows those feelings better than my client.

"This seems to be a morning of promises," he said, the slightest trickle of sweat now making its way down his brow. "And so allow me to make you a pledge as well. A declaration of innocence is one thing but verification is another, and as Judge Stein so rightly instructed, no decision should be made without the guarantee of proof.

"And so, I promise you—each and every one of you—that I shall prove my client is innocent for one reason and one reason only. James could not have killed Jessica Nagoshi because Jessica Nagoshi was murdered by somebody else. And I . . ." he began, the room so still and silent that he swore he could hear the snow falling, softly, peacefully outside. "We," he said, before gesturing at his fellow defense counsel behind him, ". . . know exactly who it is."

The courtroom exploded as David moved quickly back to his seat, the judge calling for order, Katz already on his feet accusing David of lying to the jury in his short but shocking opening address.

"Your Honor," the ADA screamed above the hubbub, "this is outrageous. Mr. Cavanaugh obviously has no respect for the good people of the jury. He insults them and he spits in the face of the police and the District Attorney's Office who have been investigating this case for months."

"Calm down, Mr. Katz. Order," Stein called to the room. "I am afraid Mr. Cavanaugh has every right to make suppositions in his opening statement, and now it is his lot to back them up." Stein turned to David.

"Mr. Cavanaugh, a word of warning, if I feel you are setting out on a path of unsubstantiated accusations, I shall shut you down before you have a chance to extend your finger and point."

But David was sure that Stein knew better. He could see it in the old man's eyes. "We have the proof, Your Honor."

Stein nodded, a nod that soon turned into a shake. "All right, but I warn you, the road you travel is a dangerous one."

"I understand that, Your Honor."

"Judge, please," urged the Kat.

"You had your fair share of airtime this morning, Mr. Katz. So I suggest you move on and prepare to call your first witness. We shall adjourn for an early lunch and then hear the testimony of . . ."

And then it hit him—as he remembered who the first witness was and realized what he had done to him. David saw it in the half-smile now spreading across the ADA's face.

"Detective Joseph Mannix," said Katz, speaking to the judge but looking at David. "We shall be calling the Boston Police Homicide Unit Commander directly after lunch."

And in that moment David recognized the trap he had set for himself—and worse, for his good friend Joe.

74

"What the hell are you doing?" asked Arthur as he pulled David and Sara into a vacant office along the Superior Court corridor.

"He set me up," said David. "I had no choice."

"Bullshit," said Arthur. "You could have conceded a loss. Katz got you fair and square, David, and you made it worse by taking the bait. This is only the first morning, we had time to make up ground."

"No," David said again. They were pacing now, around a stranger's office. "The odds are stacked against us, Arthur. We can't afford to start in second place. At least I narrowed the playing field and . . ."

"And created a massive problem for Joe." Arthur took a breath, removed his glasses and rubbed his eyes. "Having a witness for the Commonwealth on our side is a huge advantage, but you just pissed that into the wind because you cannot stand to lose to your longtime foe.

"Joe didn't hear your opening, David, he assumes you stuck to the original. He has no idea you told the world that we know the identity of the real killer and Katz is going to grill him on it within the hour. You boxed him into a corner, David. This is nothing short of catastrophic."

In all his years with Arthur, David had never seen him like this. The man had a temper, sure, but this was more than that. Arthur wanted to save James as much as he did, and he could see their chances slipping away by the minute, thanks to David's hatred for Katz, and his selfish need to challenge the clever ADA every step of the way.

"I'm sorry," said David at last, falling into the chair at the far corner of the office before burying his head in his hands.

"This is my fault. I have placed us in an impossible position. I have promised something we can't deliver. We have no *proof*."

"Then we'll get it," said Sara, speaking for the first time.

Arthur turned to her as David lifted his eyes.

"Enough is enough," she went on. "Dwelling on what is done won't get us anywhere. First, we have to work out how the hell we are going to save Joe's testimony, and then . . . then we do everything in our power to nail the real killer. That is all that is left to us, and so that is what we will do."

• • •

The Kat began slowly. He was smiling and this in itself Joe found disconcerting. He started by asking Joe to state his position and give a brief description of his duties as Boston PD's homicide chief. He even stopped along the way to compliment Joe on his "impeccable record," which was enough to confirm to Joe that something was up.

"Lieutenant Mannix," said the Kat, now parading like a peacock before the court, "I want to begin by making one thing clear. You have been following this investigation from the outset, is that correct?"

"Yes. The Wellesley police took the call, but myself and my partner Detective Frank McKay were the first homicide detectives on the scene."

"And you surveyed the crime scene, supervised the collection of evidence, organized the analysis of such evidence, conducted interviews first with Miss Nagoshi's family and then, subsequently, with her colleagues, friends, associates?"

"Yes."

"Sounds like an extremely thorough investigation to me, Lieutenant."

"Every investigation we undertake is thorough, Mr. Katz," said Joe, stealing a quick glance at David.

"Of course," said Katz. "And I would expect no less from you, Lieutenant."

The ADA proceeded to run through Joe's investigations, starting with his first interview with James at the Deane University boathouse all those months ago. Joe had expected this. He knew Katz would be determined to paint James as a liar from the get-go, and unfortunately, there was nothing Joe could do to stop him.

"Yes, Mr. Matheson lied to us on that occasion," Joe confirmed after a series of questions. "He certainly seemed to be uncomfortable given we approached him in front of his peers. Believe it or not, Mr. Katz, myself and Detective McKay have been known to trigger reactions of stress and discomfort even in the purest of innocents."

Joe said this in a manner that could have been read as an attempt at humor, but he made his point to the jury. He was giving James an out, an explanation for his lies in that first all-important interview. But Katz knew this too, and was not going to take it lying down.

"Come now, Lieutenant, embarrassment is one thing but a blatant misrepresentation of the truth—to two *police officers*, no less—is most certainly another." Katz stopped in front of the witness, shaking his head, his frame now captured in a lone muted sunbeam that streamed through the northern window, his shadow long and impressive.

"Mr. Matheson told you he barely knew Miss Nagoshi, is that right?" he asked, picking up the pace.

"Yes," said Joe.

"He said he had no idea why she would be sketching him," said Katz as he moved to his desk to pick up Jessica's sketchbook, displaying the impressive drawing for the jury before entering the sketch pad as exhibit number 1.

"That's right," said Joe.

"And correct me if I am wrong, Lieutenant, but the defendant," he said, now turning to point at James, "went on to tell a blatant lie regarding his whereabouts at the time of Miss Nagoshi's death."

"Yes, but . . ."

"Yes or no, Lieutenant?"

"Yes."

"He said he was having sex with another college student."

"Yes."

"A French exchange student by the name of Barbara Rousseau."

"Yes."

"But you spoke to Miss Rousseau and she assured you that this was not the case."

"Yes," conceded Joe at last. "But after Mr. Matheson was

arrested he made every effort to explain such misgivings. The young man lied about sleeping with an attractive fellow student, to two male friends no less. I am afraid we have all been guilty of such falsehoods, Mr. Katz. At least, I know when I was a young man . . ."

"Lieutenant Mannix, we appreciate your offer to share your no doubt thrilling tales regarding your past sexual conquests, or lack thereof, but in the interest of this court, I would ask you to stick to the questions."

Joe nodded. Katz was not giving him an inch.

"Did you have any explanation for the defendant's repeated lies, Lieutenant?"

It was a good question, because the obvious answer was that the defendant was trying to hide something.

"Well," Joe began, choosing his words carefully, "following his arrest Mr. Matheson explained that his falsehoods were founded in a desire to honor his girlfriend's wishes to keep their relationship secret."

"But there you go," said Katz interrupting, raising his right hand to scratch his head as if unable to solve the puzzle before him. "You see, this is what I don't understand," he said, looking up at Joe as if he might be able to shed some light on this frustrating conundrum. "When Mr. Matheson told these lies, when he stared you and your partner in the eye and told untruth after untruth, Miss Nagoshi was dead, was she not?"

"Well, yes, but . . ."

"So, you can see my problem, Lieutenant. I find it difficult to conceive why Mr. Matheson was so concerned about her wishes, so desperate to protect her from scrutiny, when she was no longer alive to protect. Having said that, Lieutenant, I do see the irony—the fact that the defendant has a propensity for keeping secrets—that he expressed a desire to protect the ideals of a life that he so heartlessly extinguished in one of the most brutal executions this state has ever seen."

"*Objection!*" screamed David. "Your Honor, the ADA is engaging in blatant grandstanding. Mr. Katz is taking advantage of the court's license by attempting to weave his own agendas into the testimony of the witness, leaving the jury with the impression that the lieutenant has similar views in regard to my client's motives."

"He's right, Mr. Katz. The objection is sustained," said an
obviously annoyed Stein. "You know better than that, Mr. Katz,
and if I catch you at it again I shall hold you in contempt. The
jury will disregard the ADA's last comments," said Stein turning
briefly to the twelve. "And you shall watch your step, Mr. Katz."

Katz, having made his point, straightened his tie and, wearing a fresh expression of humility, went on to ask about the
physical evidence in the case. He asked about James' Nike shoes,
forcing Joe to concede that the partial print in the greenhouse
was also a Nike, but did not push too far considering the shoe
was a popular one and the FBI had failed to find any evidence of
"greenhouse mud and/or residue" on the pair confiscated from
James' apartment.

He skirted over the other physical evidence collected but
only long enough to establish that while the police did not have
evidence linking the defendant to the murder, they had not
linked anyone else to the crime scene either. Finally, he reached
the point he was so obviously impatient to get to—the one piece
of evidence the defense would find it almost impossible to re-
fute: the fact that James' friends had given statements regarding
a confession and the knowledge of those all-important shoes.

He lumbered on about the confession for over an hour, making continual references to Jessica's missing shoes—"the highly
confidential piece of evidence" known only to the police and
the District Attorney's office. He harped on about how difficult
it must have been for Simpson and Westinghouse to speak out
against their closest friend, and touched repeatedly on their honesty and their strength of character in forgoing their instincts of
loyalty to do what they knew to be right.

By the end of Katz's soliloquy, during which Mannix hardly
got a word in edgewise despite David's repeated objections that
the ADA failed to allow the witness to answer the question,
Katz had created an almost saintlike aura around the two boys
named Simpson and Westinghouse. In short, he had done an
exemplary job of paving the way for his two young "super witnesses" to take the stand in the coming days.

And so, after seventy long minutes of having to swallow
Katz's interminable flattery of the two assholes known as Simpson and Westinghouse, Joe had had enough.

"So, Lieutenant, allow me to clarify," said Katz for the

umpteenth time. "Messrs Simpson and Westinghouse appeared genuine in their efforts. They . . ."

"Absolutely," interrupted Joe. "The minute the reward was mentioned their eyes lit up like Christmas trees. Two million bucks is a lot of cash," he said. "But I got the feeling that for these trust fund babies the thrill was more in the chase."

The crowd gasped. It was the first time the two boys had been described as anything but heroes, and it was the first time, in a very long time, that the press had seen a witness for the prosecution turn the tables on the confident ADA and slap him squarely in the face.

"The thing is," Joe went on before Katz had a chance to recover, "if I were a cynic, I might take the leap and consider these boys had their eye on the prize from the very beginning. I might even suggest they manipulated Mr. Nagoshi's grief for their own benefit—some sort of power thing, being able to control a room of experienced legal and criminal authorities and earn some extra cash in the process.

"But of course, we are not cynics, Mr. Katz, which is probably a very good thing, because if we were, we would have to admit to being had—by a pair of twenty-two-year-old college kids, no less."

The room erupted, David looked at Joe with a nod and Stein picked up his gavel and thumped it on the desk before him once, twice, three times.

"Your Honor," Katz cried above the hubbub, his voice a shaky, high-pitched staccato. "I request you demand this witness refrain from this scandalous conjecture. And I ask that his comments be struck from the record."

"Hold on, Mr. Katz," said Stein, glaring out at the crowd as if daring them to give him a run for his money in the volume stakes. "Might I remind you that you cannot object to your own witness and as Mr. Cavanaugh is still firmly in his seat I suggest you accept the lieutenant's testimony and move on. After all, Mr. Katz, you were the one who rightly described Lieutenant Mannix as an experienced, exemplary officer, and as such, I believe his observations should be heard.

"Having said that, Lieutenant," said Stein, now turning to Joe, "I might suggest you think carefully before you offer any further comments on the two boys in question. They are . . ."

"I know what they are, Judge." Mannix went to say "who" but "what" came out instead.

Joe looked back to the ADA, unable to suppress a smile. He was challenging him and Katz knew it. Joe was daring him to throw another punch, and warning him of the potential repercussions all at the very same time.

"Lieutenant," Katz gathered himself before moving on, a new fire of intensity in his narrow brown eyes. "As your grasp of the players in this case seems so insightful, I feel I would be remiss in my duty if I failed to ask you one final question—or rather a series in the same vein."

Joe nodded, his eyes never leaving the ADA's before him.

"Do you have any other bona fide suspects?"

Joe was completely taken aback. This was the last question he expected the Kat to ask. The ADA had spent the last few months telling Joe there were no other suspects—and here he was, opening the door for Joe to suggest otherwise.

Joe stole a quick glance at David, seeing the panic, the fear, the regret in his eyes and in that moment he guessed what had gone down at this morning's opening—David had let the cat out of the bag, and now the Kat was determined to shove it back in.

"No," answered Joe at last, because it was the only thing he could say.

"Did you ever, in the course of the investigation, consider another individual as the perpetrator of this heinous crime?"

Joe was caught. A "yes" would be giving away their game, but a "no" would be a blatant lie, and considering he was under oath, this alternative was unthinkable.

"We always consider a number of possibilities, Mr. Katz. That is our job."

Katz shook his head, as if signaling to the jury that he knew the lieutenant was avoiding the question.

"Fair enough, Lieutenant, I realize the police came under a considerable amount of criticism for taking so long to solve this case so in all fairness to you I shall rephrase the question. Do you have any genuine proof that someone other than the defendant killed Jessica Nagoshi?"

Joe hesitated. "No," he said at last.

"So, as far as the police are concerned the only viable suspect for the murder of Jessica Nagoshi is James Matheson."

"Well . . . yes."

"The defendant."

"Yes."

And Katz took a breath. "Thank you, Lieutenant," he said with a smile. "We have no further questions for this witness, Your Honor."

75

It was after eight. The sun had set almost four hours ago. The snow had slowed to a steady drift but the wind was still strong— enough to force a temperature barely in the positives down to a biting three below. David closed his eyes, allowing the cold crystals of frost to fall against his face. They were there and then they weren't, attempting to land where they intended only to be swept up and taken on another journey by the determined offshore breeze.

He was at the northern end of the harbor, his gloved hands clasping the chained balustrades before him, the city lights behind him hitting the squat intermittent supports that cast long thick shadows into the black water beyond. Arthur was right. This was all his fault. His inability to "take a hit" and his egocentric decision to play their cards out of order had backfired with catastrophic results.

Joe's testimony was a disaster. David had used his cross to try and reinforce Joe's suspicions that Simpson and Westinghouse's real motives were less than honorable, but the fact that Joe had admitted, in open court, that the police had no other suspects had basically painted David and his colleagues as a team of desperate storytellers. Liars representing the liar—it certainly seemed to fit.

And then the day had gone from bad to worse as Katz followed Joe's testimony with a similarly "in the dark" McKay. The ADA had started with the compliments, touched on James' Nikes once again and then built up to Frank's insightful connection between James' kayaking skills and the nature of the blows to Jessica Nagoshi's forehead. At one point he even had Frank stand and demonstrate a kayaker's motion—one, two, one, two—a theatrical performance that had the jury mesmerized and Frank turning a burgeoning shade of red.

Tomorrow the Kat would call Sawyer, and while David took comfort in the kid's loyalty and ability to think on his feet, he feared Jones was no match for the cunning ADA who would be determined to "own" this witness after today's double dose of obstinacy.

He looked up and was surprised to see stars. They were poking out in between the fast moving clouds. Gazing up like this to the night sky and beyond had always made him feel insignificant, overwhelmed. Which is exactly the way he felt tonight—small, powerless . . . lost.

He felt him before he saw him—or sensed his shadow approaching, slowly but directly, like a visitor on an unavoidable mission. The man stood beside him, leaving a good two feet between them. He had his hands in the pockets of his dark cashmere coat, his woolen scarf swallowing his neck, his back straight, his head erect.

"Is it him?" he asked at last.

And David turned to look at him.

"Is it my son, Mr. Cavanaugh? Is he the one you referred to in your opening statement this morning?"

"Mr. Nagoshi," said David, unsure as to how he should proceed. "I am sorry for your loss, but you have to understand, I am not at liberty to . . . You shouldn't be here. You should go home."

David turned to face the water once more, John Nagoshi's eyes never having left the harbor before him.

"He did not kill her, Mr. Cavanaugh, and before you protest, I must assure you I have proof. I love my children, Mr. Cavanaugh, but I have never been blind to their shortcomings. Peter is many things, many things of which I am not proud, but he is not a killer, Mr. Cavanaugh, this at least I know."

And then the multinational CEO retrieved his gloved hand from his pocket and held the thick envelope to his side, offering it to David.

"Take it."

"Mr. Nagoshi . . . I . . ."

"Take it," he said and David lifted his hand from the balus-

trade to take the envelope from the determined man beside him.

"The material inside contains transcripts of a series of telephone calls that took place in the early hours of Saturday, September 12—and I can provide you with the original recordings, authenticated by an independent technician, if you so desire."

"I read your original interview with the detectives, Mr. Nagoshi," said David, guessing this was some sort of attempt to convince David of the younger Nagoshi's innocence. "I know you told them *you* had been on the phone during the course of that night, but failed to hear anything untoward."

"I was asleep, Mr. Cavanaugh. My son made those calls—to China. You see, a man died at our plant, an electrical accident, and Peter was determined to keep it quiet, especially considering the humanitarian group known as Solidarity Global had become interested in our facility."

"You knew about that?" said David, incredulous.

"I know more than you think, Mr. Cavanaugh."

"You wired your own son's phone?"

"No, but I had my suspicions about China for some time—the unusually high productivity, the low amount allocated to salary."

"You had listening devices installed at the other end—in Guangdong?"

And Nagoshi nodded.

"Then," said David, turning to him at once, "why didn't you shut him down? Why didn't you pull him off and make him accountable? From what I hear your factory runs like some sort of concentration camp and . . ."

"I was going to," said Nagoshi who, David guessed, had dwelled on his own failure to intervene. "But then Jessica . . ." Nagoshi paused, his chest rising as he took a long, slow breath. "Peter is my son, Mr. Cavanaugh. He is young and inexperienced. I suppose I hoped, in the light of Jessica's death, he might reassess his approach to life as a whole. But I am afraid his sister's 'removal' only fed his ambitions, and I was remiss for not acting sooner."

"Forgive me, Mr. Nagoshi," said David at last, taking a step closer to the tired-looking man. "But I am afraid if you allowed him to get away with organizing the death of one of his workers, then culpability rests just as much with you as it does with your son."

Nagoshi turned to him then, a fresh look of surprise on his face. "Mr. Lim's death was an accident, Mr. Cavanaugh. I have made discreet investigations. There was a fault in the generator. His death was a tragedy but unavoidable. I have proof of this also, if you need it."

David took a second to take this in before going on. "And this?" he said, holding up the envelope in his right hand. "What will this tell me about your son, Mr. Nagoshi?"

"That at the time of Mr. Lim's unfortunate accident my son was more concerned with hiding the incident from myself and the humanitarians than offering solace to the poor man's family. That he is greedy and naive. That he has lost his way. That he cares nothing for anything but money and power and self-advancement, but that he did not murder his sister." Nagoshi took another breath, this time releasing it with a shudder.

"It will also tell you that I failed him, Mr. Cavanaugh—that I too spent many years trying to build one empire while selfishly neglecting the other."

David nodded, placing the envelope in his pocket.

"If this plays out," said David at last, feeling some need to help this poor man who, he now realized, had lost two children and a potential grandson on the night of Jessica's death, "and if you assure me you plan to deal with this correctly, then I don't see any need to speak of this beyond this evening."

"You will do this for me?" asked Nagoshi, finally turning to meet David's eye.

"If you give me your word that your son will be made answerable for his mistakes, and that the people in China will be compensated. In fact, Mr. Lim's brother is here, in Boston. Perhaps you could make a personal assurance to him that his brother's death was accidental and that he and his coworkers will be remunerated and treated like human beings instead of animals."

Nagoshi, whose eyes barely gave away his surprise at the current location of the younger Mr. Lim, nodded and lifted his head. "So you *did* believe it was Peter who killed her. You brought Mr. Lim here to testify. And if that is the case, this does not end well for you. With my son's innocence confirmed, your client is doomed."

David went to say something, but Nagoshi held up his hand, signaling he needed to go on. "Mr. Katz's intentions are not pure, Mr. Cavanaugh. But for want of a better explanation I am afraid that I must reserve from offering you good fortune. For if Mr. Matheson did what he is accused of doing, then I pray he is held accountable."

"And if I told you there was somebody else? Someone I favored over Peter from the very beginning?"

"Then . . ." began Nagoshi, his eyes now wide, like two dark mirrors reflecting the swirling snowflakes between them. "Then, I offer you my hand, sir," he said removing his glove to extend his arm toward David. "And I ask you—no I *beg* you to resolve this travesty, and give my daughter and her child the peace they finally deserve."

• • •

David was back at the apartment within minutes, anxious to tell Sara what he had learned. He put the key in his door and swung it open to see her pacing the living room in sweatpants and an old college T-shirt, a carton of Chinese takeout in her hand.

"Thank goodness you're back," she said, placing the noodles on the coffee table before walking across the room to wrap her arms around him. "I was beginning to worry, it's looking pretty nasty out there and . . ." She kissed him before looking up at him with a smile. "David we have news."

"We? Um . . . me, too," he said, taking off his coat and scarf and hanging them on the stand beside the door before looking around the room to see who the "we" might refer to. "But judging by the smile, something tells me you want to go first."

"If she is first then I am second," yelled a voice from the kitchen, and David looked up to see Sawyer approaching with two steaming cartons in his hand.

"Jesus, kid," said David, taking the stir-fry with noodles. "You shouldn't be here. Not the night before your testimony. If Katz knew you were hanging out with us, he . . ."

"He'd what?" smiled Sawyer, and David, despite himself, found their good mood contagious. "Force me to slick my hair back in a replica of his own?" Sawyer ran his hand through his unruly mop. "Not a chance."

"All right," said David at last, pointing toward the sofa. "Spill it, both of you."

Sara began with her news of James' two Australian friends—Lawson Flinn and Sterling Buntine. "Long story short, they can't make it," she said. "I know this is disappointing but according to Diane, Flinn managed to track down Buntine and has arranged for him to fly into Adelaide tomorrow—or today, being Tuesday, Australian time—so that they might give their statements, in front of a lawyer, together.

"Then, both statements will be faxed to the Mathesons' home office by tomorrow morning our time. According to Diane they are going to be glowing, and in the very least we will have them in hand, ready to be entered into evidence next week."

"It's not perfect but it's better than nothing," said David.

"If they are as good as Diane predicts," added Sara, "they are as close to perfect as we are going to get."

David grabbed his girlfriend in a hug. "Sara Davis, you have made my day."

"No I haven't," she said, discarding her chopsticks for a spoon to scoop some stir-fry from David's carton. "I am afraid that honor goes to young Sawyer here."

"Okay, kid," said David, jumping to his feet to double back into the kitchen, before grabbing three waters from the fridge and tossing them over the breakfast bar and into the living room. "Spill it," he said as he made his way back into the room.

"Well, I know my latest assignment was kinda tricky."

"Assignment," thought David. *This kid is something else.*

"Sawyer, when we asked you to find out what you could about H. Edgar Simpson's sex life we didn't expect you to actually come up with anything. According to James, Simpson is unbreakable on that front, he has never heard H. Edgar, or more to the point any other student at Deane, talk about his friend's sexual exploits. The kid is a eunuch, or the only young man I know who seems to have spent his entire time at college without making out with someone—male or female."

"Making out?" smiled Sawyer. "You hear that on *Happy Days* reruns?"

"Originals, actually," David said, and he couldn't help but laugh. "Cut the lip, kid, and tell us what you know."

"James is right, Simpson isn't banging any of his fellow students at college, and you were right too when you said any such a relationship would be beneath him."

David looked at Sara.

"Simpson is having sex all right, and rumor has it the action is pretty hot. He is banging a member of the faculty, David, and while no one seems to know who it is, the rumors favor two options—Stephen Miller or Martin Meisenbach."

"And are these teachers outwardly, um . . ."

"Gay? No one is outwardly gay at Deane, David."

"I guess not." David nodded. "You think you can find out more?"

Sawyer shook his mop with a smile. "Sure. Not a problem, my friend. Just leave it with me."

76

David glanced sideways at James with an encouraging nod. Sawyer's testimony was going just as planned. He had advised Sawyer to keep his answers short and direct and avoid getting into a rally with the experienced ADA. He told him to set himself one goal, to tell the truth about Jessica's love for James and her obvious happiness during the time they were together. He would admit to following the secretive Jessica out of "concern," but to have had any fears allayed when he saw Jessica and James together—content, in love. In fact, after the ADA played the aquarium security tape showing the obviously besotted James and Jessica together, David was considering that there may be no need to cross-examine Sawyer at all. If anything, the Kat was making their case for them—leaving every juror doubting that his young client could ever lift a finger against the girl he so obviously adored.

And so, as Katz appeared to be heading back to his seat, David began to rise to inform the judge that he had no questions for the witness. Until Katz turned, his right hand lifted above his head in a gesture that said "Just one more question for this witness, Your Honor," and sent the entire morning to hell.

"I'm sorry, Mr. Jones," began Katz, moving back toward the witness once again. "Just one more thing."

"Sure," said Sawyer.

"What exactly were your feelings for Jessica Nagoshi?"

The question took Sawyer by surprise. David sensed he was trying to look at him but the ADA was now blocking their line of vision.

"Come now, Mr. Jones, it is an easy question and there really is no need to seek guidance from defense counsel. Which is exactly what you have been doing, Mr. Jones. Is it not?"

Sawyer said nothing, so Katz pushed on.

"Where were you last night, Mr. Jones?"

"Last night? I, um . . ."

"Come now, you have been forthright in your answers so far, Mr. Jones. Once again, the question is a simple one. Where were you last night?"

"At my attorney's house," said Sawyer, and David felt himself cringe as Sara shook her head ever so slightly beside him.

"Ah, I see," said Katz. "Why do you need an attorney, Mr. Jones?"

"I don't. I mean, she is more like a friend than . . ."

"A friend, of course. And is your friend here today, to give you moral support in your testimony?"

"Um, yes. I mean, no. She is here but not because I need her support."

"Forgive me. You are right, Mr. Jones. I believe your attorney is here because she has another client involved in this case. Is that correct?" Sawyer said nothing.

"Mr. Jones?"

"Yes," said Sawyer at last, the word bursting from his lips as if Katz had prized it out personally. "My attorney, Miss Sara Davis, she represents the defendant."

And there it was, Katz's cat in the hat. And in that moment David knew Sara was ruing herself for not dropping Sawyer as her client in the first place—and David was doing the same for using this poor kid as some sort of junior deputy in disguise.

The courtroom was abuzz and Stein had to call for order. David was wanting to object but knew any word of protest would be met with animosity from the obviously furious judge who could smell the insinuation of "witness tampering" a mile away.

"Mr. Cavanaugh," yelled the judge, forcing all in the room to silence. "Is this true?"

"Your Honor," began David, rising to his feet. "Mr. Jones is represented by my co-counsel and it is also true that he was at her apartment for a brief period last night. But I can assure you, she did nothing more than encourage the witness to tell the truth."

"Permission to treat this witness as hostile, Your Honor," chimed in Katz.

"Permission granted," said Stein, glaring at David before adding, "Keep your seat, Mr. Cavanaugh. We shall have words about this later."

"Mr. Jones," Katz wasted no time as a defeated David took his seat. "Let's backtrack a little, shall we, to the question you failed to answer a moment ago, regarding your feelings for Jessica Nagoshi?"

"Ah," said Sawyer, now starting to sweat. "I liked her."

"You liked her. In what way? As a colleague? As someone with similar humanitarian interests? As a friend? As a member of the opposite sex?"

"No. I mean, yes. She . . ."

"Confusing, isn't it, Mr. Jones? Girls are like that."

"I'm not confused," began Sawyer. "It is just that . . ."

"She was a beautiful girl who showed an interest in you, Sawyer. And as such, considering your . . . um . . . unusual persona, it would be only natural for you to grasp on that attention and perhaps misconstrue her friendship for . . ."

"*No*. We were friends."

"So you didn't love her?"

There was silence. David closed his eyes knowing that beyond everything else, Sawyer would never be able to lie about this one simple truth. He loved her all right. Probably more than he had ever loved anyone in his whole entire life.

"No," he said at last. "I mean yes. I did love her. How could I not?"

"And yet here you are telling us all, thanks to your attorney's hearty encouragement, that the defendant, the young man charged with murdering your *one true love*, was nothing but the perfect gentleman in her presence. Look out, Mr. Jones, jealousy is a motive too, you know. Before you know it your own lawyers could be pointing the finger at you."

"*Objection*," yelled David now on his feet.

"Sit down, Mr. Cavanaugh," yelled Stein before nodding for Katz to go on.

"Mr. Jones," said the ADA. "This court is in debt to you for revealing the defendant as a liar, for it was you who confirmed their relationship in the first place. But I fear that beyond that you have done this court a serious disservice.

"In fact, Your Honor," added Katz, turning to Stein, "I move that this witness's entire testimony be stricken from the record. Mr. Matheson has acknowledged he lied about his relationship, so in retrospect we do not require this witness to confirm the falsehood after all."

"You were the one who called him, Mr. Katz," said Stein.

"Yes, my mistake. I apologize for wasting the court's precious time, Your Honor."

"Judge," David was up again. "Can't you see what he is doing?"

"Shut up, Mr. Cavanaugh," yelled the judge without even gracing the defense table with a look. "Your request is granted, Mr. Katz. The jury will disregard the witness' entire testimony. Is that clear?" To which the jury nodded in obedience.

"You may step down, Mr. Jones, and in doing so promise me to never grace my courtroom again."

■ ■ ■

It was a stroke of brilliance. Katz had effectively used Sawyer to get the aquarium tape into evidence and catch the defendant in his lie. It gave the jury a chance to see the living, breathing, strikingly beautiful Jessica on the arm of the young man accused of killing her—a vision Katz would soon juxtapose with the brutal pictures of her death when ME Gus Svenson took the stand.

It did not matter that Sawyer's testimony was struck. None of the twelve could forget Jessica's flawless, smiling face, no matter how hard they tried. Sawyer was in tears. In fact, he was sobbing openly, as he half walked, half ran toward the back of the courtroom like a child. David felt responsible, and he knew Sara felt even more so, as they looked at their ashen-faced client beside them and the image of the boy named Sawyer fleeing the room in complete humiliation.

And so last night's jubilation at the news of James' Australian friends, and Sawyer's findings regarding Simpson's sexuality, and finally David's report on John Nagoshi which had, in the very least, allowed them to narrow their suspects to one, was now long forgotten. The only solace they had was in the fact that Gus Svenson was next on the stand, giving David his one real chance to absolve his client before the Kat could pull him down for good.

77

They had no time to regroup, for as Sawyer's testimony ran shorter than expected, Stein allowed for only a quick ten minute recess so that they might hear Svenson's testimony before lunch.

David was worried about James. The emotional rollercoaster he had been riding for months was now obviously taking its toll. He looked tired and despondent, and, as Sara had pointed out, his right hand had started to twitch again—a nervous tic that he tried to control by covering his right hand with his left and squeezing until it stopped.

They had had no time to tell him about his Australian friends' statements, and David prayed these would give him a desperately needed lift. They also hoped that David's all-important cross examination of ME Svenson, a pivotal turning point for the defense, would provide both the jury with the much needed "reasonable doubt," and their client with the courage to take the stand at the end of this trial and inevitably see this thing through.

Once again Katz stuck to the routine. He began by asking the medical examiner to state his name and position and describe his duties as the highest ranking coroner in the county. He then went on to ask Svenson to give a detailed description of the victim's injuries, beginning with that notorious "double blow to the head."

"The blunt force trauma to the victim's forehead suggests two consecutive blows from a moving object at a time when the victim was relatively stationary," Svenson began. "The high degree of force and small area over which it was applied suggest the victim fell almost instantly.

"The pattern of blood leakage from the ruptured vessels on the front of the forehead suggest the instrument used was heavy and the skin breakage suggest direct vertical impact with the causative object, leaving its impression in the skull."

The jury winced. David saw it, and he knew the Kat saw it too. David guessed the ADA would see this as his cue to "start the show," and unfortunately he was right.

Katz asked for Svenson's patience as he called for a number of easels to be dragged from the side of the room. He took his time, walking to his desk to pick up a series of poster-sized placards from the floor, holding them face inward to his body so that each one would have its own drum roll reveal. He turned them slowly, toward the jury, placing them on their stands and angling them so that Svenson would have to crane his neck, but the jury, and the courtroom beyond, got a perfect view of the horrific representations before them.

Jessica Nagoshi was the picture of torment—her skin gray, her eyes half open, her forehead mutilated by a crisscross indentation that had crushed her otherwise smooth young brow to a pulp. Her neck was covered in deep purple bruises, her chin yanked up and across like that of some disfigured doll, her hair matted, her lips blue, and her entire silent image cried terror and agony in death.

James seemed to sink in his seat as if trying to recoil from the image before him as juror number three, Sharon Kelly, a twenty-nine-year-old child-care worker from Dorchester, covered her eyes with her hands and juror number five, Ilda de Souza, a fifty-year-old mother of four, blessed herself.

"Dr. Svenson," said Katz at last, allowing just enough time for the jury to settle, their eyes still transfixed on the heinous images before them. "The impressions you spoke of," said Katz, pointing to the two strokes of the large purple "X" on Jessica Nagoshi's forehead. "Here and here. You found the causative object that left these indentations in the young girl's skull?"

"Yes. A garden hoe found nearby on the greenhouse floor. The impressions suggest the offender use both ends of the hoe, the handle and the metallic edge, in a swinging motion bringing each end down consecutively, resulting in the cross-patterned bruise you see here," said Gus, pointing to the image to his far right.

"Not unlike the movement a kayaker uses with his oar," added Katz.

"Objection," said David. "Leading the witness. The movement may mimic those of many activities, or may simply be one the offender applied at the time. The mention of the kayak is a blatant attempt to link my client to the crime."

"I see your point, Mr. Cavanaugh," said Stein. "But the witness was not asked about your client, merely about the nature of the motion. I will allow it. You may answer the question, Doctor."

Svenson nodded. "Like a kayaker, yes," said Gus, and David took a breath.

"Or like an abseiler, hand over hand, or perhaps a window cleaner or a master of any number of martial arts. The motion is an easy one to mimic, and I am afraid does not allow us to limit our conclusion as to the nature of the offender's activities."

And David let out a sigh of relief—and of gratitude.

Katz, obviously realizing he had lost that round, encouraged the ME to move on. "And the impact of the weapon itself, does *this* tell you something about the nature of the offender?"

Svenson nodded, pointing at the picture once again. "We call this a 'Tangential Impact,' the direction of which was determined by the beveled edge of the starting descent and the heaped epidermis on the finishing edge."

"And in layman's terms?"

"Miss Nagoshi was struck twice by each end of the same instrument. The impact causing a double fracture to the skull."

"Leading you to conclude the offender was athletic, strong?"

"Strong, yes."

Katz ticked a box and moved on. "Tell us, Doctor, what did these initial blows do to the victim—outwardly, internally?"

"Well," said Gus, "the victim mostly likely fell immediately. Perhaps unconscious, perhaps not."

"Right," said Katz. "I'll come back to that point in a minute, Doctor, but first, internally . . . ?"

"Yes," said Gus. "First you must understand that the head is heavy, mobile, unstable. In the victim's case her skull was deformed by the impact—depressed. Injury to blood vessels was significant and triggered intracranial hemorrhage and subsequent pressure on the brain."

David wanted to object but couldn't; he dared not question

Svenson's medical authority as it was the ME's expert opinion he would be relying on to legitimize his all-important "bruising on the neck" theory on cross. But his incredibly descriptive testimony was hurting, there was no doubt about it. The jury were practically gray with distress and worse still, David noted, now diverting their eyes back and forth from the monstrous images before them to the defendant at his side.

"Would the blows alone been enough to kill Miss Nagoshi?"

"Yes, probably." Gus nodded. "But not for some time. The pressure from intracranial hemorrhage takes time to accumulate."

"So it was the strangulation that is listed as the official cause of death?"

"Yes."

"Even though, strictly speaking, the twofold violent blows would have been enough?"

"Yes."

"So I suppose we could say the defendant killed the victim twice?"

"No," said Gus. His negative answer being the only reason David did not jump to his feet despite his intentions to reserve his objections. "No one is killed twice, Mr. Katz. In all my experience, once is always enough."

Moments later the ADA was on to the strangulation, once again encouraging his witness to give a vivid medical description of what happened when a person's throat is squeezed until it breaks.

Gus spoke of the finger pad bruises, signaling the strangulation was indeed manual, the compression on the neck that constricted the larynx and prevented the free flow of air down the respiratory passage, and the resultant hypoxic hypoxia.

"There were injuries to the laryngeal cartilages and the hyoid bone. In fact, the hyoid bone was fractured, which is indicative of aggressive strangulation. Both carotid sinuses were compressed and there was also evidence of imminent cerebral hypoxia as a result of the restriction of the carotid arteries and jugular veins."

"And going back to my point earlier, Doctor, I assume the

finger pad bruises, the nature of the aggression, the power of the force, also suggest the offender is someone of significant strength."

Gus hesitated, his eyes flicking quickly toward the defense. And David, who knew Gus could take this opportunity to elaborate on the bruises around Jessica's neck and the size of the hands that made them, held his breath as the ME considered his answer.

"Strong, yes," he said, and gratefully left it at that.

"Is it possible Miss Nagoshi was conscious during this strangulation, despite the fall mentioned earlier?"

"Unlikely, as there were no signs of struggle."

"But she was strangled from behind—at least that is what the bruising pattern tells us. Is that correct, Doctor?"

"Yes."

"So she could have been conscious but unable to fight, given her back was toward her assailant."

"Yes. It is possible." The jury could visualize it now, and it was only getting worse.

"And so," said Katz, now clearing his throat as if to show the jury that he too found this extremely distressing. "How did she actually die then, Doctor Svenson?"

"From reflex cardiac arrest as a result of the carotid sinus compression."

"She had a heart attack?"

"Yes."

"At nineteen years?"

"Yes."

"And her unborn child?"

"Would have died within minutes. Without any oxygen circulating in the blood the fetus would have . . ."

"Gone into cardiac arrest as well?"

"Yes."

"A heart attack at thirteen weeks."

"Yes."

And Katz paused, allowing it all to sink in.

"Thank you, Dr. Svenson. I have no further questions for this witness, Your Honor."

78

The judge called for lunch—a full hour recess during which, David knew, the jury would be dwelling on the testimony they had just heard, those images no doubt turning them off their food and on to the possibility of returning a guilty verdict.

Once James had been removed to a holding cell for lunch, David and Arthur headed to the court cafeteria where they could go over David's questions for Svenson, while Sara tried to track down Sawyer who, the last time they saw him, was the picture of humiliation and defeat.

"These are good, David," said Arthur before taking a sip of the too bitter, too hot cafeteria coffee.

"They'd better be," said David. "Any word from Nora?" he added, hoping the efficient Mrs. Kelly might have called or left a message with news of any faxes from Australia.

"Not yet. But it is now the early hours of the morning Down Under, and given they did not come in this morning, I wouldn't expect them until tonight."

David looked at his watch; the lunch hour was almost up and he was really hoping for some progress on the Australian front before the day was out. The trial was moving quickly and there was every chance the defense would be starting their case before the end of the week.

"Here comes Sara now," said Arthur, interrupting David's thoughts and pointing toward the café's entranceway. They watched her weave her way around the irregularly placed metal tables before reaching them and falling into her seat.

"He is not answering his cell," she said. "And I called Deane to see if he was back in class, but apparently he didn't make his last lecture."

They nodded, each of them feeling terrible for what had happened to their eager young apprentice at this morning's mortifying setup.

"Katz is an asshole," said Arthur.

"And we are even worse for getting the kid into this in the first place," said David.

Sara nodded. "There is some good news though," she said, perhaps keen to lift their spirits. "I just spoke to Nora, the Australian boys' statements have arrived."

A relieved David let out a sigh. "That is good news. Someone down there is super efficient, faxing at what must be about what? Three . . . four a.m.?"

"No," said Sara, grabbing the coffee Arthur had brought for her in advance. "The statements are originals. They arrived by courier about an hour ago and according to Nora they are glowing."

"That was fast," said David.

"Well," said Sara, taking another long sip of the now lukewarm mud. "The main thing is that they are here, and we can enter them into evidence as an opener as planned." But she must have noted the furrow in David's brow.

"What is it?" she asked.

"Nothing, they must have . . . It was just fast, that's all."

"Which is also what this lunch break has been," said Arthur pointing to his watch. "It's time for you to work your magic, David, my boy."

• • •

The walls of the courtroom moaned like an alley cat. The heating system had obviously started to cave under the pressure, letting out a series of long, low whines, which played like background music to the setting before them. The placards, which David had personally taken down before heading out for lunch, had been reassembled, a little tactic the Kat had no doubt orchestrated before anyone returned for the afternoon session.

Judge Stein peered over his glasses at the defense table below him, obviously still angry at David after Sawyer's testimony this morning. Katz was looking particularly cocky, the jury were looking accusatorily at their client, and the only comfort David took was from a small nod from John Nagoshi, who met his eye briefly before turning to face the front of the room once again.

"Are you ready to cross-examine the witness, Mr. Cavanaugh?"

"Yes, Your Honor."

And so David took to his feet and began.

David knew the jury would be exhausted by this morning's heavy and depressing medical data, and so chose to be short and direct. While Katz had done more than a stellar job in ascertaining what Svenson *could* conclude from his examinations, David wanted to begin by dwelling on what he *couldn't*—including calculating the offender's height or weight, or determining his actual identity from the finger impressions on Jessica's neck. That done, he moved on to the perpetrator's build and strength, and ultimately his hand size.

"Dr. Svenson, you told the court earlier that the offender was most likely strong."

"Yes."

"But does that necessarily mean the man was large, or tall, or athletic?"

"No."

David looked to the jury, the answer obviously caught them by surprise so he asked the witness to elaborate.

"Strength comes in all forms, Mr. Cavanaugh. It is a fact that jockeys are some of the strongest athletes in the international sporting fraternity. The power of force does not just emanate from physical size or fitness, but also from core emotion such as anger, resulting in a physical assertion of rage."

"Objection," yelled Katz. "While I have great respect for the doctor's ability as a coroner, he is neither a sports physician nor a psychologist, and this testimony is beyond his medical expertise."

"Your Honor," countered David, "Dr. Svenson has had years of experience in linking autopsies with perpetrators. I suggest his expertise lies in the very nature of his job, and the many murders he has worked on over the past decade."

"He's right, Mr. Katz. Objection overruled, but I suggest you rephrase the question, Mr. Cavanaugh."

"Yes, Your Honor," said David, turning quickly back to

Svenson. "I'm sorry, Doctor, please allow me to clarify. I believe you are suggesting that in your experience you have seen
numerous smaller men, who may appear outwardly fragile or
weak even, capable of great strength in the perpetration of a
violent crime such as this?"

"Yes."

"So if we cannot prove the offender is of a large, athletic
build, is there anything that suggests he might be otherwise—
perhaps even the opposite—small, lean, slender?"

"Yes," said Gus.

And there it was.

The courtroom gasped—sucking in an almighty intake of
air that seemed to time itself with a long, simultaneous moan
from the heating. The press lifted their heads from their pads to
look at one another in astonishment, and the jury, almost to a
number, sat transfixed, their eyes on James, their entire predis-
position of guilt flying swiftly out the window.

"Order!" cried Stein.

"Objection!" yelled Katz, but by the look on his face David
guessed that he was not too sure what to object to.

"Sit down, Mr. Katz," said Stein. "I want to hear this. Please
go on, Doctor."

Svenson paused until the rumblings abated, before lifting
his head and moving on.

"I make the conclusion the offender is small from the nature
of bruising on the neck."

"Objection!" Katz was up again. "Your Honor, the witness
gave no testimony of this nature when asked specifically about
said bruising earlier today. He . . ."

"Yes," interrupted Stein. "But if I recall, Mr. Katz, you
asked only about the perpetrator's strength, not his size. The
witness will continue and I would ask you to refrain from ob-
jecting until you have a valid argument, Mr. Katz."

And so the Kat sat, his recent look of invincibility replaced
by a churlish scowl.

"Go on please, Doctor," said David. "You were telling us
about the neck and the bruising and . . ."

"Yes. The bruising pattern tell us the victim attacked from
behind," said Gus, holding up his hands in that circular gesture
once again. "With the neck clasped with fingers at front, thumbs

around the back. But in the victim's case," said Gus, raising his right arm to point to one of the large photographs before him, "the bruising stop at the side—there."

"So the thumbs did not reach around the circumference of the neck?"

"No."

"Only to its sides, just under the ears, as the bruising shows here," said David, now pointing to the blown up image as well.

"Yes.

"Because they were too small."

"Yes."

"And short."

"Yes."

"And slender."

"Yes."

David did not miss a beat.

"Mr. Matheson!" he called to his client, the fresh look of hope on his young face now undeniable. "Would you hold up your hands for the court please, angling them toward the jury so that . . ." David thought again. "Your Honor, if it would please the court, I would like to ask that my client be given permission to approach the jury and show them his hands."

"Objection!"

"No, Mr. Katz," snapped Stein. "You are the one who favors close-ups," he said, gesturing at the macabre images before him. "I will allow it. You may approach the jury, Mr. Matheson."

And so James rose to his feet—his right hand giving the slightest of twitches. And as he stood, he straightened his back and moved around the defense table to walk slowly, carefully, toward the twelve men and women who would decide his future.

The room was still, the heating now silent, the only sound in the room was the click of James' heels on the hard floor.

David watched the jury and was relieved to see that not one—*not a single one* of them—recoiled from the approaching stranger. In fact, if anything they leaned in, toward him, as if wanting to see proof that this good-looking young kid did not kill the girl he professed to have loved.

And so, as James held up his hands—his long, strong, olive-skinned hands—the jury stared and nodded in amazement,

Josh Bergin at one point appearing as if he was about to lift his own young hand in a high five of victory with the defendant. And James nodded, as if in thanks to each of them, for their willingness to see and trust and believe.

79

That night David caught up with Joe at Bristow's—a snug, stained-glass-windowed Downtown Crossing bar that David had been frequenting since college. They chose a corner booth, away from the younger crowd that hovered around the fireplace at the front end of the bar, drinking their beer and sharing a huge platter of French fries and onion rings to go with their ribs and burgers.

"You kicked ass today, David," said Joe, lifting his glass. "You should have seen the look on the Kat's face when Stein said your client could approach the jury." Joe and Frank had sneaked into the back of the courtroom after lunch. "I thought he was going to puke."

But David said nothing, a little uncomfortable with the praise. "What's up?" asked Joe, obviously reading the concern on his friend's face. "I know the Kat gained a little on his redirect, but that thing with the hands, David, that was pure genius."

Joe was right. Katz had opted to re-cross Svenson hoping to regain some ground—which he did, by getting the ME to admit that his assumption that the killer's hands were "small" was just that—an assumption made on the evidence available. Svenson did stress, however, that given the bruising pattern, it was "highly unlikely" the victim was attacked by a large-handed man, after which the Kat cut his losses and sat down.

"It's not that," said David.

"Is it Jones, because Sara told me she spoke to him late this afternoon and he was doing okay."

"He is. He spent the afternoon hanging out with Mr. Lim, took him out to lunch, despite the weather."

"So you told Lim what Nagoshi said?"

"Yeah, I called him early this morning. I told him John

Nagoshi would be coming to see him personally, to apologize and make things right. The guy speaks reasonable English but I still got the feeling he had trouble taking it all in. But Sawyer has taken him under his wing so . . ."

"The kid's all right," said Joe.

David nodded. "We were wrong about him, Joe."

"It happens."

They took another sip of their beers and gazed over at the young people at the front of the bar, drinking, laughing, their voices getting louder with every bitter pint.

"So what is it then?" asked Joe at last.

"What's what?"

"What's bothering you? If it's not Jones then . . . ?"

"It's nothing. Just something about one of tomorrow's witnesses, and a discussion I had with Sara a while back," said David.

"Isn't the Kat calling Barbara Rousseau tomorrow?"

"Yeah. Which is bad enough, but at least we know what she is going to say."

Mannix said nothing, allowing David to take his time.

"It's that Professor Nancy Wakeford, you know the fetal expert Katz is calling to establish viability."

"You have a strong legal argument against that one, David."

"I know, and we've prepared our cross well. In fact, I thought it might be better if Sara questioned Wakeford. You know, the female angle and all."

"So you two have been talking about this issue?" asked Joe. "The whole idea of when a kid stops being a clump of cells and starts to become a human being."

"Something like that."

Joe nodded. "This isn't what this case is about, David, at least not for you and Sara. This is about saving your client, not about what either of you may believe personally."

"And if it was you? Could you get up there and argue that some unborn kid was basically nonexistent in the eyes of the law?"

"I'm a homicide detective with four kids, David—I'm not the one to ask.

"If it helps," added Joe after a time, "there is another way you could look at it."

"How so?" asked David.

"Well, it seems to me that the child is not invalid if it saves his father's life."

And David nodded, wondering how Joe always managed to say the right thing at the right time, no matter how dire the circumstances.

"This job sucks," David responded at last, lifting his beer to his lips and draining the rest of his glass in one gulp.

"Yeah well, it could be worse," said Joe, doing the same before reaching into his pocket and throwing a fifty on the table. "Instead of sharing this fine drink with me, you could be at home giving yourself a facial and manicuring your toenails like your fancy fucking opponent."

"It's called a pedicure," smiled David. "And I was gonna get to that as soon as I get out of here."

And Joe smiled in return. "I won't keep you then."

80

The weather was closing in. David looked to the windows. The high, narrow openings on the far right-hand side of the room were now covered in snow, the result being an eerie white light that beamed directly on the jury below.

The morning session for the third day of trial had been delayed an hour to allow for all the jury to be present. There was talk of putting them up in a nearby hotel if the snow got much worse, which was looking more and more likely by the minute.

David was uneasy. They knew this day would be tough—the accomplished Professor Nancy Wakeford followed by the beautiful Barbara Rousseau. While they knew their argument for fetal viability was backed by reams of documented precedent—information that proved Massachusetts law did not generally acknowledge a fetus as a "life" until the unborn child had reached the critical benchmark of twenty-three weeks—they feared Katz would use the professor's expertise to tear at the jury's heartstrings by detailing the formation of Jessica's thirteen-week-old pregnancy—and it did not take long for them to be proven right.

"Ladies and gentlemen of the jury," said Stein after entering, flipping his robe, and taking his seat at the podium. "I want to thank you for all of your kind efforts to be here. I know it took me over half an hour to walk ten paces this morning so . . ."

And the jury laughed—appearing happy to start the day on a lighter note.

"Having said that, I know you are all anxious to get moving so . . . Mr. Katz," said Stein, turning his attention to the ADA. "Are you ready to call your next witness?"

"Yes, Your Honor," answered the Kat, looking as suave as

ever in a dark charcoal suit and a crisp white shirt. "The Commonwealth would like to call Professor Nancy Wakeford, but before the professor so kindly graces this court, I wonder if I might ask the clerk's assistance in reassembling those very helpful easels, so that this witness might refer to some highly specialized images as part of her expert testimony."

David looked at Sara, both knowing their worst fears had been realized.

"It's all right," she whispered to him as the Kat supervised the assembly of his props like a stage manager commanding his "hands." "I've got this covered."

And he nodded, hoping to all hell that she was right.

• • •

The Kat began once again by asking about the professor's credentials—a long, drawn-out process, which, in the very least, David suspected, was boring the jury senseless.

Wakeford—an attractive woman in her early forties with neat red hair and wire-rimmed glasses—spoke of her graduating with high distinction from Yale's highly respected School of Medicine where she specialized in obstetrics, gynecology and reproductive sciences. From there she had completed further courses in fetal medicine and developed a special interest in pregnancies involving children with prenatal disabilities. At one point she even pointed to her semi-regular appearances on *Oprah*, which, David noticed, had the previously lethargic jury sitting at attention once again.

"Professor," Katz went on, "you have seen Dr. Svenson's autopsy notes in regards to this case, have you not?"

"Yes, Mr. Katz. In fact, I have studied them in detail."

"Right. And you agree Jessica Nagoshi's unborn child was approximately thirteen weeks of age?"

"Yes, if not perhaps a fraction older. The fetus in question was almost four inches long, which suggests a fourteen-week-old fetus—but close enough or thereabouts."

"I see," said Katz before looking up to Stein. "Your Honor, at this point I would like to ask the court's permission for the witness to leave the stand and use this pointer," he said, holding up the long narrow stick in his right hand, "as a guide so that the jury might learn more about the child's development at the time of its murder."

"Objection!" yelled Sara, getting to her feet. David had told her to take control of this witness from the outset, and the jury seemed pleased to see this new, attractive player throw her hat into the ring.

"First of all, Judge," she began. "The fetus should be referred to as a fetus and only as a fetus. A thirteen-week-old fetus is a long way from becoming a child by pure medical definition, as I am sure Professor Wakeford would agree.

"Secondly, the ADA's reference to 'murder' is both inappropriate and extremely presumptuous. Mr. Katz promised this court some months ago that he would convince it of this fetus' viability, but unless I missed something in the last sixty seconds, I am afraid his argument is yet to be established."

The jury smiled. They liked this new girl. She was quick and smart and fast.

"She's right, Mr. Katz," said Stein. "On both counts. The fetus shall be referred to as a fetus for the remainder of this trial and you, Mr. Katz, will refrain from any dramatic hyperbole in your examinations."

"Yes, Judge," said an obviously displeased Katz. "But I am afraid you are yet to address my request regarding . . ."

"I was getting to that, Mr. Katz," interrupted Stein. "The witness may leave the partition, but the moment I sense this is turning into a three-ring circus, I will shut you down. Do you understand, Mr. Katz?"

"Yes, Your Honor," he said, before handing the pointer to his witness and ushering her on to the floor.

The next hour was nothing short of disastrous, as Wakeford described the thirteen-week-old fetus in detail, from the tip of its tiny head to the soft toenails now forming on its miniature but visible feet. The witness spoke of its weight—about an ounce, its head—now the third of the size of its body, its functioning kidney and urinary tract, and developing respiratory and digestive systems.

"The baby's face is looking more and more human," she went on. "The eyes have moved closer together and the ears are near their normal position on the side of the head. At this stage the baby's heart is pumping about twenty-five quarts of blood each day. The liver is making bile and is supervising the activity of a fully working spleen. At thirteen weeks the fetus is also able to absorb sugar and pass urine."

"Amazing," said Katz, shaking his head. "And is this . . ." he said, feigning interest in one of the blowups, "is that hair I see on this fetus' head?"

"Yes." Wakeford smiled. "And if this picture was magnified further," she said, directing her pointer to the image, "you would also see fingerprints and the beginnings of eyebrows."

"And what about its behavior, Professor? Is the child . . . I'm sorry, the *fetus*, doing anything significant that it had not been doing, say, a week or even days previously?"

"Yes," said a satisfied Wakeford once again. "In fact, thirteen weeks is a wonderful benchmark. At this stage the fetus is acquiring reflexes. It will respond to touching the palms by closing its fingers, or curling its toes if you tickled its feet."

"Go on, Professor," said Katz, milking the woman's testimony for all it was worth.

"At thirteen weeks the fetus also begins to suck its thumb, as can be seen here," she said, moving to another shot and pointing her stick in delight. "And it smiles for the very first time," she said, her eyes drifting toward the jury in delight. "And more importantly, at least for the parents concerned, thirteen weeks is the watershed for miscarriage or lack thereof."

"I don't understand," said Katz, scratching his head, David and Sara both knowing that he knew damn well what his witness was referring to.

"At thirteen weeks, Mr. Katz, the mother's chances of miscarriage falls to an extremely low 0.9 percent."

"I see," smiled Katz, like an expectant father himself. "So what you are saying is that the fetus in question, Jessica Nagoshi's unborn son, was well on the way to becoming a potentially happy, extremely healthy, little boy."

David heard his client let out a sigh beside him.

"Most certainly," said Wakeford before converting her own smile to a fresh expression of sorrow. "I have dealt with many high-risk pregnancies, Mr. Katz, but this fetus was as healthy as can be."

"Until someone killed his mother," said Katz.

"Yes."

"And shut down all those wonderful developing systems."

"Yes."

"And sent the unsuspecting fetus into cardiac arrest."

"I am afraid so, Mr. Katz," she said, shaking her head, before stealing a glimpse at the defendant. "I am afraid so indeed."

"Just one more question, Professor. You mentioned earlier that there was a possibility this fetus was closer to fourteen weeks, is that correct?"

"Yes."

"And is there anything significant about development at fourteen weeks that could be relevant to this case?"

"Yes, Mr. Katz. You see at fourteen weeks, the fetus begins to hear . . . and *feel*."

"Incredible," said Katz, now making his way across to the jury. "Can you give us an example of this feeling sensation from inside the womb?"

"Well, if a mother was to prod her belly, the fetus would be able to feel it, and respond by moving about. Some mothers even report 'quickening' or flutters of movement as their unborn child shifts about inside them."

"I see," said Katz, now standing straight in front of the twelve. "So if they can feel the prodding, would it be the case they can feel other sensations as well?"

"Yes," said Wakeford, her eyes now downcast. "At fourteen weeks they start to feel pain."

"So you are saying it is possible this fetus felt the process—the pain—of its own demise?" said Katz, now looking each of the jury in the eye.

"Possible, yes," she said.

And Katz paused, allowing the jury to take this in. "I have no further questions for this witness, Your Honor."

• • •

"Professor," said Sara, who took a long, strong breath and swallowed her burgeoning nerves before approaching the witness quickly, her high but conservative heels tapping loudly across the hardwood floor. "Where were you born?"

It was an odd first question, which took Wakeford by surprise.

"Ah—Charlestown, West Virginia."

"And you grew up in Charlestown?"

"Yes. Until I was twelve, when we moved to Richmond."

"Virginia."

"Yes."

"But you studied in Connecticut?"

"New Haven. At Yale. Yes."

"And did you know, Professor, that West Virginia and Virginia and Connecticut have different laws regarding feticide?"

"Ah, I believe West Virginia recently passed a new fetal homicide statute making it a separate offense to kill a fetus starting at conception. And as for Virginia, I believe that while they do not have unborn victims' laws, they do criminalize certain conduct that terminates a pregnancy or causes a miscarriage."

"Very good, Professor. And Connecticut?"

"I believe Connecticut is one of the few states that does not have any specific laws that recognize unborn children as victims."

"Right again.

"And are you aware of the Federal Unborn Victims of Violence Act?" asked Sara.

"Yes," said Wakeford, pushing her glasses farther up the bridge of her long, slender nose. "It was signed into law in 2004. The act recognizes unborn children as victims when they are injured or killed during the commission of a federal or military crime of violence."

"You have done your homework," said Sara who, having researched Professor Wakeford, would not have expected anything less. "The legalization of the act was, in fact, seen as a major victory for the National Right to Life Committee."

"Yes, I believe so."

"Come on, Professor, you are just being modest. You have, in fact, done a lot of work for the NRLC's Political Action Committee, have you not?"

"Ah, yes but . . ."

"What state are we in now, Professor," said Sara, having made her point.

"Massachusetts," said the Professor, shifting slightly in her seat.

"Not West Virginia or Virginia or Connecticut."

"Well, obviously not."

"And this is a state, not a federal crime."

"Yes."

"Right."

Despite David's argument to the contrary, it had been Sara's idea not to bog the jury in the specifics of precedents, but to simply establish that this was a matter of state law. A strategy she hoped was about to pay off.

"And given your extensive knowledge on this subject, I am sure you are aware that Massachusetts has its own legal viewpoint on feticide. In fact, it is one of ten states that recognize unborn children as victims, but *only* when they become *viable*."

"I believe so," said the now seemingly diminutive Wakeford.

"And would you mind defining the term 'viable' for us, Professor?"

"I . . . It has a rather general definition, which refers to the period when an unborn child can survive independently from the mother."

"That's right, Professor—a benchmark generally considered to be roughly twenty-three weeks. And in your learned opinion, is there any chance a thirteen- or even fourteen-week-old fetus could survive outside of its mother's womb."

"Well . . . no."

"It is a medical impossibility."

"Yes."

"Never happened in the history of the human race."

"No."

"Do you have strong opinions about this issue, Professor?"

"Objection!" Katz was up. "Your Honor, I appreciate Miss Davis must be overjoyed and perhaps a little overexcited at her chance to take the floor. But my witness was called to give medical testimony, not legal, nor personal, comment."

"Your Honor," chimed in Sara. "If you will allow me to continue I am sure I can quantify my queries in regards to the relevancy of the witness' personal views."

"All right, Miss Davis," said Stein. "But you overstep the mark and I'll be reprimanding you for harassment. Sit down, Mr. Katz. Your objection is overruled. But you have my word, I am watching defense counsel like a hawk."

"Let me ask you this, Professor," said Sara, swallowing her nerves and getting back on track. "You mentioned earlier that you specialize in fetal disabilities."

"Yes."

"And have you ever advised a mother not to terminate a pregnancy, despite the child's obvious physical disadvantages."

"Objection!" yelled Katz once again.

"Sit down, Mr. Katz. I want to hear this. Professor Wakeford," he said turning to the woman on his left. "You may answer the question."

And the room fell silent, as Wakeford took a breath, her previously overconfident demeanor now showing the earliest signs of insecurity.

And then her face—her pale, smooth-skinned complexion—turned a determined shade of red as she sat up in her seat and voiced the point that she had obviously been determined to make all morning.

"We do not get to choose, Miss Davis, if our child be blond or dark or have blue eyes or brown. That is nature's call, just as it is whether a child is born with a disability or not. Yes, I have encouraged mothers to bear their children when our investigations show them to be disadvantaged. And I have *never* had a mother express regret.

"Your client robbed a healthy young woman from giving birth to a healthy little boy and in the process stupidly stole the ultimate joy from himself. This is not about viability, Miss Davis, it is about *life* and the taking of it. Mr. Matheson killed his own son and in my opinion—medical, legal and otherwise—he should rot in hell for it."

And then Sara let out a breath—a lungful of air she had no idea she had been holding for the past minute. She had done it. She had forced this woman to tell the court what she really felt—an admission that gave Sara more than reasonable cause to turn to Judge Stein with the question she had hoped she could ask from the get-go.

"Your Honor," she began. "The defense requests the witness's entire testimony be struck from the record for reasons of personal bias."

Stein's entire body tensed, the frustration and fury written all over his now flushed face. "Your request is granted, Miss

Davis," he said at last. "And Mr. Katz," the judge added, turning to the now horrified ADA. "If I ever catch you trying to disguise a secret agenda in the auspices of fact, if I ever see a personal opinion masquerading as an 'expert testimony' of any kind, I shall arrest you for contempt and throw away the key, do you understand?"

"Yes, Your Honor," said an obviously livid Katz.

"First Jones and now this," said Stein, shaking his head. "Truly unacceptable."

In that moment Sara turned to look at David. And he met her eyes, a look of pure admiration on his face. She had done her job as intended—for David, for James and perhaps, even more so, for herself.

81

"It's done," said H. Edgar as he approached an extremely agitated Westinghouse at the far end of the faculty corridor.

"Did you say anything when you gave it to him?"

"I told him to read it."

"Quickly?" asked Westinghouse.

"That wasn't necessary," said Simpson, passing Westinghouse without stopping and gesturing for him to keep up. "The most important slip of paper was stapled to the front of the report. He won't be able to help himself. He'll be reading it as we speak."

Things were happening quickly. Once H. Edgar had finally convinced Westinghouse to play along, they had spent the entire week working on their "assignment," researching and triple checking their personal immunity every step of the way.

"Are you sure about this?" asked Westinghouse at last. "Heffer hates our guts. How do you know he will pass on the message?"

"Because the fat fuck is a man of principle."

"Well, he better be, because we are due on the stand tomorrow."

"Trust me, Westinghouse," said Simpson, stopping at the end of the corridor. "I can do this. You just need to sit tight and let me fix this thing for good."

■ ■ ■

Roger Katz had spent the lunch hour in the court's executive private men's room. He had commandeered the key from the clerk, saying that if it was not immediately forthcoming he would use his influence to send said clerk back to the mail room, which he could have, and would have, if the young idiot had not fished into his pocket and produced it forthwith.

He had locked the door. And then he had gone through his paces—concentrating, breathing, counting off the moves one by one. Katz did not practice yoga, that was for those piss-weak pussies with tight clothes and little rolled up mats that they carried under their arms like large colorful sausages.

No, his daily calisthenics—which he normally practiced in the privacy of his own extensive bedroom at 5 a.m. every morning, were *man's* exercises—a series of focused, specific movements that cleansed him of the bullshit of others, and focused his attention on the cause at hand, one hundred and ten fucking percent.

Wakeford was a mistake, a huge gaffe of astronomical proportions. He thought she could keep her goddamned personal views in her pocket but obviously he was wrong. He knew that righteous Cavanaugh and his stunning and (he had to admit) smarter than average girlfriend, would be patting themselves on the back—or on the pussy if Cavanaugh had the balls to give her one in the lunchtime break. And she would be ripe for the picking, fresh from the victory of kicking his own precious balls with that *A Few Good Men* strategy of forcing his witness to vomit her conscientious crap all over the witness partition like a goddamned nun with gastro.

But! *But,* he told himself, trying to refocus on the positives as he stretched both his arms above his head. The jury heard her earlier testimony and despite the fact that Stein had told them to disregard it all, there was no way the images of that half-baked bun-in-the-oven wouldn't stay with them—haunt them even—every time he referred to the Nagoshi girl's unborn kid.

In other words, he told himself, as he brought his arms down and arched his back, feeling the stretch right down the front of his body, Davis may have won the battle but he had set the groundwork for winning the war.

Katz straightened. He closed his eyes and shook his arms and legs and then took ten deep consecutive breaths, feeling the cool air feed his lungs and nourish his reserve with a fresh supply of voltage.

Time to play my next card, he said to himself. And then he straightened his tie, smoothed his hair and checked his reflection in the freshly cleaned mirror before heading for the door—

the power of self-confidence injecting him with vigor and the taste of victory as sweet as candy in his mouth.

. . .

"James, *please*," said Sara. "You have to sit down."

The lunch break was almost over, and rather than use it to go over their cross of Barbara Rousseau, they had spent the entire hour trying to calm their client. Wakeford's controversial testimony had hit him hard, finally allowing him to see his unborn son for the potential life that he was—to see him, and *feel* him, and know him as a person rather than just an idea, or a promise of a hope destroyed by tragedy.

"Did you hear what she said?" asked James for the umpteenth time. "About his heart and his kidneys and his lungs—about his eyes and his ears and his hair and his fingers and his incredible response to touch.

"Do you think he felt it? Do you think he felt himself dying when that bastard stole her life? I don't want to believe it—I still can't bring myself to accept it. But if you are sure H. Edgar killed them, then I need you to find him and bring him to justice before I break out of here and kill the goddamned traitor myself."

But David had had enough. While he felt sorry for his client he knew that if he did not keep him on track, his very distress could ruin his chances at freedom. He had been honest with James from the very beginning, telling James that while they suspected Simpson they still had no bona fide proof. And more and more, as the trial progressed, he was beginning to realize that this evidence may never come, that James' future could well rely entirely on his testimony alone—and his ability to convince the jury that he did not kill either his girlfriend or his unborn child.

"Okay," he said, rising from his vinyl chair to grab James' shoulders in both of his hands, forcing him to stop pacing and look him directly in the eye.

"This stops right here, right now! If you don't pull yourself together, if you allow the jury to see you as a young man wracked with regret, then they will simply mistake your remorse for guilt and put you away for good.

"Simpson's hands may be small, Simpson may be in love with you, Simpson may have even murdered your girlfriend and sold you out, but when it comes down to it we *still don't have any proof.* I wish I could tell you otherwise, I wish I could have met you in that too-crowded bar on that fateful night, and helped with your assignments and later, watched your blossoming career with awe and admiration, but the fact is, James, that is not how it turned out.

"You are on trial for murder, James, and double murder at that. You lost your son, granted, but if you do not wake up to the seriousness of the situation around you, you may never have the chance to become a father again."

James' shoulders slumped, the talk of fatherhood obviously wrenching at his heart.

"Katz is pissed," David went on. "No, he is more than pissed because Sara just ate his witness for breakfast and he will be set on revenge. And Barbara Rousseau is his ultimate weapon—young, beautiful and ready to tell the world what a goddamned liar you are."

James lifted his face, his bloodshot eyes set on David's similarly hued pair with a look of pure sorrow.

"I'm sorry," he said at last. And David looked across at Sara, her aqua eyes now pooling with tears.

"I will try to help you, David," James went on. "I will do the best I can. But you have to understand that right now I can't even find a reason to want to save myself."

"I know, James," said David at last, now pulling his client close, feeling the young man's body convulse with long overdue sobs. "And if you cannot do it for you, then I beg you to do it for me. For if we lose this thing I will never forgive myself, and it will haunt me for the rest of my life."

82

"Are you ready to call your next witness?" said a relatively calmer Stein as he took his seat for the afternoon session. His face returned to its normal pallor but his voice was still edged with the slightest trace of irritation.

"No, Your Honor," answered the Kat, looking remarkably well considering the morning's shellacking, and the fact that he was, without a doubt, about to set a fire under the already volatile judge before him. "I am afraid our suggested order for the afternoon will need to be changed."

"He's up to something," David whispered to Arthur, who nodded in agreement.

"Forgive me, Mr. Katz, but I believe I am owed an explanation," glared Stein, his manner barely concealing his growing rage. "I am a stickler for order, in case you haven't noticed."

"Yes, Judge. You see, Miss Rousseau's flight has been delayed due to bad weather, and she is not as yet in Boston."

"And where is she, Mr. Katz?" asked Stein, removing his glasses to rub at his deep-set hazel eyes with vigor.

"Still in Paris, Judge."

"That's a long way from Boston, Mr. Katz."

"I know, Your Honor. There are rumors Logan International may be closed by this evening and if that is the case, we have made alternate plans to fly her into New York and will attempt to get her here by other means tomorrow or Friday at the latest."

"And I am assuming you have a backup plan, Mr. Katz, that ah . . ." Stein checked the witness list before him. "Perhaps Mr. Westinghouse has made himself available so that this day is not a complete loss?"

"No, Your Honor. I did try to contact Mr. Westinghouse during the lunch break," he lied. "But to no avail." David guessed

Katz was determined to play Westinghouse and Simpson as a double-hitter tomorrow and had no intention of breaking them with an overnight lag. "Apparently he is in class, and even if he left Wellesley now, he would not be here until three."

"Are you suggesting an early recess, Mr. Katz?"

"That is exactly what I am proposing, Judge, with sincerest apologies for the delay."

"Are you all right with this, Mr. Cavanaugh?"

"Do I have a choice, Judge?" said David, taking every opportunity to stick it to the ADA.

"It appears not," said Stein, shaking his head before turning to the jury.

"Ladies and gentlemen, I want to thank you for your patience today and apologize for this senseless waste of your time. In fact, I know Mr. Katz feels so pained at this inconvenience that he would like to give you each fifty dollars apiece so that you might catch a taxi home in this dreadful weather. That all right with you, Mr. Katz?" asked Stein, peering down at the ADA in disdain.

"Ah, of course, Your Honor," said Katz, now fishing into his pocket. "But I may need an advance on some cash."

"That's all right, Mr. Katz. There's an ATM around the corner," said Stein. "And as the jury were meant to be here all afternoon, I am sure they won't mind the wait."

. . .

With the early adjournment and the weather worse than ever, David and Sara decided to work from home for the rest of the evening—Arthur having promised them he would call if they were needed back at the office. They made themselves a light early dinner and started to discuss the impact of Wakeford's testimony when David looked up from his notes to meet Sara's eyes.

"You were amazing in there today," he said.

"Thanks." She smiled, before reaching across the coffee table to rest her hand on his. "I'm learning, David," she said then. "How to separate the two."

And he nodded, knowing just how hard it was to disconnect your own views from the argument you needed to make in court.

"James was right," he said then. "That despite everything

we have to do, when it comes down to it, the world ceases to exist without the people you love."

And she smiled, before moving around the table to fall into his arms. "Then maybe we need a reminder of what matters most," she said, kissing him then.

And as he unbuttoned her blouse and took her in his arms and entered a world where he was allowed to forget, at least for a time, who they were and what they needed to do, he took comfort in knowing that whatever else, they were in this—and everything else they chose to take on—together.

■ ■ ■

When the man first walked through the door, she thought he was a vagrant seeking respite from the cold. Nora Kelly was not one to judge people, at least not by appearances alone. But this large, red-faced man looked like he had commandeered every jacket and overcoat in Boston and layered them one on top of the other, like a circus clown wearing an impossible mishmash of colors and patterns and styles.

"Can I help you?" she asked, looking over the top of her small, square tortoiseshell glasses.

"I need to see Mr. Cavanaugh," said the now puffing man, removing his purple tartan scarf and resting his hands on Nora's desk as he attempted to catch his breath.

"Ah . . ." began Nora. "I am afraid he is out of the office at present, but if you would like to leave a message?"

"What is it, Nora?" asked Arthur, now at his office door.

"Are you Mr. Wright?" asked the man, turning around.

"Yes. I am Arthur Wright, one of the partners of this firm. How can I help you Mr. . . ."

"Professor," said the man. "Professor Carl Heffer. I'm a lecturer at Deane."

"Right," said Arthur. "Well, Professor, if you'd like to come into my office, Mrs. Kelly will get you some coffee and . . ."

"I'm sorry, Mr. Wright, and I apologize for the late hour, but the boys were very specific. I need to speak to Cavanaugh and Mr. Cavanaugh alone."

"What boys?" asked Arthur, his curiosity now piqued.

"H. Edgar Simpson and Heath Westinghouse, or the master and his apprentice, as I like to call them."

Arthur nodded.

"Nora, call David, and ask him to come at once. He's not far, Professor," he said, turning toward Heffer. "It should not take him long."

"Good, because believe me, Mr. Wright, if what I am guessing is correct, then time is not on your side."

• • •

An hour later David sat stock-still across from the cherry-faced man before him—his office door closed, with Sara, Arthur and Nora waiting anxiously in the rooms beyond. And even as Professor Heffer reached the section headed "conclusion," David could still not believe what he was hearing—the scope of it all, and the arrogance it had taken to see it through.

"It's them," David said at last, as Heffer put down the report and looked up at him.

"Yes," replied Heffer, incredulous. "The names are aliases of course, but there is no doubt the two subjects in this assignment are Simpson and Westinghouse."

"And you believe them?" asked David, anxious to get the professor's learned opinion. "You think these two are capable of . . ."

"Yes," interrupted Heffer without hesitation. "Simpson is a genius, a Machiavellian mastermind with an extremely accomplished intellect. Westinghouse is also incredibly bright, but naive when it comes to his choice of friends—obviously."

The report was nothing short of extraordinary. It basically laid out their entire strategy from beginning to end. David had no doubt the boys had edited the copy to ensure their own legal protection and the work had been submitted as a work of fiction. But it was real, David could feel it, and he knew Heffer could feel it too.

"Mr. Cavanaugh," Heffer began.

"Call me David," said David, and Heffer nodded.

"David, these boys have basically admitted to concocting the entire 'confession,' to setting up your client simply to see if it could be done. And despite what you think or what everyone else would assume, this is not about the money. These boys are trust fund babies of the highest order. I believe Simpson inherited close to twenty million when he turned twenty-one, and I suspect Westinghouse would not have been far behind."

"They sold out their friend simply to get off on their superiority?" asked David.

"Yes and no," said Heffer. "As the report suggests, they believed in their friend's innocence from the very beginning and were certain the foreign 'lover' could verify his whereabouts at the time of the young girl's death. But the third friend, your client, lied, or in the very least exaggerated, leaving our two principals with a monstrous calamity on their hands."

"So this was all an exercise of 'let's see how far we can go,'" said David. "They wanted to test their manipulation abilities against the police, the DA's office, the FBI, and then use the money as proof that they pulled it off. It was all a game from the beginning, one astronomical scam that proved, at least to themselves, that they were smarter than some of the highest law enforcement officials in this city."

"Yes," said Heffer simply. "The assignment requested they be entrepreneurial, and I suppose, in a macabre sense, they outdid themselves, literally."

David nodded, while Heffer took a sip of his coffee, a long, slow slurp that reminded David of the noise kids made when they drained the bottom of their chocolate malt with a straw.

"Of course," Heffer went on, wiping a drop of espresso from his large double chin, "now they find themselves in some very deep water—about to take the stand in an extremely high-profile trial. If they lie and say Matheson's confession was real, they perjure themselves and send their closest friend to the gallows; if they tell the truth and admit to their own obnoxious lie, they come off looking like the smug manipulators that they are—and once again their future is in tatters."

"They have no way out," said David.

"It appears so, at least at face value," said Heffer, and David was beginning to see why this man was coveted by respected law schools such as Deane. "But this is obviously not the case."

"I'm sorry, Professor, I do not follow."

"They have found a way out, David. There is no doubt about that. These boys have come up with a solution and it is sitting before me as I speak."

"Me?"

"Of course. Why do you think they submitted this assignment

and added a note instructing me to contact you at my earliest opportunity."

"And the note?" asked David, who was yet to see Simpson's handwritten adjunct to the controversial report.

"It requests you meet him tomorrow—seven a.m., before court begins and Westinghouse is called to the stand."

"Where?" asked David.

"The Somerset Club, a private room no less."

David nodded. "Will Westinghouse be there?" he asked, perhaps sensing he might have a chance of winning over the less manipulative of the two. Heffer looked at him as if the question was beneath him.

"I guess not," added David. And they sat there for a while in silence.

"I don't trust him, Professor," said David at last. "How do we know that this meeting is not just another layer of their incessant deception?"

"You don't," replied the straightforward professor. "And forgive me for being blunt, David, but you have no other choice."

"They still have the money, Professor. That alone proves the motive of greed."

But Heffer shook his head before pulling a small piece of paper from one of his many pockets. "Not anymore. For this was attached to their assignment—a check for one million made out to Deane."

"A donation?"

"Yes. Very philanthropic of them, wasn't it?" replied Heffer.

"Jesus," said David, taking the check from Heffer's substantial hand—a bank check from the Grand Cayman Island Caribbean Trust and Banking Corporation no less.

"And the other million?" asked David.

"Gone to an international charitable organization, I believe. Like I said, David," said Heffer, shaking his head. "This was never about the money."

"So I meet him," said David.

"Yes."

"And negotiate with the devil."

"Yes. I have followed your career, David, and at the risk of sounding sycophantic, you are the ultimate entrepreneur. This boy is smart, but his ego will be his downfall."

David nodded, as the professor got up to leave.

"Professor," said David at last, having one more question to ask before he escorted this honest, genuine man toward the back of his office. "Is Simpson sleeping with a staff member at Deane?" He didn't mean to be blunt, but given the nature of their conversation, he felt it only fair to be straight.

"I have heard as much," said Heffer, perhaps just a touch surprised that David had heard it too. "And according to faculty gossip, it is a professor no less."

David looked at him, willing him to say it.

"Her name is Maggie Grosvenor and she has a PhD in criminal law. Sort of ironic, don't you think?"

But David heard nothing after the name Maggie—their only hope for survival now was fading before him, faster than he could blink.

83

As David approached the Somerset Club at 42 Beacon, the morning still dark, the air cool and fresh, he remembered an old and much told anecdote about the level of exclusivity at this historic establishment. From what he could recall it dated back to an event in the 1940s when a fire broke out, spreading to all three of the Club's impeccably decorated floors. The firemen apparently ran straight through the front doors, only to be told by some legendary majordomo that, as they were not members, they would have to go round back and enter via the servants' quarters—which they did, and continued to battle the fire while those in the dining rooms sat completely unperturbed.

But David's early entry was much less troublesome. In fact, he barely got the chance to utter his name before a faultlessly dressed concierge escorted him silently to a private dining room on the third floor. Although he had heard much about this elite Boston establishment, David had never been inside. The décor was rich and ornate but still subtle in a comfortable way that spoke of years of affluence and breeding. The heavy drapes, leather lounges, dark wood chairs, lush tapestries and richly colored European rugs were all accented by the effective but restrained lighting of crystal chandeliers, which hung from ornate ceiling roses, bordered by elaborate cornices that stamped the room with authenticity.

The room was empty—at least from what he could see. There was a large table set for two with silverware neatly arranged next to thick white napkins and china cups for tea. The fire in the corner was warm and inviting, burning beneath a white marble mantle that held two matching antique urns displaying some sort of colorful bird on lean leafy branches.

"Mr. Cavanaugh," said a voice, and David turned to see

Simpson—who had been seated behind him the entire time—rising slowly from his plush, burgundy chair. The boy extended his arm in greeting, his ginger hair parted neatly down the side and shining almost golden in the glint of the elaborate glass lights above.

"Welcome to the Somerset," he said as if he owned the place—his blue button-down, subtle tie and beige cashmere V-neck fitting the casual young affluent to a "*T.*"

"Please," he said. "Take a seat, I took the liberty of ordering you some poached eggs and bacon with the Somerset's delectable potato on the side. Some tea?" he asked, taking a seat at one side of the long cherrywood table.

"No," said David. "Coffee, black. That is, if they serve it here."

"Of course," said Simpson. "I expected as much so I asked William to bring a special pot of their pure Brazilian. It is nothing short of sublime."

David took a seat, feeling like he was in some strange time warp where his previous reality had ceased to exist. This was the other Boston, the historic, prosperous, upper-class world of the city's first families—where privilege and superiority seemed to come with genes on some very well-to-do strands of DNA.

He went to open his mouth, feeling the need to control this meeting from the outset, only to be interrupted by a gray-haired William who glided in, presented the coffee and poured its aromatic contents into David's china cup before turning to leave, having not made one single sound in the process.

"All right," said David at last, staring directly at the blue-eyed young man. "Your time is up, Simpson, in less than two hours your buddy Westinghouse takes the stand, and if you have something you want to tell me before I tear him to shreds on cross, I suggest you explain yourself now."

Simpson smiled. "I can see why James chose you, Mr. Cavanaugh—I mean David. Can I call you David?"

"Can I call you Homer?"

"Best not," he said.

"Likewise."

"What I mean to say is," said Simpson, shifting slightly on his emerald green silk embroidered chair, "I appreciate your straightforwardness."

"And I'm sick of your bullshit," countered David. "I read your assignment, Simpson, and it reeks of conspiracy to pervert the course of justice."

"We saw to that."

"Oh, I know you covered your asses," said David. "But I also know I am a fucking determined lawyer and if anyone can find a crack to have you indicted, it will be me."

"I believe the Somerset discourages swearing, Mr. Cavanaugh."

"Well then you will no doubt enjoy cussing your ass off when you are sipping tea in your two by four at Massachusetts Correctional."

"All right." Simpson smiled, lifting his small, smooth hands to give David a short round of applause. "Fair enough. Let's get down to business shall we, before our eggs arrive."

David nodded, grabbing his teacup like a coffee mug and downing it in one, long, strong-scented gulp.

"James is innocent," said Simpson. David was slightly taken aback from his frankness from the get-go. "We understand that. We concocted this highly ambitious, and might I add, singularly brilliant plan, simply because we wanted to explore the possibilities of testing the boundaries of justice. Which we did, quite successfully, would you not agree?"

David went to answer but Simpson held up his hand.

"We did not, however, foresee the problem relating to our good friend's alibi. We took him at his word—a word backed by our own personal observation of Miss Rousseau's obvious intentions on that night at the Lincoln. She had the hots for him, Mr. Cavanaugh, and who were we to think he would be fool enough to decline?

"That being said, our friend's lack of honesty created a fissure in our otherwise flawless plan, a gap which has unfortunately grown beyond repair."

Simpson picked up his own teacup as he said this, as if examining it for cracks.

"And with all this exceptional planning," said David, "did you ever once consider the repercussions on your friend?"

"Of course, which is why we built the confidentiality agreements into the terms of our testimony. James was supposed to hand himself in within a specified time but failed to do so.

Which I suppose is understandable, given he knew his alibi would not hold."

"You're suggesting James was in on this from the very beginning?" asked David, watching Simpson closely. He could see this question was a difficult one, and that Simpson was thinking carefully before offering a reply.

"I am suggesting," Simpson began, "that James may have misread my intent, and in the process dug himself a hole from which there appears no escape. You have to understand, Mr. Cavanaugh, that myself and Heath and James, we are different to most others at Deane. Indeed we are different to most others at any of this nation's fine educational institutions, set apart by our superior intellect and circumstances.

"We did not ask to be born into advantage, Mr. Cavanaugh, it was simply a matter of luck. But we are, at the very least, three of the few who *use* such good fortune to improve ourselves and push at the boundaries the less progressive set upon us. It is our duty, and to fail to do so would do our fortuity a gross misservice."

David shook his head. This kid was something else. "Tell me, Simpson, do you actually believe the crap that comes out of your mouth? Are you that conceited that you truly see yourself as some sort of demigod, delivered like a deity to us less fortunate individuals so that you might rewrite the ground rules of justice and . . ."

"Lord no," said Simpson. "In all honesty I could not give a crap about the masses, Mr. Cavanaugh. What they learn from my example, what they perceive from my feathering my own nest is left entirely up to them."

"Then you admit this is all about you."

"Of course, and to a lesser degree Westinghouse and Matheson. I am not a complete narcissist, Mr. Cavanaugh, more an individual willing to share with a select few who are worthy, which James is of course, a fact I am sure you already know."

Seconds later William was back delivering their steaming hot breakfasts, the aroma of eggs with Parmesan and perfectly grilled bacon strong and inviting in the cozy, softly lit room about them—a warmth so at odds with the nature of their discussion. But as William made his silent retreat, neither of them moved to consider their meal, both waiting for the other to make the first move and broker the deal they had come here to make.

"I have a proposal for you, Mr. Cavanaugh," said Simpson at last. "An offer that will be withdrawn unless you agree to it forthwith.

"I am not stupid, Mr. Cavanaugh. I know our situation is precarious and Westinghouse and I are locked in a room to which you hold the key. But my advantage lies in the fact that I hold a second key to your release—or more specifically your client's, who let us be honest, is the most desperate prisoner of all."

"What do you want, Simpson?" said David at last.

"Two things. First I want you to pull back, to moderate your cross of Westinghouse. I want you to follow the line he takes and in return you may ask the question you have always wanted to ask."

"So now you are dictating my questions?"

"Only because I can assure you of their answers."

David said nothing, finally understanding what the young man was proposing.

"Secondly and most importantly," Simpson went on, "I want you to abandon your cross of me altogether."

"What?" said David, incredulous. "I'm sorry, Simpson, but there is no way I am going to sit back and . . ."

"Actually, it is not up to you, Mr. Cavanaugh, it is up to your client."

"You are not the prosecutor, Simpson, and this is no plea bargain."

"No, but you will put it to him nonetheless, for if you don't, and he finds out about this little tête-à-tête, which I can assure you he will, he will never forgive you. One thing I know about you, Mr. Cavanaugh, is that you do not lie—an admirable quality, no doubt, and in this instance one that will work to all our benefits."

"And what about Katz?" asked David after a pause. "Are you suggesting he knows nothing of this?"

Simpson just glared at him. "I shan't go into details, Mr. Cavanaugh, for to do so would insult your intelligence, and specifics are always dangerous in a scenario such as this. But I do promise you, that in salvaging our reputations, you shall create an opening for yourselves—a window of opportunity that is otherwise unattainable."

"What makes you think I need your help?" asked David.

"The fact that you told the entire world you know the identity of the killer and cannot deliver on your promise."

"You have no idea if I . . ."

"*Oh yes, I do*," said Simpson, leaning into the table now, a fresh look of determination in his eye. "I didn't kill her, Mr. Cavanaugh. I had no regard for her whatsoever. She wasn't even a blip on my radar apart from the fact that her father is a man of great influence and success.

"You think these," he said, now holding up his hands, their meager size shedding monstrous shadows across the white linen tablecloth before them, "you think my small stature and my questionable sexuality are enough to proffer a presentable Plan B? Come now, Mr. Cavanaugh," he said, bringing both of his hands down with enough force for the china to chink in a tingle of protest. "Your little *spy* was as discreet as an elephant in a phone booth. Mr. Jones lives in his own little comic book world where the hero wins and his offsider gets to bask in his glory. Pathetic really, and you should be ashamed of yourself for enlisting him."

And sadly, he was right.

"Don't you see, Mr. Cavanaugh? In all your earnest determination to find the true killer, you have wasted nothing but precious time. Your job is to prove James' innocence not to identify the real offender—which, despite their connection are actually two different things. The girl is dead, as is the child in her belly, and finding the culprit will not bring them back."

And sadly, he was right again.

"I am not totally callous, Mr. Cavanaugh," Simpson went on at last. "I do have affection for James and would like to see him freed. The fact that I want to see to my own interests first does not discount my regard for him as a comrade, an equal even," he added.

David said nothing, just sat there staring at this fresh-faced young man with the Mensa brain and the empty heart.

"You know, Simpson," he said at last. "If you had the morality to balance your fucking intellect, you could really be something."

"A slap wrapped up in a compliment," responded Simpson. "But as I am feeling particularly generous this morning, I shall simply offer a humble thank-you."

"I can destroy you if I choose to, Simpson."

"Yes," said Simpson, perhaps the slightest trace of fear in his otherwise confident tone. "But at what price, Mr. Cavanaugh?"

And then—there was a pause.

"Will you promise that neither you nor Westinghouse will lie on the stand?" asked David at last.

"To do so would jeopardize our careers, would it not?"

"And that whatever so-called new evidence you have concocted against my client will be diffused?"

Simpson smiled, leaving David to wonder why his latest question had not taken him by surprise.

"The new evidence has been taken care of. Or rather, destroying it is now well within your grasp," he said, holding up his hand as if to indicate he had no intention of elaborating further. "And so, Mr. Cavanaugh?"

David looked at him then, realizing that this young man's entire life—his career, his reputation, his all-important social standing in a world where character was king—was in his hands solely and completely. Simpson's entire future balanced on what he was about to say.

"I'll talk to James," he said at last.

Simpson let out a poorly concealed sigh, reaching across the table to shake David's hand.

"And given I know he will agree, I will promise you, Mr. Cavanaugh, that your client will soon be set free."

84

Sawyer Jones woke to a very selfish feeling. The snow outside appeared to have abated somewhat, its thick pellets having shrunk to soft crystals that floated down on the picturesque public gardens like butterflies. It was a magical sight, the beauty of which Sawyer missed entirely thanks to his realization that he would give anything not to be where he was right now—knowing that he should be there in court, with Sara and David, as Westinghouse and Simpson finally took the stand.

He had just spent his third night at the Regency Plaza—on the couch no less—fearing the somber Mr. Lim was not yet well enough to be left alone. It was not as if the Chinese factory worker was outwardly upset, in fact, it was quite the opposite. Lim's lack of emotion was decidedly unsettling, leaving Sawyer with no idea as to how to comfort this man in his obvious hour of need. He had tried to coax him out—despite the weather— but to no avail. The man could speak English, Sawyer had at least established this much, but how much he actually grasped was still a complete and utter mystery.

John Nagoshi had been the epitome of graciousness. He had come last night, expressing his condolences and bearing gifts and a quite substantial check of compensation for the entire Lim family. He had made promises regarding the Guangdong plant, which Sawyer was sure would be forthcoming, and all in all was the picture of remorse and humility.

But Mr. Lim remained speechless throughout the entire encounter, an embarrassed Sawyer's only relief coming in the form of the Chinese man's eventual willingness to shake John Nagoshi's hand at the end of their extremely uncomfortable meeting. Nagoshi had then turned to Sawyer and taken his hand as well, a strong, determined pump that seemed to speak of the man's appreciation of Sawyer's efforts on his behalf.

"You have spoken well for my people in Guangdong," Nagoshi had said just before he left. "And you were a good friend to my daughter. You are an honorable man, Mr. Jones, and I shall be forever in your debt."

Sawyer believed it was the first time anyone had called him a "man," and he had to admit it felt good. But the feeling did not last, given the sting of her memory and his inability to forget that he should have found some way to protect her.

Sawyer rubbed his eyes and found his glasses on a side table and rose from the chintz-covered sofa to head toward the bathroom, praying Mr. Lim might be in better spirits today. But he had a feeling, deep in the pit of his now nauseated stomach, that Mr. Lim would never recover from the passing of a brother he so obviously adored, just as part of Sawyer would always wonder what might have been, as he grieved for the loss of his first true love.

■ ■ ■

"Are you sure about this?" asked David at last. He had raced to the Superior Court building from the Somerset, linking up with Sara and Arthur and briefing them on the way. They then proceeded to wait for James at the prisoner delivery dock, spiriting him away to a private conference room mere minutes before the day's session was due to begin.

"Yes," said James, with not the slightest trace of hesitation.

"I cannot promise you Simpson is not . . ."

"Do it," said James again, his green eyes unwavering.

"You trust him?" asked Sara. "After all he has done to you?"

"I trust Westinghouse," he said. "And I know Simpson will be looking out for his own interests. We are just fortunate that now they happen to be parallel with our own."

"It's a risk," said Arthur.

"But as both H. Edgar and Peter Nagoshi have been ruled out as suspects, we have no choice but to act now," countered James. "If we can end this thing before David has to follow through on his promise to reveal the identity of Jessica's killer then . . ."

He was right. And David felt a fresh sense of relief that his client seemed to have risen from the previous day's malaise with a new sense of focus.

"David?" said James, as if willing him to agree. And in that moment David knew, that despite the fact that this was James' call, deserved or not, his client had such respect for his attorney that he was leaving the final decision to him.

"Okay," said David at last, just as the clock hit nine. "Let's do this."

• • •

Roger Katz looked at the young man before him and immediately suppressed a smile. He wanted to appear dedicated and focused on this all-important day, and did not need the jury glimpsing his resplendent but justifiable glee.

Westinghouse was the picture of all-American perfection. His fair hair neat without looking over-styled, his physique toned beneath his impeccably fitted suit, his wide blue eyes speaking of sincerity and his slightly nervous demeanor suggesting a selfless determination to do his duty despite any obvious distress to himself.

Katz glanced toward the defense desk to see Cavanaugh and the old man in a tight huddle of desperation, the girl Davis now with her back to him as she whispered sweet but empty words of consolation in the young defendant's ear. Katz then moved his head to the right where he gave nods of acknowledgment to the more important members of the press, before doing a full 180 toward the jury whose eyes were fixed on the Apple Pie Adonis before them.

"Mr. Katz," said Stein with a boom, having obviously reached the end of the few minutes he requested to read the morning's notes. "I believe that Miss Rousseau is still beyond our shores."

"I am afraid so, Your Honor. But if this respite in the storm keeps up, and the airport reopens, we may have her here by tomorrow, if not definitely by early next week."

"I understand," said Stein, who seemed in better spirits today. "The court is grateful for your being here with us this morning, Mr. Westinghouse," said Stein, turning to the witness.

"My pleasure, Your Honor," said Heath, with a smile that lit up the entire room.

• • •

Katz began quietly, working up a conversational banter with the movie star witness before him. He asked about his impeccable student record, close ties to his family, dedication to sporting excellence and finally his high regard for his friends.

"I am an only child, Mr. Katz, and as such, friends have always been incredibly important to me. I am lucky to have many friends—from high school, from Deane and from other connections, who are all very much a part of my life."

"And if it is possible to distinguish, Mr. Westinghouse," Katz went on, "could you provide this court with the names of your closest friends?"

"Yes, sir," answered Westinghouse without hesitation. "H. Edgar Simpson and James Matheson are my best friends without question, Mr. Katz. We were thrown together by chance when we decided to study law at Deane, but our friendship goes beyond the similarity of our circumstances and rests more in our ability to get on. In other words, Mr. Katz, we just clicked. You know how it goes," he finished, sharing an understanding smile with the jury.

Katz spent the next few minutes asking Westinghouse to elaborate on their "friendship," detailing their similar sensibilities and goals.

"And given such closeness, Mr. Westinghouse, would it be fair to say that Mr. Matheson's failure to tell you about his relationship with Miss Nagoshi came as quite a shock?"

"Yes," said Heath, as Katz mentally prepared his next question, ". . . and no," finished the witness, causing the ADA the slightest tingle of concern.

"What I mean to say is," Westinghouse went on, "I believe James hid his relationship with Jessica at her bequest. So while his secrecy surprised me, I have come to understand its motivation."

And Katz hesitated—just a second.

"You are an extremely forgiving young man, Mr. Westinghouse," he said at last, deciding to use this slight bump in the road to build up his witness's character in the eyes of the jury. "And it is a pity your friend did not return your tolerance with the appropriate reciprocation of honesty."

"Objection!" yelled David.

"Withdrawn," said Katz, now obviously anxious to move on. "Mr. Westinghouse, on the night of Friday, September 11, you and Mr. Simpson attended the Lincoln Club with Mr. Matheson, is that correct?"

"Yes, sir."

"And during your stay, you noted a Miss Barbara Rousseau who made certain advances toward the defendant?" prompted Katz.

"Well, I suppose you could say she made her intentions known."

"She came on to him?"

"Yes, sir."

"I see," said Katz, giving the jury the slightest of smiles. "And did you see Mr. Matheson leave with Miss Rousseau?"

"No, sir. He left with us but then returned, and I assumed it was to make a connection with Miss Rousseau."

"But you did not see them leave together," stressed Katz.

"No," repeated Westinghouse. "But I didn't see him leave with Miss Nagoshi either, so I suppose his whereabouts beyond my leaving could not be verified one way or the other."

Katz looked up at the witness, now sure that something was amiss. He started toward him with the slightest look of displeasure in his eyes. He was not too sure what was going on, but feared that Westinghouse, the obviously weaker of his two shining stars, was slowly losing his nerve. His plan was to block his view of the defendant and force the young man to focus on him and him alone. And then he would have no choice but to move back on track, exactly where he belonged.

"And the following morning, did not Mr. Matheson tell you he returned to the club and later had sexual intercourse with Miss Rousseau?" Katz asked, sensing he needed to cut to the chase.

"No," said Heath.

And Katz was aghast.

"At least not in so many words. We riled him about it, and he sort of suggested he responded to her advances. But he never actually said he slept with Barbara. It was just an assumption we made."

"An assumption he did not bother to deny?"

"No, sir, and perhaps if you saw Miss Rousseau you might

understand why." And the jury laughed—at Katz's expense no less!

"Mr. Westinghouse," Katz continued, determined to make up some ground. "We certainly appreciate your loyalty to your friend, but I would not feel distress at his lack of honesty if I were you. Mr. Matheson lied to the police, which suggests you and Mr. Simpson were not the only victims of his contrived duplicity."

"Objection," yelled David. "Is that a question, Your Honor?"

"It is not, Mr. Cavanaugh," said Stein before turning to Katz who was now positioned immediately in front of the witness. "This is not some political rally, Mr. Katz. We are not here to give speeches. Objection sustained."

And Katz nodded before gathering his thoughts and moving on. His next few questions led directly up to the night of the all-important "confession," which he approached with the utmost of care. He knew that Westinghouse and Simpson's statements were extremely specific in the description of Matheson's admissions, and there was no way he would allow this fair-weather witness to suggest they were open to "interpretation."

"And so, Mr. Westinghouse, on this occasion, in a corner of the Deane University bar known as The Fringe, Mr. Matheson admitted to killing his girlfriend?"

"Yes," said Westinghouse after a beat, and Katz would have called for a high five if it would not have been extremely inappropriate.

"And specifically, he said . . ."

"That he was responsible for her death, that one moment he was holding her in his arms and that in the next she was gone, and there was nothing he could do to bring her back."

"And I believe in your statement you described his mood as intense, direct—to the point where you believed Mr. Matheson needed to cleanse his soul of the terrible crime he had committed."

"Yes, Mr. Katz," responded Westinghouse instantly. "And I also described him as drunk, emotional and wracked with an inconsolable grief."

Katz went to open his mouth, but Westinghouse was determined to go on.

"Which is why we hesitated before going to the police. We

were terrified of misrepresenting his intent and needed some time to decide upon our course of action."

But Katz had had enough. "But you *did* go to the police, didn't you, Mr. Westinghouse?"

"Yes."

"And you *did* decide to turn him in."

Westinghouse hesitated. "Yes."

"You made the decision after some serious consideration and did your duty despite your most earnest attempts to give your friend the ultimate benefit of the doubt."

Silence.

"Isn't that right, Mr. Westinghouse?" asked Katz, pressing the point, now less than a foot from the young man before him.

"Yes, Mr. Katz. That is correct."

And Katz took a breath.

"Mr. Westinghouse," he said at last, finally winning his own witness over and now wary of alienating the jury by browbeating this obviously sincere and genuine young man. "I understand how difficult this is, to be in the same room as your former best friend and admit to the world what you know to be true. But a life has been lost, Mr. Westinghouse—two lives, in fact—and your testimony to the police, and here today, does you proud.

"I have no further questions for this witness, Your Honor," he said, returning to his chair, a sigh of relief barely concealed under the release of a long, slow breath.

. . .

"Your witness, Mr. Cavanaugh," said Stein at last, glancing at his watch as if to check whether this testimony might drag them over lunch.

"Yes, Your Honor, and I promise to be brief," said David, reading the judge's mind.

David got to his feet and approached the witness calmly, slowly, like a friend wandering over for a chat.

"Mr. Westinghouse," said David at last, "I too understand how difficult this is for you, as my client has described your friendship in much the same way as you have here this morning—firm, unconditional, strong."

And Westinghouse stole a quick glance at James just as David had intended.

"Besides his parents, who I believe also include you and

Mr. Simpson as family, would you agree that no one else in this room, or even beyond, knows James as well as you?"

"Ah . . . no I suppose not," said Heath, now obviously finding it difficult not to meet his close friend's eye. "We are pretty tight." And David noted he said "*are*," not "*were*."

"And so, given you know James so well, given you have spent thousands of hours in his company, shared his confidences and allowed him to share yours, do you believe, with all the information available to you and all your knowledge of James as a person, that he is guilty of murdering his girlfriend?"

And that was it, one simple question, one almighty risk, upon which Westinghouse's entire testimony would rest.

David waited, his pale green eyes meeting the wide blue orbs of the young man before him. And in that second he saw the fear abate and an almost grateful expression move across his face as if someone had finally asked him the question he had been dying to answer for months.

"No, sir, Mr. Cavanaugh," said Heath with intent. "No, sir, I do not."

85

Moments later, after Stein called for an early lunch, Roger Katz stormed from the courtroom determined to catch his pathetic, ball-less excuse for a witness before he scampered from the building in shame. But he was not hiding! On the contrary he stood at the end of the corridor tall and satisfied—and conversing with Simpson no less—while the members of the press, who were under strict instructions not to harass the witnesses within the Superior Court building, fluttered like fascinated finches around them.

And so Katz, his teeth now set in a taut, tense grin, made his way toward them—carefully carving a swath between the obviously fixated flock.

"A moment," said Katz, steering the two young men to the private enclave by the water cooler. And then, once he was sure he was beyond earshot, he began on his fierce and merciless tirade.

"You fucking prick," he said at last. "What the hell do you think you are playing at?"

"I told the truth, Mr. Katz," said Westinghouse.

"You fucked me over and pissed on your own fucking future like an ignorant, egotistical fool."

"Mr. Katz," said Heath after a pause, "I appreciate your constant concern for my future, but I think I got it covered."

And an exasperated Katz turned to Simpson who, he noticed, could barely conceal a smile on his smug, self-satisfied face.

"Mr. Simpson," Katz began, his flush, shiny face now mere inches from H. Edgar's cool and even-pallored features. "A word of warning. You follow your retarded puppet's lead and I swear to God, I will make sure that you never work in this city again."

"I'm not working now, Mr. Katz," he said.

"You know what the fuck I mean," countered the now furious ADA. "I know what you are doing," he said after a breath. "You are attempting to cover your own pathetic piss-weak asses so that you can preserve your blessed blue-blood reputations. You think that by sitting on the fence you avoid offending everyone who is anyone and can never be blamed for backing the wrong goddamned horse.

"But don't you see gentlemen—that is a mantra spoken by cowards, not to mention the fact that, by drawing arms against me, you make a dedicated enemy for life."

And then they said nothing, Katz's eyes now fixed solely on Simpson, willing him to commit to the testimony they had planned and challenging him to suggest he would do otherwise.

"Don't worry, Mr. Katz," said Simpson at last, using his hand to shift the ADA slightly to his left so that he might pull a paper cup from the dispenser and pour himself a long drink. "Despite your suspicions we are not out to betray you. In fact, I am fully aware that it was us who ratted out James in the first place," he said, and Katz noticed Westinghouse flinch.

"I am not going to get up and call myself a liar, Mr. Katz," Simpson went on. "For that would be tantamount to stupidity. And so I will give you what you want in regards to the additional incriminating evidence, and then the rest will be up to you."

Katz could not help but smile.

"That is all I ask," said a now placated Katz, offering his hand to Simpson who chose to bring his cup to his mouth and down its entire icy contents before offering his hand in return.

"Then we are on the same page," said Katz as Simpson tossed the paper cup into the small white bin behind him.

"It would appear so," said Simpson in reply. "And now, if you would forgive us, Mr. Katz, Mr. Westinghouse and I are going to get some lunch—and I suggest you do the same. For the hour is almost gone, and there is no doubt that we face a long and laborious afternoon ahead."

• • •

If Westinghouse was the embodiment of beauty, then Simpson was the epitome of earnestness. David noted he had changed

into a conservative but expensive suit, the color a dark chocolate, the shirt a sparkling white, the tie a subtle beige with tiny
flecks of gold. The young man had the ability, David noted, to
tone down his arrogance when required, at least at face value,
so that if he sat as he did now, still, silent, upright, he looked
almost like a serious Richie Cunningham of *Happy Days*
fame—all focused and humble and ready to serve.

"Don't worry," whispered Sara as Judge Stein entered the
room. "There is nothing we can do now. James has made our
decision for us."

"We have agreed to do business with the devil, Sara," David
said, looking into her pale blue eyes.

"No," she said. "He has agreed to do business with us."

. . .

Half an hour later, the Kat had settled into a nice easy rhythm,
his questions clear and precise. Unlike Westinghouse, Simpson
appeared at ease on the stand, his lack of hesitation suggesting
honesty and certainty, his directness confirming his confidence
in every response.

And so after almost an hour of re-covering the "friendship"
issues, of revisiting Matheson's lies about Rousseau and of asking Simpson to reiterate the defendant's much talked about
confession, the ADA finally got to the much anticipated subject
of those all-important shoes.

"You are aware, are you not, Mr. Simpson, as a distinguished student of the law, that the police sometimes hold certain details from the public in an effort to identify a suspect."

"Yes, sir."

"And that in this case it was the removal of Miss Nagoshi's
shoes."

"Yes."

"And it was James Matheson, the defendant, who told you of
this detail during that all telling night of truths."

"Yes."

". . . when he said it was he who took them, as some sickening memento of his brutal and infamous deed."

"Well, not quite, Mr. Katz," said Simpson. "James told us
about the shoes but I believe his words were more to the effect
that they were taken by the *killer*, and there was no mention of
the words memento or infamous."

"Forgive me for not being plain, Mr. Simpson," said Katz, his left eye twitching with the slightest indication of irritation. "What I meant to say was that Mr. Matheson knew about the shoes when nobody else did."

"Well," pondered Simpson. "The police knew about them, as did certain members of the FBI, and yourself, and I am assuming perhaps some others in the district attorney's office. And I believe the Nagoshis were also made aware of their absence, which I suppose means this so-called secret was not so tightly held after all."

The courtroom offered the slightest of chuckles in response.

Katz paused, and David sensed the ADA knew this was perhaps just the beginning of the young man's disobedience. Westinghouse's testimony had no doubt been unsettling enough for the overconfident Katz, but now, to have his number one witness diverting from the script as well . . .

And so David was not surprised when the Kat changed tack, but did become concerned when the new line of questioning became disjointed in its lack of continuity. At first it appeared as if the rattled ADA had lost track—stepping backward instead of forward, his previous strict adhesion to chronology abandoned for an oddly timed stroll down memory lane.

"Did Mr. Matheson ever talk to you and Mr. Westinghouse about his time in Sydney?" asked Katz.

"Yes, sir. He certainly enjoyed it. He got a good education, spent time with his mother, got a chance to enjoy the fine Australian weather, made lots of friends."

"Such as?"

"I believe his two best friends were named Lawson Flinn and Sterling Buntine. Both boarders from the country—one from a place called Gundagai in southwestern New South Wales, and the other from the genuine Outback in the Mid Northern Territory."

"And to the best of your knowledge, Mr. Simpson, is Mr. Matheson still in contact with these two young men?"

"I believe not, Mr. Katz."

"And why is that, Mr. Simpson?"

"Because, according to James, they had a falling out, an extremely unfortunate argument that has lasted all this time."

"And are you aware what this argument was over, Mr. Simpson?"

"Yes, sir," said H. Edgar, stealing the slightest of glances at David. "I believe it was over a girl."

The court erupted in confusion as all present, including the now salivating press and the ever-interested jury sat up, at attention, waiting to hear more. David went to object on the basis of relevancy, but had read Simpson's glance as a direction to remain silent, and was praying his instincts were right.

"Did Mr. Matheson ever tell you the nature of this altercation, Mr. Simpson?"

"Yes, he confided in us some time ago. I believe the circumstances surrounding the cessation of their friendship were upsetting for James, and as his two best friends, he chose to share the information with myself and Mr. Westinghouse some time earlier this year."

The Kat said nothing, his silence obviously an indication that he was giving his witness the floor and so Simpson took it slowly, carefully relaying the story as it was told to him.

He began by explaining that in their final year of school, Lawson Flinn was dating a young woman of some note. Her name, according to Simpson, was Alison Saunders—the daughter of a British diplomat who attended a private girls' school not far from the one attended by Matheson and his friends.

"Long story short, Mr. Katz, the girl fell for James. According to James it was just one of those things. But the matter ended in a physical confrontation, which I believe took place late one evening beside the school's Olympic-sized swimming pool."

Simpson went on to explain how the fight—witnessed by the third friend, Buntine—resulted in the smaller Flinn losing his footing on the slippery wet tiles and falling, his head hitting the sharp corner of the pool's wet lip, his neck bending backward as he fell into the water

"According to James, Lawson Flinn lost consciousness and James and Mr. Buntine made haste to pull him out."

"And so the boy did not drown," offered Katz.

"No," countered Simpson. "But he did sustain some significant injuries, resulting in his losing the use of his legs."

"Mr. Flinn is now a paraplegic?" asked Katz in feigned incredulity.

"Yes," said Simpson. "A sad but true example of how life can turn on a knife's edge."

The crowd was silent, the implications of this new testimony creating a dark shadow over the room. Stein looked at David, almost willing him to object, but a million things were going through David's mind and he needed a moment to consider them. He wondered why James and his mother had not told him of Flinn's disability, and the reason for it. And he was concerned that his client did not feel comfortable enough to tell him either—that his tendency to see David in some "super lawyer" light had resulted in him feeling ashamed to share details that Katz was now determined to use against him. But more importantly, at least for now, David sensed he finally understood what Simpson had meant about the new evidence being "diffused" and thus sat still, silent, knowing that his time would come.

"Your Honor," said a now straight-backed Katz, approaching the bench with vigor. "I would like to submit a patient report from St. Vincent's Hospital in Darlinghurst, Sydney, dated on the night of the aforementioned altercation, as further evidence to the severity of Mr. Flinn's injuries.

"The report clearly outlines the specifics of what was no doubt a violent and vicious attack—a broken rib, a bruised cheek, a grazed hip and of course the spinal injury that has rendered Mr. Flinn immobile.

"At the time Mr. Buntine gave a statement to the Rose Bay Police outlining the details of the heated attack, including Mr. Matheson's disinclination to walk away when it was obvious Mr. Flinn was defeated.

"The district attorney's office did make contact with Mr. Flinn some weeks ago, Your Honor, and unfortunately, although understandably, he said he was too distressed to speak of the incident in this courtroom today."

And then Katz took a pause, allowing this all to sink in, before turning to the judge and taking a breath and voicing what he so desperately needed to say.

"Your Honor, Mr. Matheson's clear propensity for violence as illustrated in his aggressive attack on his ex-best friend," he said, lifting his hand to tick off his points, "his bloody and brutal temper as demonstrated in the slaughter of his so-called love, Jessica Nagoshi, and his fierce and sadistic attack on Miss Nagoshi's brother at the recent Deane Halloween Ball, not only indicate this young man has a vicious streak, but also that he has the audacity to hide it under the guise of being the all-American hero.

"But I am glad to say, that thanks to decent young men like Mr. Simpson here, his true nature has finally been revealed."

"Mr. Simpson," Katz said at last, no doubt wondering why an objection to his previous soliloquy had not been forthcoming. "I am sure if Mr. Flinn were here, he would thank you for telling his story in his stead."

"Thank you, Mr. Katz, but to be honest, my representation feels somewhat inappropriate. I am sure Mr. Flinn would have done a much finer job of expressing his own sentiments before the court." Simpson flicked his eyes at David.

"No, Mr. Simpson," bowed Katz. "You do yourself a disservice. There is no doubt in my mind that Mr. Flinn appreciates your honesty, and your determination to speak up on his behalf."

86

"To whom it may concern," David began, the room still reeling in shock.

Moments earlier, as Katz had taken his seat, obviously satisfied with his final result, and completely oblivious to Simpson's careful tweaking of his previously rehearsed testimony, all eyes had moved to David, as the room waited anxiously on his highly anticipated cross. Ever since Joe Mannix had taken the stand days ago, accusing the two boys of being the ultimate egotistical traitors, the press had marked this point—the moment where Matheson's lawyer would question the boys' motives and "finish them off" with accusations of avarice and superiority and greed—as a definite highlight of this already front-page-grabbing trial.

But when David announced he had no questions for the witness, their disappointment was soon replaced by a new level of curiosity as he requested he might read from a statement that he promised would finally put any questions about his client's character to rest.

"My name is Lawson Flinn," he read, as all eyes around him grew wide and inquiring as if the young Australian were reading from the document himself, *"and I make this statement of my own free will in front of my attorney, Rebecca Morgan, and my witness and friend, Mr. Sterling Buntine.*

"It has come to my attention that my friend James Matheson has been charged with a crime of violence and, as is so common in my profession of law, I have been called upon to give a statement regarding Mr. Matheson's character or lack thereof.

"First and foremost I wish to stress," read David, his voice slow and deliberate, his tone strong but not aggressive, *"that*

Mr. Matheson is my friend. I met him when we first attended high school in Sydney, both entering at the seventh grade.

"My first memories of him were of his enthusiasm to please, his genuine manner, his concern for the well-being of others and his immediate popularity amongst the boys and teachers alike.

"James and I, along with Mr. Buntine, all three of us from different walks of life, became immediate comrades. We were inseparable from age twelve, supporting each other in class, enjoying leisure activities on weekends and often cheering one another on the football field or tennis court or swimming pool when the opportunity arose.

"There was no doubt, to either Mr. Buntine or myself, or others who came to know James during that time, that he was, and no doubt still is, an extraordinary human being. His academic prowess, sporting talents, and social graces won him many admirers. His generosity of spirit, hospitable temperament, upbeat personality and good sense of humor made him one of the most popular boys in school, and in mine and Mr. Buntine's case, an honored and valued friend.

"Of course, there were times when our friendship was tested. There were moments when our mateship was stretched. There was even one incident when anger grew beyond intent and resulted in regrets set in stone.

"But even then, even now as I sit and record this statement, the mark of such incidents still fresh in my memory, I knew, I know, that my regrets at such times are equaled or surpassed by those of my American friend.

"And so, as I read the reports in the newspapers, as I hear the international bulletins regarding the nature of the case at hand, I sit and shake my head and wish beyond all hope that I can do my bit in informing all involved of the simple things I know to be true."

David paused there, his eyes lifting slightly toward his client, who was now openly starting to cry.

"James Matheson is a man of integrity. He is incapable of the violent act described, and perhaps more importantly, no doubt sitting before you, destroyed by what has come to pass.

"And so—as a student of the law who has witnessed and

researched case upon case where innocent lives have been destroyed, as a man who is no stranger to the sorrows of hardship, as an adult who was once a boy who sought strength in the bonds of mateship, I ask you, each and every one of you to consider the third victim in this heinous crime, and allow my good and innocent friend to grieve his losses in peace.

"Thank you.

"Mr. Lawson W. Flinn."

87

That night, overwhelmed by the intensity of it all, tired beyond all comprehension and still confused as to how all this had come to pass, David sought out his best friend—Homicide Lieutenant Joe Mannix.

Joe was on the phone when David slumped into the chair across from his birch laminate desk, Frank McKay having shaken his hand with a nod before heading off for the night. And when Joe glanced up, he finished his conversation with haste before returning the handpiece to its cradle and looking across at his obviously exhausted friend.

"I thought you would be celebrating," said Joe at last.

David shrugged. "I wanted to make sure you were okay with this," he said.

"With what?"

"With my not going after him, with my letting him off the hook when it came to the reward."

Joe said nothing.

"They donated it to charity," explained David.

Joe nodded. "What's an odd mill or two when your reputation is at stake?

"You shouldn't beat yourself up," said Joe after a pause. "You were hired to defend your client and that is exactly what you are doing."

"Then why do I feel like crap?"

"Because you are an idealistic son of a bitch and none of this sits right with your high and mighty goddamned conscience."

They sat there for a while, the vague sound of a homicide police scanner buzzing somewhere in the background.

"I am beginning to think we will never know who did this, Joe."

"Not every mystery gets solved, David, but if it is any consolation Susan rang earlier. She is going to triple test everything."

"She'll be running the bureau by Christmas," said David.

"I know."

"Did he tell you his friend was a paraplegic?" asked Joe after a time.

"No. At first he thought Flinn and his family would support him despite the troubles of their past but, when Flinn and Buntine seemed to procrastinate, James thought the worst and decided not to tell us exactly what had gone down. He was scared of what we would think of him, Joe," said David, "which just goes to show how much this whole thing has fucked him up."

"I guess," said Joe.

David nodded.

"The kid called earlier," said Joe after a time. "Mr. Lim is going home tomorrow."

"Just another one of my screwups," said David.

"Mr. Lim was gonna be suffering no matter what, David. At least you brought him and John Nagoshi together."

"Nah, Sawyer gets credit for that."

"Another genius in the making," added Joe. "And one with scruples, no less."

"When he runs for president, I'll vote for him," said David.

"Me too," said Joe. "The Kat calling Rousseau tomorrow?"

"Yeah, if she makes it in time. If not, we start our case. And James wants to take the stand right away."

"I thought you were meant to leave the big guns until the end."

"You are, but James argued that the jury needs to hear him now, while Flinn's statement is still fresh in their minds. Right now they are willing to—almost *wanting* to—see him as the decent young man his Australian friend described."

"And timing is everything."

"Something like that." They sat there in silence a minute longer, as good friends tend to do.

"Did you know," began Joe at last, "that as of this evening, a Fox poll voted you odds-on favorite?"

"Then why do I have this horrible feeling that we missed something, and that it is all going to blow up in our faces? I lose this one, Joe—I send this kid to a life in prison—and I don't think I will ever forgive myself."

"I know," said Joe.

David nodded. "Anyways, I just wanted to say, you know, thanks Joe, for everything."

"Not sure if I helped."

"You just did."

88

The morning editions said it all. "KATZ LICKS HIS WOUNDS AS AUSSIE TESTIMONY BACKFIRES, 'BEST MATE INNOCENT,' SAYS FRIEND," "DEANE'S DYNAMIC DUO DONATE REWARD TO CHARITY," and from the *Tribune*, " 'GENUINE' MATHESON EXPECTED TO TAKE THE STAND."

Sara looked up from the papers before her, a piece of rye toast going cold in her hand. "Simpson and Westinghouse leaked their own donation to the press," she said, looking across the breakfast bar at David who had barely touched his coffee.

"It didn't make it into testimony," he said. "They had to get it out there somehow."

And she nodded, finally discarding the toast. "The *Herald* calls them 'local heroes.' "

"And every law firm in town will now be flocking to employ them. I wouldn't be surprised if Westinghouse Senior has to bid for his own kid."

"Nah," said Sara. "He'll just be made junior partner before he hits twenty-three—harborview office and all."

They sat there for a moment, drinking their coffee in silence.

"Did you tell Marc about James' testimony?" she asked, referring to the *Tribune's* front page exclusive, and the fact it was written by their good friend, Deputy Editor Marc Rigotti.

"He called late. You were asleep."

"So you have decided to put him up front?" she asked, noting the trace of uncertainty in David's expression. "It's the right thing to do, David, he is up for it."

And David nodded. "Is it just my imagination, Sara," he said after a time, "or are they breeding kids smarter these days?"

"Not smarter, just with a better eye to self-preservation," she said.

"Well," he said at last, rising from his chair to lean across the bar and take her face in his hands. "When we have a kid, I'm gonna tell him that life isn't just about looking out for yourself."

"You won't have to," she said, kissing him now. "He *or she* will sense it, just by watching their dad." And then he kissed her in return.

She looked at her watch. "If we shower together, we have a spare ten minutes before we have to head out the door."

David just stared at her, a look of pure admiration on his face.

"Come on," she said at last, as she headed around the bar and took his hand. "The clock is ticking."

• • •

"All right, Mr. Lim," said Sawyer, shaking the sleet from his hair. "This is the end of the line." And Lim looked at him.

"This is where you check in for your flight, Mr. Lim. It boards in under an hour so you had better join the line." Lim said nothing.

"I want to say," said Sawyer at last, "that it has been a pleasure, Mr. Lim, and that I hope, in some small way, we have managed to ease your burdens, and that of your brother's family back home.

"And if it's okay with you, I might leave you here because I really wanted to get to court today and you know, hide somewhere at the back so I can at least hear what is going on without the judge spotting me and . . ." Sawyer paused, realizing the Chinese man before him had no idea what he was prattling on about. He looked at his watch.

"Is that okay, Mr. Lim?" he said, gesturing toward the now lengthening line. "If you check yourself in? The lady behind the counter will point you toward the gate."

"Sawyer Jones, good man," said Lim at once—"good *man*" he had said—the second time in as many days. "I thank you, my family thank you, my brother thank you."

And Sawyer nodded, taking the man's hand. "You're okay, Mr. Lim."

"You also okay," returned Lim with a rare smile.

And then Mr. Lim nodded, before offering Sawyer some small blessing in Chinese and joining the now growing line to begin his long and lonely journey back home.

89

"The defense calls James Matheson," said David, the five words the press and everyone else present had hoped beyond all hope to hear.

The room was packed to full capacity. So much so that another room, complete with video monitors and audio equipment, had been set up next door so that the additional press, who had flown in for this closing stage, could bear witness to this highly anticipated event when the real star of this show would finally get to have his say.

Stein had ordered the clerk to open the windows, an odd request considering the cold, but necessary given the stifling nature of the aged heating system and the pure numbers who breathed and coughed and shuffled in this mosh pit of legal finales.

James looked nervous. His wide green eyes were watering. His right hand was clenched, his breathing was short and his normally olive skin was almost translucent in its paleness. He got to his feet, looked behind him toward his parents who gave encouraging smiles before stepping around the desk and walking slowly toward the stand. He held his head high, never avoiding the jury's gaze and nodding at the judge in greeting as he moved behind the partition and took that famous oath.

He shifted the pants of his dark gray suit, adjusted his subtly striped green tie and ran his fingers through his short dark hair before taking his seat and looking up at his attorney with an expression that said "let's do this"—to which David nodded before opening his mouth to begin.

• • •

"Come on, Chief," said Frank McKay now standing in his boss's office doorway, a small piece of white tissue blotting the tiniest spot of blood on his lower left cheek.

"Jesus, McKay," said Joe, looking up at his partner. "What the fuck does it tell our public when the likes of us who carry *guns*, McKay, can't even control a razor?"

"It was Kay's," said Frank in explanation, "one of those cushy pink numbers with the blue strip that are meant to moisturize your skin. But to be honest, boss, the fucker tore me to shreds, and now my complexion feels like sandpaper."

"Your complexion, Frank?" said Joe, barely managing to contain a smile. "Get rid of the shit paper and we'll get going. Matheson is probably taking the stand as we speak." But just as Joe was grabbing his keys and rounding his desk to head for the door, his phone rang for the umpteenth time in the past thirty minutes.

"Geez," he said as he turned toward it. He was hoping someone else in the squad would pick it up and take a message, but the room was largely empty thanks to an apparent double suicide in Mattapan. And so he pocketed his keys and reached across the desk for the phone.

"Mannix," he said aggressively, making it more than plain to the unknown caller that they had better make it quick.

"Chief," said the voice. "It's me, Susan. Thank Christ you're still there." And then Joe felt the anticipation rise from his gut.

"What is it?" he asked.

"Wicks rechecked the prints," she said. "And he found something."

"Something or someone?" asked Joe, a curious and now clean-faced McKay now perched just inside his door.

"Both. We got a match, Chief, on a print *inside* Simpson's glass."

"Inside?"

"Yeah, a thumb."

"Shit," said Joe, wishing beyond all hope that what he was thinking was wrong. "Does the print match one from inside the greenhouse."

"Two—the one off of the flower and the one near the door."

"You sure?"

"I'm sure."

"Shit."

"Chief?" said Susan after a time, as if waiting for further instructions.

"Okay, Susan," said Joe now staring at Frank. "This is what I need you to do."

• • •

"The thing is, Mr. Cavanaugh," said James to a now perfectly still courtroom, "that Jessica was so different from anyone I had ever known. She was smart and beautiful and funny, but she was also surprising and interested and incredibly attuned to everything that went on around her. She could see things in people that I could never hope to see—like that someone was lonely or uncomfortable or depressed. And then she would seek them out and talk to them and include them without the slightest trace of pity.

"Jess was one of those rare people who saw happiness as a right, not as a luxury. She cut through the complications and stripped things bare. She . . . she," James paused there, obviously frustrated with his inability to capture the essence of his former love, and David told him it was okay to slow down, take his time.

"I remember that first weekend in New York," he said, perhaps feeling that giving an example was easier than expressing his feelings outright. "We were at the Met and standing in front of this painting and all I saw was a picture of a girl bathing. But Jess saw color and depth and light and texture. She saw that girl's life beyond the picture. The frame meant nothing to her, Mr. Cavanaugh, because she looked *into* it, not *at* it. And maybe that's why I loved her so much." James took a breath then, casting the slightest glance at his late girlfriend's father.

"I have had a lifetime of people assessing me by my achievements, not in a bad way, but just because that's the way it normally goes. But Jess, she saw beyond all that from the first moment we met, and the fact that she fell in love with me, well, that was the most amazing thing of all."

• • •

Sawyer saw the irony in it, the fact that he was now in his very own line to get past the front security checkpoint at Boston's Superior Court. Some crazy tourist had come in and pulled out her camera and started snapping away at the court's interior steps because she thought they were the ones the lawyers came down in the TV show *Boston Legal* and she couldn't wait to get all the way home to Topeka and give evidence to one and all of

her serious brush with fame. Of course the camera—complete
with shots of her entire East Coast over-fifties coach tour—was
confiscated within seconds, leaving the woman beyond consolation and causing a hell of a backlog at the court's front steps.

Ten minutes later the line started to move again and Sawyer
put down his bag to be checked, while another guard ran him
over with an electric prod.

"You here for the Matheson thing?" asked the guard. "Because it's standing room only up there."

"That's okay," said Sawyer. "I go to Deane," he added, not
wanting the guard to think he was one of those shameless voyeurs. "I'm friends with defense counsel," he added.

"And I'm Tom Cruise," said the guard. "And Katie sends her
regards."

Seconds later he was on his way and taking the stairs two at
a time toward the elevators. He was late, but at least when the
judge called for morning recess Sara would know he moved
hell or high water to be here.

■ ■ ■

"Look, Dean," said Joe over the noise. "The thing is, we can
to-and-fro this thing until the cows come home but I really don't
need your permission." Frank was at the wheel, the removable
siren light now flashing on top of their unmarked sedan.

"We have a warrant and this is nothing more than a courtesy
call. You want to meet us and show us the way to the dorm then
that would be great. But either way we are going in."

"Enter via the east gate," said Johns after a pause. "There's
a garage down and inclined to your left. I'll meet you there in
ten," he said before hanging up.

"Real charmer that one," said Frank above the siren.

"Fucking university of pricks," said Joe before rubbing at
his forehead with his right hand.

"There are a million explanations for this, Chief," said
Frank at last.

"He was in that greenhouse, Frank."

"Yeah, but maybe long before the girl died."

And then Joe's cell rang again and, expecting it to be Johns,
he pressed "receive" quickly to say: "We're almost there."

But it wasn't Johns; in fact, it was the last person in the universe Joe was expecting to hear from this morning.

"Lieutenant Mannix," said the obviously distressed girl.

"Who is this?" asked Joe.

"It's Barbara Rousseau, Lieutenant. And I need to speak with you urgently."

. . .

"Everything they said was true," said James without hesitation. The court was now reeling at this blatant admission. "Heath and H. Edgar, they are my best friends, and that night, at the bar, I was drunk and emotional and sick with grief.

"You have to remember that the last time I saw her we barely spoke. She still wanted to keep everything quiet, and that night, the last Friday before semester, she was with her girl-friends and I was with the guys, and considering we had made arrangements to hook up after the orientation the following day I never realized how much I would regret not being with her until . . ."

"It's okay, James," said David. "Tell us about that night at the university bar. Your friends said you confessed, and you just told us everything they said was true."

"It was—in that I did say I felt responsible. The truth is, if I had been with her that night this would not have happened. I *had* held her only the day before, and then the next thing I knew she *was* gone, and there was nothing I could do."

"And you expressed these feelings to your friends?"

"Yes."

"Which they misinterpreted."

"Yes. But it wasn't their fault. Like I said, I was rotten drunk." James looked at the jury as if asking their forgiveness for drowning his sorrows. "And when I look back on it now, I realize I *did* feel like I was the one who killed her."

"In what way?" asked David.

"Well, I was her boyfriend and when it came down to it I was unable to protect her. I am sure it all came out the wrong way. I had, after all, misrepresented my relationship with Bar-bara, and then there was the thing with the shoes." James took a breath.

"Okay, James," said David at last. "We can see how your friends may have misconstrued your meaning when it came to your feelings of responsibility, but that last point you made, about Jessica's shoes . . . I think the thing we all need to know,

I think the question that most begs an answer, is how did you know about the shoes?"

. . .

He was losing her.

"Miss Rousseau . . . *Miss Rousseau*. Where are you calling from? You are breaking up."

"I'm still in Paris, Lieutenant. I was meant to be on a plane to Boston hours ago, but didn't . . . I couldn't . . ."

This was useless, thought Joe as he waved at Dean Johns, who was now approaching from the other end of the garage and pointing at the entrance to the dorm. The dean joined them with a nod, obviously noting the cell now crushed to Joe's ear. Johns gestured with his head for them to follow him into the building, and Joe and Frank were flanked by two newly arrived uniforms who brought up the rear.

"Miss Rousseau," yelled Joe into his phone. "I can hardly hear you. I am going to have to call you back on a landline. I'm gonna hand you to my partner who will take down your number so that I can call you in about ten minutes, okay? Did you get that, Miss Rousseau? Ten minutes. But right now I need you to sit tight." Joe handed his cell to Frank.

"I need access to a landline," said Joe, calling out to the dean who was a good ten paces ahead of him. The corridors were now filling with inquisitive students who were obviously wondering why their honored leader was paying them an impromptu visit—and why he was flanked by two men who could only be detectives, and two uniforms asking them politely to go back into their rooms.

"There is an RA's office on every floor," said Johns. "We're headed for level three so you can use the phone up there."

They opted for the stairs over the slow moving elevator and hit level three within seconds. They pulled open the stair exit door and turned left into the gray carpeted corridor, moving quickly, almost to the end, before Johns stopped in front of a green-painted door marked with the number 312.

"This is the dorm you are after," he said.

"Open it," said Joe. And Johns retrieved a single silver key to oblige.

The room was small and sparsely decorated, the bed a single, the wardrobe old and worn. The brown calico curtains were drawn back to reveal an impressive view of the university grounds beyond—the red-roofed gazebos now covered in snow, the odd squirrel tracks forming lines like a dot to dot puzzle linking tree to tree to tree.

"Where do you want me?" asked Johns after a time.

"Outside," said Joe. "In fact, I want everyone outside apart from me and Detective McKay here."

"Frank, you take the bathroom," he said, turning to McKay and pointing to the tiny en suite. "And I'll check things out in here."

Despite its old age and small size, the room was extremely neat and reasonably comfortable as a living space for one. A computer desk sat snugly in the corner by the window, while a bedside table against the far wall held an alarm clock, a novel about the Sudan, and one of those skinny, bendable study lamps. Every second Joe searched, every time he opened a book or lifted a cushion or checked under a bed, he felt a small wave of relief—that he found nothing untoward, nothing but class notes or folded laundry or empty space in the case of the metal-framed bed.

Then he hit the closet, the oversized built-in that sat flush against the thin bathroom wall. It was one of those cheap formica structures with sliding doors that never remained on their tracks. The inside was incredibly well organized with shirts up top and pants down on the bottom and sweaters and T-shirts folded like they did in stores. The bottom held four pairs of shoes—shoes that looked small enough to be worn by a child. Two pairs of sneakers—one Adidas and one Nike, one set of dress shoes and a pair of rubber flip-flops, which sat one on top of the other with the heel part slotting into the thong.

In the far corner, under a hanging overcoat, sat a cardboard box that was only half shut, the top spouting what looked to be some old high school trophy and a rolled up certificate of sorts. Joe reached in to pull the box from its nook, the room's only sign of dust now releasing itself as he slid it across the scratched wardrobe floor.

And then he saw it. There was an uneven board that hung in a concave slump having dipped under the pressure of the box. He moved his knees forward and crawled inside the closet, before retrieving a pen from his pocket and flicking the ballpoint up so that he could use it to prize the wobbly board free.

And it came up, *pop!* just like that—so that Joe could slide in even farther and reach down with his now gloved hand, and pull out a clear plastic bag and drag it out of the wardrobe and into the light to see that it contained a pair of small and narrow, plain black women's shoes.

• • •

"You have to understand," said James after reaching for the small water glass in front of him and taking a long, slow sip, "that I wish, more than anything, that I could explain that reference to the shoes.

"I have thought about it and thought about it," he said, shaking his head, "to the point where the whole thing makes me sick. I realize I was drunk, and that all of this information about Jessica—who she was, and what she was like, what she thought and how she felt—was all pouring out of me at once.

"I am sure I told my friends that she had this thing about taking off her shoes near the water and dangling her feet in the pool, or the river, or the pond. She told me how she used to do that as a kid and how it made her feel free." James paused there, a look of pure confusion on his face.

"But in all honesty," he continued after a time, "as much as I would like to, as much as I know I *need* to," he said, sparing a glance at the jury, "I cannot sit here and provide a 100 percent logical explanation as to why I would have told them about her shoes—or more to the point, that the killer took them, as some sickening keepsake after the fact."

In that moment David felt a surge of admiration and fury all at the same time—admiration for his client's honesty in the face of devastating consequences, and fury at H. Edgar Simpson for putting James in a situation where the truth looked more like a lie than the lie. There was no doubt in David's mind that Simpson and Westinghouse had concocted the detail about the shoes. There is no way James could have known about them then, at least not at such an early stage, considering his contact with the police had been limited. But Simpson and Westinghouse had been questioned, and were no doubt being courted by a panicking ADA. And while David knew he could never prove it, he suspected a desperate Katz may well have shared some privileged information to his two star witnesses in order to guarantee their "confession" would stick.

"Okay, James," he said, needing to take this step-by-step. "Let's backtrack a little for a moment. When was the first time you were told of Jessica's missing shoes?"

"After I was arrested," he said. "I think it was Lieutenant Mannix who mentioned them first."

"And then I told you what your two friends had claimed?" added David.

"Yes."

"And your first impression was . . . ?"

"That maybe they misconstrued my mention of Jess's love for going barefoot, or that perhaps they heard it somewhere else first and then got confused as to how it came to their knowledge in the first place."

"Objection!" yelled Katz, jumping to his feet with such force that James, who was still cupping his water glass in his "safe" left hand, spilled half its contents into his lap.

"If this young man is insinuating that the police informed either Mr. Simpson or Mr. Westinghouse about this confidential piece of evidence prior to their testimonies then I take most serious offense on their behalf," he said.

"I don't think he was referring to the police," said David, simply because he could not resist.

And then the room took a universal breath, and a clenched-fisted Katz turned to face David, and Stein, clearly reading the building animosity between the two opposing counsel, lifted his arms in the shape of a "T" before calling for an immediate time-out.

"Enough," said Stein, now signaling for the ADA to sit. "Mr. Matheson," he said, turning to James. "I know you are an accomplished student of the law, and as such, understand that any unfounded speculation, no matter how unintentional on your part, can land you in some seriously deep water."

"I can't see the bottom as it is, Judge," said James, a simple truth that disarmed Stein with its honesty.

And the judge nodded, a nod that soon turned into a shake, before focusing on David once again.

"Mr. Cavanaugh," he began. "Mr. Katz's objection is sustained. Your client must refrain from . . ." he started, before changing tack. "Just be careful how you word your questions," he said.

"I'm sorry, Your Honor," said David, before catching his breath and moving on.

• • •

Sawyer had found a spot in the second back row directly under one of the narrow open windows. He shivered, the icy breeze now catching the sweat on his narrow face and licking it with a cold that seemed to tingle his spine.

He took off the Red Sox cap he had worn "incognito," realizing just how ridiculous he looked in a room full of hatless spectators. His small stature was a plus and a minus—a good thing considering there was no way the judge could spot him behind a row of taller people, and a bad thing considering he could barely make out the defense table at the far left-hand side of the room.

From what he could tell, David seemed to be doing a fine job, and James certainly looked as good as ever up there where everyone could see him. He was hoping to see Mannix or McKay hunkered down in the back as Sara said they had tended to do, but duty must have called, leaving them unable to offer support in their presence.

Well, at least I am here, he said to himself as David started asking James some questions about the Australian, Lawson Flinn. *In case there is some last errand they need me to run.*

• • •

The RA's office was small and cluttered. Joe was crammed into a corner behind the wooden rectangular desk, the plastic bag still clasped tightly in his now sweating hand, the telephone making international connection beeps in his ear. The cop in him had finally kicked in. There was a minute as he stood in Sawyer's room, holding up the bag for Frank to see, when both of them felt like a pair of useless idiots—too emotionally involved to even consider what they knew they had to do next.

"I don't believe it," Frank had said.

"Me neither," Joe had replied, still staring at his partner. "But here they are," he added, holding up the shoes, just as Johns came to the door, a look of complete shock on his puffy, ashen face.

"Dear God," the dean had managed.

"I'll be needing that phone now," Joe had replied, subconsciously putting the bag behind his back.

"Lieutenant?" said the frail French-accented voice, now on the other end of the phone.

"Yes," said Joe. "I'll be honest with you up front, Miss Rousseau. I got a bit of a situation here, so I am going to have to ask you to get straight to the point."

"Yes," she said, but then failed to offer anything further.

"You got something you need to tell me, Miss Rousseau?"

"Yes," she said again, this time without hesitation, as if any attempt to slow her down might see her backtrack for good. "I lied, Lieutenant. I lied about James."

"What?" said Joe, who at this point gestured at Frank to come in to the tiny windowless office and shut the door behind him. "Miss Rousseau, I need to you be very clear about what you are about to tell me. I need you to explain exactly what you mean." Joe looked up at Frank.

"I lied, Lieutenant."

"About Matheson," finished Joe.

"Yes."

"Regarding your testimony as to your dealings with him on the night of Jessica Nagoshi's death and the original statement you gave to the police some weeks ago?"

"Yes."

"Are you saying you *were* with Mr. Matheson on the night in question, Miss Rousseau, that you did go home with him after the Lincoln and engage in sexual intercourse?"

"No," she said, and even Frank jumped as he could hear her voice project clearly down the receiver from the other side of the room. "I did not sleep with James, Lieutenant. I wanted to but he was not interested. After he came back to the Lincoln, after his friends had left, I attempted to convince him again but he politely refused my advances."

"So you *didn't* lie," said a now frustrated Joe. "You just failed to fully explain the degree of your persistence." Joe could not believe it. The girl was so vain she had been worried about confessing the intensity of her come-on. Now she felt bad about not telling the whole story, and was holed up in Paris in a state of egotistical guilt.

"Miss Rousseau, forgive me, but to be honest we don't really care how hard you may or may not have tried to get the defendant into bed with you."

"No," she said again. "That is not my point. You see, Lieutenant, this isn't about my striking out with James, although I agree that does not happen to me often—in fact, it had *never* happened to me before and that was part of the problem. This is not about my dignity but my lie, about his alibi or lack thereof.

"I followed him home, Lieutenant, hoping I could change his mind. I knew he lived in his parents' pool house, so I climbed over a back wall and I watched him enter his home and drink some water, and strip, and eventually fall asleep on his sofa."

"You went to his house?"

"Yes. But I did not approach him. I intended to. It was my last night in Boston and I was determined not to end my stay in the United States with my first sexual rejection. I was *offensé*, Lieutenant—offended. My pride was hurt. You see?"

"Yeah, I get it," said Joe, his eyes never leaving McKay's. "Go on, Miss Rousseau."

"I was a little drunk. I should not have been driving, but in the end I suppose the trip, the cold night air, they cooled me down inside and out. I had followed him intending to give him a night he would never forget, but in the end, I sat on one of those pool recliners and watched him sleep. Pathetic, yes?"

"How long did you stay, Miss Rousseau?" asked Joe, realizing timing was everything.

"I am not sure, but long enough to see the slightest trace of light in the sky—five-thirty, perhaps six a.m."

"And you watched him this entire time?"

"Yes, in fact, it was hard to take my eyes off him. He was like a sleeping work of art. Of course if I had known he was dating Jessica I would never have done such a thing, and perhaps in a small way this stupidly gave me comfort as I realized his rejection was more to do with his love for her than his distaste for me. But, Lieutenant, I realize what I have done. What I said, and failed to say, was unforgivable. I went home to Paris and licked my wounds and even after I spoke to you never dreamed that it would come to this."

The girl took a breath and Mannix could hear the slightest trace of relief in the exhale—like she had got a weight off her shoulders by finally admitting the truth.

"James is innocent, Lieutenant," she said after a beat. "He is not capable of doing what the newspapers describe. Mr. Katz has been extremely persistent and I feel ashamed of my failure to be honest with him. He will be very angry, and rightly so," she said, and Joe could now hear the beginnings of tears in her voice. "You see, I have done a terrible thing by not speaking up for James earlier, and for that I am dreadfully sorry."

• • •

"You have no idea how sorry I was," said James, his voice still even, despite now having spent over ninety minutes on the stand. "Lawson was one of my best friends and I was the one who put him in that wheelchair. I know it was an accident, and I know Lawson doesn't bear any ill will, but I still have to live with the fact that some stupid schoolboy fight left him, well . . . the way he is."

"Perhaps you could tell us what happened after the accident, James—I mean, in regards to your friendship."

"Well, he didn't want to see me for a while, which I completely understood. And then it was time for me to move back to Boston, so I am afraid we kind of drifted apart."

"And Lawson's family, how did they feel toward you, James?" asked David.

"Well, they were extremely upset, understandably. And the hospital bills were pretty steep and the rehabilitation long and expensive."

"And how did they manage to pay for it, James. Correct me if I am wrong but Lawson's parents were farmers, is that right?"

"Yeah, they have a small cattle property in Gundagai and, considering the drought, found it tough to make ends meet. So my mother and I, we kind of pitched in."

"You paid his hospital bills."

"Yes."

"And did Lawson ever know of this?"

"I'm not sure, Mr. Cavanaugh. I asked his parents not to tell him, so I suppose they held true to their promise."

"So he never knew."

"I guess not."

"But obviously, considering his statement, and Mr. Buntine's as well, despite what occurred years ago, both young men still count you as one of their best friends."

"Yes," said James, shaking his head. His eyes were starting to water so he wiped them quickly with the back of his left hand. "Which is pretty amazing considering. In fact, this may sound crazy under the circumstances, but I gotta tell you, Mr. Cavanaugh, no matter what happens, when it comes to friends I am one very lucky guy."

Just then, as Roger Katz was halfway between sitting and standing, obviously having found something to object to, the back double doors burst inward with a bang.

The noise was like a balloon bursting in a nursery, the silence cracked with a resounding thump. The reaction was instantaneous, as heads turned, and bodies squirmed, necks stretched and some smaller members of the crowd lifted their legs so that they might kneel on the long narrow pews in an effort to see who the hell had caused such a racket.

The two men now striding quickly up the narrow aisle were the picture of a weatherbeaten fiasco, hair dripping, soaked to the skin, with large clumps of semi-melted snow left pooling in their wake. And when David turned to see them—Joe Mannix and Frank McKay—heading straight toward the judge, Joe gave him the slightest of nods before hastening his step so as not to be waylaid by the now openmouthed ADA.

"Judge," said Joe, the press now craning forward in an attempt to hear every breathless word. "We need a minute."

"What is it, Lieutenant?" asked Stein.

"It's a private matter, Judge, which has significant bearing on this case."

David, who now stood mere feet from Joe just in front of his client, shot a glance at Sara before approaching the bench as well. And Katz, not to be outdone, leapt to his feet before almost jumping over his desk in a desperate need to be included. And in that moment as the judge, the two principal attorneys, and the two detectives formed a huddle at the front of the room, and as every other pair of eyes, without exception, were focused entirely on the all-important five, another man entered from the back.

This man was tall and thin and extremely light on his feet,

so quiet and unremarkable in fact, that everyone, bar one lone spectator, failed to notice his presence.

"Mr. Lim," said the boy in a whisper, now getting to his feet. *"Mr. Lim,"* he said again, and this time louder, causing Sara to divert her eyes from the huddle to turn to the familiar voice behind.

"Sawyer?" she said, almost instinctively as Sawyer stood and pointed at the advancing Mr. Lim. And Sara, who obviously read the confusion in Sawyer's eyes, rose from her chair to meet him.

"Mr. Lim," she said, joining the dazed-looking Chinese man at the top of the aisle, the group up front now also turning to see what was causing the commotion behind them. "What is it, Mr. Lim?" asked Sara, now taking the man's elbow. "We thought you had left. Did you miss your flight? Have they closed the airport again?"

And then David saw it—the tiny glint of metal that caught the light from the window and rose like some self-motivated entity on a mission of its own. It was almost as if the object controlled the man who held it—Mr. Lim—his right arm now stiff and outstretched and making its taut, determined ascent toward something . . . some*one* on the right-hand side of the room.

Time stood still as all eyes focused on the small silver pistol. The screams rang out, the room ducked for cover, Sara grabbed at the man's arm, the judge called for security, and Lim screamed *"yāo!"* as Sawyer crawled over benches and bodies and security guards to get to the front of the room.

"Yamero!" screamed Peter Nagoshi who, in that second, finally realized the man was aiming at him. But the younger Nagoshi did not move, just stood, motionless, his face contorted in a stretch of terror, as his father grabbed him from behind trying to force him to take cover.

"Fusero, segare," yelled John Nagoshi just seconds before the shot rang out, the air already bitter with the pungent smell of gunpowder.

And then David saw Sara's body tug and lurch sharply to the right, her head hitting the corner of the prosecutor's desk as she fell. He saw the blood—the thick, red explosion as it shot up into the air and sprayed everyone within reach, the masses now cowering in the wake of the gun being fired.

As he ran toward her, his ears barely registering the crash of furniture and the shrieks of horror around him, he tripped and slid across the floor, his arms outstretched in an effort to pull her away from the fray. But then she was up and crawling, her hand slipping in a thick pool of crimson before her body fell again in the middle of the puddle, her entire torso now covered in red, her face splattered with blood and other pale yellow matter that stuck to her hair in clumps.

And then David realized what she was doing, she was determined to get to *him*—the *kid*—who lay motionless, his brown eyes wide and unseeing, his thick hair now burned and matted at the side, his skin draining of color and his mouth open in a scream that David knew had been frozen as he shouted the name of the girl they both loved.

"He was trying to save me," sobbed Sara hysterically, her hands now clutching at Sawyer's shirt, pulling him up and resting his head on her lap, the blood now gushing from the large open wound, his body heavy and limp and cold.

"Oh God, no," she cried, her entire body now convulsing. *"No, David, please no."*

And then David enveloped her with his arms, his face now flush against hers, his mouth pressed against her ear repeating, *"Shhh, Sara, Sara, I'm here, I am so sorry. Shhh, Sara, I love you. I'm here."*

And then time seemed to stand still as David and Sara and the young man named Sawyer existed as one. David and Sara's tears cutting swaths through the blood, their eyes closed to the horror around them, and all reality lost in a blur of regret and sorrow and guilt.

90

Two hours later, after Mr. Lim had been arrested, and the room had been contained and most of the building had been evacuated and the road outside had been closed; after the police cars and ambulances had filled the streets and the spectators had been questioned, and Sara had been treated for shock as David, Nora and Arthur stayed close by her side . . . Joe finally got to tell his story.

They were in Judge Stein's chambers, the only person not sprayed with the stains of Sawyer's blood being the surprisingly fresh looking ADA who, David vaguely remembered, had last been seen ducking for cover behind the judge's partition, as far away from the fracas as possible.

James had been taken to a private holding cell, his parents allowed to remain with him at least for the time being, while the jury were sequestered to a private meeting room under heavy security on the building's top floor.

Joe was slow and deliberate, beginning with their original suspicions about Peter Nagoshi and how their investigations had led them to the recruitment of the younger Mr. Lim. He spoke of their simultaneous qualms about H. Edgar Simpson and their admittedly inappropriate decision to include the young Sawyer Jones as part of their investigatory team. He told them how Jones retrieved Simpson's prints from the Deane Law School Common Room, unwittingly leaving his own print inside the glass, and how Susan Leigh had eventually identified the print as a match to the two in the Nagoshi's greenhouse.

Eventually he moved on to explain how they got a district judge to fast-track a warrant to search Sawyer's dorm, and in the process of doing so, they had recovered the long missing shoes. And finally he told the judge of his unexpected international call from Barbara Rousseau and their subsequent conversation as to what really happened on the night of Jessica Nagoshi's death.

"Miss Rousseau lied, Judge," said Joe. "She was with James Matheson when the Nagoshi girl was killed, but not in the way we originally suspected. Matheson is clean," he added. "And the real killer is, well, let's just say Mr. Jones has suffered the ultimate penalty for his actions."

And then there was silence as Arthur and David and Sara and Frank and Joe waited patiently for the judge to respond. A silence they sensed he needed, to absorb all that he had been told, until . . .

"This is preposterous," said Katz, now standing from his chair, which was a good two feet away from the others. "Secret investigations, illegally recruited deputies, pathetically assembled evidence, which has done nothing but make a mockery of this court. Judge," a determined Kat went on. "At the very least Lieutenant Mannix and Detective McKay should turn in their shields and report to internal affairs immediately. Their behavior has been nothing short of treasonous, and at your behest, I am personally willing to charge them both with conduct unbecoming, among other things, as soon as this meeting is over.

"As for Mr. Cavanaugh," the Kat continued in disgust. "The fact that he recruited a *murderer* to act on his behalf, the fact that he carried out an entire covert investigation relating to the Nagoshis' enterprises, the fact that he convinced his detective friends to do his dirty work and then failed to submit all of the above into discovery is, well . . . the man should be struck from the bar immediately and never allowed to practice in this fine state again."

As he listened, David realized one extremely surprising thing—that his normal need to throttle the ridiculous ADA, that his usual response of facing off and fighting back, that the typical rush of anger that tended to accompany the Kat's rantings were nowhere to be found. And even more surprising was the fact that his four friends had similar looks of nonchalance on their faces. The truth was, they had seen too much in the past few hours for Katz to even register on their radar, and oddly enough, this felt good.

"All right," said Stein at last, gesturing at Katz to resume his seat. "Let's take this one step at a time, shall we?" And the group nodded.

"Lieutenant Mannix, Detective McKay, I want you to hand over your shields immediately and place them on the desk before me."

David was in shock. "No, Judge," he began. "This is my fault. Lieutenant Mannix, Detective McKay, they were only trying to . . ."

"Shhhh!" ordered Stein, his long narrow finger now placed firmly on his lips. "Please, Mr. Cavanaugh, allow me to finish. I want these two obviously exhausted detectives to go home, rest and seek counseling if they need it. Then I invite them to come back to retrieve their shields when they feel they are ready for duty. If that be in the New Year, then fine; if that be before Christmas then so be it, and if that be on Monday morning, which I think more likely the case, then that is okay with me too."

And David nodded, and the Kat scowled, and Joe and Frank removed their shields with gratitude.

"As for you, Mr. Cavanaugh," Stein continued. "First up, I want you to know that I have already received a note via my clerk from John Nagoshi who not only wanted me to thank the police for their efforts in this matter but also expressed a desire that I pass on his regret at what your client has had to suffer over the past few months."

David nodded again.

"Secondly, I want you to know that I expect to be included in any follow-up investigations and reports in regards to this case. I shall anticipate a call from you daily, Mr. Cavanaugh, until this matter is finally put to rest.

"Finally," the judge continued as he sat back in his large leather chair and removed his glasses, which contained the slightest spotting of red on the corner of the right lens, "I want to direct you to undertake one more significant task in relation to the proceedings today. I want you and your co-counsel," he said, offering a smile to Sara, "to go free your client. For he has been incarcerated long enough, and right now, more than anything, he deserves to go home with his family."

91

It was two days before Christmas and the snow had finally stopped, leaving the skies blue and the air fresh with the welcome warmth of the sun taking the edge off the bitter winter chill. Night fell to a star-filled sky, the moonlight strong and white, David and Sara packing the last few things for their week in Hyannis, thanks to Tony Bishop and his generous offer that they take his beach house and "go hide from the world for a while."

"What time is it?" said David, taking another sip of his wine before tossing a picnic blanket across the room to Sara.

"Almost nine," she said. "And Tony said not to pack things like blankets and towels," she added, throwing the blanket right back at him. "The house is fully stocked."

He leapt over the sofa and wrapped the blanket around her before pulling her close. "James' big interview starts any minute."

"I know," she said, reaching up to kiss him. "Turn on the TV. I can finish this later."

It had been almost two weeks since the trial—since that shocking day when they had lost and won on so many different levels. And even now they were not sure how they felt about it all—about Sawyer's death and Mr. Lim's incarceration, about James' freedom, and Simpson and Westinghouse's victory.

It had been Nora's idea that they have a quiet Christmas—in fact, she had practically demanded they tell their respective families that they were getting away on their own. The past ten days had seen them reeling from the constant barrage of press inquiries and right now, just the idea of their imminent break was enough to make them smile.

They had barely spoken to James. Their client had been

holed up in his Brookline mansion, constantly surrounded by cameras and news crews and journalists on a rotating shift. His parents had eventually hired a "manager" to represent his interests—the publicist/protector quickly streamlining James' interviews to a series of specific exclusives, the main one of which would be airing in seconds.

"It's starting," said David, pouring Sara a water as the opening credits for the high-rating *Newsline* flashed across the screen. The anchor, a high-profile journalist named Caroline Croft, who David and Sara knew from previous cases, soon filled the frame, promising an hour of "riveting, exclusive, never-seen-before footage—the real story behind the dignified young man who never lost faith in times of unthinkable despair and grief."

And then she threw to a special opening sequence—an emotional montage of those moments on the Superior Court steps just after James' release—the imagery that showed James' brief statement, where he spoke of his heartfelt thanks to his attorneys, his love for his parents and finally his respect for his two best friends.

The piece, that fell in and out of slow motion and was set to U2's "With or Without You," had David and Sara transfixed—the close-ups of James' smiling face, the obvious magnitude of his parents' relief, the beaming expressions of his two best friends and the entire group's eventual descent down the Superior Court stairs with the crowd cheering jubilantly around them.

It was almost like watching the parting of the Red Sea, with James as Moses, literally walking into the sunset, his parents out wide, Westinghouse on his left, Simpson on his right, and an entourage of fascinated citizens shaking his hand and patting his back and offering words of admiration and congratulations and best wishes for the future.

And then the camera swung around at the joyous faces around him, doing a full three-sixty before looping back to James once again, his pale green eyes finally stopping briefly on a pretty young girl who offered the widest smile David had ever seen, lighting up the screen for the briefest of seconds, before . . .

David sat forward in his chair, the rug that was around their legs now falling to the floor.

"What is it?" asked Sara.

"Are we recording this?" he asked.

"No, but Nora is," she said. "She set the DVD at the office. What is it, David? What did you see?"

"Not what," he said, turning to her. "Who—the pretty blond girl in the crowd. Joe showed me a photo of her from a Deane University newspaper. I might be wrong, but I could almost swear that the girl beaming at James was none other than his beautiful French alibi—Barbara Rousseau."

• • •

"This better be good," said Joe as he met David at their front office door. "It's almost midnight and I just left Marie on the living room floor with at least fifty gifts to wrap."

"I'm sorry," said David, shaking his friend's hand. "Come on up," he said, pointing to the stairs. "They turn the elevator off at eleven."

Fifteen minutes later, David switched off the DVD player and turned to look Joe in the eye. "Is it her?" he asked, knowing Joe was the only one who had met Rousseau in person. Barbara had agreed to fly to Boston to give her new statement to the police personally, saying she felt it was the least she could do considering the heartache she had caused.

"It's her," said Joe.

"But I thought you said you dialed her internationally on the last day of the trial?"

"I did," said Joe, running his hands though his thick, dark hair. "But it was an international cell, which means . . ."

"She could have been next door and you still would have registered those international beeps," finished Sara.

Joe nodded. "But why would she lie about being in Paris?"

"Wait," said David, getting up from his chair to move to the drawer behind his desk. "There's something else that doesn't make sense."

"What's that?" asked Joe, now staring at the document in David's right hand.

"A courier delivery bill," he replied, handing it to Joe. "Marking the delivery of the Australian boys' statements as Tuesday morning, December eighth."

"So?"

"So, according to Diane the boys only gave their statements

on the Monday—the seventh, which is Tuesday, the eighth
Down Under."

"A courier that delivers from Australia overnight?" asked
Joe.

"Not possible," said David, shaking his head and returning
to his chair across from Sara.

"So Diane must have got it wrong," reasoned Joe. "They
must have given their statements the week before," he added,
obviously not sure where this was going.

"But then why did their witnessing attorney date them on
the Monday—an attorney by the name of Rebecca Morgan who
works for . . ."

"Let me guess," said Joe at last. "The Australian affiliate of
Westinghouse, Lloyd and Greene." He was seeing it now.

"Yes," said David. "I just called them and checked. Ms.
Morgan works out of the Sydney office but, according to her
very helpful assistant, she was in South Australia earlier in the
month."

"The reward money," said Joe. "Simpson and Westinghouse
paid the remainder of their reward to the Australians."

"That's our guess," said Sara. "Don't forget Professor Heffer
did say the boys specified the other million went to an international cause."

"Jesus," said Joe. "Their glowing statements were bought."

"Yes," said David.

"In an attempt to get Matheson off."

"Yes," said David again. "At least that's what we're assuming, but we have no proof."

"We can try to put a trace on the money," said Joe thinking
ahead. "But those Grand Cayman Banks are impenetrable. And
even if I was lucky enough to convince a judge to issue a warrant, there is no way it could happen before the holidays."

"Wait," said Sara, now shaking her head as if trying to retrieve a memory. "Didn't the boys' assignment, the one they
gave Heffer, give details of the money transfer. It was part of
the assignment brief wasn't it, to show how the money was
made?"

"You're right," said David, moving to a filing cabinet in the
corner, grabbing the assignment and leafing to the page that
outlined the original transfer to the Grand Cayman Island Ca-

ribbean Trust and Banking Corporation. "But I don't think it is going to be of any help," he said. "These records are too old. They only show the original deposit, not the subsequent withdrawals. They won't tell us where the money went after it was paid in because . . ."

And then he stopped, Joe and Sara staring at him, seeing the color now drain from his face.

"David?" Sara began.

"What is it?" asked Joe, now getting to his feet. And David finally drew his eyes away from the document in front of him.

"It's the money," he said at last. "The two million split equally between Simpson and Westinghouse." David could feel the chill start in his lower spine and rise up his back like liquid mercury. "It seems that when the accounts were first set up, there was a third one—one that was canceled before the two million was wired and split evenly between the two boys." He placed his hand on the desk before him, feeling a strange need to steady himself as the reality of what was before him finally became clear.

"David," said Sara, obviously noting his distress. "What is it?" she said, getting to her feet as well. "I don't understand."

But Joe obviously did. "Someone called and told them to get rid of the third account," said Joe. "Someone who needed to cover their tracks."

"Yes," said David.

"And you know who it was," said Joe.

"Yes," he replied, now pointing to a contact telephone number beginning with the prefix 714.

"Oh God," she said, finally getting it at last. "Sawyer was innocent after all."

• • •

The final piece of the puzzle fell into place around 5 a.m., after hours of trying to work out just how Jessica's shoes ended up in Sawyer Jones' closet. It was the one question they could not answer, the one mystery with no logical explanation—until David asked Joe to go through the particulars of his search of Sawyer's dorm room, until Joe happened to mention a tiny detail that would normally have seemed insignificant, until David made the connection with another seemingly insignificant discovery he had come across weeks ago, and eventually forgotten in all the chaos. And in the end they saw it—the incredible, horrible, genius of it all.

As the sun rose on a sunny Christmas Eve, David stood from his chair and headed for the door, Joe and Sara knowing there was no point in stopping him. And then he walked back to his apartment and got into his car, knowing exactly what he had to do.

92

He was in the water when he found him, doing lap after lap of the heated pool. The steam sat on its surface like a blanket, his arms rising like ghosts in and out of the mist as he pushed gracefully through the water, his stroke slow and long and efficient. David moved to the shallow end around the northern side of the pool house, his feet hanging slightly over its blue mosaic edge. And there he stood, patiently, waiting for James to notice him.

"David," said James at last, finally stopping to take a break. "God, you scared me. Sorry, I didn't see you there. I was in the zone you know—all the blue and the fog and, well, I cannot tell you how great it is to be home."

James jumped from the pool, his body lean and fit and strong. He ran to a deck chair where he grabbed a thick terry cloth robe, putting it on quickly as the cold began to bite at his skin.

"It's so good to see you, man," he said, walking back toward David and shaking his hand. "I am sorry I haven't called, but it has been—well, I guess you guys know how it has been. Did you see the piece last night? I think Caroline did a pretty good job. It was fair and thorough, if not a little over the top."

"You look good," said David at last.

"Thanks," he said, wrapping the robe even tighter around him. "I feel incredible. Everything looks brighter, you know—everything smells sweeter, tastes better." James considered him then. "But I have to say, David, you are looking a little worse for wear. I suppose you guys have been holed up with the paperwork while I am here having the time of it. I'm sorry."

"Aren't you cold?" asked David, noticing the goose bumps now rising on the young man's skin.

"Nah," said James. "To be honest, I can't get enough of the outdoors at the moment. I've been practically living in that pool," he said, gesturing toward the now still water. "It makes me feel alive, you know?"

"Yes."

And then there was a pause.

"So listen to me prattling on," said James with that million dollar smile. "It's Christmas Eve, for God's sake. You probably have a zillion better places to be than here. You heading down to Jersey for the holidays?"

"No."

"To Sara's folk's in Cambridge?"

"No. We are getting away on our own for a while."

"That's great, man. You two deserve a break. Everything I said in that interview last night is true, David. You guys saved my life and I will never be able to thank you enough." And then James pulled him into an embrace. "Happy holidays, man," he said.

And then David pulled back, shifting his arm so that he might reach into the left-hand pocket of his Adirondack jacket. He retrieved his hand to reveal a small slip of yellow paper now stuck to his fingers. And then he turned the slip around and stuck it firmly onto James' white cotton robe.

"What's this?" said a now obviously confused James. "A sticker for good work?" he went on, his voice now showing the slightest trace of uncertainty. James pulled the Post-it from his front, and began to read the words aloud.

"Cabot 312," he said, his face maintaining a forced smile but his voice shaking as he read the final digit "two."

"It's three twelve actually," corrected David. "Cabot is the name of a dorm house at Deane—and three twelve refers to a dorm number, as in twelfth room on the third floor."

James shrugged.

"It was Sawyer Jones' dorm, James, and I was just wondering how it came to be stuck to the back of one of the photos on your wall, a shot of you and Simpson and Westinghouse no less."

"David, I . . ." hesitated James. "I'm sorry, man, but you must be confused. I know how hard this has been on you and Sara. The Jones kid fooled you all. But to be honest, I am finding it hard to forgive him. He killed Jess, David. And she was . . ."

"Shut the fuck up," said David at last, pushing James back so that he almost tripped over the long designer pool lounge.

"Jesus, David," said a now horrified James. "What the hell is this about? I mean, I am grateful for everything you have done for me, but this is kind of out of order. I have no idea why you . . ."

"How much did he pay them?"

"What?

"How much did Simpson pay the two Australians on your behalf?"

"Seriously, David, you have lost it man."

"Well, I am sure you would have done it yourself but that would have been difficult considering you closed your third Grand Cayman account so that the money would be deposited into the other two. Did Simpson know you were doing that, James, or was that a secret backup plan of your own, in case the cops managed to do a trace on the money and see the reward was originally meant for three?"

"I don't know what you are talking about," said James, his voice now carrying a thick, hard edge.

"Are you cold, James?" asked David.

"No."

"You're shivering."

"No, David. No I'm not."

"The shoe print was too big."

"What?"

"The impression in Jessica's greenhouse. Sawyer had smaller than average feet. None of the shoes in his closet matched the partial print at the crime scene."

"That doesn't mean he didn't . . ."

"He did go to her greenhouse at some point, James. Sawyer was her friend so in many ways he had every right to be there. She must have invited him, showed him the black orchid, must have told him how rare it was—in fact, she probably told you about it too."

"I told you, David, I never went to her . . ."

"Mannix got the FBI to check the mineralogy on Sawyer's shoes with the print that was left behind. They don't match,

James—in fact, a new test on the dirt under the print found small traces of chlorine, the same stuff that they put in pools. See your Nike could have been washed . . . but the stuff that was left behind . . . ?"

"What the fuck are you insinuating, David?"

"I'm not *insinuating* anything, James."

"Jesus, this is . . ."

"When did you stash her shoes, James?" David pushed on, taking another step toward his client. "I suppose that part would have been simple given Sawyer rarely locked his door and the dorm room number would have been easy to ascertain.

"Did Jess give it to you unwittingly, James? I mean, Sawyer was her friend after all. He was the one who encouraged her to go out with you because he realized how much she liked you and . . ."

"Stop it."

"It was a gamble, of course," David went on, taking a step closer to the now clench-fisted James before him. "I mean, there is no way you could have known if or when they would be found. But I suppose you had a plan for that too, some sneaky scheme that would lead us to Sawyer's room before the jury had a chance to convict."

"Shut the hell up, David," said James through gritted teeth. "I am warning you . . ."

"Is that a threat, James?" said David, moving forward once again. "Because I really do not think that is your style. Come on, James, you are much smarter than that. You manipulate people's personalities so that they have no choice but to do as you wish. You appealed to Simpson's arrogance and you preyed on Westinghouse's loyalty and you fucked them over big time. And here was I, stupid as all hell, thinking it was the other way around.

"You killed Jessica and you had no alibi so you came up with the plan to involve your friends. They went along with it only because they thought Rousseau would give you a pass. But when she failed to come through they found themselves trapped, being portrayed as greedy traitors while you sat like the wide-eyed innocent who knew that whatever else happened, you had collateral in the form of a pair of two black shoes that sat ready to be found at the bottom of Sawyer Jones's closet. You framed a seventeen-year-old kid who loved your girlfriend, James—and now they are both lying dead and cold in their graves."

And then James lifted his arm, his movement so swift and slick and powerful that David barely had time to duck out of the way. But David recovered quickly, lifting his own right hand to grab James' fist as it swung back for another go.

"There is just one thing I do not understand," said David, catching his breath as he forced his client's arm down and pushed James backward, staying in his personal space, goading him on, wanting him, willing him to explode with anger.

"Your hands, James, they are big and powerful. How the hell did you leave such small bruises on her neck, James? How the hell did you . . ."

And then James leapt forward, his two hands now flexed and poised as he lunged at David's neck. It was if he wanted him to see it, as if he needed him to know just how perfect his crime had been.

David acted on instinct, lifting his own hands to his neck in a classic defensive pose. His fingers laced at the front, his thumbs wrapped around the side. And in that second he saw it, and the final piece of the jigsaw fell horrifyingly into place.

"They were *her* prints," he said as James lowered his arms at last. "Jessica lifted her hands in defense and you wrapped your hands around hers—strangling her from the front, not the back, looking her in the eye as the life leached out of her. You killed the goddamned love of your life, James, and the life of your own baby boy in the process."

And then James did something David did not expect. He stretched his right hand and looked down at his feet, he took a breath and shook his head, the water still dripping from the short, sharp ends of his closely cropped hair. And then he lifted his face again, his eyes now bright as his mouth broke out into a wide, perfect smile.

"You are my attorney," he said at last. "And I am not admitting anything you say is true, but even if I did, it would be under privilege.

"And, you know as well as I do, David, that the double jeopardy clause was attached the moment my jury was sworn in. In other words, that wonderful fifth amendment addition to our blessed Constitution says I cannot be prosecuted twice for the same fucking offense. I'm free, David, thanks to you, I might add, and there is nothing you can do about it."

David took a step back before falling into a blue-and-white striped deck chair behind him. He knew that was exactly what James was going to say—and he needed to look defeated if this was going to play out the way he intended.

"You're right, James," he said at last, as James perched on the end of the recliner next to him.

"I usually am," said James. "But then again, I have to admit, you've done an amazing job by figuring it all out."

"But that's just it, James," said David, lifting his hands in mock surrender. "I can't figure it out. I mean, why the hell did you kill her? You loved her, for Christ's sake."

James hesitated, as if gauging how far he should go, but his confidence in his incredible knowledge of the law was well founded, and he saw no legal recourse to his actions so . . .

"I cheated on her and she sensed it," he said, as plain as day. "She was like that—intuitive, perceptive. It was a mistake, David," he said, turning to him now. "She was in New York and the summer had been long and this girl, she was beautiful and persistent. It just kind of happened."

"So you killed her because she was jealous?"

"No. Of course not. I did love her, David. But she threw it back in my face. I returned to the Lincoln that night because I knew she suspected. We went back to her place so we could talk it out, but there was no reasoning with her.

"In the end she told me she didn't give a crap who the hell I slept with, because she had been fucking some other guy sense-less in New York. She said I was just some pathetic local diver-sion, some meaningless, passing fling.

"She said she wanted someone older, smarter, who knew how to fend for himself, someone who made his own way and was not dependent on his parents' fortune—someone with de-termination and guts and drive." James took a breath and David could sense his anger at the memory. Whatever else David knew about James, he sensed that above all else, this young man could not abide being made to feel the fool.

"And then she told me she was pregnant and that the child she was carrying had nothing to do with me," said James.

There was silence, as David took it all in, the sun now hitting the water with a vengeance, burning off the steam and sending its aqua blue surface gold.

"And you took her shoes because . . . ?"

"The keepsake stuff was a load of psychological bullshit. My mom's a psychologist, so I should know. I just figured I might need a little collateral."

"It worked," said David.

"I know." James smiled.

And there they sat, the attorney and his prodigy, the big brother and his younger replica with the brilliant mind and unstoppable reserve and a shining future ahead of him—just as David had once hoped.

"Are you cold?" asked David for a third time.

"Yes," answered James, finally admitting the truth, before rising from his seat and heading toward the pool house door.

And then David saw her, just beyond the now sliding door—the slightest glimpse of a beautiful, long-legged blond girl wearing nothing but a man's sweater and pair of fresh white underwear.

"Say hello to David, Barbara," called out James, stepping slightly aside.

"Hello, David," she said, walking toward him, her French accent strong.

And in that moment David realized that, in the end, he had pulled her in too.

"I know what you are thinking." James smiled, now reaching his large hand behind the girl's neck to pull her close. "And I believe H. Edgar did make Barbara an offer on my behalf, but she was generous enough to provide her services gratis," he said, referring to the girl's obvious decision not to accept cash in return for the recount of her "no alibi" statement.

"I really did not think she would be so generous—I mean, obviously, if I had, I would have saved myself all the trouble and got her to give me that goddamned alibi in the first place. But I guess she knows a good thing when she sees it, David, because now we are together." And then that hand reached a little farther, his fingers widening as he drew her in for a kiss.

"Your luck will run out eventually, James," said David then.

"Somehow I don't think so," replied James as he moved inside and began to slide the door back into its catches. "But whatever the case, I want to say none of this would have been possible if not for you so . . . Merry Christmas, man, and thanks again for everything."

The traffic was light until he reached the shopping strips around Copley, with hoards of animated people buying last-minute gifts and stocking up with bagloads of food before the holidays. Downtown was worse, with the malls and department stores now teeming with bodies, the fine weather dragging people from their homes, the promise of a blue-skied Christmas a welcome respite after weeks of being forced indoors.

And in that moment David felt the all-encompassing wave of envy, that he was not one of them, walking, shopping, laughing, with nothing to worry about except what to buy the kids and how long to cook the Christmas turkey. He wanted to ring Sara and tell her to meet him out front with their bags now—so that he could hit the accelerator and head south, and forget about it all, and lead some semblance of a normal holiday with the person he loved most in the world.

But he couldn't do that, and he knew why. This was his fault. If he had not been blinded by James' seeming idealism, and his own determination to see his client as a younger version of himself, this might never have happened. It was true these "kids" were masters, for they had effectively fooled David and his team, Joe and Frank and even the savvy ADA with their barrage of lies and deception.

James and Simpson, and to a lesser extent Westinghouse and Rousseau, had driven this thing from the outset—with no regard for people like Jessica and her child or Sawyer and Mr. Lim who they had destroyed in their wake.

And so he would do what he needed to do—walk that fine line between what was "right" and what was not, and in the end pray that justice had not betrayed him, just taken another track where the final destination was exactly where it was meant to be all along.

. . .

He pulled the car into the space outside his office, a small, corner spot that saw his Land Cruiser spill into a no-standing zone. It was after midday, and if Nora had done as instructed, the man would be in there alone, waiting, curious, with no idea why he had been asked to this unexpected meeting or what David needed to discuss.

David took the stairs, and as he entered the outer office was pleased to see that Nora had left immediately after the man arrived, for he knew if this was to happen, it had to be done alone.

"Mr. Nagoshi," he said at last, pushing his door back to see the distinguished Japanese businessman dressed in his usual perfectly cut suit, sitting patiently and straight-backed in the chair opposite David's desk.

"Mr. Cavanaugh," smiled John Nagoshi, standing to take David's hand. "It is nice to see you again."

"Thank you," said David. "But I must apologize for asking you here on such a busy holiday."

"It is no trouble, Mr. Cavanaugh," said Nagoshi, taking his seat once again as David moved around his now perfectly cleared desk and bent to retrieve a large thick file from his briefcase.

He picked up the file with both hands and placed it squarely in the middle of the desk before him, as if it deserved some sort of reverential treatment, some sort of ceremony in positioning, as the only thing on David's normally cluttered workspace.

"How is your son?" asked David, taking his seat on the other side of the desk.

"He is well, thank you. My son is humbled by the events of recent weeks, Mr. Cavanaugh. He has decided to slow down his progress so that he might observe and learn from myself and the soon-to-be-appointed head of our American division."

"You have a new local boss?" asked David.

"Yes, an American, named Jenkins. And we have decided to close our Guangdong plant, offering substantial retrenchment packages for all of our loyal Chinese workers, at least for the time being."

David nodded. The only sound in the room was now the ticking of the large antique clock in Arthur's office next door.

"I am sorry, Mr. Nagoshi," said David at last.

"What for, Mr. Cavanaugh? I should think you would be feeling . . . how should I say it? Vindicated?"

And David could not help but laugh. "Not exactly, sir."

Nagoshi looked at him puzzled. "Sawyer Jones appeared to be a friend, a good man," said the Japanese businessman in some attempt to ease David's obvious discomfort. "Do not feel bad for being deceived, Mr. Cavanaugh. It happens to the best of us."

David shook his head. "Sawyer was not a man, Mr. Nagoshi—he was a boy, barely seventeen, or so we discovered after his death. And as for my being duped, I am afraid that is the king of understatements."

"I am sorry," said Nagoshi again. "I do not . . ."

"I'm hungry, Mr. Nagoshi," said David at last, getting to his feet once again. "Starving, in fact. You see, we worked through the night and I haven't eaten breakfast and Sara and I are heading to the Cape this afternoon so . . ."

"I understand," said Nagoshi, rising to his feet to shake David's hand, obviously still confused as to why he had been summoned, but more than willing to wish David well and leave at his somewhat premature suggestion.

"No, Mr. Nagoshi, the traffic is horrendous out there," David said, gesturing toward the window. "I suggest you sit a while until the crowds have thinned a little."

"I . . ." began Nagoshi, as David helped him back into his seat.

"Please," said David, his eyes now shifting to focus on the lone thick file before them. "Take your time."

And then David moved toward the door, turning briefly to make one last observation.

"You know, Mr. Nagoshi . . ." he began.

"It's John," said Nagoshi, finally realizing exactly what David was directing him to do.

"When I was in law school one of my most respected lecturers told me a fact I have never forgotten. That when it comes to the civil court, justice and money are interchangeable, because they mean exactly the same thing."

Nagoshi nodded.

"It was never about the money, John, but perhaps, in the end, it will be."

EPILOGUE

December 25—Christmas Day
Hyannis Port

The sun was up. Christmas morning was cold but fresh, the breeze kissing their skin as they walked, hand in hand, along Hyannis' white-sanded Craigville Beach.

"This is so beautiful," said Sara, glancing out across the ocean, her long brown hair whipping in the wind, her skin fresh and alive, her pale eyes almost translucent under the bright morning sun.

David took a deep breath. "Smell that," he said. "The smell of pure salt minus diesel oil and gas fumes and fisheries and other city rubbish that accompanies the harbor we have back home."

They walked on for a while, their shoes now covered in sand, their faces red, their bodies energized and the memory of the past months slowly being cleansed from their souls.

"Do you think he'll file?" she asked at last, perhaps sensing that until they talked this through, it would not be put to rest.

"Yes," he said. "John Nagoshi is a good man, but if he sees a chance to avenge his daughter's and his grandson's deaths, he will do it."

"What kind of money are we talking?" she asked.

"A civil suit like this could break records, Sara, in the tens of millions at least. I guess H. Edgar wins the prize for being the smartest kid on the block after all—leaving the transaction information of the three original accounts in the assignment. He had to know we would pick it up, and find some way to . . ."

"Screw James for screwing with him," finished Sara.

"Or rather, having John Nagoshi do it for him."

"Funny how things happen," she said after a time, brushing a stray wisp of hair from her aqua blue eyes. "In lots of ways this thing started with a conversation you had with Tony all those months ago and now, if the Nagoshis decide to file, he will most likely be representing them in the civil case against James."

"Finishing what I couldn't," he said.

"No," she argued. "Just picking up where we left off."

And he nodded, squeezing her hand in his.

"In any case, it might mean Bishop will have some fun for a change," he said after a time.

"And make a packet of money in the process," she grinned.

"Tony's idea of heaven," he added.

"Whereas mine is right here, right now," she said, pulling him close.

They walked along, the sun now high enough to turn the ocean into a sea of silver, the winter holidaymakers playing catch or walking their dogs along the soft sand.

"Look," said a smiling Sara, pointing to a little blond-haired boy who, bundled up like an Eskimo, was running, tumbling and running again along the fine white sand. His beaming father jogging down to greet him, grabbing him up and lifting him high, tossing him toward the bright blue sky above, before catching him again, cuddling him in a bear hug and setting him down to repeat the same loving process over and over and over again.

"The kid can barely walk," laughed David as the kid fell again.

"He's having the time of his life," said Sara.

"No more than his dad," David added.

"You think you could do that?" she asked quickly, still focusing on the child.

"Do what?" he asked.

"You know, roughhouse with a toddler. Forget the troubles of this big bad world and focus on the important things—like playing ball, or finger painting, or sucking down spaghetti so the sauce dribbles all over your chin." She mimicked the spaghetti sucking motion, slurping sound affects and all.

"That *is* how I eat spaghetti," he joked, stopping her now, turning her face toward him. "What are you trying to tell me? I mean, are you asking me if I want to . . . ?"

"It's a little too late for that, I'm afraid," she said, looking into his eyes. "You are going to be a father, David, and a damned fine one at that."

"Me . . . I . . . ," he managed, before breaking into a smile and pulling her into him—and holding her, holding *them*, like they were the most precious beings on earth.

"You think I'm good enough to do this?" he asked.

"I think you're better than you think," she replied, and he bent down to kiss her.

"But you could use some practice," she said after a time.

"At what?" he asked.

"Roughhousing, of course," she said, grabbing his cap from his head and threatening to throw it into the incoming surf.

"You wouldn't dare," he said.

"Oh yes, I would." She grinned, running away from him now, heading straight for the freezing cold water.

And then he caught up to her and grabbed her and picked her up and ran toward the waves threatening to throw her in, cap and all.

"I love you, Sara Davis," he said at last, putting her down just at the edge of the shoreline, which lapped softly at their feet.

"You'd better," she said. "Because we love you too."

ALSO AVAILABLE FROM
NATIONAL BESTSELLING AUTHOR

SYDNEY BAUER

UNDERTOW

"Terrific legal suspense—a great debut."
—LEE CHILD

After the daughter of a powerful senator dies in a tragic accident, the witness to the accident, an esteemed female attorney, unexpectedly finds herself charged with murder by the girl's vengeful father—a man with his own twisted agenda.

"Compelling from start to finish, this fast-paced thriller combines engaging characters, sharp dialogue, and a plot so gripping that the pages seem to turn themselves."
—RICHARD NORTH PATTERSON

penguin.com

Don't miss the page-turning suspense, intriguing characters, and unstoppable action that keep readers coming back for more from these bestselling authors...

Tom Clancy
Robin Cook
Patricia Cornwell
Clive Cussler
Dean Koontz
J.D. Robb
John Sandford

Your favorite thrillers and suspense novels come from Berkley.

penguin.com